On Fortune's Tide

Theresa-Marie Smith

**Grosvenor House
Publishing Limited**

The right of Theresa-Marie Smith to be identified as the author of this
work has been asserted in accordance with Section 78
of the Copyright, Designs and Patents Act 1988

The book cover is copyright to Theresa-Marie Smith
The front cover image is credited to:
www.istockphoto.com/gb/portfolio/
alexkich?assettype=image&mediatype=photography&sort=best

This book is published by
Grosvenor House Publishing Ltd
Link House
140 The Broadway, Tolworth, Surrey, KT6 7HT.
www.grosvenorhousepublishing.co.uk

This book is a work of fiction. Any resemblance to
people or events, past or present, is purely coincidental.

A CIP record for this book
is available from the British Library

ISBN 978-1-83975-123-3

Introduction

Like many others I have a real love of Cornwall. My Cornish ancestors have left this legacy for me to follow. I love to read both historical fiction and non-fiction set within eighteenth century Cornwall. This period in time I find fascinating. A time when smugglers and excise men each sort to outwit one another. When all the fictional hero's you read about in this land of legend, including my own hero Jarren Polverne are handsome and determined to fight for the principals they believe in, and the women they love. The sea and smuggling deep rooted in their blood. In this novel there is one ruthless revenue officer in particular named Ruskin Tripper, bribed by the cruel monstrous Lord Trevoran, he is someone Jarren and Layunie need to fear, for he is just as cruel as his master.

Prologue

This novel draws you into the romance between two people who come from very different backgrounds. How they struggle to overcome those who are determined to separate them. The reader will be horrified by the cruelty our heroine has to suffer at the hands of Lord Trevoran, who is determined to make her his bride. A powerful man in Cornwall Trevoran gets his way as the lovers are hunted down and Jarren imprisoned. His lordship seems to have won the day and is heartlessly brutal as he takes his revenge on Layunie, but Layunie now has her own secret.

Will Jarren manage to rescue his love? And if so what twist of fate leads Layunie many many years later to send someone very close to her, on a mission to sail up the river Fal to Trevoran Court, there to deliver her precious diaries to the present Lord Trevoran. Her diaries she hopes will give the recipient a true insight into the events that took place so long ago.

CHAPTER ONE

A thick shroud of sea mist drifted upriver from the Cornish coast, creeping silently into the creeks and inlets of the river Fal, gently caressing the great house that peeped through the trees. No one saw the shabby craft emerge from the misty waters and tie up alongside the Trevoran Quay; the presence of the man who jumped ashore and walked across the immaculate lawns went undetected until he knocked upon the huge doors under the canopied entrance of Trevoran Court.

A liveried butler opened the door and gave the stranger a look of total disapproval, for he was poorly clothed and would not give his name. However, there was something vaguely familiar about him, and when asked, instead of saying his master was not at home, gestured him to enter and wait in the enormous marble-floored hall.

Lord Thomas Trevoran was in his study when the butler knocked, and in a discreet tone of voice described the manner of person asking to see him. Much intrigued, his master instructed that the visitor be shown in. Immediately he saw the fellow it was obvious he came from the fishing fraternity, the man looked completely lost in his present surroundings. For a second the two men looked at each other before the stranger spoke.

'Are you Lord Thomas Trevoran whose mother had the Christian name Layunie?' he asked.

The surprise of just hearing his mother's name spoken out loud came as a shock to his lordship, his late father having forbidden that anyone ever speak of her. 'I am,' he replied stiffly, mystified as the stranger came forward to place on his desk a large bundle of tightly tied leather journals.

'I was asked to give these to you in person, together with this letter.' He placed it on top of the journals. For just a moment Lord Thomas looked down at his desk. When he glanced up it was to find the stranger gone.

Immediately he summoned his servants to organise a search for the man, but there was no sign of him. Outside the mist was thickening; there was no point in looking further beyond the house.

Intrigued, he returned to his study and opened out the letter. It read:

'To my son, whom I never forgot and have thought of constantly. My journals are for you to read and only you, there are things which will shock you, but I feel you should know the truth. I shall never know what you were told of me, none of it good, I'm sure, but believe me when I say you have always been in my heart. Destroy my writings when you are finished with them, for it would not do for them to fall into the wrong hands.

Your loving mother Layunie Polverne.'

Thomas untied the thick red ribbon holding the journals together. He poured himself a liberal amount of brandy from the cut glass decanter in front of him, sat down and opened the frail cover of the top journal, knowing instinctively that someone had put them carefully in date order.

In a good hand was written:

These the journals of Layunie Polverne whose maiden name was Ledridge. I was born on the 17th August in the year 1700. In these journals I have set out for you the events in time that led me into a life so different from anything I could have possibly dreamed of, and to explain my sorrow at not being part of your life. For in all truth, I was led to believe you had died in childhood.

At which point in my life to begin my story it is difficult to decide upon, and so perhaps it will be best to tell you something of my family, my home and social standing before I made the journey which was to alter my life.

My father, brother and myself lived in a beautiful rambling house by the name of Wellowmead, situated in a hamlet not far from the southern outskirts of Bath.

When destiny struck, I had just made my come out and was enjoying a whirl of society balls and other enjoyable pleasures accompanied by my mother's much younger sister who was my chaperone, my mother having died when I was born. Aunt Sarah was still quite young and attractive herself and great company to be with, her gregarious nature ensured she had a multitude of followers all of whom she rebuffed.

Above all else she was fun to be with and I was much content with my life at that time, and if on occasion some dowager duchess looked scornfully upon my aunt I took no care, for I myself was no simpering miss. I too had a confident nature, knowing myself not unattractive to the eye, unlike some of the young prodigies the dowagers had the misfortune to chaperone!

My father said in looks I favoured my mother, for she too had been small and slender of build, with heart shaped face and strikingly blue eyes. From my father's side of the family I'd inherited the almost uncontrollable fairest of curls, causing Polly my maid endless traumas as she struggled daily to control and coax it into the latest fashion.

Already two gentlemen in particular paid me much attention and I was often to ponder what my future could have been if things had remained as they were. This then was my life at seventeen and I thoroughly enjoyed it. But quite suddenly it was to change dramatically.

One morning as I made my way downstairs, I became aware of a heated argument taking place in the study between Father and Charles. As I neared the bottom stair my father opened the study door, his face dark with anger, he merely glanced up at me and without speaking left the house, the sound of the door being slammed resounding in the hall.

Perturbed, I entered the study and found Charles slumped forward in the huge leather armchair beside the mantle, his face buried in his hands. I begged him tell me what had happened and so learned the terrible truth.

Over the last few weeks, he had gambled away everything he possessed and much more besides. He had made pledges of payment he couldn't possibly meet. Heavily pressed to repay his debts, he'd been forced to confess all to Father, such were the amounts in question.

Bad news it seems travels fast; soon not only Charles's debts were being asked for, but tradesmen who dealt with Father, and usually paid monthly or even annually, were now asking for immediate settlement of their accounts. Father was desperate, suddenly confronted with demands for payment from almost everyone. It was just too much. The magnitude of what Charles owed mounted, and the final blow came when the Cornish Shipping Company, in which Father was a large shareholder, went into receivership. Even under normal circumstances this would have been cause for worry, but in the present circumstances it was a disaster. The money was running out.

Invitations to society gatherings became fewer and fewer, and those that came I had to turn down. The happy atmosphere in our home had gone. Charles talked of suicide, and Father hardly spoke at all. I did my best to keep the house functioning, for now only Alice Stowe the cook remained. Having been with the family since the days when my mother was alive, she went on working as usual and would accept no payment. Aunt Sarah offered to help, but we knew her income was only just sufficient for herself. My suggestion that I find work was scorned by Father as being out of the question. And so our fortunes steadily worsened.

Then it came, the morning I shall never forget. Lord Trevoran, an elderly landowner from Cornwall who had been a friend of my grandfather Oliver Ledridge, paid Father a visit. Lord Trevoran had known my grandfather since they were boys growing up on adjoining estates beside the river Fal. Alas, by the time grandfather inherited the Ledridge estate it was heavily in debt and he was forced to sell to Lord Trevoran. Father had thus moved to Somerset and purchased our beloved

Wellowmead House. Not since my grandfather's funeral, two years before, had we seen his lordship.

As soon as his surprise visit was announced I retreated upstairs for I had always had a dislike of him, even as a little girl when he reached out to touch my tumbling curls or tried to lure me on his knee.

Once his lordship had left I was summoned to the study by Alice, I found my father sitting behind his desk, he was ashen, his once robust frame seemed shrunken; the sadness in his eyes as they met mine brought sorrow to my heart.

'Sit down, maid,' he began, lapsing into the Cornish way of speaking which he did only on the very rarest of occasions. I could tell how serious the matter was, for his voice trembled as he spoke.

'Layunie my child, you know the wretched situation we're in today. So many debts, alas, it seems probable that shortly I must lose even Wellowmead.'

A discreet cough from the doorway announced the arrival of Charles. Half turning, I saw the look that passed between them, as impatiently Charles asked Father, 'Have you told her she can save you totally?'

Father shook his head, and deep inside I felt the first stirring of misgivings. I looked to him for an explanation. It was then I learnt the purpose of Lord Trevoran's visit. Word had reached him of Father's financial difficulties, and he had come here to offer him a solution: my hand in marriage. After twenty years married to a barren shrew now deceased, he needed a young wife who would, God willing, produce an heir for the Trevoran Estate. In return, he would settle on Father a large sum of money, and a partnership in a new Bristol Merchant Venture on the understanding that Charles be employed therein, the said young man to give his word that he would gamble no more.

I sat speechless, numbed by the implications, aware only of the ticking clock on the mantle and the turmoil I felt inside. To find myself placed in such a position appalled me. The prospect of marriage to such a man was beyond words. I pictured him in my mind's eye, small, thin, his face resembling a bony skull, his teeth worn down to blackened stubs. And above all else, he was old, so very, very old. I swallowed hard, unable to utter a single word.

At that moment I think I hated Charles more than anyone in the world, for it was he who had put me in this dreadful position. Looking at Father, I could see what a tired man he had become, the worries of the past weeks written across his face. We sat in silence until I managed to ask, 'Is there no other way?'

Tears came to his eyes and with both hands he gripped his desk. 'No, Layunie, I can see no other way. We shall lose the house soon, all will be lost, your brother and I taken to the debtors' prison.' With that he turned away from me, ashamed that I should see him weep.

Leaving the study I fled upstairs and into the sanctuary of my own bedroom, throwing myself on the bed, there to weep helplessly for the life I so recently had, for the excitement and promises of a future that would never be mine. There was no way of escape; I could not let my father be ruined. I would have to make this marriage.

After the engagement was publicly announced, telegrams of congratulation began arriving from the very top of society, also from those who had rejected our family so very recently. Once again visiting cards were left; all these I cast aside together with the congratulations, how fickle indeed was society. Now I was to become Lady Trevoran I was once more acceptable.

Lord Cedric Trevoran I had met only once since that fateful visit. I was called to the study and inspected up and down as though I were a prize he'd won. I noticed his lizard-like skin as he reached out and took my hands in his. A shudder passed through me at contact with his person, and aware of my discomfort, I saw a gleam of malice spread across his face.

The following day both Father and Charles's debts were settled together with a financial settlement which would allow Father to take his place once more in the business world. A very generous amount was made available for me to purchase the necessities I should require for my new life and position in society. My bridal dress, a Trevoran heirloom, was to be altered by a seamstress in Truro ready for my arrival in Cornwall. I had money to buy anything I wanted, but found no pleasure in doing so, as with leaden feet, together with Aunt Sarah I bought what was needed, feeling totally detached from those around me.

The dreaded day finally arrived. Looking down from my window I saw the coach with the Trevoran crest approaching. Slowly I made my way downstairs tears brimming in my eyes. In the hallway Mrs Stowe stood weeping, she wiped away a tear with the corner of her apron and reached out taking both my hands in hers.

'Goodbye, my dear, and God go with you,' she sobbed, trying as best she could to give me an encouraging smile, and with a rush of emotion I kissed her velvety cheek. Alice Stowe had been a part of my life for as long as I could remember. A lump came to my throat as I took my leave of her, trying to hold my head up high as I walked on past the two new maids we could now afford. Each bobbed a curtsey as I passed, watching as I made my way further down the hall to where Charles stood by the open door. A distance had grown between us since that fateful day I was summoned to the study, for I felt quite unforgiving of him. We looked at each other, both knowing there was nothing he could say or do to right the harm he had caused. Abruptly he stepped back hanging his head in shame unable to meet my gaze any longer.

Finally, I said goodbye to Father, who with Charles was to journey down to Cornwall for the wedding in four weeks' time. He stood bravely trying to mask the overwhelming sadness that touched his very soul, then as if a child once more I stepped into his outstretched arms, momentarily comforted as he held me to him, postponing the inevitable parting for as long as he could.

'My own precious maid, tis an awful sacrifice you've had to make, and I thank you for it from the bottom of my heart.' His voice faltered; I could not speak so choked was I with emotion. For one brief moment the desire to turn and run away seemed too powerful to resist, but I knew for the sake of my father's honour this to be impossible. Thus, with great sadness, accompanied by Aunt Sarah, I left Wellowmead forever.

CHAPTER TWO

The condition of the roads worsened the further west we travelled, the coaching inns we stopped at overnight a welcome break on what seemed an endless journey. Each morning I found my appetite depleted by the knowledge of what lay ahead, knowing the deep furrows in the road would cause our coach to be tossed about in all directions.

It was after we left Launceston that once again one or more of the wheels became bogged down in the mud or stuck fast in some deep furrow. It mattered not to me, for indeed I was in no hurry to complete this journey, loathing what lay ahead. But Aunt Sarah was feeling unwell and frustrated at the delay, I opened the door and enquired of the coachman and his companion who'd climbed down and now stood ankle deep in the mire, spade in hand, 'Pray how long until we reach Bodmin?'

'Tis the other side of the moor, miss,' he grunted, glancing up at the darkening sky, a look of apprehension on his weather-beaten face.

Quickly I snapped shut the door, wishing we could be on our way. The look on the fellow's face had filled me with a sense of unease. Shortly afterwards the coach swayed as the horses heaved us out of the mud, and our journey continued. With each mile we travelled, the landscape became ever more bleak and barren. Although quite early, darkness was closing in, and with it a cold swirling mist.

'Surely we should have stayed overnight at Launceston,' Aunt Sarah muttered, knowing full well why we had not. No way would the surly coachman defy his master's instructions.

'We must hope Bodmin's not too far,' I replied, trying to calm her, uneasy myself at the reckless speed at which we seemed to be travelling, despite the weather conditions, and prayed inwardly that the man responsible was familiar with the road before him.

Then suddenly the coachman hollered at the horses and the pace slackened, muffled voices could be heard some way off, but looking from the window I could see nothing but the swirling mist. Abruptly the coach jolted to a halt. The voices grew nearer.

Never in my whole life had I been so frightened, and clung to Aunt Sarah absolutely terrified, as did she to me. Some kind of a dispute was taking place and we strained to hear what was being said.

Without warning, the door of the coach was suddenly wrenched open, and we screamed in alarm. I edged even closer to my aunt and stared wide-eyed at the man who stood before us. Boldly he watched me, so intense his gaze, I felt yet more fearful, but unable to look away.

Mesmerised, I found myself staring into the darkest pair of brown eyes imaginable, a large black handkerchief hid the remainder of his face together with a wide-brimmed battered hat. The dark clothes he wore were well made but very worn. In one hand he held a long-barrelled pistol, and lowering the step, he gestured us to step down from the coach, holding out his hand to assist me to do so. I declined his offer of help and almost tripped as I stepped down, horrified now to feel myself blushing. Aunt Sarah was not so foolish and in the most gracious of fashion he helped her alight, returning his gaze upon me once this was done.

The cold swirling mist engulfed us, and I shivered as the biting cold penetrated my lightweight cloak. I looked up at him and for one brief moment I could almost sense he was smiling beneath the mask, for indeed what a sorry sight I must look in my delicate footwear, together with the hem of my skirts and petticoats engulfed in mud.

Diverting my eyes from his, I saw just visible through the mist a covered wagon. Lord Trevoran's coachman and his companion were being forced to hand over one of our horses in exchange for another poor creature that had obviously gone lame.

Someone called, 'Tis done, let's be on our way.' But the man with the dark brown eyes continued to stare at me, it was unnerving. I felt my face blush scarlet under his scrutiny and saw a glint of amusement in his eyes. Although his companions were eager to be away, he showed no sign of joining them.

'So, tis true his lordship has got himself a pretty miss to marry, well tis my duty, lads, to save this poor damsel from such a—'

But his words were interrupted by the sound of pounding hoofbeats fast approaching. He didn't hesitate, but thrust the pistol in his belt, and came forward plucking me from the mud and running to join the others. I had no time to protest, so swift was my removal from my aunt's side.

'You're mad, his lordship'll kill you, leave her behind, man,' I heard one of the men shout to him, but he didn't heed the speaker's words, and without ceremony, I was almost thrown in the wagon, lying amidst umpteen kegs, with Aunt Sarah's screams fading further and further away.

We were fleeing across the moor, and for what seemed an age I hung onto the kegs terrified of losing my grip and falling. Grateful when at last the sound of our pursuers became fainter until they were no more, then came the realisation I'd been kidnapped. Too tired to cry, my whole body began to feel numb. It began to rain, dripping onto me through holes in the threadbare canvas, adding to the cold. My fingers felt they could hold on no more, and this is my final memory of that journey.

How far we travelled I could not tell and awoke the next morning at a complete loss as to where I was, knowing only that I ached from head to toe. The memory of what had befallen me followed swiftly, and in a state of panic I struggled to sit up, recalling what had taken place, confused as to where I was now. I knew Aunt Sarah must be beside herself with worry, and hoped the Trevoran coachman had escorted her safely on to Bodmin, from where, no doubt, she would send a message to Father.

I shivered, feeling frightened at the prospect of meeting my dark eyed captor again. Obviously, he'd brought me here, and carried me up to where I lay on a makeshift bed amongst the straw in a low vaulted loft, my head barely beneath the rafters. A tiny window at floor level let in faint rays of light, and through its cobwebbed pane, I could see a narrow track below with a ragged row of cottages on the opposite side. I sank back against the rough pillow finding it difficult to fathom out exactly how I felt, for indeed the nearer my bridegroom's estate had become each day, so too had my dread of what lay ahead. I knew in my heart I felt a guilty relief to no longer be heading for Trevoran Court, this though replaced by apprehension as to where I was, and what was going to happen next.

Instinctively, I felt no harm would come to me by the man who'd brought me here, but how would his lordship react when I didn't appear, and what of Father? Above all, I wanted to know who was this man who dare make off with the bride of Lord Trevoran? He was either very brave or a fool.

I lifted the coarse blanket aside so I could crawl over and take a better look from the window and discovered I was wearing a very large much-patched nightgown. My face flared crimson. Pray God it wasn't him who'd removed my clothes! Mortified I lay back once again on the sweet-smelling straw, pulling the blanket up tight beneath my chin, wondering how I could possibly face him again, such was my embarrassment. Finding myself drawn to think the unthinkable, what would happen should I not demand to be returned to my future husband's estate forthwith? After all, my kidnap had nothing to do with Father. Thoughts such as these were swiftly followed by the knowledge that Lord Trevoran was powerful and ruthless; when grandfather was alive, I'd often heard him telling Father of men ruined because they'd dare cross his lordship. I wondered if by now he knew of my kidnap and what terrible retribution would be brought against my captor if he were caught. My heart hammered in my chest as I realised how much I feared for this unknown man. I pictured his dark eyes looking into mine, and felt goose bumps creeping up my arms, recalling conversations held daily by myself and friends whilst in attendance at the Bath Ladies Academy on the subject of love at first sight.

Suddenly I became aware of whispered voices drifting up through the open hatch, and sat wide-eyed looking up at the rafters, almost holding my breath as I listened, alas unable to hear clearly anything that was being said and after a while the voices ceased. Eager to discover the whereabouts of my clothes, I decided to try, whilst it was quiet, to find them. A heavy ladder was propped up against the edge of the loft and although there was insufficient room for me to stand, I gathered the vast nightgown around me and stooping, quietly made my way towards it. It seemed no one was about, so with great care I slowly climbed down.

When I reached the bottom, I found myself to be in a cottage with tiny windows set deep in thick cob walls, woven rugs some more worn than others covered the floor. A huge fireplace dominated the single room with a cloam oven built into it on one side, a large steaming pot hung over the brushwood fire. There was little furniture, a table, four stools, a bed of sorts, other bits and pieces, pots and pans and two roughly made chairs on which my clothes were laid out before the fire. I reached out to feel if they were dry enough to wear, and as I did so, heard a sound behind me and I turned round, catching the hem of my nightgown with the back of my heel, this caused the wide neck of the gown to slip from my shoulder exposing my right breast. I clutched the offending garment to me, hastily pulling it up, trying to restore my dignity in front of the man with the dark brown eyes. His name I would know soon enough. Jarren Polverne.

It was a strange meeting. I blushed scarlet and felt incredibly shy, turning my back on him pretending to rearrange my dress on the chair, somewhat flustered at my instant attraction to the man whose handsome face had gazed upon my naked bosom, the slow smile which spread across his face as he did so, telling me the attraction was mutual.

'I have seen so much of you and I don't even know your name,' he teased, breaking the awkward silence as still I busied with my clothes on the chairs.

'It's Layunie,' I replied trying to sound much more confident than I felt and turned around, raising my eyes to meet his.

'Come here,' he ordered and obediently I stepped towards him as though sleepwalking. Gently he tilted my chin upwards and in seconds I found myself crushed in his arms, being kissed like I'd never been kissed in all my life, held in a timeless world of passion, responding to the urgency that erupted within both of us, ended only by a very discreet cough from one of the two people who stood in the now open doorway of the cottage.

Abruptly he let me go, and I stood reeling with discomfiture at being caught in such an unladylike manner before strangers. Not him though, he just grinned at me most wickedly.

'Jarren Polverne, you leave the poor girl alone, you rogue, just out of bed and barely decent she be, and you taking advantage of her already, shame on you.' The woman scolded him in familiar banter and he just smiled wickedly, looking over towards where I stood, red faced.

'I'm Tilley, my dear,' she said warmly, taking off her worn bonnet and placing it on the table. 'Have no fear, I'll see to it Jarren behaves himself in my home and that's a promise, maid.' Jarren went over and put his arm around the little plump figure hugging her to him, pretending to feel duly chastised.

'Pray meet my good friends Tilley and Jack whose hospitality I accepted on your behalf when you were in dire need of shelter,' he gushed, patting Jack on the back whilst I somewhat nervously thanked them for letting me stay, suddenly feeling rather silly standing there in just my nightgown. Tilley came over and ran her hand along the hem of my dress, feeling to see if it was dry, then gave me a knowing smile and took charge of the situation, shooing the men from the cottage whilst I dressed.

A short while later I sat down at the rickety table with Tilley and Jack, listening as Jarren explained what he had planned, taking my hands in his as he made it clear that if I wished to be taken to Trevoran Court it would be arranged thus.

'The choice is entirely yours,' he insisted. 'You're free to make your own decision, twas rash of me to make off with you in such a fashion, but seeing the crest on the coach and knowing to whom it belonged, I had to do it.'

It was time for me to decide, I had escaped that which I feared most, marriage to a man I loathed; this was my last chance of freedom. I looked across the table at Jarren, our eyes met and I felt a rush of love for this man I scarcely knew, and that I'd agree to whatever he had planned so long as I was with him, thus sealing my fate forever.

There was so much to discuss and arrange that the day sped by. Midday, Tilley prepared a simple meal of vegetable broth and freshly baked bread. The long journey that would take us down the coast needed careful planning. It was decided we would set out for

Gwithian early the next morning, Jarren knew of a place I could stay much safer than here at Tremaron. He tried his best to reassure me that Trevoran could not retract from his agreement with Father for indeed my abduction from the moor could not have been foreseen, a fact his own coachman would vouch for. I felt an overwhelming sense of finality, for fate had intervened and now I must prepare for whatever adventure lay ahead.

By the end of that first day I'd learnt little about Jarren himself, making him still a man of mystery, a smuggler yes, but his voice was cultured, his manner that of a person used to being obeyed and those dark eyes were more foreign than English.

After we ate a simple supper, the men folk left us almost immediately. Tired after a day that had passed so quickly, still aching from the rough journey here the night before, it was a relief when the time came once more to climb the ladder and crawl into that soft bed of straw.

Sometime, how long I can't be sure, but it seemed long after I'd fallen asleep, I was startled into wakefulness. I sat up in bed and listened, realising at once what had woken me, the sound of wheels on the rough track outside. Leaning over, I looked out of the little window, cobwebs caught in my hair and I brushed them away, watching intently as a shadowy procession of horses, wagons and men made their way past. The moon shed little light, I could scarce see those who passed below my window before they melted into the darkness once again. Surely all the men in the village must be in on tonight's smuggling activities; for this was without doubt what I was witnessing.

Beneath the loft I heard movement and guessed that Tilley was waiting for Jack's return; indeed, he soon appeared, leading his horse and laden wagon towards the side of the cottage, two others were with him. I sat back on my straw bed and listened. Downstairs there was a great deal of noise and movement with hushed voices and soft laughter. Crawling over I peeped down from the loft, disappointed to find the activity out of sight with nothing to be seen just flickering candlelight. Speed it seemed was all-important and soon the sound of heavy breathing replaced the laughter I'd heard earlier. Then came a loud bang followed by a slow grating noise. Footsteps made towards the door and I looked out through the window once again, watching as the men who'd been with Jack became shadows in the night.

A few last wagons rolled by and then silence even in the room below; but sleep seemed impossible now, somehow my mind was so full of what I'd witnessed. At last when tiredness must have overcome me and I was almost asleep, a horse being ridden for all its worth shattered the silence. Still half asleep I took little notice until the pounding hooves stopped right outside, and someone beat upon the door with great urgency. Jack must have opened the door, for immediately I heard someone breathless, talking very fast. The door banged shut, and looking out through the window, I saw Jack and another man knocking at cottage doors and giving the occupants a hasty message. When Jack returned, the row of cottages opposite were in complete darkness.

Awake now, I sat up in bed completely still; below I heard Jack and Tilley whispering quietly. Moments later the sound of another horse ridden at breakneck speed thundered past, I heard a heavy thump; either the rider had jumped or fallen from the horse, for the sound of its hooves just carried on into the night.

An urgent hammering on the door assured it was quickly opened. Short of breath a voice gasped, 'Tis here they're coming; dragoons along with Ruskin Tripper, making their way to the village.' There was no mistaking the voice which sounded so desperate, it was Jarren's.

'God knows why Tripper's this far up the coast, I've warned all on tonight's run,' was all I heard Jack utter as the door slammed shut.

The blood in my body seemed to run icy cold. I'd heard Jack and Jarren talk of Ruskin Tripper earlier today. Excise officer and friend of Lord Trevoran he was someone Jarren feared, knowing with a certainty he would likely be summoned to find me, and would try any means to do so. A ruthless predator of the smuggling fraternity, the powerful bond between him and his lordship guaranteed him the hatred he deserved. A shiver ran up and down my spine, as almost immediately the top of the ladder began to move and Jarren called softly out to me.

'Sorry, my lovely, but it's the hidey-hole for the likes of us.' And before I could so much as utter a word, I was taken by the hand and ushered towards the ladder. At the bottom, Tilley held a tallow candle, her hand hiding the dull yellow light from the windows. Led by Jarren, I was hurried through a gap in the stone wall which now stood open beside the cloan oven.

There was little room inside, for the hidey-hole was full of brandy kegs from tonight's endeavours; only a tiny spot was free for us to stand in. Jack passed Jarren the candle and banged shut the entrance, moving something heavy in front of it. I heard Tilley's cooking pots clink together as they were re-hung along the rail outside. Just then the candle flickered and went out, leaving us in complete darkness.

In the pitch black, sheer panic overcame me and sensing this, Jarren pulled me towards him holding me tightly.

'Have faith, little one, just remember if anyone comes, tis important we keep deathly quiet.' I felt his strong heartbeat through the cotton of my nightgown, felt his arms go around me holding me tight against him, he kissed my forehead, his hand gently caressing the back of my neck. I went to speak and was silenced as he pressed his lips on mine, caressing me gently with an intimacy none had dared before, and I feeling not the slightest inclination to pull away and deny his pleasure.

The silence beyond our dark world was soon shattered by a loud hammering on the door. It sounded as though the cottage was being entered by an army of men, the very floor of the hidey-hole vibrated. A sharp and commanding voice sounded above the others. I heard Jack protesting and Tilley's cries of anguish as their possessions were roughly cast aside and searched. The bed must have been upturned for something thudded against the wall. My heart pounded and I hung onto Jarren as the heavy table in the middle of the room was surely being dragged across the flagstone floor. Gasps of satisfaction were followed by the sound of more upheaval, then moments where only Tilley's sobs could be heard. A clamour of footsteps came, seeming to come so close to the very spot where we stood. Terrified, I let out an uncontrollable gasp. For a moment I felt the man beside me tense and a firm hand was placed over my mouth, I could hardly breathe. Thus, we stood for what seemed an age until further orders were shouted, the footsteps retreated, the intruders gone.

Jarren took his hand away and whispered, 'What they found was the decoy cellar, it served its purpose well.' He gave my hand a squeeze, and I knew we were safe for the moment.

At last Jack opened the hidey-hole, I stepped out into the dimly lit room and gazed around me in disbelief. The cottage had been totally ransacked; overturned furniture lay where it had been carelessly thrown aside. Running over to Tilley, I put my arms round her giving her as much comfort as I could, whilst the men set to work placing the furniture back in some kind of order. Each was questioning how the excise knew of tonight's run, was it chance or something more sinister, just why was Ruskin Tripper here on this stretch of the coast, this was Robert Readers territory. The questioning of it went on between them with Jarren adamant it was too soon for him to be here because of my abduction, but Jack insisted, as he placed the last chair in its place.

'That man wouldn't be this far up the coast without good reason.' It was no good though, Jarren couldn't be persuaded to agree.

A trundle bed was pulled out for Jarren and he kissed me lightly on the forehead before I climbed gratefully back to my bed in the straw.

Early the next morning and feeling barely awake, Tilley fitted me out with a heavily patched cloak, grey dress, woollen shawl and bonnet, together with the oldest boots I'd ever seen. I hoped one day I could repay her for such kindness. My hair she scraped back into a tight bun, but what altered my appearance most was the padding tied round my waist under the dress, making

me seem very pregnant. I felt shy when Jarren knocked
and walked in, but his expression clearly showed a
liking for what he saw, and he gave Tilley a nod of
appreciation.

'You'll do as a little wife.' He grinned, dark eyes
sparkling with amusement. He was in a hurry to be off
so there was little time for conversation. Jack had harnessed a horse to a small cart and Tilley handed me a
basket of food, giving me a last hug of reassurance. I
kissed her rosy cheek and thanked her from the bottom
of my heart for all her help.

'Good luck to you both and God's speed,' her final
words as Jack steadied the horse, and Jarren's strong
arms helped me up onto the wooden seat. It was time
to go.

Earlier, Jarren had told me ahead of us lay a long
journey, much of it along rough tracks that wound
themselves around the coast. I looked back and waved
Tilley a final goodbye as we made our way out of
Tremaron, so very grateful for the shelter given me in
that tiny cottage. We headed westwards along the
blustery cliff tops and I tasted salt sea air on my lips for
the very first time. Jack rode alongside us on horseback
for a while, before wishing us farewell and heading
back. I felt strangely alone when he'd gone, suddenly a
little afraid of what lay ahead and of my future with this
man who sat beside me.

It was a slow journey and I wished it over, for the
rutted uneven tracks were sometimes perilously close to
the cliff edge and the pounding sea below. This together
with the knowledge that by now his lordship would have
organised a search for me, led me to cast my eyes around
in all directions, expecting any minute that someone

would approach us. After a particularly steep descent, the track levelled out, here the ground although stony was much better. When it widened out into a clearing, I ventured to ask Jarren where exactly he was taking me, conscious as I spoke of my voice sounding childlike and unsure. How dependent I was on him, and how my heart skipped a beat as he turned to me and smiled.

'You've nothing to fear; I'm taking you to a place called Chy-an-Mor high on the headland at Godrevy. Kate Penrose who lives there is the widow of my old friend Adam, you'll be quite safe, little one, I promise.' He put his arm round me and pulled me closer.

'It's been a home to me whenever I've needed it, a safe haven to return to. Kate's husband was my best friend going way back when we were but boys growing up in St Ives. Twas natural for us boys to help out on smuggling runs, it made us feel like men, and so we carried on until we were men, escaping the revenue many, many times; silly chances we took, then one night our luck ran out and Adam was killed.'

He paused and I sensed his sorrow, watched a tiny nerve twitch beside his mouth as his jaw tensed. Gently I laid my hand on his arm.

'I'm sorry. It must have been dreadful to lose such a good friend,' I stated softly, knowing no words could quell his anguish.

The ground still flat, he let the horse choose its own pace and relaxed the reins. 'A sad time it was, afterwards Kate moved up to Chy-an-Mor when old Mrs Raddy died, and now Kate plays her part in keeping us one step ahead of the excise. She lights a lantern and places it in an upstairs window which faces out to sea, a warning should she see or hear the excise or dragoons searching the cliff top or gathering in wait for men coming up from the beach. Many a life she's saved. Tis the best place to take you, the old house has some secrets of its own, I wouldn't take you there if I thought you wouldn't be safe.'

'It's foolish of me to be bothering you with questions, I shouldn't have asked.'

'Tis as it should be.' Jarren smiled, pulling me even closer. I lay my head on his shoulder and fell asleep wondering about my mysterious destination. Much later when I woke, we were travelling along a narrow lane between high hedgerows. Briefly I caught glimpses of an enchanting sea hardly ruffled by the breeze, it looked like a blanket of soft blue velvet. I was grateful when Jarren, realising I was awake, decided to stop awhile and we ate the food Tilley had prepared for us before continuing.

As the light began to fade so the breeze suddenly seemed to gather strength, in truth I was glad to hear our journey was all but through. In the distance dotted about I saw a few faint lights which Jarren said came from the cottages at Gwithian, then just as I thought our way would lead us through the village itself we turned off, making our way up a winding track which seemed barely wider than a path, leading towards the headland jutting out to our right. When we came to the end, there standing like a shadow against the sky was Chy-an-Mor.

A dog barked furiously, and a curtain moved just a little before the front door opened and Kate stood in the doorway. Jarren jumped from the seat of the wagon and lifted me down.

'Tis good to see you, Jarren, you too, miss.' The smile Kate welcomed me with made me feel like an old friend rather than a stranger. Once in the parlour, Jarren wasted no time before asking if I could stay awhile.

'Of course, she can stay.' Kate held out her hands and grasped mine. 'It will be nice to have some company. If you are who I think you are, you've caused quite a stir even down in these parts, we've all heard about Lord Trevoran's bride being taken off the moor.' She glanced at me and smiled.

'Now I've seen the maid myself it's no wonder you made off with her, Jarren. Mind you they're searching everywhere for you, his lordships made it clear there's money for whoever finds his bride and money for the capture of her abductor. So far, I haven't heard your name linked with the deed, Jarren, but one thing's for sure they'll never find her here.' Jarren bent over and gave her a friendly kiss.

'You're a good woman, Kate,' he declared, giving her another kiss and smiling broadly over towards me. At Chy-an-Mor I could tell he felt quite at home, going over now to crouch down beside her newly kindled fire and throwing on more brushwood.

'Making yourself at home as usual I see,' Kate exclaimed in a voice which told me she was happy to have him here, then she turned her attention to me and picking up a candle from the mantle beckoned me follow her up the steep staircase. 'Best get you settled.'

At the top of the stairs she opened the door to the right, and from her candle lit the lamp on the table, by its cosy glow I could see a pretty blue and cream room furnished with everything I could want.

'This is lovely, thank you for letting me stay, Kate,' was all I could say, overwhelmed, tears prickling behind my eyelids. I sat down on the bed feeling quite lost, overcome by all that was happening, and the kindness complete strangers were showing me.

'I'll enjoy having you here,' Kate replied, and seeing I was near to tears passed me a handkerchief before her broad little body vanished downstairs returning with a pitcher of hot water which she placed beside a pewter bowl, laying out on the bed a nightgown, hairbrush and other items I should need.

'Come down whenever you're ready, they'll be supper shortly,' she said softly. 'You can take that bundle from under your dress now, you'll be more comfy.' And closing the door she left me alone.

I got up and went over to look in the oval mirror above the mantle dismayed at my bedraggled appearance, hastily pouring water from the pitcher and splashing it on my face, unpinning my hair and tugging at my unruly curls with the hairbrush. There was so much I wanted to know about Jarren and longed to find out. But above all, I wanted to look my best before I saw him again.

When the time came to go down to supper, I felt extraordinarily shy as he stood up as I entered the parlour. Feeling my cheeks redden as he pulled out a chair for me to sit on and stole a quick kiss from me behind Kate's back. She ladled out broth into bowls and cut thick chunks of bread that we ate with relish, asking me questions about the circumstances that led me to Cornwall. When I'd finished telling her the sorry tale she reached across and patted my hand.

'I'm glad you're here, maid, tis a sorry plight you found yourself in. It's a young husband you need not an old goat like his lordship, despicable man he is, tis only a little parcel of land he owns in these parts but he treats his tenant farmers real bad, he's not fit to wed anyone, and as for your brother he should be ashamed of himself, well and truly.' She gathered up the plates and left us alone, purposefully closing fast the door behind her.

Seconds later, Jarren had me in his arms, his lips brushing my hair as he held me tight, drawing away and looking into my eyes before holding me tighter and kissing me again, his mouth forcefully probing mine. His grip on me tightened as I responded, overwhelmed by the passion I felt, having no desire to flee as his hand gently slipped beneath my bodice. I could have stayed in his arms forever but finally, gently, he set me free.

'Layunie, my darling girl, sadly I have to leave you, its time I was gone. I'm to join Giles Galley aboard the *Rosemary* for we sail for France on the morning's high tide.'

I went to protest but once again his mouth covered mine and I found myself responding to the probing of his tongue, responding to the feel of his hands upon my breast, abandoning any ladylike notions I'd been taught, caught up in a flurry of desire too fierce to dampen. I loved this man.

At last we drew apart and I buried my face in his coat.

'I'll be back; then you'll be mine. I'll not be gone long, I promise. Stay here with Kate and wait for me, twill be but a couple of weeks at most.'

He gave me one last lingering kiss before Kate returned and with arms still entwined, I went with him to the door. Moments later my eyes brimmed with tears as I stood beside Kate, watching as he disappeared down the lane and into the night.

Even as Kate closed the door, I was already worried, and seeing my troubled expression she put a friendly arm through mine. 'Now, maid, don't you go worrying, he'll be back safe and sound, Jarren can look after himself. You go on up to bed now and get a good night's sleep, we'll have a good talk in the morning.'

Indeed, the hour was late and the thought of the comfortable bed waiting for me upstairs very welcome, gratefully I took the candle Kate offered and said goodnight.

I awoke to the sound of seagulls and getting out of bed opened the lattice window letting in the fresh salty air, only a faint breeze ruffled the sea and I thought of Jarren out there somewhere on his way to France.

A short while later Kate knocked and came in with freshly laundered clothes and combs for my hair, on the washstand she placed another pitcher of water, and as if reading my thoughts, she came over to the window following my gaze out to sea.

'Don't worry, it won't be long before Jarren's back and the two of you can make plans. Best get dressed now and come down when you're ready, fretting by the window won't bring him back any quicker. Just one thing I'd best mention, be sure to always to keep your personal items in my room. There's a little chest of drawers behind the door, keep them there just in case we have unwanted callers.'

It felt good to be in clean clothes and able to run a brush through my untidy curls, I took heed of what Kate had told me, stopping just briefly once more at the window to glance out to sea thinking of Jarren and trying to convince myself he was in no danger.

After we'd eaten, impatient with curiosity, I asked Kate to tell me about Jarren eager to hear everything she knew about the man I loved but hardly knew.

'It's difficult to know where to begin,' she sighed, tracing a pattern on the wooden tabletop with her finger. 'I've known Jarren for years, even before I married Adam, I'll tell you as far back as I know. Adam lived in a huddle of cottages just off the harbour in St Ives, the Polvernes lived there too. Adam was friendly with all the Polverne brood, but the streak of recklessness he shared with Jarren as they grew from boys to men bonded them together.'

I tried to picture the younger Jarren, but it wouldn't come, all I could picture was the man he was today.

Softly Kate continued, 'Even after I married Adam the two were inseparable, it seemed lady luck was always on their side. Then, one night—' Kate stopped and her voice began to quiver '—one night, the revenue surprised them, high tide it was near Sennen, a good little boat they had, the *Ann* she was called, slip through the sea like an eel she could. They'd painted her black, so she was practically invisible on a moonless night, with her dark sails rigged fore and aft. That night a storm was brewing so speed was essential, smaller boats had already begun to ferry the goods ashore and the tub men had waded out to the shallow water ready to get the brandy ashore. It was then the dragoons and revenue led by Ruskin Tripper came upon them. Adam was rowing ashore in one of the small boats and in the mayhem that followed, the boat hit a sunken rock ripping it apart.'

I begged her not to go on as clearly these memories upset her, but bravely she wiped away her tears with the tip of her apron.

'Adam tried to swim ashore, but the incoming tide carried him forward smashing him against the rocks further in. Jarren tried to save him, but the revenue seemed everywhere both on the beach and in cutters firing shot after shot.' Getting up, she walked over to the window.

'My life seemed to end that day. Twas Jarren that told me Adam had perished, and others that told me how he'd risked his life to save him, searching for Adam amongst the swirling waters regardless of the danger of losing his own life. It was a hard time that followed, none could help his sorrow nor mine but we both survived. Jarren saw I needed for nothing, and when old Mrs Raddy who lived here died, I moved up from St Ives to continue as the old lady had been done for years; keeping a watchful eye from this vantage point, ready to give warning to ships anchored offshore and those in the small boats waiting to come ashore.'

I joined her beside the window, silently looking out at the wild deserted cliff tops and sea beyond. Then as if out of nowhere an old woman appeared, black cloak billowing in the wind as she struggled up the overgrown path leading to the back door. In panic, I turned to run but Kate clasped my arm and stopped me.

'Now here comes someone who can tell you more than I can about Jarren! It's old Martha, she lived nearby to the Polvernes in St Ives, known Jarren all his life, don't worry there's no danger in her seeing you here, there's no fear of her telling.' She opened the door at the back of Chy-an-Mor and helped the breathless woman in. To me, she looked likely to expire at any moment so rasping was her breath as we helped her into a chair. I was aware of her scrutiny and felt a trifle unnerved by it.

'Well, Kate,' she declared. 'I'm an old woman but I think I know who this is.' She pointed a bony finger at me, her concern for Kate clearly showing on her wrinkled face. 'Johnny Fisher told me the *Rosemary* sailed on the high tide, so I take it Jarren was here and this young maid is the one they're all looking for, am I right?'

'And it will be my pleasure to have Layunie here until Jarren's back,' Kate emphasised, and I knew then that Martha felt it too dangerous for Kate to have me here.

It took a while to break down old Martha's wariness of me, but as we talked slowly she began to accept my presence, sensing with the help of some strong hints from Kate, that Jarren was much taken with me and I with him. I was told quite plainly then.

'If it's notions of taming him, maid, you've an impossible task, he's wild is Jarren, foreign blood, comes from his mother, poor soul, father too maybe, sets him apart from others, those dark looks of his, he's handsome right enough, too handsome!'

Did I detect a warning look from Kate or was it my imagination? However, she did seem a trifle anxious to change the course of the conversation.

'Tell Layunie about the day they found Jarren's mother,' she prompted, and clearly fond of him, old Martha settled back in the chair remembering.

'Nigh on thirty years ago it must be now, us old folk will never forget it, washed up on the beach she was, the sole survivor of a ship pounded to pieces on the rocks.' I listened intrigued willing her to carry on.

'Sam Polverne found her, a bundle of rags he thought at first, barely alive. Sam carried her back to his cottage and his wife tended to her and weak though she was, the poor soul, she gave birth to a son, dying soon after. Buried up at St Mark's, she was at first, God rest her soul. Mary Polverne named the baby Jarren after the wrecked ship the *Jarrenmayne*, brought him up with the rest of her brood, telling him when she felt the time was right about his birth, and how his poor mother feebly cried out in a foreign tongue as she gave life to him. Gave Jarren the gold coins the poor maid had sewn into the hem of her dress, along with the rings she'd round her neck on a gold chain, twas his, they said, not touched since they'd placed them in a wooden box hidden away in a cubby hole all those years ago.'

I wanted to know more, ask questions, but Martha slowly eased herself up, holding the table to get her balance, she looked straight at Kate.

'Them searching all over for this young miss, I'll tell you plain, Kate, tis foolish what Jarren's gone and done, tis a hanging offence, does he know that?' She exaggerated her words and looked over at me. I bit my lip with fear, her words sinking into my very heart.

'I've said what I feel, that's not to say I don't wish you well, I know how headstrong Jarren can be when he takes a notion to do something.' Martha tugged her cloak around her and started making her way towards the door, glancing at me one last time.

'Don't go fretting I'll tell no one you'm here be sure of that, they'll not hear it from my lips.' As Kate lifted the latch, I overheard her say, 'For heaven's sake, Kate, take extra care,' and felt dreadful that I was here placing her in danger. I watched as the two of them walked down the path wondering what else old Martha was saying.

Where the path narrowed Kate stopped, she turned back and I watched as the little old woman continued, and gradually vanished from sight between the hedgerows.

I was to learn nothing more about Jarren, for when Kate returned, firmly bolting the back door, she said calmly, 'I've taken Martha's advice and have decided it's best I show you where to hide should we have unwelcome visitors.' She led me over to what I thought to be a cupboard but was in fact a fairly large larder set well back in a recess to the left of the wide hearth. When she opened the door, I saw inside a mixture of household items including preserves and cooking implements, on the back wall several aprons hung from hooks.

'Watch.' Kate turned the hook furthest right and the wall swung forward leaving a gaping black opening. I stood open-mouthed in astonishment, stepping forward to peer into the darkness, just able to see that a flight of steps led downwards, and smell the pungent musty air. Kate was lighting a small lantern and I stood aside as she passed in front of me.

'You saw how I opened the back of the cupboard, come now and I'll show you how to close it.' Stepping through after her, by the light of the lantern I watched as she pulled a rope fastened to a pulley at the back of the door and it clicked shut; by pulling the rope upwards the door reopened.

'Can I try?' I asked. Knowing how important it would be I do this properly, and Kate watched until she saw I was familiar with how the mechanism worked.

'Good, now we'll continue on.' She smiled trying to reassure me as I peered into the darkness.

'This is the way you must take if you need to escape.' Holding the lantern high she began making her way down the well-worn steps and I followed just a little way behind.

The passage was extremely narrow with very little headroom. The winding steps grew steep and uneven, carved out of sandstone and in places solid rock. The walls and ceiling were wet and glistened in the light of the lantern. Obviously, Kate was quite used to coming here, but in all truth, I was glad when at last we stepped down into a lofty cavern. On an old table was a larger lamp which Kate lit, and by its more powerful light I saw fully the extent of smuggled goods hoarded away here. Barrels were stacked high against the walls, casks of all kinds piled one on top the other. I felt a kind of strange excitement mingled with a chill of fear, a shiver went through me and I felt scared of the risk the smugglers must take. Jarren among them.

Kate picked up the larger lamp. 'I'll just show you a little way further on and then we'll go back,' she coaxed.

Another passage led off at the far end of the cavern, and following Kate, I set off down more rough uneven steps until I knew we must be getting nearer the beach below Chy-an-Mor, for in the distance I could hear the sound of waves breaking against the rocks. We came to a part of the underground passage where the sloping floor was much steeper than before, here, thankfully, thick ropes hung from hooks embedded in the rock wall. Carefully I made my way down until standing beside Kate on a rocky ledge, we reached a point where the present tide flooded our way ahead. Before us was a cavern of churning water.

'This passage continues until it descends into a small cave well hidden by boulders on the beach. The only problem you could find—' but she didn't finish the sentence for a huge wave surged through the cave soaking us both in spray. Wet through, we quickly made our way back, I should have asked what it was she'd been about to say, but didn't.

* * * * * * * * * * * * * * * * * * * *

The days of isolation passed quickly, for there was much to keep me occupied, the long hours spent as a child over my needlework were well put to use altering the different items of clothing Kate had given me.

One afternoon though, we did have a visitor. Jack, who'd ridden down from Tremaron, bringing news of my aunt who'd been left stranded on the moor. She was safe; the riders we'd heard approaching that night had been revenue officers returning to Bodmin. Jack scowled when he mentioned them, showing his obvious dislike of such individuals.

'They discovered your aunt in a state of great distress beside the coach, she was crying and hysterical with worry. Having calmed her they discovered what had taken place, and recognising the importance of just who you were, they gave assistance to the coachman, then escorted your aunt to a coaching inn just outside Bodmin. The innkeeper's a friend of ours, customer like, that's how I knows. Immediately word was sent to Lord Trevoran who duly arrived in great temper the next day, accompanied by Ruskin Tripper and around fifty dragoons. A search was ordered immediately.'

Kate placed a tankard of ale on the table and thankful of it, Jack reached over and took a hearty swallow. Looking up, his kindly face broke into a smile. 'My Tilley, miss, she insisted I came, knew you'd like to know about yer aunt.'

I was indeed delighted; this would be the one and only time I should ever be grateful to men of the revenue.

'Thank you, Jack, for coming here, tis good to hear all's well.' I held my hand out to him and he took hold of it, squeezing it softly between his large rough hands. And tentatively I asked, 'One thing, Jack, something I never had a chance to ask Jarren, just what exactly was it that he and the rest of you were doing out on the Moor that night.'

He grinned. 'We were on our way to make a delivery to the 'The Black Boar' near Bodmin, the very inn your aunt was escorted to after you were kidnapped. I delivered the consignment of brandy there three days later, and so t'was Oliver Penhale the innkeeper who warned me your aunt had been brought there, and that revenue were still lodging there. Out searching for you they was, so I made great haste in unloading, but not before a door opened and your aunt came out, catching her breath as she recognised me from the moor, it proper frightened me I'll tell you.' He took another sip of ale.

'Scared, I was, she'd call out so I ran over and begged her not be alarmed, knowing I had to convince her you were safe and well and that no harm had befallen you, poor lady she was visibly shaken. I begged she kept her silence for your sake, Miss Layunie, told her you had decided to stay with my good friend of your own free will, so t'was in her power to let matters rest as they were, you'm no wish to be found.'

At this I smiled, Aunt Sarah shared my dislike of Lord Trevoran, Jack couldn't have put things in a better manner.

'Well, miss,' and here he paused, clearly pleased with himself. 'She agreed to say nothing, only to tell your father and brother that she'd had word you were safe and well.'

'Well done, Jack, you're a friend indeed.' Impulsively I leaned over and kissed his weather-beaten cheek.

'Tis a shame to spoil things but I've brought other news too.' His expression changed and I saw him cast a solemn glance in Kate's direction before looking across to me.

'It's a word of warning for Jarren to take extra care. Oliver Penhale overheard his lordship and Ruskin Tripper talking as he served them supper, he plainly heard Jarren's name mentioned along with others. Oli managed to linger long enough to hear Tripper summon three dragoons who'd just entered the tap room and issued them with a succession of orders. One of these was to find Jarren Polverne, and named places where to search.' A look of hesitation crossed his face before continuing.

'Given the wealth and amount of men his lordship can put at Tripper's disposal, things could get very dangerous.' As Jack disclosed his thoughts to us, I felt terrified for Jarren, together with an overwhelming hatred of this man Ruskin Tripper who'd sent men out to find Jarren, a hatred matched only by my feelings towards Trevoran himself.

Too soon it was time for Jack to leave, we stood waving as he set off. His brief visit leaving both Kate and myself worried and frustrated, but there was nothing we could do for the present. She tried to reassure me. 'If there's the slightest suspicion of danger, usually a signal is sent well before the goods are brought ashore, and the run abandoned.' Far from comforted I now dreaded the consequences should something go wrong.

During the following days all we could do was wait. Kate told me sometimes contraband was brought ashore elsewhere, and a messenger sent telling her she need not keep watch, perhaps this would happen now. And I prayed Jarren was safely back upon Cornish soil taking safe refuge from those who would seek him out. Each night we stood before the upstairs window, looking out upon the ink black sea, but the silhouette of the *Rosemary*, which Kate knew so well, failed to appear.

Frustrated, I longed for word, but when it came, found myself taken by surprise. Calling out to Kate in alarm when I saw a large well-built man with a profusion of whiskers and beard making his way up the lane in a pony and trap.

'Tis Jenkins,' she exclaimed, having peered out cautiously from behind the drapes. 'He'll have brought news with him for sure.' We watched as he climbed down from the cart, and Kate drew me away from the window.

'Best you stay out of sight; the fewer people know you're here the better.'

Moments later came several heavy raps of the doorknocker, by which time I'd quickly made my way upstairs. Kate unbolted the door and ushered our visitor in, his booming voice filling the hallway as he lumbered through to the parlour.

'Good morning to you, mistress, thought it best I come and tell you the *Rosemary*'s been sighted at last, long ways off at present, but by old Jacob's reckoning she'll be here tomorrow night.' His husky tones were cut short as Kate repeated what Jack had told her. A man of optimism, Jenkins seemed unperturbed.

'Kate, listen,' he soothed. 'I know you're worried but just think, tis a long coastline and would be bad luck indeed if we were caught making the run. Ruskin Tripper's no idea where Jarren is, and remember, the last time he slipped Tripper's clutches was down in Hope Cove, miles away.' I couldn't hear exactly what Kate replied, but the booming voice became softer, conveying in it a touch of sympathy.

'Tomorrow I'll tell the men waiting down on the beach, and them above with the mules to take extra care, if you've the slightest notion of trouble, light the lamp in the window, that'll give us good enough warning.'

After Jenkins had gone, we both felt tense and restless. To ease this, I teased Kate a little for as I'd listened to them talking, something in Jenkins manner led me to believe he was more than a little fond of her.

'Don't be so silly,' she laughed. 'That's ridiculous, Jenkins indeed.' She busied about as if not giving the matter a second thought, but underneath I knew she was. We laughed about this on and off for the remainder of the day, diverting our thoughts from the worries of tomorrow night. I tried to keep busy but attempts at re-stitching a lace collar on my dress went unfinished, for I found myself quite unable to concentrate on the tiny stitches.

It was late when finally I wished Kate goodnight, only to lie abed unable to sleep. Somewhere at the back of my mind I kept hearing the vile voice of Ruskin Tripper as he'd entered the cottage at Tremaron and

Tilley's screams as the place was searched, imagining what would happen if his despicable men found Jarren. Above all, I wished tomorrow night was over, and my love safely home.

Kate had long gone to bed but still I couldn't sleep. Getting up, I wrapped a shawl around my shoulders and crept across the landing to the room with the lamp on the stone sill, here I stood staring out to sea. No ships were on the horizon tonight, the shimmering water lit by a mellow moon. A clock on the mantle downstairs chimed two, making me jump, and hastily I crept back to bed trying my hardest to cast my fears aside, maybe Jenkins was right, and everything would go as planned. My heartbeat quickened and a thrill of anticipation surged through me. Tomorrow I would see Jarren.

CHAPTER THREE

The following day was full of anticipation; by the time evening came I had changed into my favourite dress and arranged my hair with the utmost care. Far too early I stood looking out at the empty sea, and watched the sun set over Godrevy Island, the mass of rock a little off-shore, and waited. As the hour grew late, Kate joined me and together we watched until surely it seemed the *Rosemary* would never appear, then suddenly she was there, rounding the headland, sails full blown in the wind, slowly making her way closer into shore. Kate put her arm round me.

'You'll have to be patient, maid, it'll be awhile til you see Jarren, there's work to be done first, tis a big con-signment for um, most of the men in Gwithian are down on the beach.' She felt me tense, for unlike her all this was new to me.

'Don't fret, maid, tis nothing to them, they've done this many times before, and once the cargo's in the small boats, Jarren will come ashore and Giles Galley will sail the *Rosemary* into the harbour at St Ives.'

Only moments later Kate's calm countenance changed for like me she saw dark figures stealthy creeping along cliff top, saw the glint of a silver blade as the crescent moon came out from behind a cloud, then a hammering came on the front door, shattering the silence of Chy-an-Mor.

'Quick, you know where to go, wait there until they've gone,' Kate whispered, as she propelled me forwards, following as in terror I ran downstairs. She lit a candle from one on the mantle and handed it to me, throwing open the larder door and ushering me inside, closing it and dropping the latch into place as the hammering became more persistent.

I heard the wooden front door splinter and Kate angrily shouting at the intruders, it was then I realised she'd had no time to light the lamp upstairs. With a heavy heart I turned the hook and gained access into the darkness beyond, the flame of my candle dancing madly in all directions but thankfully remaining alight. As I placed my hand on the pulley to shut the hidden door, I heard one voice raised above the others, brusquely commanding Kate's silence, it was the voice of Ruskin Tripper, well remembered from that night at Tremaron.

Someone came and searched the larder, their footsteps echoing loudly on the stone flags and I almost stopped breathing for fear of being discovered. I heard a furious Kate demand to know the reason why Tripper and his men were here. 'A scoundrel by the name of Polverne, madam.' I could hear the sneer in his voice as he spoke.

'Polverne's one of those I suspect of kidnapping Lord Trevoran's future bride, but there's another reason for my visit tonight. Many times, my men have been patrolling these parts, and indeed, several times been close to capturing vessels engaged in the business of smuggling. My men have almost caught them when suddenly, as though warned, they've made off, I find this rather curious.'

'Mayhap your men were detected before they thought and therefore the smugglers, if indeed they were smugglers, reacted in the obvious way.'

There was a long pause before Tripper replied. 'I alas cannot dismiss this matter so lightly, in the absence of the usual cliff fires or any of the other methods used to warn the free traders, the only light my men have seen has been from your window upstairs which faces the sea, so answer me this, pray, do you warn the smugglers of my men's presence? I want the truth from you now.' A sharp sound like that of a whip brought down with force upon the table rang out, sending a shudder though me. I heard Kate bravely answer him, her voice betraying none of the uneasiness she must be feeling.

'You have sorely misjudged me, sir, if that's what you think.'

'Well, mistress, we shall see if my theory is correct,' Tripper replied. 'Word has reached me a run has been planned for tonight and a ship sighted. I have positioned my men along cliffs and two revenue boats are close at hand, I shall make sure no light show forth from here tonight.'

He called two of his men by name and harshly ordered them escort Kate into the front parlour and to guard her until his return. Two others he ordered to make sure no lights were visible from Chy-an-Mor. I heard movement and more orders given, then all was quiet.

My heart sank, knowing it was crucial I get a warning to those on the *Rosemary* and the men on the beach; I must do something and quickly. Holding tight to the candle, hastily I began to descend the worn steps at the beginning of the passage, peering down into the yawning pitch darkness. Normally I should have been fearful venturing down into such a place, but I had no choice; Jarren's life may depend upon my actions.

I hurried on; the damp musty atmosphere caught in my throat, clogging my lungs. More than once I stumbled, the steps more uneven and slippery than I remembered. At last I reached the lofty cavern where the contraband was stored, thankful to see the lantern with its shutters remained where Kate had replaced it on the table. Carefully I lit the wick and let the full strength of the light shine though before blowing out my candle.

Holding the lantern high I entered the steeper narrower passage leading down into the cave and the beach beyond. I remembered Kate telling me only the day before of the fires the lookouts lit on cliff tops as a warning if they felt a run had been detected and knew I must try and do the same.

By the time I reached the hazardous part of the passage where the thick rope hung from iron rings in the walls, I had already decided on my plan. My greatest fear now was that the furthest part of the passage and cave itself would be too flooded for me to continue. For I hoped to be able to make my way onto the beach and build a fire with gorse and coarse grass from the cliff face, lighting it from the lantern, and return to the passage hopefully undetected.

Fraught with anxiety over whether the cave would be flooded, I stumbled blindly on, the mossy damp walls narrower in places and snagging at my skirts until I came to the final rough-hewn steps which led down into the cave, hanging onto the rope trying to ensure I didn't slip for fear the lantern should fall and shatter, leaving me in complete darkness without the ghostly shadows cast about by its flickering light.

On my previous visit we'd found the cave impassable, tonight though the sea water was less deep, churning against the side of the cave but well below the tide mark on the rocky wall. I stepped down and waded in my wet skirt and petticoats, heavy now and slowing me down as I dragged myself towards a shaft of weak light ahead. A waft of sea breeze and the sound of waves told me I was nearing the beach.

Chilled, my feet turning to ice in the freezing water, I stood and carefully closed the shutters on the lantern, it would do no good if I was spotted by the revenue emerging from the cave.

With hardly any light from the lantern and only muted light seeping in from the beyond the cave, I felt my way along slowly until I managed to find the entrance of the cave, its sandy floor rising slightly as it came within reach of the beach, water now barely covered my ankles.

The cave was so dark because its entrance was blocked almost entirely by a wall of rocks piled high in front of it to disguise the entrance. Was this what Kate had been about to tell me last time we were here, when her sentence had gone unfinished? Slowly as my eyes grew more accustomed to the dim light, I found a stout ledge on which to set the lantern down, dismayed to discover it would take more than one pair of hands to move any of the rocky boulders however hard I pushed against them. Panic rose inside me; nothing must stop me now.

There were small gaps on each side of the huge rocks, but these crevices, like those at the bottom where the sea flooded in, were tiny. At the top only barely could I glimpse the sky.

I had no option other than to see if there was any way I could get out and watched as the tide swirled in at intervals spilling down into the far reaches of the cave. I looked closer at the largest ragged crevice, and kneeling down on the sandy floor peered out into the night beyond, completely drenched as a wave forced its way through, knocking me backwards, seawater stinging my eyes as hurriedly I scrambled to my feet. Somehow, I must squeeze through this tiny space, it was my only hope of escaping.

Hastily I retrieved the lantern, knowing I had no option but to try. Aware I had but one chance, knowing if the lantern got wet and the flame quenched, my plan was useless. I watched and waited, getting a pattern as to how long it was between the waves, then after the next wave came bursting through and the white froth disappeared, I quickly lay face down in the wet sand, holding the lantern out in front of me as high as I could, and with all my strength dragged myself though the gap. Sharp edges of the rock tore at my dress, scraped the skin from my arms, but somehow, I managed to clamber to my feet just as the next wave came tumbling towards me.

Wet through though I was, the lantern remained thankfully dry and with skirts and petticoats clinging to me I stood still for a moment and looked out to sea. Godrevy Island was to my right. Thankfully the *Rosemary* still looked to be a fair way off.

I began walking along the narrow stretch of sand, cautious now, keeping tight in against the cliff face, desperate to find a place where I could climb. Here the sheer rock made it impossible and the grassy ledges were too high and out of reach. With feet silent upon the wet sands, I walked further, weaving my way between the huge black rocks, desperate to find a suitable place. I began to run, knowing with certainty I'd be unable to recognise my way back, for the huge rocks with their dark alleys and pools all began to look the same.

At last I found a place where it would be difficult but not impossible to clamber up, here the wild grass and gorse grew down almost to the beach and I began to climb. Suddenly from somewhere above me, shattering the intense silence came the clatter of loose stones tumbling downwards. I stopped, holding my breath waiting for more to follow but there were none. I hurried on in fear someone knew I was here. Holding onto clumps of long hardy grass with my free hand, I pulled myself up, tightly clasping the lantern, thankful little light escaped the closed shutters, for clearly I was not entirely alone.

I paused only for a second and took refuge between a scrawny tree and clump of gorse bushes and took a look out to sea. The *Rosemary* was much nearer the shore now and I realised there could be only a short time left to give a warning. I tore hurriedly at the wild grass and gorse about me, heaping one upon the other, ignoring the prickles as they tore my hands to pieces and began to make a pile of it. Finally, I wrapped my skirt around my hand to protect it and opened the shutters on the lantern, lifting the hot glass high enough to let the flame escape, throwing it downwards and within seconds, the fire burst into life.

A shot was fired, and men shouted across to each other through the darkness. I crouched down behind the tree and froze, heart hammering, frightened what would happen next. For an eternity I stayed there, scarce breathing. Apart from another shower of loosened stones that rained down from above, the voices died away, and all was quiet. To my great joy as I looked out to sea, slowly the *Rosemary* altered course. My mission to stop them had been successful. Looking up I could see now that thankfully the cliff face above me was too steep for men to venture down. The beach below seemed deserted.

Tendrils of loosened hair clung to my face and purposefully I brushed them aside, it was time I tried to find my way back. The climb downwards seemed almost impossibly steep. Many times my red slippers slid from beneath me as I sought out niches where my tentative hold on the cliff seemed safe, and I was indeed nearly halfway down when suddenly I felt the ground beneath me begin to crumble. I managed to stifle a cry as terrified I began to slither downwards unable to stop, sent crashing time after time against the rough cliff, my skirts and petticoats though snagged and torn by gorse and brambles, failing to stop my fall. Then at last, bruised and bleeding, I tumbled with an almighty thump onto the soft sand below.

I lay in a heap, dazed. My head throbbed and warm blood trickled down my face. I wiped it away, my hands torn by gorse, stinging with pain and like an injured animal, I crawled into a hollow near the foot of the cliff.

Out of breath, I sat leaning against the rock clutching my skirts about me. Dazed it took a while before I realised my nightmare was far from over, numb with disbelief when I saw that encircling the tiny patch of beach where I'd fallen were huge boulders. Somehow, I struggled to stand, limping and barely able to walk as I searched in vain for some place I could escape, but there was none.

I had no time to ponder this new dilemma, for the sound of a voice somewhere nearby sent me scurrying back to the foot of the cliff, to lie curled up, helpless, and beyond afraid.

Silence followed then another sound, the unmistakeable creaking of oars and the dapple of water as they sliced through it, steadily getting louder, coming closer, filling me with a new terror, making me jump when the same voice shouted.

'Can you see anyone one?'

I held my breath.

'No.'

'Shall we take a look, put out the fire?'

The pause that followed seemed to last forever.

'It's too late, they've done what was intended, the ships gone, we'll turn back.' Once again the oars dipped in the water, until the sound they made finally faded into the night.

A deathly quiet followed, except for the murmur of the sea and the odd screech of a gull.

Freezing seawater began to swirl around me, getting deeper, rising above my ankles, the incoming tide finding its way between thin clefts in the rocks. I sought somewhere to climb up to safety, but it was impossible.

Above me high on the cliff the flames of the fire began to fade as wearily I sought refuge on a rocky ledge barely higher than the seawater. Trembling with cold, all manner of thoughts surfaced in my mind for surely I would drown, soon my life would be over. Just as I had found the man I loved, my beloved Jarren with his wickedly inviting brown eyes and special smile. If only he could rescue me now. I remembered his lips on mine, and tears trickled down my face at the thought of never seeing him again. I lost track of time and my mind wandered through a maze of memories. My father waving me goodbye, Aunt Sarah's screams as Jarren carried me away, even Charles came unbidden to my mind. Until at last all thoughts began to fade.

How long I remained thus I do not know only that as though through the fuzz of a dream I heard my name softly being called over and over again, knowing instinctively it was Jarren who called me. I opened my eyes and shivered, feeling deathly cold. Had it been a dream? No, I heard it again and it was real.

'Layunie.' My name was called softly once more and I managed a weak response. Slowly I got to my feet, steadying myself by leaning against the cliff behind me.

In dazed disbelief I watched as Jarren appeared above one of the rocks and crawled towards me. At the sight of him I found the energy to lower myself down into the waist-deep water, wading through it submerged now almost up to my neck as it grew deeper. I reached the rock where he was, and tears of joy filled my eyes.

'Come, be quick,' he urged. 'Thanks be to God I've found you, tis no time to waste, my love.' He threw a rope down into the water, and ignoring the searing pain of my hands, I held on to it tightly as he pulled me up, so relieved to escape my watery prison.

When I was close enough, he grabbed me by the arm, dragging me to him, briefly kissing my forehead. Carefully he held on to me, helping me down into the water that was much deeper on this side. The tide beat in covering us with violent spray as Jarren swam holding on to me to where a boat was tied up on a jutting of shaft of rock. He handed me into the outstretched arms of his companion, who placed me gently onto the wooden seat in the bow, whilst Jarren pushed the boat further into the churning waves before climbing aboard.

Each took up a set of oars and began to pull away from the shore, heaving with all their might to hasten our departure from this stretch of beach.

I went to speak, but the wind took my breath away, and silently begged that the moon disappear behind the heavy veil of clouds drifting across the sky. The sea now seemed to hold a violet anger as we thrust our way along the coast until Godrevy Island and the cliffs below Chy-an-Mor drew further and further away.

The shot when it came pierced through the night, shattering any illusion we'd held of being undetected. The black outline of a revenue boat bore down upon us and another shot rang out.

Jarren reached over and dragged me off the seat and down into the bottom of the boat.

'We'll beach at Porth Ripler and make a run for it; take a chance they'll not get through Gerrans gap,' Jarren yelled at his companion, and seemingly only moments later the sides of our boat scraped between a band of rocks. I felt a terrific jolt as the boat struck the beach. Lifted quickly onto the sandy beach, my legs felt weak as hand in hand with Jarren I ran towards the vast grassy wilderness beyond. Jarren somehow managing to keep me on my feet. The three of us then began to climb a seemingly endless wall of sand, when we reached the top, I looked back, the revenue men were just landing.

We ran on, the voices of our pursuers getting ever closer. A sudden dip in the dunes surprised even Jarren and we found ourselves helplessly slipping down a vast slope of sand until finally we came to rest. Nearby was a scattering of trees and thick gorse which gave us somewhere to crawl behind for cover.

'Where's Matt?' Jarren queried, and went to stand, anxious to know what had become of his friend, but now the voices were much closer, each becoming more distinguishable as they came nearer. We had no choice other than to stay where we were and await our fate. I felt Jarren feared we would be captured for he reached out and brushed aside my wild curls, pulling me closer, kissing me with a passion.

'I love you, I love you,' he whispered over and over again as the sound of footsteps tramping through the sand came closer.

He released me slowly when a figure appeared over the top of the dune; musket in hand, sand began to slither down towards us as his heavy boots displaced it. I closed my eyes and waited hardly able to breath, until at last Jarren whispered.

'He's gone.'

Then from somewhere came a holler, the sound of shouting increased, and a shot was fired followed by a shrill cry. I felt Jarren tense, cursing beneath his breath, and I prayed that Matt had escaped.

Much activity followed until gradually all was quiet. We crawled to a vantage point and watched as the dark figures made their way back over the dunes and across the sand. There was no sign they'd captured Matt for we saw no prisoner being hauled along by them, perchance the shots we'd heard had wounded but not killed, for thankfully none carried a body either.

We watched in silence as the last man climbed aboard the cutter. With precise strokes they struck off from the shore and began making their way back up the coast, finally disappearing from view, no doubt to report to Ruskin Tripper waiting anxiously on some deserted beach for their return.

Jarren gazed thoughtfully towards our boat which still rested on the beach.

'Luckily, they thought we'd made a run for it inland, so they didn't bother to scuttle her,' he murmured as much to himself as to me.

'It's crucial we get to St Ives before dawn, I've friends there who'll provide us with a safe sanctuary, by daylight these dunes may well be crawling with dragoons.'

Taking hold of my hands, he turned them over and saw just how raw they were, he reached down and tore strips of material from the hem of my dress and wrapped them round my palms.

'I'll need your help, Layunie. If you can find the strength to take the second pair of oars and row, if only a little, it will help bring us more quickly to safety.'

I looked out across the bay, in the distance just a few faint lights could be seen across an expanse of sea, which looked dark and forbidding.

'I'll do my best,' I answered, and as my eyes met those of the man beside me any doubts I had were cast aside.

We crept down to the boat, easily pushing it off the beach and into the pounding sea. I struggled to control the heavy oars as they creaked against the wood, on many occasions my efforts wasted as they only skimmed the water as desperately I fought to keep pace with Jarren. Storm clouds gathered overhead, and it began to rain; the sea grew boisterous with sudden gusts of wind pitching the boat precariously over the rough sea. My faith that we should reach our destination began to falter along with my strength.

'Keep rowing,' Jarren shouted time and time again, and I did until wet through and chilled to the bone I began to feel too weak to row. Another wave broke over us, now it was an effort even to hold the oars. Then just as desperation grew to despair Jarren shouted, 'We're almost there, just hang on.' Finally, the boat bumped against stone steps leading down from a quay. I was too exhausted even to move, and once he'd secured the boat, Jarren picked me up and carried me up onto the harbour. Quickly he made his way through a narrow maze of alleys until we emerged at the top of a cobbled hill and passed beneath a wide arch, above it on a weather-beaten sign swinging wildly in the wind I read the words 'The Star Inn'.

Jarren pounded on the door with the side of his fist and a faint light appeared in the casement above. A face peered briefly down at us and in no time at all the heavy bolts on the stout oak door were drawn back. Hastily we were ushered inside, Jarren having to bend his head as we passed under the low doorway.

I noticed little of my surroundings save for the heavily beamed ceiling and pungent smell of tobacco and ale which hung in the air. Jarren carried me between the cluster of tables and chairs, placing me carefully on a settle beside the dying embers of the previous evening's fire. He began explaining to the stout bearded man in his nightshirt all that had happened. Whispered words were spoken which I couldn't hear, but turning my head, I saw their look of grave concern as I began to shiver uncontrollably.

Jarren placed more logs on the fire urging it back to life, but to little avail. He squeezed my hand.

'George has gone to fetch his daughter Nancy, she'll help you to bed, you'll be safe here, I promise.' He kissed me briefly as footsteps sounded on the stairs.

Nancy followed behind her father, and by the light of the tallow candle in its holder, I could see the look of bewilderment on her face as she gazed at my torn and tattered form seated before the fire.

Swooping down, Jarren lifted me up and carried me upstairs, many stairs it seemed, before at last we came to a tiny bedroom where gently I was set down on a narrow bed. Bending over he brushed my cheek with the back of his hand, about to kiss me when Nancy bustled in and shooed him from the room.

Soon I was eased out of my wet cloths and into a dry nightgown, my wet hair rubbed through with a towel and plaited, my hands bathed in warm water and palms covered in a soothing salve. At last I lay exhausted between clean sheets, thick woollen blankets were placed on top but nothing could stop my violent shivering. During all this time and although few words had been spoken between us, I felt I had found a friend in Nancy. When Jarren came to say goodnight, discreetly she left us alone together.

Kneeling down beside the bed, he cradled me in his arms, his wet clothes replaced with others, his tousled black hair still damp as I reached up to touch his face.

'Lovely Layunie, all this because of me, I'll never forgive myself for the danger you've been placed in.'

Reaching up I put my arms round his neck pulling his face close to mine silencing him with a kiss.

A discreet cough and we parted. Nancy came in and went over to the table and blew out the candle; I could see she was trying desperately hard to conceal a smile.

'Sorry, miss, but Father says it's time we all got some sleep, you too, Master Jarren, off with you, you know where to go, goodnight, miss.' She left leaving the door open and I reached up for one last stolen kiss from Jarren, feeling an awful pang of emptiness as I watched the door close behind him.

Three days passed of which I have just fleeting memories, aware only that I was tossing and turning in a never-ending nightmare, waking briefly to feel completely disoriented. Faces swam before my eyes, muddled words heard in disjointed sentences until at last a calm came over me. I woke and realised someone was wiping my brow, as I opened my eyes, I saw Nancy, who called out excitedly.

'I think the fever's broken, come quickly.' Moments later her father's ruddy face appeared looking round the open door, smiling at me with a slightly embarrassed look as if he felt uncertain at entering the room.

'Good to see you better, miss,' he said, with genuine warmth.

'I'll get Jenny to bring you up some broth, tis a pity master Jarren's not here, only been gone this last hour he has, but there's a note he left for you, Father's got it I'll get Jenny to bring it up with her.'

Nancy brought an extra pillow and helped me sit up.

'Oh, miss, you've been so ill, a right fever you've had, crying out something dreadful these last few days. Master Jarren's been here worried out his mind, but never fear you'll be alright now, the worst is over.' A weak smile was all I could give in reply for I had not the energy even to speak.

I would have taken little notice of the dark haired girl who brought the broth had it not been for the change of atmosphere I felt as she entered my room and the sly glance she shot at me with her dark sloe eyes. Neither did I miss the look which passed between her and Nancy as she placed the tray clumsily on my bed.

She brought no note and Nancy herself went to fetch it from her father. I broke the wax seal and found Jarren's scrawny writing hard to read.

"Dearest Layunie," he wrote. "I must leave for St Agnes, the brandy destined for Gwithian has been landed safely near there, but the curate in whose church it's stored insists it be moved as the Bishop is due to visit any day. I have no choice but to go and make the necessary arrangements. Tis in good health I hope to see you when I return. Jarren Polverne." Nancy watched patiently as I read it over and over again.

'Best tear it up and destroy it, miss, it always pays to be careful.' Her matter of fact voice made me aware she'd spent her entire life surrounded by those involved in smuggling, something which until recently I had very little knowledge of, and tore the note into many pieces, handing over the torn fragments which she tucked safely away in her pocket. She drew the tray closer and with an encouraging smile lifted a spoonful of broth to my lips. Much to my surprise I found myself quite hungry, the broth tasted good and warmed by it I felt much better.

Later I drifted back to sleep, waking with a much clearer head. Nancy fetched her father and it pleased me to hear that word had been sent to Chy-an-Mor telling Kate I was safe. She in turn begged I be told that once the excise men watching over her had left Chy-an-Mor, she'd immediately searched for me. Jenkins had arrived to find her frantic with worry. He told her about the fire on the face of the cliff, this she had no knowledge of having been kept prisoner in the parlour. Both realised I was responsible for the fire, and deeply thankful for the bravery I'd shown. So many could have been lost that night if the run had got underway and the revenue come upon them. She gave Davy, the ostler sent from the Star, my few possessions and a bundle of clothes she wanted me to have, sending me God's blessings for the future and the gratitude of all those villagers who'd been down on the beach that night. When visiting St Ives, she'd no doubt see me should I still be there.

As I recovered, Nancy recounted all I had missed during my days of fever. The troop of excise and soldiers who'd come galloping into St Ives at dawn that first morning. Two had come here hammering with rifle butts on the door, searching the Star, tumbling tired honest travellers from their beds. They'd come up onto the top landing and thrust open the door of my attic room, looking in as I tossed delirious in my bed. A white cap kept my wild curls safely unseen; droplets of sweat lay on my brow, my pale complexion totally transformed by fever. They saw the sparse furnishings and servant's clothes hanging on a hook and fearing my affliction may be catching, taking me for what I appeared, just a servant, they'd quickly retreated.

The whole of St. Ives had echoed with dragoons and excise knocking on doors. Angry cries from the inhabitants could be heard as their cottages were thoroughly searched. It was a dawn the inhabitants of St Ives would remember for a long time.

Ruskin Tripper had taken rooms at the Eight Bells, his men billeted throughout St Ives, Nancy's father George mightily relieved that none had come here.

Thankfully all his rooms were taken. Ruskin Tripper had followed us to St Ives.

Thankfully, the fever once broken quickly began to pass. When I felt better and could leave my bed, the first thing I did was push aside the thin piece of cloth covering the tiny window and look down over the grey tumble of rooftops to the sea beyond, watching the bustle of life in the busy street below, longing for the Jarren's return.

I readily agreed to wear the same grey dress, cap and apron as the other girls working here, Nancy's father had let it be known his niece was down from Lanner to help Nancy, hoping this would quell speculation as to who I was.

Now that I felt better, one night when no travellers were staying, Nancy took me on a tour of the Star. It proved to be an intriguing place with its honeycomb of rooms. Straddling a hill, it had many levels and three staircases, a maze of rooms used by travellers linked by narrow passages with low ceilings. There were doors that led nowhere, built to confuse and delay those who came in search of smuggled goods. Most importantly there was a secret panel built into one of the walls on the top floor, this led to the hiding place in the rafters where Jarren had stayed the night he brought me here.

* * * * * * * * * * * * * * * * * * * *

During the following days I spent much time with Nancy, helping her with the mending and sewing, of which there seemed an endless amount. Thankful that the skills learnt at the academy for young ladies were at least of some good to me.

I had found a friend in Nancy; with her cheery round face covered in freckles and mop of ginger hair as unruly as mine. I loved her sense of humour, but above all she was kind. Like me she was waiting for someone she loved to return. John Penrose had gone home to Sennen to help his father repair the damaged hull of his fishing boat; and like me she was impatient for his return.

I knew it grieved her when Jenny slighted me, which was often. I'd catch those green eyes burning into mine telling me without words that she bitterly hated me being here, but why?

Unaccustomed to doing nothing, for even at Wellowmead I was always busy, I began to wander from the confines of my room and take the back stairs down into the kitchen and help, I disliked being idle. In doing so my encounters with Jenny Weaver increased, and although at first I made attempts at being friendly, these were always ignored and a cold stare all I ever received from her. It was when she contrived to spill slops down my dress that Nancy decided it was time I knew why.

I fled to my room, anxious to rid myself of the foul-smelling dress and Nancy followed grumbling.

'Take no notice of her, proper nasty piece of goods she is to you, all this and them nasty looks she gives you tis because she's jealous, you coming here like you did with Master Jarren, she's taken with him herself. But tis like this, Jarren's known Jenny since she was a child almost, treats her like a younger sister, never given her any encouragement in that way.'

At last I knew why Jenny so resented me, and having picked up my discarded cloths, I took a peep out the window, watching as the subject of our conversation boldly made her way down the cobbled hill. A fresh thought occurred to me as I let the cloth fall back over the window and couldn't help but ask, 'Do you think Jenny hates me enough to tell of my being here? Do you think she knows who I am?'

Nancy's freckled face beamed at me. 'Have no fear she'll not betray you, her brothers are all friends of Jarren's and help out when there's a run, she'd not want to harm Jarren either, she knows what's done to traitors in these parts.'

Although Nancy was convinced in what she said, somewhere inside me the fear of betrayal still remained.

That night I tossed and turned unable to sleep, and finally when I did, was awakened by the echo of a single horse's hooves upon the cobbles. I sat up listening as they came down the hill, ever closer, until they passed beneath my window and clattered under the archway leading to the stables. Getting out of bed, I opened the door and crept to the top the stairs. A solitary candle flickered on the landing below. I stood and listened; faint voices drifted up from the taproom. My heart beat a little faster, could it be Jarren?' My first reaction was to run downstairs and into his arms, but caution was something I was beginning to live with, so silently I crept down to the next landing, disappointed to discern whoever was with George Tought, it wasn't Jarren. Then as I made to go upstairs, I heard his name spoken and remained where I was, far too inquisitive not to stay. The now slightly raised voice of whoever was speaking sounded angry, declaring impatiently.

'Does he realise the danger? He must be mad!'

I couldn't hear the reply so crept down the next flight of stairs to be closer.

'In God's name, does he know what kind of man he's dealing with? Tripper's ruthless, different by far to the other riding officers. Ruskin Tripper was posted here from Sussex for his own safety, the men there having made a pact to kill him; the man's hatred of free traders is legendary, let alone this other business.'

The speaker sounded totally exasperated. I heard George grunt in agreement, as his visitor's depth of feeling continued.

'Now it's said Tripper's in the pocket of that fiend Lord Trevoran, and totally obsessed with finding and returning the old devil's bride, for a very high fee, no doubt.'

'Keep your voice down, man,' George urged, but there was no abating the other's fury.

'Jarren best think of somewhere very safe to hide when he gets back, only he would do something so insane as kidnap the bride of one of the most powerful men in Cornwall!'

'But, John,' was all I heard, just a name for there was movement now, the scraping back of chairs. Frightened at the prospect of being discovered, and feeling somewhat downcast, with a heavy heart I returned to bed. At least I knew who George Tought's visitor was, Nancy's John Penrose.

I was to meet John the next morning; he was seated in front of the huge range in the kitchen. Nancy proudly introduced him to me and although outwardly his manner towards was friendly, I felt he was somewhat guarded, and understood why, having heard him share his views with Nancy's father the night before. His scrutiny made me shy and I felt a blush creep up from my neck, wondering if perhaps he thought me unworthy of the trouble I'd caused his friend. Just as I was thinking this, George sent Nancy out on an errand and I found myself left alone with John, whilst those around us were busily preparing for the day ahead.

Neither of us spoke until at last I could bear the tension no longer.

'I know you're worried about Jarren, I overheard you telling Nancy's father last night,' I said boldly, and he looked up and smiled.

'Then you were mighty quiet for I never heard a sound, and yes I am worried. But I've heard more of how things stand between you and Jarren, and what you did out at Gwithian, Nancy's told me. And now that I've met you, I can see why he did it, I myself would not have let you continue your journey knowing for whom you were destined.'

These words dispelled the tension between us, and I warmed to this fair-haired young man who was Nancy's sweetheart.

It was to be through John that over the next couple of days I acquired a deeper understanding of how dangerous smuggling was, and that in recent months things had got steadily worse with Ruskin Tripper planting more spies in the little villages around the coast. Men pretending they were travellers, prying into the smuggling activities of the community and pointing the finger at the ringleaders who were subsequently seized. Gone now the games they'd played and usually won with Tripper's predecessor David Joy, a man easily outwitted. Then few were caught, or goods seized. One night, Jarren and his fellow smugglers even managed to retrieve captured contraband from the Penzance Customs House within hours of it being taken there.

Times like these were gone now, Ruskin Tripper was devious and clever. John warned me to stay out of sight from those drinking in the taproom and be ever wary. I was still worried about Jenny Weaver and seized the chance one day when Nancy wasn't present to voice my fears to John.

'Jenny Weaver's one of us, Layunie, she knows the meaning of loyalty, tis Tripper's spies to watch out for.' His reply broached no further discussion, and I wished I'd never mentioned my mistrust of her, recognising the fierce loyalty that existed in these parts.

That same evening, I crept through and joined him and Nancy in the parlour. It seemed that John himself was to be gone the next day, the *Lillyanne* would be anchoring off Zennor point and many men were needed to help with the run. A discreet knock came on the door, and I stood out of sight behind it, relieved it was only one of the serving wenches asking John go through to the tap room, for there was a friend, she emphasised the word, asking to see him.

I waited with Nancy, both of us curious, until finally John returned.

'Twas Simon Jago with a message from Jarren, he'll be at Zennor tomorrow night.' And he looked at me and grinned. 'News which will bring a smile to that sad little face of yours, after the run he'll be returning here, he says you must be ready to leave immediately so best be prepared, maid.'

It was indeed good news and I could not help but go over and hug him, so pleased to hear word from Jarren. Shortly afterwards, I left the two of them alone to enjoy the rest of the evening together. Much later, Nancy came to my room in a state of great excitement for John had proposed and her father had given them his blessing.

We talked long into the night like two friends who had known each other a lifetime, I shared her hopes for the future, both of us wondering if somehow Jarren and myself could be at their wedding.

I woke late the next morning on this my last day at the Star and although I tried to keep busy it seemed the longest too. The tedious afternoon broken only by the unexpected appearance of Jenkins who Nancy ushered through to the kitchen. He'd come, Kate's friendly giant, to tell me Kate felt sure she was being watched. Worried it could be one of Tripper's spies it was best she not visit St Ives. A man of few words, Jenkins hadn't stayed long, anxious to get back to Gwithian. Feeling tiny as I stood beside this huge man, as he turned to leave, I meekly touched his arm.

'Give Kate my love and tell her I'm grateful for the time I spent at Chy-an-Mor.'

He heard the anxiety in my voice and put a reassuring hand on my shoulder. 'I will, maid, and don't worry, I'll look after Kate she'll be quite safe.' A gentle hug and he was gone bending his huge frame as he passed under the doorway.

That night there were but a few drinking in the tap-room, but it seemed as noisy as ever. I was used to all the rowdiness downstairs by now and took no notice. I sat sewing in my room, surprised when suddenly the voices below ceased and sensed something was amiss. I sat still as though turned to stone waiting, wondering what could be happening, not daring to get up and leave my room in case it was the excise. I heard running footsteps on the back stair and George Tought's voice, though when I opened my door he was nowhere to be seen, something was very wrong.

I crept out from my room and stood on the landing, a murmur of voices drifted up from below, then a sudden clatter of chairs and shuffle of footsteps. A door was loudly banged shut, and I crept down the back stairs into the silence. By the time I peeped into the tap room it was deserted, only Nancy was there, heaving the two heavy bolts across the door. As she turned, I could see from her face something was amiss, and ran to her through the abandoned chairs and tables begging to know what was wrong.

'Them in real trouble out at Zennor.' Her voice trembled and she wiped away a tear. 'Its bad out there; young Harry's come back with Davy to summon help.' The tone of her voice left me in no doubt, whatever had befallen them was serious.

'What's happened?' I felt desperately afraid for Jarren.

'Tis the excise, they were lying in wait and ambushed our men. First we heard was when Davy and Harry rode into the stables, with Davy so weak he could barely hold on to the horse's mane. Tis Harry as told us of the bloodshed out there, the men from here have all gone to help.'

A trickle of fear ran down my spine. 'Did he mention Jarren?'

'No, nor John; twas the first question I asked.'

I looked on the floor and saw a trail of blood leading across the flagstones and up the main stairs.

'We'd best clear this up in case anyone comes calling,' Nancy said in a matter of fact voice, and I followed her into the kitchen and out to the well to get water.

As we scrubbed away at the floor, desperate cries came from upstairs.

Nancy glanced over and saw my look of bewilderment. 'That's Davy you can hear, Harry's helping to get him to bed, the poor lad's in a bad way, he's lost a lot of blood. Jenny's tending him, no doubt like me she'll try and stop Harry going back to Zennor for he's exhausted but determined to return. Father left with the others; God knows what they can do to help.'

For a moment she stopped scrubbing. 'It's said the excise ambushed the lookouts before they could light the warning beacon. It seems the excise and dragoons stayed hidden, watching the ship until the men set out to bring the goods ashore.'

She began to cry, and I put my arm around her shaking shoulders, there was nothing I could do to comfort her, for inside I felt the same cold fear as she did. We continued cleaning away the incriminating blood until all of it had gone, and bit by bit Nancy sobbed out what she knew.

'Harry told the men here that the first boats were being rowed ashore when Tripper's men opened fire. He made a run for it, but a dragoon caught up with him, beating him to the ground with the butt of his rifle.'

I thought of the lad I'd often seen from the parlour window, so kind and gentle with the horses and felt so much anger.

Nancy's red-rimmed eyes blinked back more tears. 'Harry managed to clamber up the cliff and seize a stray horse, he was riding back to summon help when he came across Davy left for dead and hauled him up before him on the horse. When they reached the quay in

St Ives, they'd stopped first at The Sloop to summon help and then came on here.'

She stopped and we listened as the storm that had threatened all night broke at last, thunder overhead made us both jump and the Star groaned under the strong winds sweeping in from the sea. Rain beat heavily against the windows, and I silently prayed for Jarren and the others out at Zennor.

As we took the leather pails back to the kitchen another shrill, seemingly unending cry came from upstairs, and I followed Nancy as she ran to the passage at the end of the taproom and up the dark unlit stairs.

Harry was making his way down; I could tell even in the dark he was limping badly.

'Don't worry, Davy's alright, Jenny's doing a fine job,' he half whispered to the both of us. 'I'm off now back to help bring any home I can.' Nancy went to protest, and Harry put his hand on her shoulder. 'And nothing you can say will stop me.' Reluctantly Nancy followed him downstairs and I heard the bolts shoot firmly back in place as he went out into the yard.

I went on up, a faint light came from a small room; here Jenny sat beside Davy, a single candle by his bed. He lay with his head to one side, a wad of rag between his teeth, writhing in pain as Jenny cleansed a dreadful wound to his neck and head. Feeling totally useless I stood looking down at him. He was little more than a boy really, barely thirteen or fourteen, his clothes saturated in blood. Nancy poured water from a pitcher by the bed and placed a cloth across his forehead, his eyes opened, mirroring the pain he felt, and I knelt down beside him holding one of his hands in mine. His eyes closed once more, his face tensing in pain.

I asked Jenny my voice a whisper, 'Is he going to be all right?' Half expecting a sarcastic reply, but it never came, the old hostility swept aside by the magnitude of tonight's disaster.

'He'll be fine now,' she replied softly. 'The wound's clean, just the bandaging to do then he can sleep.'

When this was finished, she helped Davy have a drink of water, and together we watched as he drifted off to sleep. In silence we sat, each with our own fears as the light from the candle grew less. When its flame began to splutter sending strange shadows on the walls, Nancy left to fetch another, and so we continued our vigil watching over Davy until the faint light of dawn slowly filled the room, only then did we make our way downstairs leaving Davy still sleeping peacefully. Our thoughts focused on the men we loved and prayed we'd see again.

There was little conversation while we waited; how slowly time was passing. Frustrated and feeling the need to do something, Nancy picked up her shawl intending to go down to the Sloop when we heard a sound outside, and a hammering came on the door. She shot back the square shutter and looked out, hastily drawing back the bolts. A surge of men pushed past, Harry stumbled in carrying Simon Jago, his right leg a mess of bloodied flesh. Other injured men were helped in, their clothes blood stained and torn, they made a pitiful sight these tired dispirited men. To my dismay neither Jarren or John were among them, though to Nancy's joy her father appeared banging shut the door and swiftly ramming home the bolts and checking the shutters.

They carried Simon through and laid him down on one of the long tables. Without hesitating, Jenny ran forward tearing back more of the bloody cloth to expose the deep wound to his leg, whilst I ashamedly turned away in horror. Nancy ran upstairs to find linen to bind the wound and Jenny issued orders for water to be fetched in from the well. Two young boys set off to do this while the others sat exhausted, grateful to have escaped and glad to be here in the relative safety of the Star.

When she came downstairs Nancy called to me, 'Get the men some ale.' And I made haste to do so, stealing a quick look in Simon's direction, almost fainting at the sight I saw, before turning away to fetch the tankards. As I walked back, I diverted my eyes feeling queasy having seen the bloody water in the bowl. I knew Simon through his frequent visits to the Star and to the kitchen in particular, he sensed my unease, his eyes half closed as I handed him a tankard.

'It's not that bad, maid, Jenny'll soon have it looking better, won't you love?' And glancing back I saw the look he gave her.

Not until the last man had his ale did I ask the question burning in my heart, 'Did any of you see Jarren?'

My desperate tone made the men look at me for the first time. I didn't care that I shouldn't be seen, should stay hidden away, my fears for Jarren made me forget about this. Some spoke in hushed tones and others looked at me warily for after all I was a complete stranger. I saw them look to Nancy and Simon, saw Simon nod by way of approval, and one of the men spoke up in a hesitant voice.

'I don't know if this will put your mind at rest or make it worse, I saw Jarren fighting on the cliff top and winning by the looks of it. I can tell you he wasn't with the prisoners being marched off inland, and beg your pardon, miss, to mention this, but he wasn't with the dead or wounded I seen laid out on the grass. Nor was John, of that I'm sure.'

Relief swept over me. 'Thank heavens.' Tears of relief welled up in my eyes and I sat down opposite the man who'd spoken, felt his gnarled old hand reach out and pat mine in an effort to comfort me.

Once his wound was tended it was Simon who broke the news to Jenny that her father and uncle had both been captured, he sat hugging the sobbing girl to him, holding her tightly, his strong arms stroking her back knowing no words could lessen her pain.

Although we tried hard to dissuade her, Jenny wanted to go home to Treveany to be with her mother. Simon told her it was too dangerous to make the journey, besides the weather outside was still dreadful, but Jenny was determined. She made her way upstairs to gather a few things together. Someone came forward who knew her father; setting down his ale he offered to take her if George would lend him his cart. As she hurried past him, Simon reached out and took her hand.

'Thank you, tis well you've tended me.' He pulled her towards him kissing her lightly on the cheek. 'Take care and God's speed, maid.'

There was silence as the door closed behind them, Simon eased himself off the table and onto the nearby settle, he looked over to me. 'Don't go fretting about Jarren, I'm sure he'll be all right, and John.' He gave Nancy a smile of encouragement as she refilled the tankards, and I fetched his ale over and placed it on the table beside him.

'If you're not too tired can you tell us more of what happened?' I asked anxious to know how bad things were.

For a moment he didn't speak just looked at Nancy as she began raking out the embers of the dead fire, keeping busy, unable to cope with not knowing whether John was safe.

'It was going well; the sea was a bit rough but nothing to worry about was it.' He looked round at the others. 'Then came an explosion of musket fire and everyone ran for cover.'

He stared down at the flagstone floor, when he looked up, his face was ashen. 'Those near the top of the cliff hauling kegs up from the beach were taken prisoner, they had no chance to flee, those further down were trapped, forced to turn and join those on the beach.

'I was on the beach and made to escape by running across the rocks. Glancing up I saw the devil himself Ruskin Tripper standing on the cliff overhead. He took aim and fired, that's how I got this.' Simon stopped and winced in pain as he eased his leg into a more comfortable position. 'He fired again but missed and somehow I stumbled on. I was saved by Jacob and Matthew here; they grabbed my arm and pulled me into the cave where they were hiding. Injured and unarmed there was nothing we could do to help.'

The taproom was silent as he paused and took a sup of ale. 'From there we watched men desperate to escape push two boats of ours into the water, too many struggled onboard; the boats capsized. Most were seized by the dragoons and dragged from the sea.' He stopped, took a deep breath and I refilled his tankard. 'Some I fear are lost forever in the clouds of foam beating against the rocks, growing more ferocious by the minute. When at last the fighting on the beach was over and the storm moved inland, we crawled to the top of the cliff, what we saw was a procession of men tied to ponies, being led inland towards Penzance destined for the watch house.'

I could barely conceive what these men had been through and prayed that Jarren was safe.

Nancy got up from the hearth, leaving the newly kindled fire; she sat silently waiting for Simon to continue.

'When we were sure both revenue and dragoons had gone, the three of us made our way back to the beach, joined by others as they came out of hiding. He looked at Nancy. 'Tom Pardoe and William Cage from Madron were among the dead.'

I saw the look of distress on Nancy's face.

'The last man pulled from the water was old Joe, his yarns us all have heard time and time again, but no more. Lucas here'—he nodded over in the direction of a young man at a nearby table—'you tell them, Lucas.' With that, Simon lay back exhausted and closed his eyes.

The young faired haired man struggled to speak, clearly distraught, trying to find the right words to describe the horror he'd witnessed. 'I seen Joe's body floating in the sea, his patched and darned jacket recognisable even though the moon gave little light. I waded in, pulling the old man onto the beach. One of his buckled shoes came off and lay upturned on the wet beach, sea water washed over it, dragging the shoe back over the sand tossing it over and over as the sea reclaimed it. I held Joe in my arms and looked down at his weather-beaten face, the white whiskers yellowed with snuff, finally I closed the sightless eyes.' He gulped back tears and so did I my heart going out to these strangers whose lives were now entwined with mine.

Blood seeped through the bandages on Simon's leg, and getting up I went over to him, but received a look that made me stop where I was.

'Don't go fussing, maid, leave me be.' He was clearly in pain but the anger which darkened his face wasn't caused by his leg. 'In a sudden explosion of emotion, he lifted his fist and banged it forcefully down on the table.

'Good men we've lost this night and by God I'll find the person who informed, for its mighty clear Ruskin Tripper knew exactly where we'd be.'

Simon's fury spent he fell silent. What he'd said caused much discussion throughout the taproom. The hostile mood amongst the men almost frightening as half whispered names of possible traitors were voiced openly.

We waited on into the night, then dawn, hoping for further word to come; none came and finally I fell asleep there in the tap room.

CHAPTER FOUR

On waking, my first thoughts were of Jarren, I prayed he was safe and dreaded the thought that he was out there somewhere injured and alone. I went quietly up to sit beside Davy watching as he tossed and turned, the fever unabated. Gently I wiped his brow with cool water praying his young life wouldn't end.

George had gone to fetch Davy's mother from Porth Mear; her cry of dismay as she entered the room and saw her son, was heartbreaking. I looked at the still form on the bed, Davy's shallow breathing almost undetectable, my faith he would recover wavered. Nothing I could say would comfort this poor woman, her son so obviously near death. I offered her my seat beside his bed and crept from the room.

'No news of Jarren, maid,' George said softly. 'Nor John either.' His voice faltered, and blinking back tears I made my way downstairs.

The hour was still early but I found Nancy red eyed and as anxious as myself pacing the kitchen. I put my arms around her, no words were needed, each of us knew how wretched the other was feeling, all we could do was wait to hear further word from Zennor.

The men were stirring now, and to keep ourselves busy we began to gather up tankards and straighten out the tables and chairs. All was quiet a strange kind of melancholy hung over the place, an echoing silence as the wooden tables and chairs were scraped into place over the flag floor.

We had all but completed this task when the door leading into the courtyard was pushed open and a tall fair-haired youngish man stepped inside. Taken by surprise, wary as to who he was, we both stopped what we were doing. Those in the tap room rose as though to confront him. Nervously he ran his fingers round the rim of his felt hat, looking uneasy as he cast his eyes around the room.

'Can I speak privately with George Tought the innkeeper?' he enquired, having cleared his throat, and addressing neither of us in particular.

'Why?' Nancy asked wiping her hands on her apron.

''Tis only to him I'll speak,' was his reply.

She gave me a look that plainly warned I was to say nothing whilst she was gone; an unnecessary precaution for by now I knew not to do so without being told. Nancy returned with her father who although somewhat puzzled at his being here, clearly recognised the young man, and ushered him through to the private parlour.

After only a few seconds the door opened, and George gestured for us to join them, introducing us in turn to Callum Dann the parson's son from Nancledra.

George looked at his daughter. 'Callum's come here to let us know John's safe.' Her relief was visible, and I too shared in her delight, anxious to hear if he'd brought news of Jarren too.

He turned to me. 'My dear, not such good news of Jarren, I'm afraid, he was wounded, and is in a bad way.'

A sense of numbness and dread assailed me; I wanted to run, to escape whatever I had to hear. I caught a flickering look of pity pass between the two men. 'How bad is he?' I needed to know the truth and noticed Callum Dann took a deep breath before replying.

'He received a wound to his shoulder through a cowardly attack by another during the fighting, someone came up behind him with a dagger intending to stab him in the back, but Jarren turned and the dagger penetrated deep into his shoulder, his assailant fled and Jarren withdraw the offending weapon himself. The wound is deep with much loss of blood, tis nothing short of a miracle John found him and carried him to Nancledra and the rectory. My mother has managed to stem the bleeding but the loss of so much blood has left him very weak. It was impossible to tell at first whether he had any chance of surviving.'

I looked him directly in the eye and asked, 'Will he be all right?' I willed his eyes to return the reassuring message I so desperately yearned to see, but it wasn't there, instead only a look of concern.

'My mother's taking good care of him, he needs rest, that's why it's best for the present he stay hidden at Nancledra, all we can do is pray he pulls through.'

Reaching into his jacket, he pulled out a tiny blue cloth purse and handed it to me. 'Jarren asked me to give you this.'

Inside was the gold ring with its intricate engraving Jarren wore on the little finger of his left hand, unbidden the thought came. *Jarren thought he was going to die.*

I sat down staring at the ring; a tear fell silently onto the little purse leaving a dark stain; but tears would do no good, a determination that Jarren must survive surged through me and I struggled to pull myself together, listening as Callum Dann began talking to George Tought.

'As I was leaving, my father and John were making arrangements to move Jarren to a vacant cottage. It belongs to a relative at present in Truro, he can rest safer there than at the parsonage. The cottage is in a dell surrounded by trees it is easily passed without being seen.

'I must go there,' I pleaded, looking at both George Tought and Callum Dann in turn, so forceful and stubborn my manner they knew there'd be no way of stopping me.

'I wish to go also if John's there,' Nancy added, giving her father a pleading look.

'Did you see any revenue on your way here?' George asked.

'None, sir, not up on the cliff,' Callum replied.

A discreet knock on the door and Mary came in, warning us the revenue were gathered down on the harbour. Hasty arrangements were made before Callum bade us farewell. Soon after, George gave into our beseeching and promised to take us out to Nancledra.

'Don't know what the parson's going to make of it,' he warned us firmly. 'Don't like the man myself, you can't stay that's for sure, he won't take kindly to the likes of you two females being unchaperoned at the cottage. Not too sure I approves of it myself.'

First, we had to make arrangements about Davy who thankfully did seem a little better, his breathing stronger. And although he had not wakened, his mother insisted she'd felt him squeeze her hand. Thankfully, Mary said she'd tend him. Abigail, Jenny's younger sister, came offering her help in the taproom; help George was very grateful to accept. This made it a lot easier for George to take the time to accompany us to Nancledra.

A succession of folk came to the Star seeking word of those who had perished the night before, telling us of some who'd survived, speculation was rife as to who'd informed, each with a mind as to what punishment should be dealt this traitor.

It seemed an age before we could leave. I paced the floor, impatient to be gone. Then at last all was ready. Only a small cart remained in the yard, all the other wagons had been in use the night before. George harnessed the one remaining horse, and we loaded into the cart the provisions Nancy and I had prepared.

George lifted us into the back of the cart, here we sat facing each other trying as best we could to get comfortable. He took hold of the reins and climbed up to perch precariously on the rickety seat in front. We told no one where we were going and thankfully, as George guided the horse and cart out through the twisting back lanes of St Ives, we passed but few folk.

We headed west, the lane now a narrow track and very muddy, we entered an area of silent, barren moorland covered with gorse, moss and bramble. Only two or three isolated cottages were dotted about on the bleak landscape. The track was rough and twisted in all directions. Above us the sky was leaden, heavy with the promise of more rain to follow last night's storm, occasionally we glimpsed the iron grey sea, the turbulent waters reaching out to blend with the sky in a lost horizon.

The bumps and potholes sent the wagon swaying from side to side whilst Nancy and I held on the best we could. We followed the coast westwards until at the top of a small rise George branched off inland and began following a winding lane that seemed endless.

Only on Bodmin Moor had I sensed such total bleakness, huge grey craggy rocks broke the skyline here and there. The journey seemed to be taking an incredibly long time, I felt impatient, helpless as we struggled on so slowly. Time and time again the cart became bogged down in mud. Finally, Nancy and I trudged along on foot, the hems of our dresses dragging in the mire, thorns plucked and pulled on our skirts as we struggled on.

Forced to stop once again we helped George as he tried to free the cart. He swore with frustration as the three of us heaved the wheel with all our might to free it.

'I wouldn't have come if I'd known how bad the track was, and I'll tell the pair of you I've a mind to turn back.'

Nancy tried to calm him. ''Tis only a little way to go now, let us carry on, please.'

George grumbled beneath his breath but continued to lead the horse forward as we stumbled on with mud-sodden feet, the shrill cry of a single gull swooping low above our heads shattering the silent landscape.

Tendrils of escaping curls fluttered across my face and with muddy hands I brushed them back, only just managing to hold back the tears of frustration. At last after what seemed an eternity, we came upon a cluster of grey cottages grouped around a tiny church. The rough track widened, and the ground became firmer making it possible for Nancy and me to ride in the wagon.

As we made our way along the solitary street, children scurried indoors, a group of women glanced at us warily. And suddenly I realised why. Being so close to

Zennor, everyone here knew of the disastrous happenings the previous night, no strangers would be welcome.

Once through the village, George found the landmark which would bring us to our destination. Here we
left the track, the cart bumping over a patch of rough
uneven stones to begin the gentle descent into a tree
lined dell. A little in front of us we saw a lone cottage;
no smoke issued forth from the chimney and as we
approached no movement came from within. I felt a
quiver of apprehension, dreading I find Jarren's condition had worsened or worse still that he was dead. As
we stopped, I jumped down running forward, swallowed up in the long, wet grass. Just as I reached the
threshold, the door scraped open and behind me I heard
Nancy's cry of joy as John emerged from within.

'Where's Jarren?' I asked, and followed his gaze
looking through the doorway into dimness beyond.
Jarren was lying on a makeshift bed on the floor, his
eyes were closed, and he looked to be in an uneasy
sleep. Perspiration covered his face, his fringe of dark
curls glistening with sweat. I watched as he twisted and
turned in obvious pain. For a second, he opened his
eyes, a faint smile touched the corner of his lips. I ran
over and sat on the floor beside him leaning over to
gently kiss him.

'I love you,' I whispered as his eyes closed once more
and knew at once no matter what convention demanded
I would stay here with Jarren, come what may.

The provisions unloaded, I wondered when would be
the best time to tell the others I intended to stay, indeed
I had just plucked up courage to do so when without
warning someone tugged open the door of the cottage

and came in, startling us all. After the shock subsided, George greeted the newcomer warmly.

'Morwenna, we cannot thank you enough, nor Callum, tis a sorry circumstance that brings us here.'

'I'll do all I can and hope to God it's enough,' she sighed. John stepped forward and took her basket as George walked with her to where I sat with Jarren.

'And you must be Layunie.' She gave me a smile of encouragement.

Kneeling down she laid her hand on Jarren's brow. I prayed, fearful she should think him worse, but she made no comment only looked at me and said softly, 'Jarren called your name over and over last night, it will do him good to have you here, maid.'

She began unpacking her basket, placing fresh dressings beside the makeshift bed. 'Would be good for him if the fire was lit, but that cannot be, the smoke would be spotted and a careless word fatal. Alas, I must dress his wound now not later for I cannot stay as long as I planned to.'

I saw the look which passed between the others and wished I had the courage to speak now but stayed foolishly silent, watching as from the depths of her basket she brought forth a covered bowl and began gently to wake Jarren. John placed an extra pillow behind him before Morwenna encouraged him to sip some of the broth before it went cold. She was younger than I expected, small and neat, her hair drawn back into a loose bun, an apron covered her plain black dress, and when she smiled, two deep dimples transformed her plain face into one of beauty.

It was pitiful to watch, Jarren having used all his energy in taking just a few sips of broth became too weak to take more and slumped back, his eyes closed.

Morwenna let him rest and looked up at George her expression serious.

'The plans Callum told you about earlier will have to be changed, two strangers have come to the village, dubious creatures likely as not spies for Ruskin Tripper. They arrived after Callum had left for St Ives and rode off about an hour ago down the coast towards Sennen, but they've booked a room at the Feathers so they'll be back for sure. Nettie ran over to warn me that's why I slipped over here now; I can't come again today it will be too dangerous.' She began to lay out fresh dressings.

George scowled. 'The revenue play this trick, Layunie. After the likes of what took place last night, they send spies to watch, waiting for someone to do something or go somewhere they wouldn't normally, they follow hoping to be led to wounded men hiding out like Jarren, that's why for the present all in the village must go about their business as usual.'

Morwenna placed her hand once again on Jarren's brow. 'He shouldn't be so hot,' she said quietly, as if to herself. But I heard and the pit of my stomach turned over, my heart full of questions I dare not ask. She stood up and looked down at Jarren, her hands flattening out the ruffles in her apron and skirts.

'I fear for Master Jarren should he be found here, but there's no way he can be moved at present, all we can do is pray he's not discovered. Alas there's others in the village I'm afeard for too, like Tom Salt at the Feathers. His foot's twisted and swollen from climbing the cliff last night, and him knowing it mustn't show. Old Greg from Moses Cross is there, hidden upstairs with a broken leg, not so much as a hair's breadth away from the room where the strangers will dwell tonight. The old man's son is beside him with hand at the ready to shut his old dad up should he so much as mutter the slightest cry of pain. The sooner these strangers leave the village the better.'

'Tis a sorry business indeed,' George said, his voice full of sorrow. 'You'd best get on now and change Jarren's dressings, so you'll not be missed. We'll discuss then what's to be done after.'

John fetched water from the well behind the cottage and Morwenna asked me to help raise Jarren forward and hold him still so she could unwind the bandages. I knelt beside her, pleased I could help, but as she removed the bloody dressings I had to looked away. Bright red blood had soaked through them, and I'd glimpsed the raw torn flesh beneath. With the ease of someone used to tending others, Morwenna cleansed the wound, and encouraged by her I overcame my fears. When the wound was cleansed, I followed her instructions and replaced the dressings myself, relieved when finally the task was complete. My beloved Jarren was now barely conscious.

'I'll come tomorrow early before the strangers are up,' Morwenna stated.

Now was the time to speak for I could stay silent on the matter no longer. 'I'll stay here with Jarren tonight, I'll take care of him.' I waited for condemnation at such an idea, more so from Morwenna being a parson's wife than from the others, knowing full well George had told Callum this very morning we must return to St Ives by nightfall.

Morwenna's face at first held the look of disapproval I expected. Nancy offered to stay with me, but George said that would be impossible; if people asked where she was, what could he say? Ruskin Tripper would have informants everywhere and with Jenny gone for the present Nancy would surely be missed and questions asked. John said he'd stay but I told him there was no need and an uneasy silence followed.

'It's against all I know that's right and proper, but with four young children at home besides Callum and my husband, and with his livelihood to think of, if that's how it's going to be then I'll gladly talk you through what's to be done for Jarren. I'm sure the young man's far too ill to take advantage of the situation.'

I thanked her, listening as she continued. 'You must be strong, for it won't be easy, I'll come over tomorrow when it's safe, but you must understand just how seriously ill Jarren is and prepare yourself to accept whatever is to be God's will.' I nodded in agreement and listened intently as she told me what I must do.

Nothing could have prepared me for the silence and sense of isolation I felt following their departure. Having eaten, I lay down fully clothed on the makeshift bed Nancy had prepared. The light that shone through the two small windows began to fade, leaving no doubt in my mind I should keep at least one tallow candle burning for I had no wish to lie here in pitch darkness with only the occasional cry of a bird or animal to keep me company as I watched over Jarren.

Next morning as the pale light of dawn streaked its way across the flagstone floor, Jarren's tortured cries woke me. Disoriented, I jumped from my bed horrified to see his face burning with fever, his whole body shaking as if freezing cold, he was mumbling deliriously between agonising cries of pain. I stood hand to mouth watching in horror feeling pure panic, Jarren was sick, more so than Davy back at the Star and I didn't know how to help him. I dipped a cloth in water and tried wiping his brow hoping to cool the raging temperature but he tossed his head from side to side, arms flaying about pushing me away, he needed help and I felt a total failure, Jarren was dependent on me and I was useless.

I must fetch Morwenna. I thrust my feet into cold muddy shoes and knelt down grasping one of Jarren's hands and holding it still, staring into the tortured face of the man I loved.

'Oh God, let him survive,' I murmured, snatching up my shawl and fleeing from the cottage, traipsing through the soggy grass and along the rough uneven ground until I reached the village.

The rectory, I hoped, was the square solid house beside the church that I'd seen as we passed by yesterday. In sight of the church, I paused for breath, realising the front of the rectory was in the direct view of the Feathers Inn. I drew back retracing my steps, stepping sideways into a narrow alleyway, for I had no wish to endanger Morwenna and her family.

Glancing down the alley, I saw it curved round disappearing between a row of tall trees, even now with dawn firmly established on the horizon the alley was dark and daunting, but I had no choice other than to find out where it led and ran on through the canopy of dark trees to emerge with relief at the back of what I hoped was the rectory.

A white wicket gate opened into the garden and I walked across the lawns towards the one window through which I could see a faint light. Creeping up, I peered in and saw the kneeling figure of a man, bible in hand. Before tapping on the window I hesitated, feeling it wrong to disturb his prayers but at that moment he must have sensed my presence, his head jerked up and he looked over to the window, rising hastily to his feet. In the half-light the thin face I glimpsed appeared sallow and waxy and there could be no doubting his look of displeasure. Moments later he appeared at a nearby door and with an impatient flick of his wrist bade me enter; meekly I followed him down the cold unlit passage into what I presumed to be his study.

'I need your wife's help; pray can you fetch her for Jarren fares much worse, and I don't know what to do.'

He made no reply, but walked over to a dark oak cabinet opening wide its doors, reaching inside to bring forth a tumbler into which he poured a good measure of brandy, this he swilled down his throat in one swallow, then slammed the tumbler down on the cabinet with such ferocity I thought the glass would surely break.

It seemed the Reverend Dann could not bear to bring himself even to look upon my person, for having refilled his tumbler he walked over and stood gazing out of the window, whilst I was left with no other option than to stand looking at the back of his head, wondering momentarily if, like the Reverend Fox at Wellow, this man gave his old clothes to the parish poor. But as the silence continued and I stared at the unmoving figure in his long black clerical coat, glanced down at his tailored knee breeches and fastidiously clean shoes, I thought this most unlikely, this was not a man to think of others' needs.

To my dismay his presence overwhelmed me, held me here waiting when time was so important, Jarren needed help now, every moment precious. 'I beg you—' He raised his hand to silence me and so great his dominance, I obeyed. This man was unapproachable, I must somehow find a way to ask Morwenna herself.

The gloomy rectory and dour man in whose presence I stood was not at all as I expected, it seemed unthinkable that Morwenna with her pretty dimples and friendly manner could be the wife of such a man. He who so rudely stood with his back to me no doubt thought himself to be very godly, very superior.

Was his treatment of me because he had learned from his wife of my being left alone with Jarren? Had he already convinced himself I had committed a grievous sin and endangered my soul, was a fallen woman? His manner towards me bore witness he must believe this to be the case. A growing anger was seething beneath my outward calm, then abruptly he turned to face me. 'I take it you are from the cottage.'

His voice was direct and carried with it no warmth; I nodded tongue tied, never before being the recipient of such a hostile greeting. He walked round me keeping his distance, the glare from his hollow eyes only leaving me once he'd passed through the door. I heard his heavy tread upon the stairs as I stood shivering with cold, shaken and dismayed at this my first meeting with Morwenna's husband.

Minutes later, Morwenna came running down the stairs her face full of anxiety, somewhere upstairs a door slammed shut and I saw her flinch. 'Layunie, what is it, maid, has Jarren taken more poorly?'

With motherly tenderness she put her arms round me and I blurted out between sobs why I had risked coming here. 'I'm so worried, please come back with me.'

'I'll come, don't you worry, it sounds as if the wounds become infected and Jarren's developed a high fever, follow me whilst I collect some things we need to take with us.'

She busied herself in the huge chilly kitchen, exclaiming as she hurriedly put on her cloak and bonnet, 'My husband, as you may have sensed, disapproved of you, an unwed girl, being alone with Jarren, no doubt he made his feelings known to you, he knows not how ill that poor young man is. Principles are all very fine, but they don't stop him enjoying the spoils of the free traders when it comes to filling his own weakness for brandy.'

My heart went out to her, realising life at the rectory must be far from easy and I hoped with all my heart that the Reverend Dann would break no retribution on her for helping me.

As we were about to leave, footsteps sounded on the stair, to my relief it was Callum not his father who came down them, he looked anxious when seeing me there.

'Is Jarren worse?' he queried, genuinely concerned, and the notion came to mind maybe he envied Jarren and the free traders the freedom and adventure they enjoyed, his own life here must be exceedingly dull. I wondered what plans the Reverend Dann had for his son's future.

'I'm going back to the cottage with Layunie,' Morwenna told him. 'Wait here until Polly and cook arrive and then join us. Be mindful of those two strangers over at the Feathers; don't let them follow you. If Jarren's worse, we'll have to bring him here whatever your father says.'

'I'll remind him who supplies his brandy and that it was Jarren who fought off the ruffians who attacked him last summer as he rode home from Penzance. I'll stand up to him, Mother, I mean it.'

Morwenna tenderly laid her hand on her son's shoulder. 'I know you will, son, we'll do what's right by Jarren, let's waste no more time here but be on our way.'

We left by the door that led out into the alleyway, a window opened, and the Reverend Dann shouted down to his wife forbidding her go with me. We quickened our pace and she took no notice.

Thankfully, Jarren was no worse than when I'd left, briefly his eyes fluttered open and I sank down onto the cold floor beside him, running my hand gently across his tormented brow, pressing a fingertip kiss to his lips. Morwenna removed the bandages. A green pus oozed forth from the wound, and I saw a look of dismay in her eyes.

'Tis as I thought; the wound's infected.' She sounded troubled but looked up and tried to hide this with a smile, bravely trying to reassure me that all would be well. 'I'll clean it for now and put some of old Bessy Tree's salve on it, it needs to be done properly with warm water which we haven't here and we dare not light the fire to provide, somehow we must take Jarren back to the rectory with us.'

I held Jarren to me, cradling his head in my arms brushing back the wet curls from his forehead and trying to still his shaking limbs.

'Whatever Bessy puts in her salve the smell of it is dreadful,' Morwenna declared. 'But there's nothing round these parts better for curing infected wounds.'

I sincerely hoped this was true as I placed my hand in front my nose, almost retching as more of the disgusting salve was rubbed onto Jarren's freshly cleansed wounds.

Callum arrived and Morwenna told him of her decision to take Jarren back to the rectory. 'Tis too cold here,' she sighed.

Mother and son looked at each other, I read their thoughts and could not help but ask, 'What about your husband, pray what view will he take on this matter?'

It was Callum who answered. 'He's done well out of the free traders, charged them he has for hiding contraband in the vaults and the hidey-hole beneath the font, tis right and Christian he give refuge to one of them who's needing it.'

With the wound rebandaged, Jarren lay exhausted. I wondered how we were going to get him back to the rectory, for Callum surely lacked the strength to carry him. I needn't have worried, for an old handcart was propped up against the back of the cottage, and this he wheeled round to the front door. Morwenna quickly gathered her things together and I tidied away anything that would show someone had been here recently.

Placing spare blankets on the handcart, Callum gently lifted Jarren from his bed and carried him from the cottage. We closed the door behind us and wasted no time in leaving, Callum trying his hardest to find the most even ground on which to make his way.

We kept well back from the track leading to the village, taking a longer way round, and at times it needed the strength of all three of us to make any progress, my heart going out to Jarren for the unevenness of the grassy slopes and dips jarred his tortured body. At last I realised where we were, the way we had come led in through the gates at the back of the cemetery well away from any living souls. A cold sun lit the sky and the tall trees we passed beneath cast gloomy shadows in this hallowed place. We stopped in the farthest corner behind a huge vault, grateful to rest at last; concerned too that Jarren seemed so weak, his eyes half closed.

'I'll go home and make sure no one's there, Polly should be out with the children, she was due to take them over to Paulton's Farm for some eggs. It's best the younger ones know nothing of Jarren's being here, young Paul hero worships Jarren, talks about him for days after he's visited.'

Whilst she was gone, I fetched a cloth from the basket and wiped the sweat from Jarren's face, praying Morwenna would be back soon, my senses on edge listening to every sound around me. Relieved when Callum told me his father had gone to the Blessing of the Sea in Penzance along with others from the village, they'd be long gone by now, and although this only delayed a confrontation with him, it pleased me to know it would not be now. I heard the rustle of Morwenna's skirts as she threaded her way back, she was running and out of breath, holding her side as she called to Callum, 'Quickly now, son, whilst no one's about.'

Callum bent down struggling as his young frame lifted the weight of Jarren from the cart. Morwenna and I followed as swiftly he half ran, half stumbled in and out between the tombstones, as though the burden he carried would surely fall to the ground should he stop. Indeed, I was thankful when he reached a small gate leading into the alley, for I knew now he had but a little further to go, and hoped with all my heart that the rectory would prove a safe haven.

CHAPTER FIVE

Much later that evening, the Reverend Dann returned from Penzance having dined with the Bishop of Truro. I heard raised voices coming from the study, the outcome of which was the Reverend Dann condescended to our being housed beneath his roof on the understanding I was chaperoned and never alone with Jarren.

I waited and in due course the expected summons came. I went down to the study and like a schoolgirl stood before him head bowed. There was much I wanted to say, but knew timidity was what he wanted and for Jarren's sake I complied. Agreeing to everything he said.

Morwenna told the children I had been hired to help Polly but was poorly at present and must keep to my room, no one must know I was there. She assured me they would stay silent, but the deception weighed heavily on my conscience, it seemed dreadful to tell these falsehoods and no doubt the Reverend Dann was appalled.

For almost a week I sat beside Jarren in the sparsely furnished room on the half landing, staring out at the gravestones below, as slowly, slowly, his fever abated.

On my first day here, Callum had struggled in with a comfortable chair that he placed beside Jarren's bed. To fill my time whilst Jarren slept, Callum showed me his father's splendid library of books, books which I borrowed in his absence.

In compliance with the Reverend's wishes, I was not often alone with Jarren. Thus, if Morwenna wasn't sitting with me then Polly, who they'd taken into their confidence, took over this duty, the two of us frequently joined by Callum. Soon it became clear to me the Reverend's son was much taken with Polly, though I doubted his father would approve.

When Morwenna was out fulfilling her duties in the village, I kept to my room, even when I knew the children were out. I had no desire to meet with the Reverend Dann, his attitude towards me was totally unchanged and the atmosphere between us very frosty on the few occasions our paths crossed.

Word reached us from the Feathers that Lord Trevoran had increased the reward for the recovery of his fiancée, and also the capture of her suspected abductor Jarren Polverne. I did wonder if maybe the Reverend would be tempted by this and voiced my fears to Morwenna.

'What!' she exclaimed, astonished at my thinking such a thing. 'And have Jarren tell how he'd helped the free traders in the past, the Bishop would have us out of here within a week and then what would we do? Don't worry, maid, he'll tell no tales.'

It was two days after this conversation, as I sat chatting to Morwenna beside Jarren's bed, that he reached out his hand and held mine. His turned his head, and with eyes now open gave me one of his familiar smiles. Overjoyed, I leant forward, kissing my beloved tenderly. Too weak to speak, he mouthed the words 'I love you' and I lay my head on his chest.

'He'll be alright now,' Morwenna vowed, as overjoyed as I at his recovery, and indeed each day following this his strength improved.

The strangers stayed on at the Feathers much to my discomfiture, and indeed called upon the Revered Dann one afternoon, masquerading as mine agents. Thankfully, protocol in this tightly governed house meant the children were kept well out of their sight, which was just as well for information, if coaxed skilfully out of them by those accustomed in doing so, would spell disaster.

That evening was to be the first time of many when I glimpsed the Reverend Dann completely intoxicated stumbling up the stairs holding tight the bannisters for support. And my heart went out to Morwenna.

I shall never forget the following days. Waiting, as slowly Jarren's strength returned. An innocent kiss snatched behind Morwenna's back, the touch of Jarren's hand reaching out for mine. His breath warm upon my cheek awakened passions that sent my pulses racing, emotions I saw mirrored in Jarren's dark brooding eyes. His shattered body was on the mend, each day he was a little better, the wicked smile that first melted my heart did so again, the old Jarren was returning, vibrant with life. But all desires, however passionately felt, must be controlled at present, already we had suffered the wrath of the Reverend Dann.

For a fleeting moment earlier in the week, Morwenna left us alone. Jarren had been asleep when we'd taken up his supper tray of cold mutton, bread, and tankard of ale. She had much to do but declined my offer of help, so I stayed content to be with Jarren. I placed the tray on a table beneath the window and was standing looking down into the garden when he woke, reached out and seized my hand. He tugged me towards him and onto the bed, kissing me with a passion I eagerly return-ed. For just a few seconds I laid my head on his chest, nestling snugly into his encircling arms, a rare moment of shared contentment as I listened to the rhythm of his beating heart, happy at being so close to the man I loved.

'I love you,' he whispered, and lost in our own private world we missed the tread on the stair and thus entwined we were discovered. How quick can fear strike? The silence that followed the creaking open of the door made me tear myself from Jarren as though he were the devil.

The Reverend Dann stood looking at us his face contorted with anger, the ugly vein in his forehead standing out more so than ever I'd seen it before. He struck the door with his fist. 'I will have none of this sinful behaviour in my house.'

He focused his bulging eyes on Jarren, then upon me, and my face flamed crimson. 'As for you, miss, never again will you be alone with Jarren whilst under my roof, and you, sir, must give me your word that this person here—' He walked over, swinging me round by the arm so I faced Jarren, who angrily tried to rise from his bed. 'You will give me your word that this individual will leave my house as intact as the day she came here, for I'll not have it said by his lordship, should heaven forbid you be discovered here, that his intended bride was defiled whilst under my roof.'

Furious, I went to pull my arm from his grasp but his fingers bit into my flesh.

'You have my word on that, sir,' Jarren replied, clearly outraged that circumstance had forced this issue to be discussed so.

We had let Morwenna down, after all she had done for us. The risk we brought to this household by just being here, it was a shameful way to repay her kindness by being discovered thus. I looked away determined not to let the Reverend Dann see that I was close to tears. He let go of my arm and thrust me away, striding out of the door, placing his hands on the bannister rail as he leaned over and shouted down for Polly, who ran up the stairs only to stop upon reaching the landing and creep past her employer looking terrified.

He jabbed a finger over towards the supper tray. 'Take over here, and, you, out of there now.' But I stood unmoving, stubbornly defiant, returning his stare; in temper, he descended the stairs bellowing for Morwenna.

She, we knew, would bear the brunt of the Reverend's anger and indeed moments later we heard raised voices.

Polly closed the door and leant against it as if placing a barrier between us and the awful shouting of the self-righteous man downstairs. 'Believe me,' she sighed, 'that man is no saint, I'll tell you something, not all his thoughts are godly.' She lowered her voice and came over to sit at the bottom of Jarren's bed, trembling. 'It's more than once he's come up to my room befuddled with drink and I've woken to find the covers being pulled from my bed, his hand reaching down beneath my nightgown; I've threatened to scream the place down and he's stumbled away. If it wasn't for Callum I'd be gone from here, like the last poor maid who worked here.'

We were both shocked by what she said, the relief of telling us this dreadful secret left Polly weeping and I passed her a handkerchief asking if Callum knew of this, but she shook her head and beseeched us not to tell.

That day I will always think of as a turning point in our stay at the Rectory. When Morwenna came in later to collect Jarren's supper tray, her eyes were red from crying. Discreetly, Polly quietly slipped from the room as both Jarren and myself begged her forgiveness reassuring her that her husband had caught us doing nothing inappropriate.

'There's no need to say more, Jarren, you're both young, like I was once.'

She glanced down at her hands, and I glimpsed a look of sorrow, wondering how on earth she came to be here, married to her tyrannical husband. She looked up and must have read my thoughts, smiling, her cheeks dimpling, she said softly, 'Take all the happiness you can while you can, for who knows when it will end.' She sat down on Jarren's bed and began to smooth the covers.

'I too was happy once; there was a young man, we were very fond of each other. I lived in Fowey then, he was a boat builder's son and wasn't deemed suitable for a merchant's daughter, even though I was the youngest. To ensure we were parted, I was sent to Penzance to my uncle, who wasted no time in finding a match for me with the son of his closest friend. I had no choice, nor did I care, for I only wanted him who I loved.'

She stood up and looked at us both in turn. 'So be happy together the both of you, true love may only come once, so grasp it and hold on to it tightly. I'll tell Callum the same when he sees fit to tell me that Polly and he have feelings for each other.'

She paused; there were tears in her eyes. 'My husband saw fit to act in such a righteous manner earlier out of fear of your being discovered here. Nettie's been over from the Feathers, those men staying there are from the revenue, been boasting, they have, that a reward has been offered for your return and the capture of your suspected kidnapper Jarren Polverne, once again that sum has been doubled.'

Morwenna didn't miss the look of apprehension I felt on hearing this and reached out her hand to pat mine. 'Have no fear, my husband's love of brandy and fear of Jarren's free-trading friends will keep his tongue stilled.'

Later as I lay in bed, sleep eluded me, I felt confined in a nightmare desperate for escape and wished Jarren fully recovered. I longed for us to be gone from here, for the guilt remained deep within me about the manner in which the Reverend Dann came upon us.

The following days passed uncomfortably slowly. I received from the Reverend Dann an unpleasantness of manner and regard I found quite wearisome and partook of meals in my room to avoid contact with him as much as possible. But I was unable to escape the overlong prayers both morning and evening held in the bleak study. I would stand head bowed, trying my hardest to look suitably subdued and grateful the wellbeing of my soul was so earnestly attended to. Aware too of the glances that passed between Callum and Polly, fearful that the reverend Dann would see them too.

Each day, Jarren's wound pained him less; he was growing restless, especially so since Captain Galley's visit two nights ago. That evening, long after I'd gone to bed, something wakened me. The sound seemed to come from outside, so I went over to the window and drew back the drapes peering into the blanket of darkness shrouding the cemetery. My eyes were drawn to a faint flickering light in one distant corner. From beneath the window came a sound, the closing of a door, and craning my neck I saw the Reverend Dann walking quickly away from the house, striding through the iron gate leading to the cemetery, and watched as he disappeared in the direction of the dancing light. Intrigued, I remained by the window and watched the light of the lantern dipping and weaving until it finally disappeared from sight. Soon afterwards the familiar figure of the Reverend Dann returned and with him a slightly smaller man with whom he was clearly at ease, their pace was quick and it was so dark I had no chance to see his companion clearly, but minutes later I heard a single set of footsteps pass up the stairs. I had no fear for Jarren's safety for without doubt I guessed the reverend Dann had taken delivery of smuggled goods, and whoever the visitor was it was friend not foe.

The next morning, I was curious to know more, but the day began as usual, though after prayers the Reverend Dann left for Lelant and a meeting with the new incumbent there. After he'd gone an unmistakeable feeling of relief was shared by everyone.

As usual every morning, I helped Morwenna and Polly in the kitchen. As I turned to place a plate I'd dried on the table, I saw Callum, he came in and gave Polly a quick kiss behind his mother's back. I blushed stupidly and hoped with his father gone from the house Callum would find it possible to share his feelings for Polly with Morwenna.

As Polly and I tidied away the last of the dishes, Morwenna took a basket and went out into the kitchen garden. Callum was stacking the newly dried crockery away when we were all startled by a gentle tap on the door. Then to my joy Jarren walked in, his eyes twinkling with merriment at our obvious surprise, with a roguish grin he declared, 'I was impatient to leave my bed and having been informed that the good reverend is away to Lelant, thought today would be a good day to do so.'

I ran towards his outstretched arms, closing my eyes as he bent down to kiss my brow. A discreet cough from Callum parted us and looking out the window we saw Morwenna making her way back up the path. Jarren's eyes smiled down into mine and looking up he winked at Callum. 'Tell Morwenna I've taken Layunie out a while so I can catch a breath of fresh air, don't worry I'll be careful we're not seen.'

He took my hand and we were gone, along the hallway and out through the door, almost running down the back path and through to the cemetery. Weaving our way between the tombstones until laughing and breathless we paused, Jarren breathing in the fresh air like a man taking a magic cure. With his arm round my shoulders we walked on until well out of sight of the rectory.

When we stopped, Jarren pulled me closer, I felt the warmth of his body against me, and as his lips sought mine, the kiss which followed more passionate than I had ever enjoyed before. Abandoning all that was proper, I matched his passion with my own, leaning my body into his. Such was our desire neither of us noticed the rain until Jarren pulled away, our eyes spoke what no words could adequately convey, he held out his hand which I grasped firmly, knowing without doubt the huge step I was about to take. My heart raced knowing where he was leading me as through the rain we half ran, half tumbled down the steep uneven grass until we came to the slope leading down to the cottage.

Jarren pushed against the door with his good shoulder and it scraped open; nothing was changed. We stood before the hearth that was bereft of any warmth, but I had no need of such comfort. Jarren reached out and cupped my face in his warm hands, I closed my eyes as his lips found mine and returned and sought his kisses, until at last he led me over to the makeshift bed in the corner. Now his strong hands nimbly released the tiny fastenings of my bodice and in a matter of seconds this, together with my skirts and petticoats, lay abandoned along with our wet footsteps on the flagstone floor. My arms went around his neck as he kissed my cheek, then neck and shoulders, venturing down between my breasts until I felt oblivious to the world around me, our passion and lust for each other insatiable, until at last we lay at peace.

Turning my head, I glanced at the discarded clothes on the floor, our wet footprints long since dried. I nestled my head against Jarren's chest, and a smile formed on my lips as I felt the warmth of this man who'd made me a woman. As though he knew what I was thinking, Jarren reached for my hand bringing it to his lips, just his touch brought the tingling sensation of desire and a longing that led me to beg my love to satisfy the burning need in me once more.

Thus, all passion spent, with reluctance we knew it was time to return. Hastily we dressed, and with Jarren's help, I pinned escaping strands of hair safely back beneath my little white cap. Then, after one last lingering kiss, hand in hand we left the cottage to walk back to the rectory.

Too soon we were pushing open the iron gate and walking up the path. Jarren held the door open for me to enter and as I stepped over the threshold, I felt sure the truth I was no longer a maid could be seen written boldly on my forehead, and blushed crimson when Polly came hurrying down the hall carrying a pile of linen. Jarren appealed to her, 'I need to talk with Layunie. Can we sit awhile in the parlour? I don't think Morwenna would object.'

Polly nodded in agreement, her eyes darting between us, I was sure in that instant her smile grew wider, but no doubt it was just my imagination.

Jarren ushered me into the parlour and closed the door.

'Now, my sweet, alas we must talk seriously.' We sat opposite each other at Morwenna's highly polished table, my heart thudding with anticipation. For a moment, Jarren sat head bowed, fingers smoothing the top of the table, his tumbling black curls shielding his face. I reached across to touch him, and he raised his head, his brown eyes burrowed deep into mine.

'It's time we made plans, Layunie, tis time to move on.' He took a deep breath. 'My cousin Giles was here, there's been another search of St Ives, your intended bridegroom has raised the reward money and people have reported sightings of you all over Cornwall. Tis said on many occasions his lordship has gone in person to retrieve his promised bride only to find the information false. He is beside himself with fury. Ruskin Tripper has been put in charge a small army of men concentrating entirely on finding you, he seems convinced also that it is I who abducted you.'

He paused, all warmth had faded from my face, it seemed I had been transported from the ecstasy of this morning back to reality so swiftly it was unfair. Jarren took my hand. 'There's something else, Trevoran has sent for your brother. Charles is staying in Penzance, his debts were paid in full with Trevoran money given to your father, so he had no chance to decline the order, in fact his lordship sent a coach for him, now he too must help in the search for us.'

I remembered the glimpse of remorse I'd seen on Charles's face the day Aunt Sarah and I had set out for Cornwall. I wondered what his true feelings were and how committed he felt in the search for his sister, who he must know from Aunt Sarah was content to remain free.

Jarren fell silent and I glimpsed a look of hesitation, some inner instinct telling me I wasn't going to like what was coming next.

'Tomorrow I'm going back to St Ives.' His troubled eyes looked across the table from under the heavy fringe of curls and reaching across he wrapped his strong hands round mine; my sharp intake of breath had registered my dismay. 'It's only for a couple of days, then I'll come back to collect you, don't worry it's for the best, I promise.'

'But why?' The question burst forth, the last thing I wanted was for him to go away again.

'There's things I must do, Layunie, arrangements to make, other business I must attend to.'

Suddenly I felt frightened, torn apart by a mixture of emotions. I looked at Jarren too restless to remain sitting, standing now beside the casement window, a man eager to take charge of is life once more, a life like the wild rugged moorland surrounding us that would never change. He'd never cease the life he'd chosen and I who loved him must accept that and overcome my fears.

'Will you stay, at the Star?' I asked quietly, and he nodded searching my face for approval, and a shadow seem to pass over me, a memory. 'Then I'm coming with you.'

'No, Layunie, it's not safe, stay here I beg of you.' A deathly silence filled the room; somehow before morning I would persuade Jarren to take me away from the stifling atmosphere of the rectory. I knew too the other reason I so desperately wanted to go with him. Jenny! I still remembered the look of joy on her face as Jarren picked her up and whirled her round and round, the last time she'd greeted his return to the Star, remembered too the feeling I'd felt as I watched.

Much later, reluctantly and only after much pleading, Jarren agreed to take me with him. And early the next morning we bade goodbye to Morwenna, Callum and Polly, thankful that the reverend Dann was shut in his study at private prayer. Twas a tearful leave-taking for no words could convey our thanks strongly enough to Morwenna, who'd nursed Jarren back from the brink of death when first we'd come here.

With tears still in my eyes, we started out on our journey, Callum's aged grey mare plodding along steadily carrying both of us on its back, the tracks winding endlessly on until at last we entered St Ives and passed under the arch of the Star into the courtyard. The bolts were drawn back, and George Tought appeared, quickly ushering us indoors whilst Davy, now fully recovered, led Callum's horse into the stables.

'Tis good to see you both, though I'm a mite surprised to see you, miss.' He turned and looked at me briefly, as purposefully he led us on through the deserted taproom. Capt'n Galley's here waiting, thought likely t'would be today you came back.' Dutifully we followed him up the far stairs, then along to the end of the passage and the room I'd occupied during my stay here, knocking lightly on the door twice before it was opened.

As discreetly George slipped away, so Jarren ushered me inside, and a few seconds later I found myself being introduced to this man of whom I'd heard so much. Captain Giles Galley.

He was much as I'd imagined, this cousin of Jarren's, with the same dark rugged looks, for like Jarren's father, Matthew, William his younger brother had taken a Spanish wife also. Giles stepped forward and took my hand, kissing it, his gaze travelling swiftly over my body as if taking in every little detail before he looked at Jarren and with a roguish grin remarked, 'So this is your fine little lady from London, you're a lucky fellow for I swear I'd have rescued her myself from old Trevoran had I had the chance.'

I felt my face redden, embarrassed at such scrutiny, pleased though at the obvious pleasure Jarren felt, as possessively he put his arm around my waist, smiling broadly at this cousin.

'You must have much to discuss so I'll go now and find Nancy.' I began, hastily disentangling myself from Jarren's grasp. And as I did, he caught my hand.

'Be careful, go down the back stairs and stay out of sight.' His dark eyes bore into mine demanding obedience. 'Be mindful of what I say, tis more dangerous now than when we were here last.'

'I will, don't worry,' I replied, feeling the heat of his hand as he squeezed mine before letting it go. He opened the door a fraction to make sure no one was about. I smiled at Giles, desperately hoping he truly believed

Jarren had done the right thing in kidnapping me, glad to leave the two of them alone and go in search of Nancy.

Downstairs, I slipped quietly into the kitchen, disappointed to find her not there, even sloe-eyed Jenny was missing. George Tought came hurrying in, greeting me with genuine warmth, and assuring me in his usual jovial manner, 'Nancy'll be back soon, maid, she's been gone the best part of an hour now, down at that busybody Daisy Borlase the dressmaker, no doubt learning all the local tittle-tattle.'

I couldn't help but ask, 'Is it far?'

He shook his head. 'Young Jarren wouldn't want me telling you where it was, for fear you'd be tempted to go finding her on yer own, maid.' He gave me a stern look and went back into the taproom, leaving me to sit alone, waiting for Nancy. Faint strands of sunshine filtered through the tiny panes in the window and formed a pattern on the grey flag floor. I traced them with my toe, becoming bored, getting ever more restless. I couldn't resist wondering if I might, if I knew where to go, chance to seek Nancy out and hurry her home, for I longed to talk with her and had no idea how long we should be here.

The voices were faint at first but as they came closer, I withdrew from the window and stood out of sight behind the door leading to the courtyard, flustered as the latch lifted. I heard giggling and had no option but to remain hidden as first Jenny came in followed by Simon, neither saw me.

Simon caught her round the waist whirling her round in flurry of dusty petticoats and grey skirt, kissing her firmly on the lips for what seemed an eternity.

They'd left the door wide open and the sound of the whistle Billy gave as he caught sight of the embracing couple drew them apart, Jenny picking up a cloth, making to throw it at him. She relented and pulled a face instead, firmly closing the door; it was then they saw me. Jenny opened her mouth in surprise, there was none of the usual wariness in her eyes and, stifling a giggle, she explained the two of them had just become betrothed. They looked so happy I felt a real delight at their joy, tinged maybe with just a little relief, her easy manner with Jarren meant I could never have trusted her. She was eager to tell George, and it was just as they were going out the door I asked Jenny where Daisy Borlase the dressmaker lived, looking back she called out the directions before together they vanished into the tap room, where soon could be heard cheers of congratulations.

I knew even as I lifted the latch and stepped out into the yard that what I was about to do was wrong. Nervously I glanced up at the window above, in the room beyond Jarren was talking with Giles. Without doubt he'd disapprove most strongly of what I was about to do, but it was only a short step away. I'd be back before he realised I'd ventured out. Determined to continue, I hurried across the courtyard, it felt so good to be out in the sunshine. Having peeked out from under the archway, I briskly started walking down the hill towards the sea following Jenny's instructions.

Gulls screeched noisily overhead and the salty sea breeze that brushed against my face carried with it the smell of the sea. As I reached the turn at the bottom of the hill, I saw fishermen on the quay mending their nets and old women huddled together gossiping. Mules with fully laden carts struggled as they started to climb the steep hill, their owners swearing as ragged children darted in and out between them, whilst I in my old tattered shawl, drab dress and servants cap drew not a single glance.

The narrow alley which led to Daisy Borlase's cottage in Hedders Court was exactly where Jenny said, but on impulse I continued further on, wanting to glimpse just for a moment a wider view of the harbour. Just as I set foot on the cobbled quay, I saw him, sitting astride a huge black horse. He was shouting orders at two dragoons who began clambering aboard a schooner moored nearby. The blood ran cold in my veins; I recognised that voice, and all confidence in my disguise was forgotten, for the man in the three cornered hat and black cloak whose boots gleamed against the horse's black flanks was Ruskin Tripper.

His orders given, he sat scrutinising the quay his mount remaining majestically still. I stood as though a statue exactly where I was watching him, hoping for some distraction to stop his intense search of the quay, but inevitably his eyes came to rest in my direction and instinctively I began to turn and in doing so I caught his eye. He looked directly at me, briefly our eyes met, but it was enough, he knew in that instant who I was. I ran, and he followed shouting to others as his horse clattered over the cobbles. Footsteps came running from all directions, getting closer as frantically I darted into the sunless warren of high stepped cottages searching for a place to hide.

Lost in the maze of dwellings, I ran on through the alleys terrified should I become trapped in some courtyard that rendered no escape, I saw no one, the inhabitants of St Ives had melted away. I was alone except for my pursuers. The shouts I heard came from them alone, desperate for my capture.

Sheer exhaustion forced me to stop and seek somewhere to rest, and glancing frantically around, I saw a tiny nook between two cottages and tucked myself into it gasping for breath. I listened, the shouting seemed further away, and I began to relax a little, maybe I'd lost them. Then I heard it! The echo of a single horse's hooves picking their way over the echoing cobbles somewhere close by.

My life, my being, stopped; I pressed myself back against the cold grey stone, holding my breath, my heart beating wildly as horse and rider came ever closer and stopped almost beside me. I trembled with fear as the head of Ruskin Tripper's horse came just within my vision, its left eye seeming boldly to stare straight at me.

I stared back; the handsome head lifted as though sensing my fear. Silence, the rider cussed beneath his breath before urging the animal forward, for a second only I glimpsed my enemy, his ferret face passing by so close. His eyes looking thankfully straight ahead.

I waited, loath to leave my safe sanctuary, no one ventured forth from the muddle of cottage surrounding me, no face could I glimpse even at a window. And so I stayed where I was, fearful Jarren would get caught if he set out to find me, afraid too of his anger at my foolishness.

Dusk came, I felt wretched, hungry and ached with the cold, I'd disobeyed Jarren and he would be furious, all I longed for now was to find my way back to the Star. I crept forth from my hiding place and made my way along the narrow alley that gradually began to slope downwards with deep uneven steps cut into rock itself. At the bottom of these I found myself in a court-yard full of handcarts that held an overwhelming smell of fish, from here I could see the quay and a maze of masts.

A sudden holler startled me, the arrival of fishing boats returning on the high tide had brought a rush of activity. From here I could see the hill leading up to the Star and hoped to thread my way back up through the alleyways and be quickly home.

I pulled up my shawl so it covered my head and walked briskly on. A few folk hurried by but took no notice of me nor I them, for I was lost within my own thoughts, angry with myself and distressed at my folly, fearing Jarren's justly deserved wrath, when suddenly I realised I was hopelessly lost.

Shivering and chilled to the bone, I hurried on hoping to find some way out of the warren of cottages and onto Skidden Hill and the safety of the Star, but this was not to be. The alley I followed widened out and ran along-side a small brook. A little way ahead was a narrow stone bridge that I decided to cross; maybe this would lead to some landmark I would recognise.

As I stepped onto the bridge, I heard a movement, two men stood up and stepped out of the shadows, blue coats! I ran back the way I'd come but they were too quick, rough hands reached out and seized me. Like a wild animal I fought to escape, but it was useless, my efforts in vain, for the more I struggled the more the brutes enjoyed it. The smaller of the two held my hands behind my back whilst the other with the scar running down his cheek pawed at the bodice of my dress.

'Well, and who have we here!' he drawled leering at me, his breath stinking of stale ale, and all the while his friend tightened his grip on my wrists until the pain was unbearable.

'It's her, I reckon, the miss we've spent all this bloody time looking for.'

Savagely, scar face forced his wet lips against mine, as desperately I fought to pull away, struggling as he tore at the neck of my dress. The thin material ripped as he burrowed one hand deep inside my bodice, dismayed I felt his other hand tugging at my skirts, he reached beneath my petticoats and hoisted them up, now his hand clawed at my thigh.

'I'll give you a taste of what's to come, shall I, miss high and mighty.'

He spat viciously in my face and as the foul saliva trickled down my cheek, his hands sought to violate my person in the most disgusting manner.

As he tried to force me to the ground, one of my hands slipped free, so I dug my nails into his cheek and felt the skin rip beneath my fingers, he lashed out in anger, striking a blow which sent me tumbling to the ground. 'Hold her,' he yelled, and began loosening his clothing.

I struggled and kicked out as he reached down and took hold of my petticoats, lifting them high above my waist, whilst I pinioned to the ground by his companion could do nothing to cover my modesty. It was then came the sound of approaching horses. Abruptly I was released.

'Best leave her, case tis the Tripper.'

Scar face hauled me up and gave my right breast a final squeeze as an assortment of men, some on horseback, some not, came as if from nowhere, parting as the man on the black stallion made his way through. The sound of his whip whistled through the air, and dust rose from the stone wall as he struck it.

'Leave her,' he ordered. 'This is no ordinary trollop you've caught and can have your fun with; this is a real lady we've got here!'

Someone sniggered and once again Ruskin Tripper hit out at the wall. 'Our task, gentlemen, is to deliver her safely to his lordship, a virgin bride not defiled and showing no signs of being mishandled.'

The cynical tone and manner in which this was said brought howls of laughter and my face flushed red with anger. I placed one hand over the torn neck of my dress drawing the two remnants of it together, unable to disguise how much my hand was shaking as I did so.

Ruskin Tripper leaned forwards and stared down at me, his gloating satisfaction plain to see, behind him others looked on with faces cold and without expression. Caught like a wild animal, I made a bid for freedom darting between those who surrounded me, but much to their amusement I slipped and fell.

Tripper eased his huge horse forward, leaned down and as I struggled to get up caught hold of me, and in one violent move brought me to my feet, his raisin eyes stared into mine. I stared back steadily and defiantly without so much as blinking, so this was the man who would steal away my new found happiness, for the price of Trevoran's gold.

He looked over to my two captors. 'Good work, you'll get just reward, so too the rest of you, so don't fret.'

A cheer went up. 'She's a vixen, sir,' scar face bellowed, his face bleeding from the wealds left by my nails, but Ruskin Tripper ignored his comment his mind on one thing only, he glanced round at the men.

'Lord Trevoran's staying at Carradale Manor, we'll take her to him tonight.'

He ordered two men to go on ahead to inform his lordship of my capture, and then looked at me his mouth twisting with sarcastic cruelty. 'Well, well, at last we meet, Miss Ledridge. He let go of me and thrust me backwards.

'Hold her tight,' he ordered, and from his pocket withdrew a miniature. 'A good likeness indeed,' he sneered, 'well, men, we'd best get the bride to her eager bridegroom, he's waited long enough to get her in his bed.'

To the sound of sniggers and lurid jokes, kicking and struggling I was ungraciously picked up and placed before Ruskin Tripper on the huge black stallion. He held me within his iron grip, there was no escape. Thus, with leaden heart my journey from St Ives began.

CHAPTER SIX

Sick at heart, at last I sensed we were nearing our destination. Ruskin Tripper's iron grip around my waist never lessening during all the time we travelled. Eventually someone spoke the words I dreaded to hear. 'I'll go on ahead and make sure the gatekeeper's about his business.'

I glimpsed the outline of a high stone wall, then a pair of elegant wrought iron gates that swung open as we approached. A man stood to one side touching his forelock in respect as we passed by. I felt sure his wife standing beside him gave me a fleeting look of pity, and tears came to my eyes; I felt a numbness both of spirit and limbs.

This was a journey I wished would never end; yet even as these and other thoughts tumbled through my mind it was too late. Dusk fell incredibly quickly as we rode on in silence up the seemingly never-ending tree lined drive, until through the gently swaying trees the great bulk of the house itself came into view.

'Pengoweth House at last, Miss Ledridge,' the menacing voice beside me rasped in my ear. 'Journeys end.' His foul breath wafted across my face, and I turned away repulsed.

We were clearly expected for candlelight shone from a good many windows. We halted in front of the impressive entrance. Ruskin Tripper jumped down from his horse and without ceremony hauled me down to stand beside him. The massive doors of Pengoweth had already been opened and a middle-aged woman dressed in grey, her dark hair pinned neatly into a loose bun, descended the steps, keys on her belt jangling as she did so. She'd witnessed my rough treatment and shot a look of condemnation at Ruskin Tripper.

When she spoke, it was in a clipped precise manner with none of the Cornish warmth I had come to love. 'I'll take care of Miss Ledridge now,' she asserted, aiming a cool glance at my captor, adding, 'Lord Trevoran's waiting to see you in the library, sir.'

She turned her head and as if waiting for just such a summons a young footman stepped forward.

'Show Mr Tripper through to the library,' she ordered, returning her steely gaze upon Ruskin Tripper, who with a final look at me and a mock bow took his leave and dutifully followed the footman up the stone steps to go on ahead of us into the house.

Mrs Penglasse introduced herself as the housekeeper and formally welcomed me to Pengoweth House. She said briskly but not unkindly, 'Lord and Lady Carradale left for Bristol but yesterday. Lord Trevoran has asked me to make all the necessary arrangements, therefore if you'd kindly follow me, I have had a room prepared for you, which I hope you will find to your liking.'

Meekly I followed her into the house and up the huge carved staircase lit by a profusion of candles, and down a long gallery hung with paintings, presumably of the previous owners of Pengoweth, finally she stopped and held open the door of the room prepared for me. It was the most lavishly decorated room I had ever beheld, the richness of the decorations and elaborate red materials used in its furnishing quite breathtaking, the furniture of the most highest quality. Behind me the click of the door closing brought me swiftly back to reality. Mrs Penglasse walked past me and went over to the long casement window pulling together the heavy drapes, shutting out the enclosing darkness beyond.

'When Lord Trevoran is ready to see you, miss, I will take you down, in the meantime warm water will be brought so you may freshen up after the journey, on the bed is a selection of dresses and other garments which his Lordship hopes will be a good fit.'

Just then a knock came on the door and a maid hastened in head bowed, she handed the housekeeper a note, the contents of which seemed to puzzle her. 'It seems his lordship has changed his mind, miss.' Mrs Penglasse folded the note in half and cast her eye over the dresses laid out on the bed. 'A maid will be sent shortly to put these away, the hour being so late his lordship's instructions are that you rest tonight and then he'll see you tomorrow.'

I watched her retreat from the room, saw the door close and heard the key being turned in the lock. I sat down on the huge four-poster bed, not caring if I crease the clothes beneath me. I felt totally alone and in the overwhelming silence, the unbelievable reality of my situation took hold. How stupid and reckless I'd been. How angry Jarren must be.

My eyes filled with tears and in temper at my foolishness, I quickly brushed them away, going across to the window and opening the drapes to peer out. Far below I could see a paved terrace and knew escape from this height would be impossible. I placed one hand against the glass feeling it cool beneath my fingers. I dreaded to think what was happening in St Ives. I imagined Jarren's anger at my foolishness, how long would it be before he knew I'd been caught by Ruskin Tripper, would he know where I'd been taken and praise God what would he do to get me back? I turned and leant my back against the window, downhearted and despondent I may be, but at the same time resolutely determined to escape.

A timid knock came on the door and a maid came in instructed to prepare me for bed. This was the last thing I desired, for weary though I was my mind was fully focused on escaping, to be stripped of my clothes and made ready of bed not what I wanted at all, so it was somewhat stubbornly I complied with her ministrations, for there seemed nothing else I could do. A tray was brought, and I was urged by Mrs Penglasse to eat, but I ate only a sparse amount of the creamy broth and refused to speak to either her or the maid. When Mrs Penglasse left, taking my clothes with her, I lay in the huge bed my head resting against the soft lace edged pillows, and cried until finally racked with despair I slept.

It was past dawn when I woke, startled from my sleep by the sound of children's voices and the patter of feet running past my door, the imploring commands of some poor servant beseeching them to slow down, ignored amidst the laughter of those she pursued. Pushing aside the bed coverings, I got up and walked over to the door knowing in my heart even before I tried that it was locked. The giggling children's laughter disappeared along the passage and into the depths of the great house to be replaced by approaching footsteps coming from the opposite direction. I fled back to bed pulling the bedclothes high about me. The key turned and the door opened revealing to my relief only a maid carrying a breakfast tray, this she placed on the table beside the bed and said shyly trying not to look directly at me, 'Mrs Penglasse asks that having breakfasted you ring for someone to come and assist you dress, miss.'

She bobbed a curtsey and was gone leaving me alone once more. Although the last thing I wanted was to partake of any hospitality here, it was a long time since I had last eaten, and lifting the lid on the silver dish I helped myself to a little of the scrambled eggs and had a small glass of cold water. With reluctance I then complied with Mrs Penglasse's instructions. A jug of hot water was brought in together with other necessities, brushes and combs were laid out upon the dressing table. The two young maids who brought them eyeing me with curiosity, my arrival must have caused much gossip to those below stairs. I duly washed, letting the same maid who'd helped me to bed the previous night assist me into an elaborate blue satin gown. She brushed my hair and pinned it up leaving soft ringlets around the nape of my neck. I made no conversation, for as she tended to my needs, I felt totally indifferent, it mattered not how I looked.

As she finished, she hesitatingly said, 'You look lovely, miss.' And somehow, I forced a smile, but her kind words had prompted a lump to come in my throat, it was all I could do to hold back the tears as she left. Soon I would be summoned downstairs whereupon Lord Trevoran would no doubt gloat and ridicule me, trapped here, his possession to do with what he liked. I bit my lip as I gazed back at the frightened stranger whose reflection stared at me from the mirror.

Alone I waited, every single second crawling by, and with its passing, the tension I felt within began to rise alarmingly, the palms of my hands grew wet with sweat. I could no longer sit down even for the briefest of moments but paced the floor, the childhood habit of biting my nails having returned unbidden in the hushed quietness of my solitude. Still I waited, luncheon was brought, this the only interruption. Convention forbade me to beg the mob capped maid to tell me what she knew of matters concerning those above stairs, though my mind cried out to know.

In my nervous state I listened intently for any sound that would herald my summons to his lordship's presence. Numbed by boredom, I thought of ways to escape. My eye was caught by movement outside and I saw from the window four children, their black-clad figures running across the lawns, two maids in grey dresses and white aprons running after them, another holding her side in pain stumbling behind. These children seemed without governess or tutor. I paused momentarily to watch, and for some reason my thoughts drifted to Callum and the dismal life he and Polly led at Nancledra with the Reverend Dann. Callum would make a very good tutor. Thoughts of their kindness to me, all that had happened during my stay there and the overwhelming sadness that I had ruined everything, left me feeling bereft, my composure disappeared.

I wept uncontrollably, the tears staining the blue satin of my dress. How far off now that day Jarren and I had run carefree hand in hand through the sunshine at Nancledra, down through the long grass to our secret place, the cottage in the dell. Remembering too the passionate lovemaking which left us craving to return there.

The children and the maids disappeared from view and I waited on and on.

It was mid-afternoon when Mrs Penglasse came to my room, over her arm she carried a dark blue velvet cloak with a lining of ivory silk, she appeared flustered and announced briskly, 'Mr Tripper and his men are to escort you to Trevoran Court, you're to prepare for the journey now, miss, in as much haste as possible.'

My room filled with scurrying servants, two maids began carefully folding the clothes that had been acquired for me, laying them in the wooden travelling chest placed beside my bed. I stood watching all this commotion as if in a trance, waking from it only as Mrs Penglasse's deft fingers placed the heavy cloak around my shoulders.

'This is Lady Carradale's cloak, miss, I know she'd not mind you borrowing it, for it is a fair journey you're making and much of it by sea.' She fussed around me, and I asked her what was to happen next.

'The coach will take you from here at Gulval to Penzance.'

'Is it far?' I asked and she shook her head.

'No, miss, after only a short while you'll pass over a stone bridge by the old mill, after that you'll be entering Penzance, where by all accounts down on the quay the *Trevoran Star* is waiting, tis a long ways round the Lizard you'll be taking to get you up to Falmouth, best pray for a calm sea.'

She sighed as we watched the maids scurrying about. 'Taking you across country and up through Helston would have been simpler, but this way's been chosen for a purpose, no doubt his lordship felt t'would be harder for you to run off. Done the journey myself years ago. I accompanied Lord Carradale's mother on a visit to Trevoran Court same ways you're going. Once we'd reached Falmouth it was but a short trip up the Fal but I was mighty glad when we got there, the old lady made sure we came home across country, that I do remember.'

Impatient with her reminisces I asked her softly under my breath, 'Can you help me escape before I leave here, please there must be a way?' I knew in my heart what her answer would be.

'No, maid, that I cannot do, it's a shame Lord and Lady Carradale's not here for things would have been handled better, that sly devil Ruskin Tripper's got too much say in matters for my liking.' For a moment she looked contrite. 'I'm sorry, miss, if I've spoken out of turn but it's how I feel.'

She bent down pulling out the folds in the cloak making sure they fell uniformly over my dress, I saw sympathy in her eyes when she stood up and realised how dismayed she felt about the manner in which I was being treated.

From somewhere quite near I heard the brusque voice of Ruskin Tripper shouting orders and asked her quietly, 'Is Lord Trevoran to accompany me also?'

She shook her head and looked down at the floor before answering. 'His lordship's been gone since shortly after you arrived, miss, I was told you weren't to be informed.'

Avoiding my gaze, she moved over to help the maids pack away the last dress before leaving to summon those who were to take the chest downstairs. I stood seething with anger.

How dare Trevoran treat me so shabbily, knowing full well the anguish he'd cause me, here alone waiting for his summons, waiting, waiting and waiting. I felt nothing but hatred for him, a hatred so strong that for a time I was quite lost in these thoughts, only the sound of Ruskin Tripper's raised voice matched by the irate tones of Mrs Penglasse's caught my attention, dragging me back to the present. Her voice came from the passage outside and was sharp with rebuke.

'Of course, she must have a female escort, Lady Carradale would forbid her to leave here without one.'

Her outburst was followed by a pregnant pause before Ruskin Tripper drawled, 'That will not be necessary, you take too much upon yourself. The conveyance of Miss Ledridge to Trevoran Court is not your concern and I give you my word nothing will stop her arrival there, myself and the dragoons will make perfectly sure of that. So I suggest, madam, you get back to your duties and fetch Miss Ledridge to me now.'

All at once the sound of children's voices echoed up from the huge hall below followed by several pairs of feet pounding up the stairs and running along the passage. I glimpsed their curious faces as momentarily they stopped and looked in as they passed my open door, the last little lad giving me a cheeky grin before following the others as they ran along and clattered up more stairs to what must be the nursery floor.

'And keep those damnable children quiet,' Ruskin Tripper shouted exasperated. Mrs Penglasse hurried past muttering under her breath, continuing up the further flight of stairs in pursuit the children and those who should have been in charge of them. Ruskin Tripper retreated downstairs shouting further orders to his men.

My eye was caught by the writing desk in the corner of the room supplied most thoughtfully with paper pen and ink, an idea sprang to mind and before Mrs Penglasse returned, I quickly scribbled two notes, the first for Lady Carradale recommending Callum Dann the rector's son at Nancledra as a most suitable tutor for her children and Polly Mayo a servant at the rectory who would make a good nursemaid, the other note I addressed to Callum Dann himself, informing him I had recommended him for the position here. I dated the note, and in it also said that I was leaving today to travel to Trevoran Court by sea from Penzance. I knew not if he would ever receive this note, that would depend on Mrs Penglasse, nor did I know how long it would take for the message conveyed within this note to reach Jarren, but I had to take this chance to do something.

Only just had I finished writing when Mrs Penglasse returned. 'It's time to go down, miss.' I glanced over towards the writing desk and was about to speak when to my dismay I heard heavy footsteps coming closer and Ruskin Tripper's voice. I ran across the room and pressed the two notes into her hand, thankful as she skilfully slipped them in her pocket just as Mr Tripper himself entered my room and ordered me downstairs.

On the drive the damask coloured Carradale coach was drawn up waiting for us. Grouped a little way off, six dragoons already on horseback waited ready to escort us. Ruskin Tripper took hold of my elbow and led me out to the coach where, in his usual unmannerly fashion, he hurried me up the lowered steps and thrust me inside, taking his place beside me. The whip cracked and I was thrown back against the seat, thus I had but a fleeting glance of Mrs Penglasse as she stood on the steps. I raised my hand to her in a gesture of farewell, and she did likewise, now all I could do was hope she'd help me, would understand the importance of my note reaching Callum in Nancledra.

I sat with my head turned towards the window. It was hard not to come into physical contact with my detestable companion, for having left the smooth gravel of the drive we were thrown together by the motion of the coach as the wheels caught in the rutted road. Only the slight wheeze of his breathing cut the edge off the silence, together with the thumping of the horses' hooves.

Just as Mrs Penglasse described we ascended into Penzance. With the sea to our left we entered the crowded streets causing considerable attention for the dragoons rode without care through the throng of people. Their presence together with the elegant Carradale coach drew curious glances and I drew back as eager eyes darted up in my direction.

At last the coach lurched to a halt and we alighted onto a wooden wharf, a cool fresh breeze brought with it the smell of the sea, of tar and rope. Gulls squawked overhead as fish were unloaded from an array of small boats. Firmly taking hold of my elbow, Ruskin Tripper strode forward into the mass of people, the sight of the riding officer brought forth jeers and crude shouts, a women bawled out, 'Release her, you bastard,' only to be pushed back into the crowd by the butt of a rifle. Others grew wary as we approached, scuttling away as the dragoons still on horseback forced their way further along the wharf. We passed many craft, their crews busy about their business, then I saw it, the schooner with Trevoran Star emblazoned on her bow. The sight of it filled my heart with fear of the unknown terrors which lay ahead.

The dragoons slowed and two dismounted. Ruskin Tripper turned to give them orders, his grip on my elbow slackened and with senses racing I pulled free, running back through the crowds. Some folk tried to help me by forming a barrier in front of my pursuers so I might get away. Then I heard their screams, the dragoons were using whips to clear them out of the way. I had no choice but to stop and was soon seized and brought back to where the black cloaked figure with his tricornered hat stood waiting, there was no disguising the fury on his face. Those gathered in readiness for us to board were waved impatiently aside, with both hands firmly held behind my back I was led up the roughly hewn gangplank and on to the deck.

The sails were unfurled, overhead the heavy canvas flapped softly in the breeze. The order was given to cast off.

Someone in command bellowed, 'Roper, show the young lady to her cabin,' and a squat little man his face wrinkled and weather-beaten by the seasons came over and motioned me to follow him. He stood aside where the square opening in the deck showed steps leading below, I peered down quite overawed by their steepness, and although clearly impatient, Ruskin Tripper standing at my side made no move to assist me, it was Roper who stepped forward and suggested how I descend them. Once below deck, Tripper snapped at Roper, 'Which cabin, man?' and Roper shot out a brown arm hastily pointing to an open door a little way off.

'Capt'n says the young miss to have this one, sir.' He broke into a toothy grin. 'It's all ready and I hear cook's prepared her a fine spread.'

The cabin was dark with mahogany panelling, it smelt of pipe tobacco and beeswax, the furnishings were basic, below the porthole a small table was laid as if ready for a meal with a carafe of water and glass inset beside it, the narrow bunk made up with freshly laundered linen. A sallow little man nervously crept past Mr Tripper and deposited a tray on the table, he lifted the silver lids on several dishes just a little, turning his head and smiling at me, I imagined he expected some show of appreciation, but in all truth I wasn't hungry but managed to murmur a quick, thank you.

Ruskin Tripper hastened him out, he himself making a mock bow before he too took his leave of me, the cabin door closed, the key was turned in the lock.

I stared at the closed door, a prisoner now, alone and isolated. In my heart a cold terror of what lay ahead, this journey would lead me to that place where my greatest nightmare must surely begin. Soon I would come face to face with Lord Trevoran whose wish was to possess me both body and soul. I bit my lip. Oh God, let Jarren save me before that dreadful day occurred.

Whilst my mind harboured such thoughts, through the porthole I watched the rise and fall of the sea. The further we ventured from shore, the more I felt the ship pitch and roll as her bow ploughed its course through the waves. The tray set in the raised rimmed table attached to the cabin's side stayed put and now the smell of food mingled with that of pipe smoke and beeswax. My empty stomach heaved, and I was engulfed in a wave of nausea, I could but lie on the bed praying with all my heart this part of the hateful journey would soon be over.

I can tell you little more only that I did not sleep, night came and after an endless wait the dawn, yet another day passed, how many I cannot tell, only that it seemed an eternity I felt so ill. Finally, Ruskin Tripper came to inform me we were entering Falmouth harbour and to make myself ready to transfer to the smaller craft waiting for us there. Indeed, he returned only minutes later to escort me on deck.

With arms resting on the dark wooden rail, I stood looking towards the harbour. A strong wind loosened my hastily secured hair and I struggled to control the wild curls blowing about my face, tucking them back haphazardly beneath an insufficient number of hairpins. The sights and sounds I saw before my eyes almost familiar, learned from the tales Grandfather had told of Falmouth, in truth his heart had never left his beloved Cornwall.

We had already sailed between the castles of Pendennis and St Mawes to enter what grandfather had called the most beautiful of harbours. Never had I seen so many ships and small craft going about their daily business. Others majestically still, their masts and rigging casting patterns across each other in the early morning sunshine.

On board it seemed preparations were being made to drop anchor. Drawing my cloak tight around me, my eyes searched the waterfront. I saw them then; the two tide mills Grandfather had so proudly spoken of. Here Ledridge corn had once been ground and stored, before being loaded onto boats and taken upriver. The two old wooden buildings looked somewhat unsteady now, their huge wheels beside them. I knew now where we were, we must be sailing past Bar Pool.

It was difficult to imagine our family had once owned the mills; sadly Great-grandfather's debts had forced their sale. I stared out across the water, my grandfather's stories bringing no warmth to my soul in this unwelcome sanctuary.

We sailed on through the harbour to drop anchor some little distance up the river Fal, sailing past the harbour's broad grey quay with its profusion of small wooden jetties. Obviously, Ruskin Tripper was taking no chances, and I saw both he and the dragoons anxiously studying the waterfront as we passed.

A small boat headed out towards us and came alongside. A bearded sailor jumped down into it and caught the ropes thrown down to secure it, two others unfurled a rope ladder, which Ruskin Tripper swiftly descended. The dragoons came to escort me into the smaller craft, but once again it was Roper who stood at the side of the deck and helped me nervously climb over the side as ordered by Tripper. Patiently, Roper guided me down, protecting my modesty by making sure my skirts stayed in place by standing behind me on the somewhat fragile ladder. Hesitantly I made my way down into the smaller boat as it rose and fell in the water. Just before I reached the bottom of the ladder, Roper's hand closed over mine and I felt a note pressed into my palm. Shocked I held it tight, as now he took my arm and steadied me over towards a place where I could sit.

'Thank you,' I whispered.

'Tis my pleasure, miss.' He turned to climb back up the ladder and I saw on his face the hint of a smile. A warm glow crept through my body, indeed I was grateful, so grateful for the glimmer of hope the yet unknown contents of the note had sown. My beloved Jarren was out there somewhere.

With no thought to those already aboard, the dragoons descended the ladder jumping down into the boat. It rocked from side to side provoking Ruskin Tripper to issue forth a tirade of outrage. Unseen I tucked the note safely down the bodice of my dress and watched Roper haul the ladder onto the deck of the Trevoran Star, whilst Ruskin Tripper irritably issued orders for this the last part of our journey.

The busy harbour was left far, far behind as we entered the more tranquil waters of the Fal. On either side of the river trees swept down from the wooded banks and touched the rippling water. Here and there tiny beaches were scattered along its banks, a few cottages lined small granite quays. Ruskin Tripper came over and sat beside me, his eyes dancing with amusement. 'Look to your left, young lady, and soon you'll glimpse the first sight of your new home.'

He returned to sit at the bow with the others, and alone I studied the wooded banks, my heart pounding when at last I saw it. A huge grey house with many windows, the house itself seeming to peep from between the trees, as if it was watching for me, waiting.

We pulled alongside a wide wooden jetty, and an unusually courteous Ruskin Tripper helped me from the boat. His manner most respectful as he introduced me to Mrs Treave, Lord Trevoran's housekeeper, who was waiting to welcome me. I wondered how long she'd been waiting there and trembled inwardly as she greeted me, the severity of her dress and hair in striking contrast to that of Mrs Penglasse at Pengoweth. She walked beside me up the winding path leading towards the house, vaguely I heard her words of welcome but in my heart, I wanted to run, run anywhere just as long as it was away from this living nightmare.

All too soon we reached the pillared entrance at the front of the house and much to my horror saw the servants were lined up to formerly greet me. Mrs Treave continued talking to me, but I took in little of what she said. I cared not a dolt about the house, its history, acreage or deer park. I saw Ruskin Tripper watching me sensing my apprehension; saw the unmistakeable twist of pleasure on his face.

Outraged I held my head high and when we reached the assembled servants recalled Miss Daisy's teachings at the Academy for Young Ladies and greeted them in entirely the proper manner, fully understanding their curious glances for no doubt every one of them knew the circumstances which brought me here, and no doubt thought me soon to be their mistress.

This task complete, bowing formally, Ruskin Tripper took his leave. I dutifully followed the housekeeper into the vaulted hall, it was stark and cold. The vast area of grey marble floor surrounded by a circle of statues, carved from the whitest marble imaginable gave the whole place a chilly atmosphere. Mrs Treave walked at a naturally brisk pace up the wide cold staircase and I found myself having to catch up my skirts and almost run up the stairs behind her. At the far end of an austere panelled corridor she stopped, and we entered the room that had been chosen for me by Lord Trevoran.

My first reaction was one of surprise for the room was really quite beautiful. Through the casement windows I could see across the lawns down towards the river. The walls were creamy yellow much the fashion of the day. In comparison the furniture was dark and heavy, of a style favoured in the past century. The imposing canopied bed took up most of the room, hung with beautifully draped lemon and plumb brocade. But all I desired now was to be left alone, my heart ached to read Jarren's note.

Impatiently I watched as livered servants deposited my trunks in the room. I untied my cloak and handed it to Mrs Treave who carefully placed it over her right arm, saying as the smoothed the blue velvet, 'I'll go and ensure hot water and refreshments are brought to you right away, miss.'

As the door closed behind her so I snatched the note from my bodice and read Jarren's scribbled hand. *Layunie, trust me, all is arranged, dearest sweetheart. I love you. Jarren.* I ran my fingers across the paper and held it to my lips glancing towards the door as I carefully folded it once more before hastily tucking it back inside my bodice.

My heart raced with expectancy, everything would be all right, Jarren was coming to rescue me. I paced the room, fearful now, wondering how it could be done, finally standing before one of the casement windows pondering upon what might happen and when.

A maid knocked and entered bearing a silver tray, but as she lifted the teapot from its stand to pour the tea, so Mrs Treave entered, holding open the door and stating briskly, 'Miss Layunie, come at once if you please, Lord Trevoran is waiting for you downstairs in the library.'

The moment I so dreaded had come at last.

Obediently I followed Mrs Treave downstairs, across the great hall and on into the very heart of the huge house. Finally, her pace slowed, and she stated solemnly,

'The library, miss.' She knocked twice on the ornate door, gave me a thin smile and retreated down the passage. I stood alone before the imposing door, shaking so much I could barely hold myself upright. From within a voice bade me enter. I opened the door and stepped into the library to face my future husband, unless by some miracle Jarren could save me from that dreadful fate.

Lord Trevoran was standing with his back to me facing the fire, he wore no wig and I stared with distaste at the sparse grey hair that covered his bony head and fell in thin strands over his wrinkled neck. He turned around and I shuddered with dismay, he was even worse than I remembered! The room seemed to close in on me, its book-lined walls, heavy furniture, dark drapes and stifling heat so unbearably oppressive.

'At last I can welcome you to Trevoran Court, my dear,' he mocked. 'Come closer so I can take a good look at you.' His eyes darted up and down taking in every detail of my person, lingering for some moments upon my breasts. I stared boldly back, perceiving how the fashionable clothes he wore ill became this old man with toad-blotched skin, his eyes piercing in their scrutiny.

'Ah! Yes,' he jibed, 'I can see I've chosen my bride well! Indeed, I have been looking forward to your arrival and now that you are here at last, you will be pleased to learn there shall be no delaying our marriage, we shall be married in four days' time in St Feock's Church, already the arrangements have been made.'

I gasped in dismay, but Lord Cedric Trevoran took not the slightest notice and carried on quite unruffled. 'Your wedding dress will arrive here tomorrow, made by the finest seamstress in Truro from the measurements your aunt gave me when we were first betrothed. The dear lady is residing at present in Truro and a message was sent to her upon your arrival, no doubt she will not delay in accepting my invitation to join you and help in the preparations. Your father and brother, alas, will not be here for the happy occasion, your father is not in good health, a long journey out of the question, and your brother on hearing of your being safely in Mr Tripper's custody fled back to London.'

Numbed by what he'd said, I stood speechless, to my horror he raised his bony hand and beckoned I go closer. Taking my hand, he raised it to his wet fleshy lips and kissed it, my shudder at his touch going unnoticed by the sudden arrival of a tall ginger-haired man who strode into the room without knocking.

'Ah, Mr Saffrey,' his lordship drawled, eyes sparkling with menace. 'Come, sir, and meet my future wife.'

The man with the ginger hair made an exaggerated bow, whilst Trevoran squeezed my hand until I winced in pain. The ginger-haired man looked at me insolently without hiding a contemptuous smirk. His lordship squeezed my hand once more and then curtly dismissed me.

Nursing my bruised hand, I fled, thankful at being able to find the way back to the sanctuary of my room, lying for the rest of the day curled up on the bed sobbing. All entreaties by Mrs Treave to partake of refreshment I refused. She saw my distress but offered no words of comfort. Much later a maid was sent to help me undress and prepare me for bed, I could see the pity in her eyes as she gently bathed my swollen hand. 'Tis shameful, miss, and that's a fact,' were her parting words, leaving me alone with only Jarren's note for comfort and the thought that Aunt Sarah would soon be here to suffer my nightmare with me.

In the morning having dressed and partaken of a solitary breakfast, I went downstairs and out into the gardens making my way slowly down towards to the river, conscious as I did so that Lord Trevoran must have informed his servants I was to be closely watched. I could see them, my watchers, but could easily exclude them from my thoughts, they need not worry. I knew already there would be no use in taking flight, there were too many of them to outrun. A light breeze carried with it the smell of the river, a gull squawked causing me to turn suddenly and I spied Ty Saffrey standing on the path someway behind and quickened my pace, walking on until I reached the river itself, fast flowing on the ebbing tide. Turning around, my eyes explored the lawns and gardens, I saw no one but knew they were there. I gazed across the swiftly flowing waters at the dense woods opposite where the trees crept down steep banks, their branches dipping into the river, there was a quietness here, but I could feel no peace.

A while later I made my way back choosing to take another path which led me through a coppice. It was here I heard the horn and hurried on until I saw the driveway that wound its way up to the house. A sudden glint of red through the trees and I caught sight of a coach coming up the drive. I knew Aunt Sarah would waste no time in getting here and ran frantically through the trees and across the dewy grass just as the horses slowed in front of the house, hoping with all my heart that it was her. The door was opened, the steps lowered, and Aunt Sarah's familiar form came forth. Forgetting any kind of protocol, I ran forward and into her outstretched arms, she held me to her and whispered softly, 'Everything will be alright, Layunie, be strong, child, be strong.' Words so welcome that I hugged her even more tightly.

The rustle of Mrs Treave's skirts informed us of her presence. I drew apart from Aunt Sarah as the house-keeper stepped forward to bid my aunt welcome. We followed her into the house, and she led us to the room that had been prepared not far from mine, which pleased me greatly.

Mrs Treave adjusted the drapes letting in more light, informing us as she took her leave, 'Lord Trevoran's away to Falmouth at present but will join you both for supper.'

She stood aside as a young maid brought in a pitcher of hot water. 'If there's anything else you want, be sure to ring the bell.' She made a last cursory glance round the room to see that everything was in order before withdrawing, leaving us alone.

To my surprise, as soon as Mrs Treave shut the door Aunt Sarah put her finger to her lips and led me over to the window, which unlike mine overlooked the rect-angular courtyard at the back of the house. 'Do you recognise anyone down there?' she whispered.

'No,' I replied, for in all truth I could not.

Two men were unloading a large box from the rear of the coach. Mrs Treave, head held high, came into sight issuing instructions. The heavily bearded man with the wide-brimmed hat glanced up as he lifted down a smaller trunk, and immediately I knew who it was.

'Jarren.' His name escaped my lips before I could stop it and I clasped my hands to my mouth with joy. Quickly Aunt Sarah drew me away from the window and across into the farthest part of the room. She held me by the arms and looked steadily into my eyes.

'Is it Jarren you truly want, Layunie? If it is then I'll go along with his plan, if not we'll find some other means of escape.' There was no need for words she saw my expression and smiled.

'I thought as much, then there is little time to waste.' Enthralled I listened as she explained the plan Jarren had in mind.

It transpired Aunt Sarah was to tell Mrs Treave there were things I needed, and that whilst the coach was still here, she'd visit the local village and purchase these personal items for me. In fact, it would be me, dressed in her clothes that Jarren would drive away in the coach. I was to summon Mrs Treave and tell her I should not be needing anything to eat midday as the excitement of my aunt's arrival had given me a headache, informing her I would like to lie down and get up when my aunt returned. Aunt Sarah herself would lie down in my bed at the appropriate time, per chance anyone should look in on me, the likeness in our hair colouring a blessing. A hefty payment had been made to the real coachman that Aunt Sarah had hired. Almost certainly Mrs Treave and the other servants would expect Aunt Sarah to leave by the main entrance, but I should slip out and into the coach at the back of the house and be driven away.

I sighed exasperated. 'This plan can never work; I am watched constantly. What of the servants? And there's a most abominable gentleman Mr Saffrey who I feel spies on me constantly.'

'Have faith, child, we must trust to luck and hope that all goes well.' Aunt Sarah then revealed the last part of the plan. The real coach driver would bring the coach back at precisely 4.00pm and pause briefly at the front entranceway before bringing the coach round to the yard to water the horses before returning to Truro. She would then hopefully be able to contrive it so it would appear that she has just returned to Trevoran Court.

'Alas what a shock awaits me for whilst I was out on my errand, you have escaped. There is precious little that Lord Trevoran can hold me accountable for if the plan works, or for that matter if it fails, but it shall not, you'll see, and this way it's quite some time before your disappearance will be noticed.'

The plan seemed too simple, and I begged her tell how Jarren came to be here.

She smiled and her eyes twinkled. 'Luckily, the messenger Trevoran sent to where I was staying in Truro stopped off on his way at the Three Coins. The landlord being a beneficiary of the free traders and Jarren in particular, listened as with tongue loosened by ale the young man let slip his mission and the address for where he was bound. The good landlord aware of rumours linking his old friend and you, knew how to get word to Jarren and quickly dispatched to him the facts he had learnt. Jarren was much relieved for none knew for certain where Ruskin Tripper had taken you. Trevoran's got houses in Bath and London, you could have been taken who knows where if not Trevoran Court, now though Jarren knew where to find you and me.'

Her excitement in telling me all this suddenly faded, and her face filled with anxiety. Once again, she led me over to the window and we peered down into the courtyard. The men were finished now and one of the maids came out with some refreshments, we watched as she handed it to them, and Aunt Sarah touched my arm. 'It's time, Layunie.'

My heart thumped as I rang for Mrs Treave, she came in a trice, and holding my head as though in pain I informed her of my sick headache, followed by my speech about Aunt Sarah going into the village whilst the coach was still here. She argued I shouldn't need anything that wasn't here at the Court so my aunt's journey wasn't necessary, but Aunt Sarah emphasised that it was purely personal items I required and this finally won her over. Reluctantly the housekeeper agreed Aunt Sarah herself would inform the coachmen of the change of plans, and at last she left, confirming I shouldn't be disturbed. After she'd gone, Aunt Sarah went downstairs to check access to the courtyard, she saw no one, only a maid on her hands and knees busily working away.

It was difficult whilst she was gone to resist the temptation of taking another glimpse out the window, but I was wary in this great house of many windows of who could be observing me.

'There's no time to lose, Layunie, we must be quick. Did you not think I had put on weight?' She saw the bemused look on my face.

'I had my dressmaker work through the night till the good woman's fingers were sore, you'll soon see why, be quick and unfasten my dress.'

Quickly my fingers undid the tiny buttons and she slid the dress to the floor, amazed I saw underneath the damson dress, fashioned I was sure in the very latest of London styles, an almost exact copy. 'Get me out of this and untie the extra petticoats, this dress is the one you'll be wearing.'

Wasting not a second, I slipped out of my own dress and was tying the tapes of the extra petticoats round my waist, struggling hurriedly into the damson dress. It lacked the elegant lace trimmings on the half sleeves, and patterned detail and lace to the bodice on aunt Sarah's, but would easily pass as the same if only glimpsed beneath a cloak. Once both of us were dressed, and Jarren's note re-tucked inside my bodice, Aunt Sarah picked up her black cloak and placed it round my shoulders, raising the hood so it discreetly hid my face. My own dress she neatly put away.

'What if it all goes wrong?' I blurted out in a last-minute attack of panic. Patiently Aunt Sarah tried her best to calm me.

'Have faith, child, hold your head high, walk with confidence, you can do it, you know you can.' I took a deep breath, and listening to her instructions, pulled on my gloves.

Slowly she opened the door. I stepped forward my heart beating wildly with a mixture of excitement and pure terror. I felt her arm go around my shoulders and a squeeze of encouragement as I peered out and into the deserted passage.

'Good luck, be off now, child, and don't stop until you're in that coach.'

I kissed her warm cheek and after a moment's hesitation set off down the less elaborate stairs that led into a rear hallway. One of the double doors that led outside was ajar, but also half open was a panelled door on my right which I had to pass. My heart stood still, and I stiffened in dismay as from within came the un-mistakeable voice of Ty Saffrey. He was arguing with someone, both voices raised in anger, and I prayed the heated discussion would not cease as I took the decision to tread softly past. Having achieved this soundlessly, I eased the outer door open further, stepping forth into the autumn sunshine with confident step, graciously nodding to the man with dark brown twinkling eyes who stood holding open the door of the coach.

Neither of us spoke as he closed the door, but Jarren winked at me most wickedly and foolishly I felt myself blushing. For the briefest of moments our eyes held each other's, before in an instant all the happiness that had welled up inside me vanished as Mrs Treave's voice rang out from somewhere nearby. I didn't catch what she said but without hesitating, Jarren swung himself up to join his companion.

'Four o'clock sharp, ma'am, I'll be sure to be back on time,' he called cheerfully as the approaching footsteps on the gravel grew closer, the whip cracked and the coach lurched forward, and without any show of undue haste we set off down the drive and out through the main gates which were swung open for us. The horses were urged on, their pace quickened, taking us further and further away from Trevoran Court.

I held on to the strap hanging from the door for dear life, frightened for the new life that grew within me as we bowled along the uneven road. Then at last the horses slowed, I looked out and could see we had turned into what could barely be described as a track leading through dense woods. The trees on either side formed a canopy of golden branches making an arch under which the horses were guided with the greatest of care. We came to a clearing, the coach pitching forward as we stopped. Moments later the door was flung open and I was in Jarren's arms, being lifted down, pulling him tighter to me as his mouth closed on mine. 'I'm sorry, I'm sorry,' was all I could say when we drew apart.

A familiar voice called out a greeting and reluctantly we drew apart, both looking across the clearing, our view momentarily obscured by the coach as Jarren's companion wasted no time in turning the horses for the return journey, a difficult task in the tight space at hand. I tensed, suddenly anxious, and Jarren drew me close. I knew not the hour, but that the coach must return on time for my escape to work in such a way no blame attach itself to Aunt Sarah, all important to me.

'Will he make it back to Trevoran Court by 4.00 o'clock,' I queried, tilting my head upwards relaxing as the comforting smile on Jarren's face quenched my fears, his eyes held mine.

'Yes, my sweet, there's no worry on that score.' His finger stroked my cheek and once more his lips met mine. The coach halted a little way off the horses stamping at the ground impatient to be off once more.

As Jarren released me, I looked over beyond the clearing delighted to see our good friend John Penrose leading two fine horses towards us. I ran to greet him so pleased to see this dear friend, my days at the Star seeming a lifetime ago.

'Tis good to see you, Miss Layunie,' he called out handing over the reins to Jarren and grasping my hands warmly. 'Nancy sends her love, George, Jenny and the others too, we've all been that worried about you, maid.'

I looked at both men thinking of the danger I had brought by my foolishness. 'It was stupid of me to go looking for Nancy. I'm so ashamed, all this has been caused by me.' I felt wretched with guilt, why had I been so thoughtless?

'Hush, tis safe you are now, that's what matters,' Jarren stated calmly, then with John began walking over to the coach.

'All's gone to plan then?' John asked him. 'Time now for me to take your place and go back with the coach.' He grinned, and Jarren described briefly how the house-keeper very nearly foiled our departure from Trevoran Court.

Jarren handed John a small leather money pouch. 'Tell the coachman he'll get his money at the Three Coins when the rest of the plan is done. Tis good you'll be with him to keep an eye on things, you know what I mean.'

'Indeed I do,' John replied looking over to where the man sat hunched over, reins in hand.

'A fine pair of horses you've brought with you, John, I feel somehow its best I enquire not from whence they come.'

A knowing looked passed between the two of them before Jarren declared, 'Time you were off, my friend, make sure the fellow understands his task and good luck.' My heart went out to him, knowing the risk he was taking and all for me.

'Take care, I'll never be able to thank you for this,' I gasped, choked with gratitude and affection.

But he merely put his hand on my arm and said softly, 'God is on our side, maid, he'll not have you mar-rying that devil of a man and nor will we, tis Jarren here you're meant for, miss.'

Jarren took off his hat and heavy black coat, unfastening his false beard and handed all these to John, who put them on and strode over, heaving himself up beside the rather dour looking coachman hired for today's deception.

As we watched them go the sky clouded over and needles of rain began to fall. Jarren reached out pulling me to him, cradling me in his arms, I nestled close against his chest, comforted by the warmth of him, oblivious of the rain, as we stood completely alone in this wilderness of trees enjoying a lingering kiss. When we parted, he held me close and stroked my hair hugging me even tighter murmuring softly in my ear, 'Don't ever take a risk like that again, twas foolish, maid, I could have lost you forever.'

A rumble of thunder unsettled the horses and the rain fell even heavier. 'I'm sorry, twas foolish of me, so much danger and all because of my reckless behaviour.'

'There's no going back, you've learnt from it.'

We drew apart and Jarren looked up at the darkening sky and brushed back a mass of damp curls from his forehead. 'We'd best be on our way, my love, it's not far now.' He cupped his hands together for me to mount the smaller of the horses and swung himself up on the other, leading the way as we went even further into the dense forest.

We rode in silence taking the utmost care; progress was slow for the horses had to pick their way through the trees and undergrowth. Jarren often had to hold aside the branches of trees so I could continue. Ahead came a glimpse of light that grew steadily larger, then a sparkle of rippling water. Finally, we emerged out onto the bank of a narrow creek. Jarren helped me dismount, and I threw back the hood of my cloak, thankful that the rain had ceased. He kissed my forehead, his hazel eyes now searching mine, concerned. 'You look tired, my love, do you want to rest here awhile, we're all but there.'

I reached up and kissed his cheek, saying nothing of the nausea that still remained, caused by the motion of the coach and replied, 'I'm fine; let's carry on.'

We set off on foot leading the horses through the trees following the contours of the creek. We made our way past an old wooden jetty, so neglected that in places only baulks of timber remained standing upright in the water. Shortly we came to what once must have been a wide path between two stone walls, crumbling now after years of neglect.

We followed this neglected path until at the end of it we came upon the ivy-clad ruins of a once grand house. Jarren stopped. 'Rosecarren,' he said softly, and I looked up at him bewildered, watching as his gaze swept over the buildings, saw his jaw set tight, the muscle in his cheek quiver. He squeezed my hand, looked at me and smiled. 'There's no time for explanations now, t'will be plenty later.'

The sadness I sensed in him touched me greatly. We walked on through the great wilderness which once must have been the gardens. Two cottages came into view, set back against a high bank of trees, greenery sprouted from the chimneys, ivy covered the walls and clawed its way across the windows. Beside one of these was a lean-to shack into which Jarren led the horses. I waited outside, the atmosphere of mellow sadness which dwelt in this deserted place quite overpowering. A strange quietness, a stillness broken only by the lapping water against the muddy banks of the creek, the solitude engulfed me, holding me with dreamlike intensity.

Jarren reappeared and instantly these feelings were forgotten. God, how I loved this man. He walked towards me and gave one of his whimsical smiles. 'Your castle awaits, ma'am.'

We made our way up the wet, moss covered path to the nearest cottage. Jarren pushed the door open and I peered into the yawning darkness, a strong dank smell escaped from within. Inside, the walls shone wet in places and the floor dipped, sodden underfoot. I crossed to stand in the middle of the solitary dark room, its low beamed ceiling and walls blackened by smoke.

'It's not for long, love, tis the best John and I could do, it's isolated enough here to hide us for a while and that's what matters.'

'It's fine,' I whispered in a rush of gratitude, over-whelmed with love for this man whose life I had turned upside down for loving me.

Slowly my eyes became accustomed to the lack of light, I glanced at the old table onto which provisions had been piled, the row of tallow candles lying on the rotten window seat and the logs stacked beside the hearth. A couple of old chairs and few oddments, the only furnishings.

The dampness of the place as I stood surveying my new home, as well as my wet clothes, made me shiver and Jarren rubbed my cold hands. 'Upstairs I made up a bed of sorts and Nancy sent some clothes over with John, get out of those wet things whilst I set the fire.'

He turned me round untying my cloak and setting it down on the table, quickly undoing the buttons of my dress and slipping it from me. Showering my neck and shoulders with passionate kisses, his hands caressing me, sending a warm blush of pleasure sweeping over my body, and the pain of desire stirred deep within me.

'Go now, before I can't wait for you,' he implored, his breath warm on my shoulder, and to my shame I wished he'd taken me then for I so wanted him.

He opened a narrow door beside the hearth and watched as I made my way up the tiny curved staircase. Only a few rays of light penetrated the ivy and came in through the tiny window, but enough for me to see the bedding laid on the bare boards and the bundle of dry clothes.

As I was about to untie my petticoats suddenly my pulse quickened, for I heard Jarren's step on the stairs, my heartbeats increased with the creaking of every tread. At the top he paused, his strong muscular frame seemed to fill the tiny room, his presence thrilled me, the smile that lifted the corners of his mouth enticing. Our longing for each other needed no words as I ran into his arms, and our lips met in fervour of desire. We wasted no time, both tearing at our clothes eager to be rid of them in a frenzy of passion, the coarse blankets on to which we lay going unnoticed as we abandoned ourselves to the task of satisfying our lust for each other, not once but many times as night fell that first day at Rosecarren.

I slept late and woke to find myself alone amid the disarray of our makeshift bed. I sat up startled to hear voices drifting up from the room below, and anxious to find out who it was, dressed hurriedly in the clothes Nancy had sent, and crept halfway down the stairs to listen. Jarren was clearly at ease with our visitor which somewhat quelled my misgivings.

'Pray, my good friend; keep a look out for the *Rosemary* she'll be returning shortly, Giles'll bring her into the creek if the tides right, otherwise it'll have to be Trehallan's Quay, if it's got to be Penrin then the unloading left till high tide. If you see her tied up at Trehallan's, I beg you tell Giles I'm here with Layunie, take care, Josh, there's bound to be enemies around aplenty looking for us.'

At this, his companion laughed and said something under his breath I couldn't hear, and after a brief exchange of friendly banter, they made as if to leave the cottage.

Venturing down to the bottom of the stairs, I pushed open the door just as Jarren followed the other man outside. Stepping lightly across the room, I peeped out of the window, my eyes searching through its covering of ivy, but could see no one. Cold despite the fire in the hearth, I went upstairs to fetch my shawl and looked from the tiny window down through the screen of trees to the creek itself, until presently I saw Jarren making his way back.

I ran downstairs and out into the crisp autumn sunshine to meet him, as the breeze brushed my face all I could think was how good it felt to be free. Jarren held out his arms to greet me, picking me up and swirling me round, holding me tight as if never to let go. Long and hard he kissed me before setting me down and pulling me close. 'Good news, my sweet, I've had word all went well when the coach returned to Trevoran Court.' He took my face between his hands and kissed away the tears of relief that came on hearing these glad tidings.

'Aunt Sarah knew it would work; I shouldn't have doubted her,' I said, hugging him with happiness. And overcome with curiosity asked, 'Did he tell you this, the person you were talking too earlier?'

'Indeed he did, my sweet, and it was good news to hear.'

We began slowly walking towards the ruins of the old house called Rosecarren.

'Have no fear, the man who came here was old Joshua, he may well come again, don't take fright if he suddenly appears, he's quite harmless, just old and a little strange in his ways. Josh keeps an eye on the place for Giles and myself, stays here awhile now and then, keeps a presence so to speak, so none who may make it their business could say the land's abandoned and make claim to it themselves, and my pretty maid, tis a handy spot to hide the *Rosemary*. Some nights when the tides high and all's quiet, Giles sails her right into the creek out of view of the river, the ruin's a good cover for other business, and if smoke's seen above the trees local folk think its old Josh.'

My eyes opened wide with amazement. 'So does Giles Galley own this land?' I queried, and he smiled.

'Only half, the other half is mine.' I stopped walking and waited for him to continue.

'It's a long story, but first there's things you must know about Rosecarren, Layunie, sad things from the past.'

We walked on and he fell silent. Holding my hand firmly in his, he led me around the outside of what was left of this once grand house. The overgrown grass and brambles caught at my skirts, Jarren forever having to stop and detach them from me. We walked under a stone arch into what once had been a walled garden. The trees here were less dense now and the smell of roses filled the air, protected in this secret place undaunted by the end of summer. They were everywhere, mostly white, unpruned growing wild and free here in this neglected garden, long ago reclaimed by nature. I looked at the house almost hidden beneath the ivy. Clusters of weeds shrouded the stone corners of hollow empty windows.

Jarren walked ahead of me now and we came to a wide portico with shallow stone steps, a gaping hole all that remained where once had been an arched doorway. I wanted to stop and linger but Jarren was impatient for us to walk on. 'Come, there's something but a short distance further I want you to see.'

We came to a high wall that divided the garden, here the tangle of brambles grew less. After but a short distance Jarren knelt down, brushing aside the thick covering of leaves blown by the wind into piles upon the ground. He tore away at the lichen beneath them to reveal a heavy slab of grey stone, engraved into this the words: *Rosario Maria Jose. Born 27th June 1671 Died 3rd October 1690.*

I knew whose grave this was and knelt beside him remembering what Kate had told me of his poor mother, gently I placed a comforting arm on his shoulder.

'How come your mother rests here?' I queried softly. 'Kate told me she was buried at St Ives in the churchyard overlooking the sea.'

Jarren took my hand and I saw his eyes were glazed with tears. 'Nearly a month after the shipwreck, word reached my uncle Gabriel in Truro and he journeyed down to St Ives, sadly to discover my father, his older brother Matthew, was feared drowned, his body never found and that Rosario his bride of a year had survived only to die soon after in childbirth, by then I'd been placed with the Polvernes and he could see I was being well looked after.

'At that time, he'd no money himself only this land, he resolved to keep a watchful eye on me, finally making himself known to me a little before I was seventeen. I never asked how, but five years after the shipwreck he arranged secretly to have my mother's body moved here to Rosecarren, to rest in peace at the home she was destined for that fateful night. My uncle never came back once the stone was laid, only Giles and myself apart from him know she rests here in the place my father so loved. My uncle has handed over this land to Giles and myself knowing we will always protect it.'

I knelt beside him watching in silence as he gathered up handfuls of leaves scattering them across the stone, covering it once more. I felt his pain but knew there was nothing I could do to ease it. Deep within his own thoughts he looked towards the ruins. 'As you can see, gradually the place fell into disrepair and when it came about I met my uncle's son, Cousin Giles, there seemed no point in changing the way things were here.'

He stood up and pulled me up beside him. 'Unlike my father whose happiness was but short lived, I'll not be parted from you again, Layunie, with Giles's help we'll be married before anyone can stop us.'

He tilted my face upwards; kissed the tip of my nose and sought my lips with such desire my body swam with hunger. When at last he let me go I knew the time had come to tell him about the coming child and slid my arms round his waist smoothing the linen of his shirt and said softly, 'There's going to be a child.'

He looked down into my upturned face and brushed back his fringe of unruly curls, his eyes searched mine as if there could be some mistake in what he heard, then the corners of his mouth tilted upwards and that familiar roguish grin spread across his face, swiftly he gathered me in his arms holding me tightly against him, murmuring into my hair. 'Precious maid, I had no idea.' I looked up and saw his dark eyes sparkled with mirth, in a trice we were laughing and hugging each other as the sun rose high above the trees, its rays warming us, the sunlight brightening even the house with its hollow windows which stood behind us.

CHAPTER SEVEN

The bliss of living here however primitive was a joy. We saw no one except for old Josh who came shuffling up to the cottage bringing with him the odd brace of rabbits, or more likely fish. He was wary of strangers, cautious when speaking in my presence, his eyes darting in my direction ever watchful as he talked to Jarren, raising his battered old hat to me briefly as he left, disappearing with surprising speed back to his boat pulled up on the bank of the creek. I stopped myself from asking Jarren what was said between them, fear of what lay ahead held me back for I knew instinctively something was being planned.

Thus, three weeks slipped quickly by and the weather began to change. There were days when drifting sea mists made all things silent, the birds hushed. If you listened you could hear just the whisper of the changing tide, the smell of the tidal water as it filled the creek creeping slowly in until it trickled up the muddy banks. The trees were yielding up their leaves, battered by the wind they grew bare against the sky. Now, from the ruins of Rosecarren and from our little cottage, you could see beyond the trees to the river Fal itself. Our precious haven was becoming more exposed and Jarren was getting restless.

One night I suffered true anguish. That was the night; soon after we arrived when I'd lain curled up in

Jarren's arms before the kindled fire. It was then he told me of everyone's dismay when I failed to return to the Star. Of the frantic search made of the alleyways leading down to the harbour, of his coming almost face to face with Ruskin Tripper, and later the search made of the Star by the revenue as Tripper waited on horseback in the cobbled yard outside.

Jarren had hidden in the secret room, he'd heard Nancy's cry of dismay when word came that I'd been captured. When it was safe, he'd set out with John on horseback for Trevoran Court, only by chance had he got the message from the landlord of the Three Coins and found Aunt Sarah, so making the plan to rescue me possible.

'The landlord will be repaid, and handsomely, just as soon as Giles returns from France,' he'd said wiping away my tears and putting his finger to my lips, kissing away the words of remorse I tried to speak. My foolishness and what had happened that night in St Ives was never spoken of again.

Early one morning, Josh woke us with the rattle of stones against the window, shouting up to Jarren as he scraped it open and leaned out. 'The *Rosemary*'s been sighted off Falmouth.'

Roused from a deep sleep this news though expected, still came as a surprise. Hastily Jarren pulled on his clothes then came over to the bed briefly brushing his lips against mine. 'Rest now, go back to the sleep I've things to arrange with Josh, don't fret I'll be back soon.'

I sat up as his footsteps disappeared downstairs, my back resting against the wall listening to the murmur of their voices below, ashamedly resentful that our days here would be over the sooner now because of the

Rosemary's return. The door banged and struggling to free myself from the bedclothes I went over to the window, watching the two men walk away disappearing through the trees as the first rays of dawn heralded in a new day.

Much later as I fetched water from the well, I saw Josh heave his boat into the creek and begin rowing towards the open river. I wondered where Jarren was and set down my heavy pail on the rough stone wall.

Purposefully I began walking along the path beside the creek, wrapping my shawl tightly around me against the chill wind. There were deep ripples on the water and sudden gusts blew the very last of the leaves from the trees. Still there was no sign of Jarren. I reached a curve in the path knowing this led on until it followed the banks of the river Fal itself. I felt too exposed here and turned to walk through the trees towards the ruins, pondering if it was tonight the *Rosemary*'s cargo would be landed.

My thoughts turned to that night on the beach below Chy-an-Mor and the horrors at Zennor, of Jarren lying wounded at Nancledra. I started running, anxious to find Jarren; where on earth was he? Suddenly I felt very alone. I wanted Jarren, wanted to feel safe, wanted to know what he had planned. Thus impatient to find him, I took a way unknown to me, scattering the carpet of golden leaves beneath my feet. Out of breath at last I reached the ruins. Jarren must be somewhere close by but I knew better than to call out. My eyes focused upon what had once been a window, the sill and wall beneath it missing. By this means I entered the old house and was soon hopelessly lost, immersed in tangled undergrowth, cross now as I fought against a mass of prickles. A thorn dug deep into my arm and I cried out in pain, tearing away the offending branch and stemming the blood with the hem of my petticoat.

Angry that I had come here, knowing I should have waited for Jarren to return to the cottage, I turned to battle my way back, floundering amongst the wild brambles, stumbling over the uneven ground, hearing my dress tear, beginning to panic, unable to find my way out. From somewhere to my left came a faint sound and I stopped petrified. My heart thumped as though about to burst as I turned and watched in disbelief as a narrow door shrouded in creeper began to open. At the same time came the murmur of voices close by and I spun round.

Overhead, birds deserted their perches and for a moment the sound of their flapping wings obliterated everything. I looked through the swaying trees bowing their heads in the wind and out through the hollow house in the direction of the river. A cutter, her deck full of dragoons was sailing upriver.

I stood terrified unable to move as it disappeared around a curve in the river. Moments later a hand was placed firmly over my mouth. Roughly I was pulled backwards through the narrow door that was silently shut. I strived to loosen my captor's hold on me, trying to bite his hand as I was half carried half pulled downwards in pitch darkness, my feet rubbing against the rocky floor until abruptly I was set free. By the light of a battered lantern I saw it was Jarren who'd pulled me into this dark hole, for he gazed down at me his face a mixture of anger and exasperation. 'What were you thinking of coming here? You know how exposed it is now, how close it is to the river.'

The fury in his voice unnerved me. 'Tonight is important, and your thoughtlessness could put everything in jeopardy, lives as well, pray God you weren't seen.'

Contrite with guilt, I raised my voice and told him in as bold as voice I could muster, 'You had no need to treat me so, I came looking for you, I needed to find out what Josh said about the *Rosemary*, I was worried about you.'

Jarren's expression changed from anger to frustration. 'No, Layunie, you don't need to know.' He hung the lantern on a large hook protruding from the ceiling sending shadows dancing round the rocky cavern. 'Its business, Layunie, nothing for you to get involved in, tis men's work plain and simple, it doesn't concern you.'

I stared back defiantly, bending down to rub the back of my ankles and saw his expression soften, reaching out he gathered me tight against his broad chest, gently stroking my face. 'Layunie, Layunie, when will you ever learn, maid?' His dark eyes looked down into mine and gently he kissed my forehead, setting me back from him holding my shoulders firmly like a spoilt child. 'Don't concern yourself with tonight, tis nothing happening here any different from times past, don't fret, what happened over at Zennor was just bad luck. I'm all mended, besides we need money, my share of tonight's cargo means we can move on, leave these parts.' He took a deep breath and sighed, pacing the floor running his hand through his hair. 'If it pleases you and keeps you out of further mischief, I'll tell you what's happening tonight.' I listened duly chastised.

'High tide is late, the *Rosemary* will sail into the creek, the cargo will be unloaded, what can be will be moved tonight and what's left stored down here to be moved later.' His tone was sharp, and I could tell he was still angry and offered up a silent prayer that the cutter with its hated dragoons was now well and truly on its way upriver.

Jarren placed a hand on my shoulder and with his thumb gently rubbed my neck. I stood forlorn, silent and obedient as Jarren shut the lantern extinguishing its flame. He took hold of my hand and led me back up to the narrow door, slowly easing it open.

'Just now I saw a cutter going upriver carrying dragoons, they never saw me of that I'm sure.' It burst from me and he stopped. I heard his sharp intake of breath, heard him curse under his breath. Abruptly he thrust the shuttered lantern at me and cautiously went outside to check it was safe for us to leave. Thankfully there was no sign of any vessel, but I could tell Jarren was cross. He stayed silent as we made our way back along the creek. The tide was rising. I smelt its scent and listened to its almost silent sound, watched as leaves fluttered down onto the water. Wretched with myself for causing ill will between us.

We came to the cottage and I made my way over to the well, but as I reached for the pail, Jarren took it from me and set it down on the ground as mellow sunlight crept from behind the clouds.

'Come, I want to tell you something and it'll be far warmer inside.'

We went inside and he motioned me to sit down with him on the threadbare rug before the unlit fire. 'Layunie, we can't stay here, you know that!'

I put my head on his shoulder, so he couldn't see the tears in my eyes and nodded in agreement, thankful as his arm went around my shoulders.

'My sweet, be glad the *Rosemary* returns tonight not just because of its cargo, but because of another reason which I've not spoken of before in case it isn't possible. When Giles came to the Star that day I asked him to do something for me, to ask his father a favour, he said he was meeting him in Penzance before he sailed. Hopefully tonight he'll bring word this favour has been granted.'

He paused and I nestled closer. 'My uncle gambles, cards mostly, last year in St Austell he gained a property, the old boy he was playing threw it in when he'd lost all else in a futile attempt to win back his money. He lost and honoured the debt. The house is in a part of Cornwall I've seldom ventured, where I'm not known.' He lifted my chin and kissed the tip of my nose.

'Go on,' I whispered.

'Giles visited the place some months ago when the *Rosemary* put into Portlooe, the house is run down but sturdy built, its somewhere where we could build a life for ourselves, Layunie, change our names; with a child on the way we cannot run forever in fear of Lord Trevoran.' I nodded in agreement.

'Don't concern yourself with tonight, all is arranged, this is my way of life, Layunie and always will be, it will never change, I've told you this before. After the run tonight I pray Giles has good news for us about the house at Port Tallus Bay.' He held me from him at arm's length, his eyes imploring mine to acknowledge what he was stating. 'I must know I can trust you to stay put here inside the cottage. For God's sake our lives and the lives of others may depend upon it.'

'I promise, believe me, Jarren, I promise, a thousand times I promise,' I whispered back, feeling thoroughly chastised.

Long before dusk, Jarren dampened down the fire, no smoke must be seen later, and tired of trying to end the bad feeling between us I sat downcast watching as Jarren placed what remained of the wooden shutters across the windows. Much of the wood had rotted away, the gaping holes he filled with pieces of timber wedged firmly in place, no flicker of tallow candle must be seen, this was not a night to take chances. And all the while the tension between us simmered.

Whilst the embers in the hearth were still glowing, I warmed what remained of the rabbit stew, this we ate in silence until abruptly Jarren pushed his plate away and sat back, staring across the table at me. 'The truth of it is, above all else tonight my greatest worry is you, can I trust you to stay in the cottage, not venture out and do something silly.'

Dismayed, I got up and walked round the table, Jarren's eyes dark and questioning never left mine, as gently I eased myself onto his lap. 'I promise, I'll cause you no trouble. I beg you, Jarren, forget about what happened earlier.' My arms went around his neck and I buried my face in the dark curls at the nape of his neck, praying I was forgiven. I felt him sigh, felt his arm encircle my waist, he moved his head and once more our eyes met, mine imploring forgiveness, he reached out and brushed away tendrils of my hair which had become loose.

'Come here,' he coaxed, passion catching on his breath as his lips sought mine and I knew once more that all was well between us.

Evening came and with it a hint of winter; from the river, fingers of mist reached into the creek and ghostly shapes entwined themselves between the trees. The door was open and Jarren stood, his back resting against its frame, together we watched the tall trees sway in the chill wind.

'Tis a good night for a landing,' he murmured, pulling me closer as he gazed towards the creek filling now with the incoming tide. The crescent moon shed little light upon the rippling waters for clusters of fine clouds drifted across the sky. 'Tis getting late and time I was on watch,' he sighed.

'Stay safe inside til morning, twill be late tomorrow before I'm back, there's kindling aplenty but best not get tempted to light a fire.' I rested my head against his chest my arms tight around his waist, as gently he ruffled my hair.

'Promise me you'll stay inside once I'm gone,' he coaxed, gently untwining my arms.

'I promise; take care, my love,' I pleaded holding his hand unwilling to let him go.

We shared one last lingering kiss before he was gone.

'Keep safe,' I whispered into the crisp night air as I watched him walk away, engulfed in the misty darkness as he strode through the trees towards the entrance of the creek.

For a moment I stayed in the doorway filled with a mixture of anxiety and strange excitement, my eyes searching the shallows and deep water beyond, trying to imagine the outline of the *Rosemary* with her tall masts moored in the creek, of the many men who would come tonight to unload her precious cargo, and longed for Jarren's safe return when all was done.

A gust of wind rustled through the trees, breaking the silence intruding upon my thoughts, the trees which shrouded round the cottage became a little frightening and with relief I closed the door and placed two sturdy wooden slats firmly across it before going upstairs.

I lay down on our makeshift bed covering myself with blankets and reluctantly blew out the candle; shivering, so cold it was without the fire. Through small spaces in the shutters tiny shafts of moonlight seeped in tempting me to look outside, I did, but could see nothing, and lay down once more huddled between the blankets, listening, but the only sound I heard was the wind rattling against the windows. At last my eyes grew heavy and I slept, the shadowy procession of men and the muffled feet of the pack ponies as they passed, going unheard in the dead of night.

I woke the next morning cross with myself for having fallen asleep. Slithers of light shone in and rested on the dusty floor, I sat up restless, daring myself to believe all had gone well. I looked out through a chink in the boarded window, no telltale signs remained of the men who'd passed this way the night before. For the first time since we came here I felt lonely, for I knew that now even the horses had gone, taken by Jarren and the free traders moving their precious cargo, and although it was Jarren who tended them, the place seemed deserted without their presence.

The hours spent waiting for Jarren's return were unbearable, so slowly the day dragged on, the midday sun bringing no warmth with its rays, then finally I heard the thud of galloping hooves and peeped curiously down from a tiny gap in the shuttered window upstairs, and my heart leapt with joy, it was Jarren and John Penrose.

By the time I'd hurried downstairs both men had dismounted and were leading their horses into the makeshift stable, as they came out, I ran to meet them and Jarren swept me off my feet. 'Missed me.' He grinned, as I raised my face to be kissed.

'Only a little,' I teased, as John stepped forward holding his arms out to embrace me. I greeted him with much joy so pleased to see this true friend. I received a quick kiss to my cheek then he stood back smiling down at me.

'I shall tell Nancy you're blooming, there's a blush to your cheeks twas never there in St Ives, maid.' I saw him wink at Jarren, whose face broke into a roguish grin and I knew without doubt Jarren had told him of the child I carried.

That night the fire was slow to catch, it gave little warmth but yielded plenty of smoke which blew back down the chimney with gusto. As we ate, talk between the two men was of the run last night. Relief expressed that it had gone well, their business safely conducted without incident. It came as no surprise to learn that John and Nancy planned to marry in the spring of next year, and that Jenny, my one-time foe, and Simon where courting. Even the mention of her name still brought a pang of jealousy I felt ashamed of. That night as we ate together our world seemed at peace and as John regaled us with the tale of how George Tought had caught two ragamuffin thieves upstairs in the Star searching through his possessions and sent them packing, having first paraded them before the tap room customers to much banging of tankards and jeering, I felt truly happy.

Josh came after we had eaten, bringing with him a small boy looking much like him, his son Michael who spoke even fewer words than his father. As always Josh spoke to Jarren alone standing just inside the door, but I could tell by the tone of his voice the news he brought was good. He didn't linger long, and we stood and watched from the doorway as he rowed into the encroaching darkness. Soon after John too took his leave, taking with him my congratulations and best wishes to Nancy. He took the horses with him also, riding one and leading the other. Jarren and I were alone again.

He picked me up and carried me upstairs, laying me down on our makeshift bed, a rush of colour coming to my face as with haste he unbuttoned his shirt and shed his breeches. Early rays of moonlight filtered through and onto his strong body, my dress I unfastened in haste and cast aside as Jarren made love to me and I him with total abandonment for what would be the very last time here at Rosecarren.

'Lay still and close your eyes,' he commanded when finally our lust for each other was satisfied, he reached across and I heard the rustle of paper. 'You can look now.' I opened my eyes and saw in the moonlight he was holding a piece of paper. 'Tis from the Bishop of Truro himself, a man who appreciates a good drop of brandy, and this, my dear, is his given authority that we may marry, God bless him.'

I sat up looking at him in disbelief. My heart quickened with the shock and happiness I felt within.

'Tis good friends us free traders make, and many an appreciative person in high places. Thanks to such a fellow, little maid, we shall be married tomorrow on the night of the Fortune's Fair.' I nestled down enclosed within his arms and begged to know more, then saw his eyes were closed, sleep had overtaken him and it was morning before I learnt fully what was planned.

How quickly that last day at Rosecarren passed, by dusk no trace of our having been here remained. When we were ready to leave, Jarren covered the well, and although I knew this was a new beginning, and looked forward to our future life together, a great sadness engulfed me at living this so special place.

I stood ready to depart dressed once more in Aunt Sarah's damask dress. I wrapped her thick velvet cloak about me as I waited in the doorway whilst Jarren walk-ed across to the ruins one last time. I knew where he'd been and saw the sadness in his eyes when he returned, saw too he'd brought back with him a few remaining white roses from the wild garden, their stems wrapped in a piece of white cloth. He came and stood close to me; his breath warm on my face as he murmured, 'I love you Layunie,' and gently placed four of the smaller blooms in my hair. The freshness of their scent and the look of love in Jarren's eyes made this a moment in time I shall never forget. His lips sought mine and here beside the rippling waters of the creek with the trees swaying in the light breeze, it seemed that destiny had sealed our love and future together forever, tonight we would be man and wife married in the eyes of the church. A new beginning and sad though I was at leaving this sanctuary I looked forward to going far away to start our new life together.

The spell of these last moments at Rosecarren was broken by the thud of Josh's boat as it beached on the bank close by, we tore apart startled for neither of us had heard him coming. Jarren's hand sought mine and we made our way down to where Josh waited. The moon slid under a scattering of silvery clouds, everything was still, the creek took on an eerie feel, the trees casting giant shadows as it reappeared settling its reflection upon the rippling water.

This was a bigger boat than the one Josh usually brought, and having sat me down in the bow, Jarren took the second set of oars. They wasted no time in pulling away from the shore. The oars rhythmically dipping in the inky waters made hardly a sound and soon we were at the mouth of the creek. I took a furtive look back and a lump came to my throat, in my hands I held tight the posy of white roses, already the cottage was swallowed up in the darkness, the ruins unseen amongst the stark haunting outline of the trees that bent and bowed their heads, swaying as if in a final gesture of farewell.

'There'll be other craft out on the river,' Jarren said softly, 'hopefully we'll be just one of many.' We crossed the creek and kept as close as we could to the bank on our right, where the twisted branches of ancient oaks reached far out over the water. We were now following the dark waters of the river Fal downstream between wide thickly wooded banks, the pungent smell of tidal water strong in the night air.

'These waters the Carrick Roads will take us down to Penryn,' Jarren told me between breaths, as both he and Josh pulled hard on the oars.

From tales of the Fal lovingly told me by my grandfather I knew that already, what I really wanted to know was how long it would take. But instead of asking, I pulled my cloak more firmly around me, raising the hood and holding it in place beneath my chin.

As though sensing my thoughts, Jarren rested his oars and leant forward. 'Do I sense you're impatient to become my wife?'

I saw the wicked look on his face and stole a quick kiss before he began rowing once more, content to observe the strength in his powerful body as he strove to row against the incoming tide.

The waters of the Fal became rough, as the freshening breeze turned the ripples on its surface into waves which lapped against the banks, and after a while I could see that both Josh and Jarren were beginning to tire. A scattering of other craft could be seen as we made our way further downriver, many were shadows barely visible, one though was strewn with coloured lanterns. From someway off in the distance came the sound of music played on a fiddle, muffled shouts and laughter. The smell of wood smoke and roasting ox drifted towards us carried on the breeze.

At last the river opened out and was joined by another, its wide mouth edged in steep granite quays that jutted out into the Fal. 'The Penryn,' Jarren shouted, his words carried away on the wind. We changed course and I held tight the wooden seat beneath me as our boat was tossed wildly about on the crosscurrent. Pain was etched on both men's faces as they heaved on the oars plunging them rhythmically in the turbulent water.

It was now I saw the glow in the sky caused by blazing torches placed in sconces along the furthest quay and many more in the meadow beyond where the fair was being held. I was shocked suddenly to see so many people. The music mingled with the cries of the crowd and grew louder as we neared the quay, all manner of voices shouted their wares and could be heard amongst the cheering revellers.

We were joined on the river by a flotilla of other boats, like us headed in the direction of the quay nearest the fair and I wondered for a moment if we too were to alight there, for surely this would be dangerous. My stomach churned as we drew closer, the blazing torches sent shimmering reflections dancing on the water, cast light too on those both on the quay and on us folk in the boats. I took comfort in Jarren's words of reassurance spoken earlier in the day, 'Fortune's Fair is one place you'll not find the revenue, and if you do they'll be as drunk as all the rest,' he'd said, but still I felt uneasy.

As we drew closer alongside the quay, water slapped against the hulls of larger vessels as they rocked in their moorings, ropes creaked. The occupants of the smaller boats jostled noisily for space to tie up near the granite steps. But not us.

We slipped with ease unnoticed into the gloom where the quay ended to glide unseen under a web of overhanging trees. Josh pulled in his oars and let Jarren guide the boat between the tangle of wooden tree stumps and dead branches, which rose from the jet-black water. We followed close the contour of the bank until Josh reached over and grasped hold the edge of a protruding granite slab. The boat rocked from side to side as Jarren helped me out, lifting me over the side, his grip firm as my feet rested on the slippery bank.

Quickly Josh secured the boat and we began to climb up a steep densely wooded hill, the layers of decaying leaves mulched under foot. Aunt Sarah's satin shoes had not been made for this kind of adventure and soaked in the moisture; my dress and cloak already damp with spray from the river were now edged in mud. One of Josh's huge calloused hands held mine, as we struggled upwards through the undergrowth, Jarren going ahead snapping away dead branches of thick foliage to make a way through. The night air caught in my throat and I gasped for breath, exhausted, about to ask Jarren if we could stop awhile, when we came upon a narrow set of steps, green with mildew, that wound their way upwards. At the top for a moment we paused. Jarren drew me to him and gently kissed my forehead, he pulled back the hood of my cloak, tucking one of the white rose buds more firmly in my escaping curls.

'Not much further, lovely maid, I promise,' he said softly, 'but come we must not delay.' And taking my hand firmly in his, guided me through the trees until we came to the graveyard at the top of the hill.

A sound close by caused us to stop, I looked back, moonlight shone on the river below and in the far distance the faint glow of light towards the sea heralded Falmouth. Silence now, apart from the music in the distance coming from the fair, we waited, but all seemed quiet around us and Jarren urged us on for indeed we were nearly there.

The church with its tall steeple stood stark against the sky, a small arched door to the side opened and Jarren hastened me forward. I recognised the figure standing anxiously waiting for us, it was John Penrose. He came forward greeting us eagerly, quickly ushering us inside glancing out into the darkness before closing the nail-studded door. The church was lit by two solitary candles placed one each side of the altar it was very dark and intensely cold.

With one hand in Jarren's I walked forward as my eyes adjusted to the sparse light, our every move, the rustle of my dress, our footsteps, emphasised in the dark vaulted chambers of the church. An aged priest with long wisps of grey hair either side of his balding head hurried towards us and bid us welcome, he mopped his large forehead with a white handkerchief and anxious to get on made his way towards the altar. Jarren squeezed my hand, our eyes met and held, my lover of so many nights to whom I'd soon be wed. I glimpsed a twinkle in Jarren's eyes and just briefly laid my head on his shoulder, before we walked further down the aisle, John followed a little way behind.

The priest picked up his prayer book and turned towards us, carefully finding his place, then standing for a moment, the bible open in his hands. A kindly smile caught the corners of his mouth as he began the words of the marriage service, this truly a moment when my heart stood still.

Clutching tight my posy of white roses from Rosecarren, trembling with emotion I made my vows, and when the priest asked of me, 'Will you take this man to be your wedded husband, to honour and love in the eyes of God,' twas my greatest joy to reply, 'I will'. My heart thumping with joy as unhurried the priest continued. Jarren looked straight into my eyes as he made his vows. From his pocket, John drew out a gold band and Jarren slipped it on my finger, kissing my fingertips as he did so, our simple ceremony was over. The priest replaced the black ribbon marker and carefully closed the prayer book as Jarren put his arms around me and claimed the first kiss from his bride.

The priest made his way down the altar steps, taking our hands in his, he wished us well. Hastily papers were signed and witnessed, there was little time for congratulations, a kiss from John and a shy squeeze of my arm from Josh, who I warmly embraced, kissing his rugged weather-beaten cheek, this strange little man who I'd grown so fond of, who no longer mistrusted me as a stranger, whose loyalty to Jarren I so valued.

Thanking the priest once again, Jarren took my hand, our secret wedding over, and with the others we made our way towards the door. John raised the latch and the priest snuffed out the candles. As I stepped outside, I felt the thrill of a new beginning, the excitement and promise of a future still unknown.

We stopped for one long lingering kiss as John and Josh discreetly went on ahead. Jarren held tight my hand as we retraced our steps back down the hill, taking care to avoid the hollows beneath the fallen leaves. Many times, I wrenched free my cloak from the tug of brambles catching at the heavy velvet, treading a path the others decreed, slowly down until we reached the boat waiting at the water's edge. John untied the rope and took the oars with Josh. Jarren lifted me onboard, sitting beside me as slowly now the boat edged forward under the gnarled old trees. From inside his jacket he pulled out his battered wide-brimmed hat and put it on. We emerged once more from beneath the safety of the trees to mingle with those travelling by river to the fair.

The hum of voices and laughter mingled with merry music, along with the cries of pedlars shouting their wares on the quay anxious to sell gingerbread and jaw breaking toffee to new arrivals. The flickering light cast by the torches fastened high in the huge sconces showed a throng of people. From two shore boats with lanterns at bow and stern a gang of rowdy sailors were climbing an iron ladder, calling out to a group of young girls getting down from a wagonette. A giant of a man standing beside one girl, her auburn locks tied up in scarlet ribbon, turned and angry words were exchanged, he began walking back along the quay, head thrust forward on his thick neck, so focusing the eyes of those around us on the two men, whilst our boat with its gently creaking oars slipped past on our way to Trehallan's Quay.

Here schooners and larger ships were tied up, some three deep against the wooden wharf, their masts stark against the sky. Now and then muffled voices drifted down, but most were silent, their rigging jangling in the wind, rocking gently with the swell of the river, seemingly deserted on this night of the fair.

'There she lies,' Jarren murmured, and ahead of us I saw Giles's ship the *Rosemary*, the name emblazoned on her stern, how much bigger she looked now. The last time I'd seen her was from the beach at Gwithian last spring when she'd been but a silhouette far out to sea, thankfully then I'd deterred her from coming any closer inshore.

We drew alongside and Jarren gave a low whistle, seconds later a rope ladder was thrown down which John caught and held. Jarren urged me to stand and nervously I held tight the ladder's rough sides, he placed my foot on the first rung and as the others steadied the ladder, bade me climb upwards, following close behind as it twisted and swung against the ship. I looked up delighted to see Giles leaning over waiting to help me, his strong arms gently pulling me over onto the deck, jesting as Jarren jumped down beside him, placing an arm round his shoulders. 'You a married man, never thought I see the day, if I'd made it here sooner, I'd not have missed it for the world.'

Laughing they hauled the others on deck and together pulled up the ladder. On board the *Rosemary* all was quiet as Giles quickly led us below.

This was far from being the stark, bare place I'd imagined on a ship used for smuggling. Giles's quarters were most plush, with wood panelled walls and other furnishings of a very high quality. In the centre of the room stood a large oblong dining table with eight chairs neatly positioned around it, on this was laid out a fine spread of food together with a plentiful amount of brandy and wine. Silverware set upon the table twinkled in the light of oil lamps hung from two beams overhead, upturned on a silver tray were six crystal glasses. From a decanter on a side cabinet Giles poured me a glass of wine before handing each of the men a brandy.

'A toast to my cousin and his bride,' he declared, raising his glass, and was joined by the others. Their glasses clinked together as Jarren proudly put his arm around me, tilting my face upwards and kissing my lips.

'A toast to you, Giles, and my two most trusted friends, and to all our futures,' he replied, as the glasses were raised once more.

Blissfully happy, my hand sought Jarren's, thankful all had gone well tonight, eager to begin the new life that awaited us tomorrow when we set sail.

Giles gestured us to sit and bade us eat. 'Twill be plenty time afterwards to talk of tomorrow.' He grinned as we gathered round the table all of us hungry, our eyes devouring the cold fowl and other delicacies with relish. Each man laid his pistol on the table's shiny surface, the hint of danger which could appear to spoil this our wedding breakfast ever present.

At last when we had partaken of our fill, Giles rose and we followed him to the far end of the room to sit on two red opulent couches, a small table between us. He laid out on this a sketch of Port Nadler Bay that showed the dwelling his father had won at cards from the old boy in Truro.

'Boswedden will be easy found, but alas in sad need of repair, tis best I drop anchor off Tallus, for the cliffs at Port Nadler Bay are too steep to climb and the walk from Tallus is done in minutes, my men will row you ashore. As luck would have it, in Fowey last week I met with an old seadog I know from Looe. I set out to him the story of my old friend Jago Pearce who'd done a great service to my father, he in gratitude for this had made Boswedden over to him by way of thanks. No doubt the local hostelries around Tallus will be recounted of this, they all know how my father came about the place, so none will query your arrival, it's up to you then, what story you tell. But Jago Pearce is the name you must go by.' His eyes, so like Jarren's, twinkled as he rolled up the sketch of the coast.

'Jago Pearce, it is then, and Mrs Pearce of course.' Jarren grinned raising his glass to toast our new name. 'Tis sad I'll be to leave these parts and indeed know twill have to be forever, I'll not risk coming back.'

I looked at Josh and felt a pang of regret, this was a parting of friends, like me he'd heard Jarren say he'd never visit this part of Cornwall again. He sat head bowed, I knew he rarely travelled far from waters of the Fal, the vital part he'd played in our wellbeing and escape was over, words could never be said that would thank him enough. Such an out of the ordinary little man, how much love I felt for him, how I appreciated his loyalty and his help. Jarren reached forward, his hand on Josh's arm. 'Old friend, this isn't the last time we'll meet, Port Nadler's not the other side of the world, you must come, Josh, pay us a visit.'

'Please do,' I pleaded.

His head lifted, and a rare smile crept across his rugged face. 'Sorely I'll miss you both, tis been a long few weeks, and yes maybe, if tis at all possible, I'll pay you a visit someday.'

Giles's eyes twinkled mischievously. 'Jarren, it's late, man, take your bride off to her marriage bed.' I blushed as Jarren took my hand, kissing it with a flourish.

'Come, wife, to bed with you,' he joked roguishly, looking at Giles, leaving me time to say but a quick goodnight before I was led towards Giles's sleeping quarters. Once outside, Jarren lifted me up in his arms twirling me round with a flourish before opening the cabin door to where we were to spend the night.

'Come here, I want to kiss every inch of my bride,' he whispered, kissing my ear, whilst with one hand he pulled back the crisp linen sheets, laying me down on the broad bunk, undressing me slowly as I reached out and began unbuttoning his shirt, the rest he finished for me with an urgency, blowing out the single candle and slipping his warm body beside mine. For a moment I stopped his eager lovemaking and laid my hand on his chest to feel his heartbeat, wanting to savour every moment of this night. Gently he pushed my hair back kissing my brow, slowly, tenderly, before his ardour devoured every part of me and I him, like that first time at Nancledra.

When I awoke it was still dark, a lone star was all I could see through the tiny porthole. Jarren lay sleeping, one arm thrown carelessly across the pillow. I lay content to watch him sleep, tracing the line of his lips with my finger, reaching out to kiss his handsome face, and about to snuggle back between the sheets when a heavy thud sounded on the deck above, followed by running footsteps. Jarren woke instantly flinging back the bedclothes.

'Get dressed now,' he ordered as more footsteps pounded overhead. Once fully clothed himself, he helped me on with my dress as frantic banging came on the cabin door. Reaching for his pistol, Jarren open the door just a little. It was Giles.

'Tis a riding officer with a company of dragoons come searching for a fellow free trader by the name of Jack Swannell, captured during a run near Falmouth, he escaped the lock up at Greenbank last night, they're searching all ships for him. There's no place to hide you, we're full laden with hidden brandy, tis best you don't risk staying, you and Layunie must be gone before they reach us.' He paused and drew breath. 'John and Josh have gone on ahead to wait in the boat, I've told them to row up river and across to Sweets Wharf, cut across land towards Mylor and Bessy's cottage, he knows where it is, if all's safe I'll send word so you'm back on board before we sail midday.'

Thankfully, it was still dark when we emerged on deck, the ship creaked as it rocked rhythmically on the water, we heard a low curse and looked over the side. Some way below, Josh was struggling to untangle the ropes securing the boat, John drew a knife from his belt and began frantically cutting away at them.

I started shivering, terrified as faint voices heard in the distance became ever closer. A concerned look passed between Jarren and his cousin.

'You'll have to trust me, Layunie, we must go before it's too late.'

However fearful of what was planned, I daren't ask, instead peered over the side of the ship breathing in the pungent smell of the river as Jarren lifted me into his arms.

'Hold tight, my darling,' he coaxed, and with Giles help I eased myself over the rail and held tight the ladder. The boat below and the inky black river seemed along way down, but there was no time to dwell on this. I felt for the rung beneath my feet and began lowering myself down. Jarren followed. Giles leaned over the side watching our progress. I paused and Jarren dropped down into the boat desperately trying to help Josh unravel the knotted lines, but time was running out.

'It's too late to tarry,' I heard him tell the others. 'Help Layunie into the boat and then hand her down to me.' With that he dived into the river.

Josh's strong arms reached up and took hold of me, setting me down in the boat before gently lifting me over the side and into Jarren's outstretched arms. I felt his grip tighten as I slipped into the icy water, the skirt of my dress and petticoats billowing out in the river, weighing me down as the pull of the current below the surface took its hold. Hastily the others eased themselves soundlessly into the water.

'Put your arms round my neck and hold on,' Jarren ordered. He began to swim, staying at first close to the hulls of the other ships, before making for the other side of the river. More than once, numb with cold, I sank beneath the surface to emerge spluttering out the foul water, my lungs bursting for air, as Jarren struggled on, battling against the current in the swirling river.

At last we neared the other side; all three men were tiring now. Jarren swam exhausted between the towering hulls of two large schooners moored beside the wharf. We passed several stout wooden bulwarks and on through the murky water until we were underneath the wharf itself, here the river was shallow, and my feet rested on its gravely bed.

I held tight Jarren's hand as he waded on through the dank waist-deep water. We came to a place where the rotten boards overhead made it possible for Jarren to heave himself up, and thus satisfy himself we would be hidden by the ships tied up alongside. He lifted me up and catching hold a ragged edge I clambered onto the wharf dragging my sodden skirts behind me. Jarren joined me and pulled Josh and John up too. We paused only for a few seconds. Just time enough for me to wonder how long it would be before the riding officer and dragoons reached the *Rosemary*.

We were all exhausted and freezing cold; we fled the quay and crept between a collection of tumbledown boatyards, into the welcome sanctuary of the wood beyond.

It was difficult to run for my sodden petticoats and skirt wrapped themselves round my legs. Sensing this, when finally Jarren deemed it safe to stop, he ordered me take off the petticoats, and with no minds to modesty helped me remove them, rolling them into a ball and stuffing them under a pile of rotten wood.

I squeezed the river water from my hair as we made our way deeper into the woods. Exhausted, finally we stopped and Jarren wrapped his arms round me in an effort to keep me warm, trying to still my uncontrollable trembling, whispering gently in my ear, before asking Josh how much further we must go.

'Soon we'll be safe, tis but another mile to Bessie's,' Josh wheezed, fighting to get his breath. 'You best go on I'll only be a hindrance, leave me behind, I'll to follow you later.'

Jarren took a deep breath about to answer when the sound of gunfire came from the direction of the river, it was time to be on our way. We ran on, John beside us, Josh a little further behind. There was more gunfire, we ran for our lives, the lace edging on my sleeves ripped from the satin as brambles tore into my arms as we fled. I kept pace with Jarren until the stitch in my side slowed me down and concerned, he caught John's arm slowing him down.

'This way,' Josh spluttered, as he saw us stopping. 'I know a place we can hide.' He set off purposefully through the trees, pausing as we reached a dell overhung by trees.

'It's only a stitch,' I breathed looking at Jarren, praying inwardly it was nought to do with the child I carried, and that the shouts we could hear in the distance weren't from anyone pursuing us. Josh led the way down and into a hidden cave, here, relieved, we all slumped down onto the earthen floor to rest.

Jarren rubbed my hands in his to warm them, then looked at my fingers. 'Tis important you take off these rings.' He slipped off my wedding ring, together with the blue sapphire. Reaching forward he tucked them deep within the hem of my dress. 'If we're caught say nothing of our marriage or Ruskin Tripper will have us both shot, believe me.'

'Come we must go, it's dangerous to tally here,' John begged, and reluctantly Jarren agreed. We emerged from the dell into a welcome silence. We ran on through the tangle of undergrowth, weaving our way forward desperate to get further away from the river. One sodden slipper fell from my foot, and as I tugged on Jarren's hand to tell him, he stopped anyway. All four of us stood still, Jarren cursing under his breath. There could be no doubt; we were no longer alone on this side of the river. Suddenly voices could be heard not far away, a shot was fired, and the birds fled the trees as we ran blindly on. Jarren almost dragging me through the trees.

The sound of splintering wood as those pursuing us desperately fought their way through the trees was unmistakeable, followed by an eerie hushed silence. Only the tops of trees swayed in the breeze as we silently picked our way through the wood, Josh leading the way. Could it be they had abandoned their quest? Jarren raised his arm and motioned us to stop, from somewhere behind us a twig snapped underfoot. With beating heart, I gazed back through the labyrinth of trees.

Then in the rays of misty first light seeping through the canopy of trees, I caught the glint of silver as a knife sped through the air and plunged into the back of Josh's neck. He cried out in agony, stumbled and fell forward. I screamed and broke free of Jarren's grasp, mortified to see blood oozing from Josh's mouth, his eyes wide open beseeched me for help. As gently as he could, Jarren withdrew the blade with its ivory handle, tearing at his shirt and holding the cloth against Josh's bleeding wound. John scrutinised the trees and scrub from where the knife was thrown, nothing stirred to betray the attackers' whereabouts. With haste, Jarren picked Josh up and ran on, all had gone silent, the stark freshness of a new day casting its spell, holding a sense of terror in its coming.

We came to a thicket, here reluctantly Jarren stopped for it was clear the little man was in deep distress. John lifted him from Jarren's arms and lay him down beneath an ancient oak, even this late in autumn its gnarled branches still hung with brown leaves, offering us a sanctuary. Josh's face was suffused with pain, a ghastly gurgling sound came from his throat, blood spewed from his mouth. Jarren knelt down and tore another strip of linen from his shirt; he lifted Josh's head trying to stem the flow of blood from the wound. *God, don't let Josh die*, I prayed silently, stifling my sobs, turning away lest he saw my tears.

'We'll take care of you, old friend,' Jarren told him. But Josh's head lolled to one side, he was dying. I reached out and took his hand, felt his fingers grasp mine just briefly before the light faded from his sorrowful eyes; our good friend had gone forever.

John set about covering Josh's body with leaves whilst Jarren held me tight. I clung on to him and wept, sobbing at the overwhelming sense of loss, remembering the happy times Josh had shared with us at Rosecarren, and his loyalty to Jarren that had cost him his life.

Too late, I saw a movement in the trees, it was the blue coats, their slow advance deliberate and terrifying. One man detached himself from the rest, his pistols aimed directly at us, there was no escape.

'Well, who have we here? Methinks I've got a richer prize than Jacky Swannell.' He motioned one of his men to come forward. 'Go back to Trehallan's Quay tell Ruskin Tripper, the money's mine, for if I'm not mistaken, we have here Jarren Polverne and the piece of skirt so sought after by Lord Trevoran.' He looked me up and down, and his mouth twisted into a cruel sneer. 'Tie em up,' he commanded.

It was Jarren who struck the first blow, savagely hitting the first man to approach us, striking the soldier's jaw, sending his opponent reeling backwards in pain. The man holding the pistols looked on, his face white with fury. 'Get on with it, you fool,' he growled, as the blue coat scrambled to his feet, and I could do nothing but watch in horror as we were surrounded by his men.

'I don't care what you do to them, but don't forget, Tripper'll want them alive.'

Jarren tried to shield me, at the same time resisting capture, fighting the brutish blue coats with his bare hands. Alongside him, John struggled with a giant of man twice his size. Hopelessly outnumbered it took little time until they were defeated, beaten until they were unable to stand, kicked repeatedly by the soldiers in their heavy boots, until they lay almost dead on the ground.

'Leave them.' The order came and the men backed away, I saw John given one last brutal kick to the ribs, before like Jarren he was hauled to his feet.

I ran forward and was dragged away from Jarren by two of his tormentors. Somehow Jarren managed to stand and limped forward until he stood before the captain head held high looking defiantly into the other's cold eye. 'Don't let any harm come to her,' he demanded, his voice strong and controlled as the captain transferred his gaze to me. Blood slowly trickled down Jarren's face from a cut above his eye; with the back of his hand he wiped it away.

'Harm, you say, sir,' the captain gloated. 'Unlike Ruskin Tripper I'm not in the pay of his lordship, not obliged to play by the same rules, and if I desire to see what pleasures Miss Ledridge has in store for his lordship, believe me I will.' His eyes roamed critically over every inch of my person, in a quick movement he thrust his pistols beneath his coat and walked towards me. I tried to step back but was held firm, my heart began to beat wildly as I resolved to defend myself from this uncouth creature. It took three men to hold Jarren as desperately he struggled trying to free himself and protect me. As the captain came closer, I kicked him viciously. Caught by surprise in anger he raised his hand and struck my face. I bit into his plump hand with all the force I could muster, and he stepped back muttering an oath before looking at me with distaste.

'I must teach you some manners, miss,' he spat, and with his right hand clutched at my throat, thrusting his face close to mine, laughing, whilst his other arm went round my waist as he crushed himself against me. One of the embossed buttons on his uniform pressed hard into my chest. Lust glinted in his eyes as he released my throat and began to nuzzle my neck, his wet lips moving down over my soft skin. I felt his hand upon my breast, heard the fabric of my bodice tear, sickened by his touch, I twisted and turned seeking to escape his probing hands.

'Leave her, pray God leave her,' Jarren beseeched, and by some miracle shook free his captors. He grasped hold the collar of the captain's coat tearing him away from me before he was cruelly beaten to the ground.

'Take them back to Falmouth,' the captain ordered between clenched teeth, glaring at his men, eyes bulging with anger. Forcefully Jarren was jerked to his feet to stand alongside John, who I'd heard shouting for me to be spared the indignities the captain would so willingly have subjected me to.

Jarren continued to protest twisting and straining his hands in an effort to dislodge the rope now around his wrists. He cried out my name before being dragged away still struggling, hauled through the trees scarce able to stand on his feet, roughly pushed and prodded back towards the river.

I was chilled to the bone, my wet dress clinging to me. My limbs felt numb my heart thumping with fright. Once they were out of sight I stood as if made of stone, shivering as the captain swaggered towards me. He reached out and cruelly pinched my face, so I spat at him. A bitter smile spread across his face. 'I can wait, miss high and mighty, hold her,' he ordered, and willing hands seized my wrists and ankles. His florid face came close to mine. 'Methinks I'll have a nice feel of you tonight, missy,' he drawled laughing out loud, signalling his men to follow as at a brisk pace he set off following the others back through the woods.

The dark shapes of the boat yards had just come into sight when Ruskin Tripper strode towards us through the trees. His fox-like features missed nothing, his current eyes fixed upon my dishevelled appearance as I clutched desperately at the remnants of my torn bodice in an effort to cover myself, a fragment of lace hanging from one shoulder.

Tripper's harsh voice rang out through the cold autumn air. 'I hope, sir, neither you or any of your men has done anything to defile this young lady, be sure you'll pay, so too your men if they have.' I began to struggle but was held even tighter, as he continued, 'I must congratulate you, sir, in catching Jarren Polverne and so enabling the return of his lordship's future bride, but Trevoran's a hard master as well you'd find out should I tell him she's been ill used in your keeping.' His mouth tightened. 'Believe what I say to be the truth.'

'You've no authority over us,' came the captain's sourly reply. And his men chorused their approval gathering close in around him.

Ruskin Tripper's eyes held his. 'Oh! but I have, Captain, you're not from these parts I wager, so I doubt you've had dealings with Lord Trevoran. Powerful man Trevoran, rules this part of Cornwall with a will of his own, not someone to be crossed.' Tripper motioned to his own men. 'Seize the captain, escort him back to Falmouth, his fate lies with his lordship.'

He turned and took off his cloak, throwing it down to me. 'Take this and cover yourself,' he ordered, the mockery in his voice unmistakeable.

'Lead on, men, back to the river.' Two of Tripper's men stepped forward; one of them raised his boot to the captain's back when he failed to move. Meanwhile his men demurred, pondering what fate awaited them in Falmouth, formed a ragged line and began to follow their captain. Ruskin Tripper firmly took hold of my arm and we followed in their wake. 'Try to escape and you'll regret it,' he advised, roughly dragging me along beside him, the ruthless edge to his voice one I remembered so well.

Barefoot by now, my feet were cut and bleeding, relentlessly I was propelled forward. I could smell the river long before we finally emerged onto the wooden quay. My eyes frantically searched for Jarren, it was daybreak and on the opposite side of the river men were already about their business, ships being loaded, and sails unfurled. The *Rosemary* I could not see. In a revenue cutter, Jarren and John sat bound back to back. The captain and his men were led down a short flight of steps and bundled aboard the cutter; just then it began rocking violently in the wake of a lugger passing by on the river. Her sailors stared at us in silence. I was helped aboard. My eyes sought Jarren's as Tripper bade me sit down, then his men took the oars.

On Tripper's orders they rowed with the greatest of speed for Falmouth. Bile rose in my throat as we made our way through the choppy waters. Jarren still fought to free his wrists of the rope, but it held firm. John sat eyes cast down deep in thought, a desolate expression on his face and I knew he must be thinking of Nancy.

The captain of the blue coats began to cause a commotion in the boat and Ruskin Tripper stood to shout orders, time enough for Jarren to lean forward and whisper, 'It seems, this time neither of us can escape, if you're forced to marry Trevoran say nothing of our marriage, he would have me hung and heaven knows what would happen to your father and brother over their debts he paid, I implore you pretend the child you are expecting is Trevoran's.'

I shrank back from him in horror, but his eyes pleaded with me to obey and as Tripper sat down beside me, I knew he spoke the truth.

Our boat passed out through the entrance of the Penryn and into the Carrick Roads, all too soon we would reach Falmouth where Jarren and I would be parted. Tripper's men rowed on in a steady rhythm, the spray created as the oars dipped into the choppy water drenched Ruskin Tripper's cloak, and beneath it I shivered as the first cluster of boatyards, warehouses and other buildings straggled the shore. A strong sea breeze blew inland from the wide mouth of the harbour. We were nearly there and our boat had to weave its way through a maze of ships, the horizon hidden by masts and lines, the wind rattling in the rigging of those anchored offshore, whilst fishing boats went about their business this crisp autumn morning.

Ruskin Tripper stood to shout instructions and whilst he did so I reached across to Jarren, crying out in agony as my hand was seized and roughly pushed away. I screamed in protest and Jarren tried to stand his face etched with anger. He was struck down by one of Tripper's men who held a knife against his throat.

The knife remained held at his throat until we reached our destination only then as we disembarked and Jarren was dragged up the deep stone steps onto the quay was the knife removed. As I was helped from the boat I looked up, our eyes met, there were so many unspoken words. In desperation I tugged furiously to free myself from Tripper's grasp and succeeded, running wildly up the steps to cling to Jarren sobbing until Ruskin Tripper tore me away unclasping my hands finger by finger from my beloved's coat. Tripper's face was suffused with a mixture of hatred, contempt and a horrible gleam of triumph.

He barked an order and we began to move on. Jarren and John, their faces bloody, clothes seeped in blood from the beatings they'd endured were pulled along the cobbles by the ropes attached to their wrists. I half walked half ran beside Ruskin Tripper my arm held in his vice-like grip. A sorry sight I must have looked, shoeless, with my dress in tatters, the black cloak almost slipping from my shoulders. My limp hair hung down to my waist a mass of tangled curls, sodden by river water. The captain and the others now under guard followed on behind.

The quay with its smell of tar and rope was already busy, our path along it made almost impassable by a multitude of handcarts and wagons. We wove our way along the wharf past coils of rope, nets strung out to dry and baskets of fish over which gulls screeched and swooped, the smell so strong I felt nauseous. Tripper increased his pace, those busy about their days toil stopped to stare, even those high above on rigging stopped to watch us pass.

As prisoners of the revenue the three of us received pitiful stares, conversations ceased as they boldly gawked at us, but there was nothing but ridicule and laughter at the captain's plight. Word spread and a crowd began to gather, outside the tannery the captain and his men were jeered at, they shouted back obscenities and an old woman selling fruit spat at them. A little way off a coachman helped a corpulent couple and a snivelling servant to alight, but on catching sight of us and hearing the commotion they retreated hastily into their coach, from where the woman stared out from behind a handkerchief held to her face.

Ahead of us a larger crowd waited outside a square solid building, bold letters carved in stone above the entrance proclaimed its purpose. Curious to see our progress, some craned their necks for a better view, but wary as ever of the revenue, as we approached, they drew back, the babble of their voices dimmed to a hushed silence. I saw sympathy in their eyes and swallowed hard in an effort to control my despair.

Jarren and John had already been led inside when Tripper's grip of my arm lessened and his hand on my back urged me on through the doorway into the stark Customs House. Prodded forward I made my way along a low-ceilinged passage until we came to a small windowless room, here Tripper took his leave of me, posting a guard each side the open door. The room was bare and icy cold, it held only one item of furniture, a wooden settle on which I sat, dispirited, isolated and alone.

Little sound penetrated the stout walls, once or twice I heard raised voices, then nothing until two soldiers passed laden with chains. My senses reeled in horror; aware for whom these were destined. In dismay I ran to the door. The guards barred my way. 'Pray don't do that to them,' I screamed, but as they turned to stare at me their faces bore no sign of compassion.

They still had hold of me when Ruskin Tripper returned; he stopped and brought his face close to mine. 'I should look away if I were you,' he sneered. 'Or you'll see a sight you'll not want to remember.'

Repulsed by his closeness I drew back.

'Bring em out,' he ordered.

From further down the passage came a dragging sound and rattle of chains. The guards pushed me back into the room. I strained to look past them and cried out in anguish as I caught sight of Jarren being hauled along the passage. He was shackled hand and foot, a short chain linked the two and caused him to be bent almost double, he stumbled. 'Jarren,' I screamed, incensed at this indignity.

A dirty hand quickly clamped over my mouth. 'Be quiet, missy,' the guard shouted in my ear and as Jarren neared the open doorway I was held even tighter, just for a moment as he drew level, he raised his pitiful face, so bloodied and bruised.

'Remember it's to be as I said.' In his eyes I saw a look of determination, unyielding to pain, and a love none could deny us.

Ruskin Tripper saw this too, he caught hold the short chain linking Jarren wrists and ankles and violently jerked him forward out of my sight, leaving me but to call his name. More of Tripper's men followed, two half-dragging John between them. 'If you can, get a message to Nancy,' he managed to mutter, as they passed. Then all were gone. Briefly I heard the sound of horses' hooves echo on the cobbles outside, then the door leading onto the quay was slammed shut.

Silence; the guards let go their hold of me, I made no bid for freedom, they had taken Jarren from me, escape, it seemed, was impossible. Despondent and with my heart filled with overwhelming sadness and defeat, I sat to await my fate, knowing full well in whose hands it lay.

If I had thought Ruskin Tripper gone with the prisoners I was mistaken for in a short while he returned accompanied by a young servant girl carrying a jug of hot water. The guards brought in a small table onto which this was placed together with a large pewter bowl.

I watched as over the back of the settle the maid carefully laid out a blue day dress with black embroidered edging, together with petticoats and a pair of velvet shoes. Tripper rebuked her for being too slow. I wondered where the clothes had come from and hoped no one had taken much trouble in their choice, for it mattered not to me what I looked like. Beside the bowl she placed a towel, hairbrush and a number of hairpins, then withdrew and stood to one side, demurely awaiting her next order. Tripper looked me up and down.

'Wash yourself, dress and attend to your hair, we leave immediately this is accomplished, I'll get no good money for you as you are.'

He turned on his heel and made to leave, pausing in the doorway. 'If you need help, the girl will attend you.'

I remembered the rings hidden in the hem of my dress and stole a look at the girl's bowed head, clearly she was fearful of Ruskin Tripper but there was no way I could search for the rings with her there, and could only hope by some miracle they had not been lost. I heard Tripper's retreating steps and set this worry aside, impatiently begging the girl tell me what I so badly wanted to know. 'Where have they taken the prisoners?'

Her eyes darted warily towards the door; she came closer though and said softly, 'Twill be Bodmin or Launceston, the assize is held at each in turn, twill be wherever soonest, most like.'

I touched her hand. 'Thank you.'

Her plain face with plump cheeks softened. 'Best hurry, miss, Mr Tripper's one of those who don't take kindly to be kept waiting.'

I undid the clasp of the black cloak and with a heavy heart asked her to unhook my dress, and as she did so, I said by way of dismissal, 'I'll call you when I need you,' and thankfully she obeyed without question, bobbing a curtsey as she took her leave, closing the door behind her.

Hastily I removed Aunt Sarah's tattered dress, retrieving the rings from the mud-soaked hem, quickly tearing a small opening in the waistband of the expensive lace trimmed petticoats placed on the settle. Hurriedly I poured icy water from the pitcher into the bowl and with a rough cloth tried to rid my skin of the grime and stench of river water, shivering with cold, afraid any moment Tripper would walk in. The tears I'd bravely tried to hold back stung my eyes and trickled down my face, I dreaded to think what harm Trevoran could inflict on Jarren. A bang on the door made me jump.

'Hurry up in there,' Tripper shouted, and thrust the servant girl into the room. In all truth I was so dirty I bade her bring fresh water several times, but still was far from clean. Finally, as Ruskin Tripper paced up and down outside, she helped me to dress, tying the tapes on my petticoats, my precious rings now held tight to me. It was whilst I stood her fingers fastening tight the bodice of my dress that I remembered the mother of pearl hairpins I'd left onboard the *Rosemary*. My face flushed with a rush of guilt and hoped with all my heart they'd been found before the ship was searched.

There was no time to dwell on this for now the maid took a brush to my hair, hair so tangled I cried out in pain as she tried to brush it through, she struggled to remove the white roses deeply embedded in my curls, their lifeless petals falling to the floor around me. Unable to stand the agony, in temper I snatched the brush from her hand and pinned up my damp straw-like hair, jabbing the pins she handed me in without care.

'Pray tell Mr Tripper I'm ready,' I told her.

'Yes, miss,' was her somewhat sharp reply as she gathered up my wet clothes and left the room, moments later Ruskin Tripper returned.

'A mild improvement,' he snapped. 'Come, we have a distance to travel.'

The girl hurried in and placed a thick blue travelling cloak around my shoulders. I followed Ruskin Tripper along the passage and out onto the quay where a crowd of townsfolk were still gathered. A coach with four restless horses straining on their harnesses jerked their heads, impatient to be off. The door of the coach was opened, and the steps lowered, held by the elbow I was thrust up these and into the coach, the crowds on the quay jeering as Ruskin Tripper took his seat beside me. I heard a commotion and saw a man roughly pushing his way through the crowd, it was Simon Jago. The injury to his leg sustained that terrible night at Zennor still caused him to walk with a limp. He stopped a short distance from the coach, and I managed to mouth the words, 'Tell Nancy,' as the coach jolted forward over the cobbles and once again, I set out on the journey to Trevoran Court.

CHAPTER EIGHT

No journey had ever seemed so long, we sat beside each other in stifling silence, travelling companions bound only by our destination. The sound of the horses' hooves sharp upon the cobbles, gone once we left Falmouth. The coach jolted and swayed along the deeply rutted roads, our shoulders involuntarily leaning one against the other as we made our way towards the end of our journey and Lord Trevoran who was both our masters. We stopped once for the carriage lamps to be lit before resuming our journey and for a while I must have slept, for I awoke with a start as the coach rumbled across a wooden bridge. A short while later the horses slowed. I peered out into the darkness as the iron gates of Trevoran Court loomed up before us. A man holding a lantern hurried out of the gatehouse to open them.

As we passed through, the coachman exchanged a few words with the gatekeeper before once again we moved on, a thick blanket of clouds obscured the moon as we travelled up the tree lined drive. As the drive weaved its way round, so Trevoran Court its windows ablaze with candlelight came into view, and the horses slowed drawing to a halt in front the canopied entrance of the great house. Ruskin Tripper stepped down from the coach and held out his hand to help me down as Mrs Treave emerged from the house solemnly walking down the steps with no look of greeting for the man who waited at the foot of them. Her eyes took in my appearance; clearly, she was dismayed.

'Tis a good job the master's not out here to see the state you've brought her to him in,' she sniped at Ruskin Tripper throwing him a look of contempt, whilst I gazed at the house aware the menacing presence of Lord Trevoran lurked within its walls. My heart filled with fear, this hateful man held my husband's life and that of John's at his whim, mine too. My spirits sank with despair for I held no doubt for one moment how cruel he could be.

Mrs Treave rounded on Ruskin Tripper. 'If it's payment you're waiting for, tis best I hurry her upstairs before his lordship catches sight of her bedraggled state.'

She turned her back on Tripper, ignoring him, as she bade me accompany her up the steps and on into the house. As I passed through the open door I cast a look back and saw him still standing at the foot of the steps. He raised his hat and made a mock bow, sharply I turned back to follow Mrs Treave whose black skirts rustled as we made our way across the lofty hall and up the oaken staircase.

'His lordship has given me strict instructions as to your welfare,' she advised without the slightest warmth. I wondered if Aunt Sarah was still here, her presence would be a comfort at this most dreadful time, but such was Mrs Treave's manner there was no way I could ask her this question. Not a soul did we see as we journeyed on into the great house along a maze of endless candlelit passages. She stopped abruptly before a pair of panelled doors. Upon opening them I was ushered into a dark bedchamber lit by only two candles, the room smelt damp and unlived in, the flames of a newly lit fire in the wide stone hearth gave out no feeling of warmth. Mrs Treave lit a candelabra and placed it on a small round table. She stood beside me watching as I gazed about the gloomy room with its dark heavy furnishings. I looked down at the carpet beneath my feet and saw it was faded and worn. A huge four-poster bed with thick brocade drapes took up most of the room, faded grey tapestries hung on all four walls. I sensed a smugness in the housekeeper as she went about lighting more candles, for this bedchamber was indeed very different to the one I had occupied before, no doubt his lordship saw it as a punishment, my discomfiture in such a room would give him pleasure.

'You'll find all you need is here, miss, in the small dressing room adjacent, clothes have been laid out for you. I shall send servants up with hot water for you to bathe in. The hour being late, his lordship wishes me to inform you he will see you in the morning.' She reached down and selected a key from those hanging on her belt and without saying another word was gone and the key turned in the lock.

In a daze I went over to the window, parted the drapes a little and stared out into the darkness. Alone now my mind fell prey to all kinds of fears, especially for Jarren. I remembered the two rings hidden inside the band of my petticoats and retrieved them, sitting on the bed holding them tight in my hand as my eyes searched the room for a safe place to hide them. A knock on the door startled me; I heard the key being turned in the lock and thrust the rings beneath a pillow as two servants entered.

How unreal everything seemed! Last night I was aboard the *Rosemary* with the man I loved, a new life awaiting us. All this was gone now and as though in a trance I bathed in the rose petal water and let Decima – the older of the two maids who I recognised from the last time I was here –wash and plait my hair. 'Is my Aunt Sarah here?' I asked, and she nodded.

'Yes, Miss Ledridge, but at the moment she is not lodged in this wing of the house.' No more was said and uncertain how to treat me the servants were coldly civil as they prepared me for bed. It was a relief when they'd gone, and I was alone with my thoughts once more. Glad to know I had one friend here and wondered when my aunt and I would be reunited. Deep in thought I retrieved the rings from beneath the pillow and hid them behind the tapestry opposite my bed, tucking them well in behind one of the corners securing it to the wall, safer hidden there than about my person. Once this task was done, I tried the door which was locked, then sat dispirited on the huge bed, it was now the tears came, and were unstoppable, for sadness filled my very being. The younger maid returned and snuffed out the candles, leaving just one alight. No words were exchanged between us and when at last I climbed into bed and slipped between the sheets they were icy cold. The fusty smell of disuse and neglect suffocated my senses as I shivered beneath the thin coverings. Sleep was impossible and I prayed over and over again that Jarren and John were safe, before finally I slept, tossing and turning amid the terrors of my nightmares.

In the morning I awoke as Decima unlocked the door and came in carrying a breakfast tray. 'If you please miss, Lord Trevoran requests your presence in the library in one hour's time, as soon as you ring, miss, I'll help you dress and pin up your hair.'

She set the tray down and pulled back the drapes before withdrawing.

I ate but a sparse breakfast before ringing the bell to summon her, dressing quickly in the cold room for the fire had not been lit. When she'd finished I stood before the mirror smoothing out the skirts of a fashionable jade dress very like one I'd once possessed. My reflection was much the same as it was before I left Wellow, that of a fashionably dressed well brought up young lady, only the dark rings under my eyes gave a hint of what I had so recently been through.

Decima gave a discreet cough and walked over to the door holding it open; I smoothed my skirts once more and took a deep breath. I could delay no longer and set off following her along the unfamiliar passages until we came to the great staircase. From here I needed little guidance for this part of the house was familiar to me, but I said nothing. I found her solid figure, with mop cap and flowing apron strings, somewhat of a comfort in this lonely mansion.

At the bottom of the stairs my heart thumped with apprehension as we made our way down the oak panell-ed passage that led to the library. Decima knocked on the door, waited and then opened it. I stepped inside and felt the draft on my neck as it was closed behind me. I stood in the middle of the room; hands clenched as I waited head held high. His lordship stood with his back to me looking out of a long window.

He turned abruptly and walked towards me, his face surely a caricature of the devil, so evil the look in his beadlike eyes. 'So, you are a schemer,' he spat viciously. Too late I saw the gloves he held in his right hand, he struck me across the face, the force so great it caused me to lose my balance. I staggered backwards my arms flaying out wildly in the hope I could grasp some piece of furniture in a bid to stop my fall. There was nothing and I fell awkwardly, crying out in pain. Trevoran came over and placed one booted foot on my arm. 'If it wasn't that I have urgent business to attend, I'd take you now on the floor like a common whore.'

Terrified I could but stare up at him as he bent down and roared in my face, 'That half breed friend of yours is as good as dead, and if it wasn't I had need to beget an heir, and paid out good money to settle your father's debts, be sure I'd not want anything to do you with you. You could rot in jail alongside him for all I care, instead you can count yourself fortunate, tomorrow I shall make you my bride, in the fullest sense of the word, and be sure, Miss Ledridge, you will have no further chance to escape.' I held my hand against the burning skin of my face and slowly moved in an effort to get up. He removed his foot and roughly grasped my arm pulling me to my feet, his face so close to mine I could smell his putrid breath, my eyes unable to divert themselves from his yellow wizened face, the black stumps of his teeth revealed as his mouth twisted into a cruel leer. 'Look to your aunt for help with your wedding preparations, tomorrow you will be mine to do with as I wish, good day to you.'

He thrust me from him and strode out of the room. I heard raised voices from beyond the door and recognised one to be Ty Saffrey's, the despicable man must have been listening. The sound of their voices gradually grew distant and I began to make my way towards the door when suddenly a searing pain tore through my body. I slumped down onto the nearest seat, heart pounding, eyes closed in agony. *Oh no, please God, no, the fall. I mustn't lose Jarren's child.* Somehow, I staggered from the room and made my way up the staircase, where to my blessed relief I saw Aunt Sarah hurrying towards me. When she reached my side I leant against her for support, and when a flustered Decima came running along the landing, my aunt calmly explained to her that I felt a little faint, and together they helped me back to my room.

Once there, and Decima dismissed, Aunt Sarah clicked her tongue in disapproval as she looked around the shabby bedchamber. She guided me over towards the bed and held me gently as I lay back against the pillows, brushing away loose tendrils of hair from my face, whispering soothing words, holding me close in an effort to stem my tears as I clung to her for comfort. After a while, the pain dulled, and I told Aunt Sarah what had happened earlier.

'The man should be horsewhipped,' was her horrified retort, her face a picture of shock and compassion when I told her my worries for the child I carried.

'Child, oh! My poor darling.' Quickly she put her finger to her lips and crept softly across the room opening the door, closing it gently. No one was there; she came back to the bed. 'We must be careful, Layunie, the walls here have ears, we must speak of this only where we are certain we cannot be overheard.' I recounted to her then what Jarren had said.

'Make no mistake, Layunie, he's right; the old goat must believe the child is his. We shall talk and make plans once tomorrow is over, you must rest now, child.'

She rang the tapestry bell pull beside the bed and the little maid I knew to be called Florence, for she'd brought up the hot water for Decima the night before, came scurrying in. Aunt Sarah ordered fresh water be brought so she could prepare for me an infusion of herbs, and hurried off to fetch these from her room, reassuring me when she returned that it would ease the pain. As usual her concoctions tasted most vile, but I found my eyes closing as she sat beside me patting my hand. I felt drowsy, in my dreams last night I had relived the moment Josh was killed, terrified as I saw over and over again the look in those kindly eyes as his life ebbed away.

Thankfully, with the help of the infusion, I drifted off into a deep sleep, waking in the early evening to find the pain low down in my stomach gone, and prayed to God it would not come back.

We ate together in my room that night, Aunt Sarah and myself, my mind fearful of what Trevoran planned for Jarren, John too, wondering how they fared. Although she had tried hard, Aunt Sarah had learnt no details of tomorrow's arrangements whilst I'd been asleep. Mrs Treave had blatantly dismissed her questions and although she'd tried hard to probe Decima who she'd caught kissing one of Trevoran's valets, the girl although deeply embarrassed had quickly excused herself. All the servants so it seemed were rushed off their feet, busy getting the great house ready for tomorrow.

I refused to let my thoughts linger even briefly on my wedding to Trevoran, and in all truth was not in the slightest bit disappointed to hear Aunt Sarah knew no details of what time or where I was to be married. I didn't care. After the wedding would come the wedding night, a most revolting prospect.

At the end of the day, Aunt Sarah helped me undress and ready myself for bed, kissing my forehead softly before leaving. When she'd gone, I rested my head against the pillows and stared into the darkness with eyes I never wanted to shut. The sooner I slept the sooner tomorrow would come and I knew however much I prayed and how ever hard he may try, this time Jarren would not come to save me.

I must have slept eventually for when I did wake, on opening my eyes I saw that the drapes were already drawn back and the fire lit. I looked over and saw Florence kneeling before the grate placing another lump of coal on the back of the fire with the tongs. I closed my eyes and lay still as if asleep. I heard the hushed voices of other servants, who came and went as I lay trying to pretend the day hadn't begun, but it had and after a while I felt a hand upon my shoulder gently shaking me awake. Opening my eyes, I saw Aunt Sarah looking down on me her face grim, there was nothing either of us could do to prevent what lay ahead.

As if in a waking nightmare I went through the rituals of the morning, withdrawn into my own world as others fussed about me, finding myself at last standing before a long mirror as two maids made the finishing touches to my elaborate wedding dress. It was indeed a beautiful dress of white brocade, on to which was embroidered a delicate floral design in ivory. The sleeves tightly fitting to my elbow, with treble flounces, the tightly fitting bodice edged with lace. But as the last tiny button was fastened, I felt imprisoned, trapped, and longed only to escape, to free myself of the dress and flee far from away from here.

My aunt sensing another flood of tears sent the servants away. 'I don't think I can go through with it; I'd rather die.' I wept, wiping away a tear and blowing my nose on the handkerchief she produced.

'Layunie, you must be strong today, especially tonight, a virgin bride he expects to bed, indelicate as it is to speak of such a matter, be sure he believes that is what you are, child.' She picked up the wedding veil from the bed and pinned it into place with tiny diamond encrusted pins. 'Remember you are doing this for Jarren and the child, your father also, for the moment it is all that can be done.'

Decima knocked lightly on the door and came in. 'His lordship wishes you informed the guests have arrived; they await you in the hall below, miss.'

I got to my feet slowly; there could be no mistaking my unwillingness to comply with this request. Aunt Sarah stepped forward and gave me a hug, before with downcast eyes I made my way towards the door. Decima gave me an encouraging smile as I passed, then suddenly I felt a tug on my arm as Aunt Sarah paused just inside the doorway. She stopped Decima as she followed behind us. 'Please, I beg you tell my niece something of today's arrangements, you must know something of them, we've been told nothing, it is quite disconcerting and not the done thing at all.'

Decima's composure relaxed at little, Aunt Sarah's presence overcoming her reluctance to speak out, and she looked at me with pity. 'You are to be married in the little church on the estate, I know only that his Lordship's best man is to be Lord St. Erran and that his lordship's godson Pierce Tredavik is to give you away, tis all I know, miss.' She bobbed a curtsey and grateful for at least this little knowledge of what lay ahead I made my way downstairs.

A sea of faces looked up as slowly I walked down the grand staircase. Lord Trevoran stepped forward and held out his hand which I had no option other than to take. He wore a striking blue coat the edges and cuffs heavily embroidered with gold, a plain waistcoat and white satin knee breeches; he introduced me to a sallow unsmiling young man.

'My godson Pierce Tredavik,' he advised, 'he will accompany you the short distance to the church.' He looked round at the other guests. 'My bride, ladies and gentlemen, come let us waste no more time, there will be time a plenty for introductions later.'

One of Lord Trevoran's most splendid coaches awaited us outside. I was grateful that Aunt Sarah was allowed to travel with me, gathering the plentiful materials of my dress and arranging them carefully as I sat in silence beside Pierce Tredavik. He spoke not one word during the short distance we travelled, watching patiently under indolent drooping eyelids as his lordship and other guests entered the church ahead of us. Then without the slightest trace of enthusiasm helped Aunt Sarah and myself alight.

I noticed from the small huddle of estate workers gathered outside the church there was no great cheering for their master as he passed, and it was a dour silent group of villagers who peered over the top of the boundary wall watching. None thought to shout and wish him well, and as I walked up the short path to the portal of the church, I caught only glimpses of sympathy in the eyes of those I passed.

The doors were opened and on the arm of Pierce Tredavik I made my way up the aisle, past the garlands of fresh flowers hung from white ribbon at the end of every pew. A small group of choristers were singing, the wedding guests turning to stare as I progressed onwards to where his lordship stood waiting. I was glad neither Father or Charles were here to bear witness to my final surrender to the fate which circumstance decreed, and held in check the tears which threatened as I remembered another church such a short while ago, where Jarren, eyes twinkling in the candlelight, had reached out and kissed me as our marriage vows were blessed.

My limbs felt weak, legs trembling as the service began. On the black and blood-red chequered floor, set in stone either side of the altar lying side by side, their cold hands touching, lay the tombs of Lord and Lady Trevorans of long ago. I focused my eyes on their peaceful effigies, trying to concentrate, so to obliterate the present. Only drawing myself back to reality when it was time to make my responses, trying to divert my gaze from the triumphant eyes of Trevoran as his bony hand took mine and he slipped the wedding ring on my finger. Unable to turn away as he drew me towards him, his hot fleshy lips on mine as the ceremony ended.

The autumn sunlight had clouded over when we emerged from the church, a heavy downpour of rain scattering those gathered outside. A liveried servant in maroon and gold rushed to open the door of the coach. Trevoran brusquely waving Aunt Sarah away as she stepped forward to help with my dress.

I feel certain for the rest of my life I will associate the smell of new leather with the interior of that coach, and the revolting manner in which Trevoran thrust his hand down my bodice once we had drawn away and were out of sight. I struggled to free myself from his claw-like grip, managing to tear his hand from me just as the coach halted, the yellowy-whites of his eyes maintaining their malicious glint as he spat the words, 'Until tonight, my merry maid.'

Mrs Treave took leave of the servants lined up under the great canopy and hurried down the steps to welcome us. It was hard to regain my composure and a great relief when all the formalities and introductions were over. The local nobility were most eager and curious to meet me, and it felt most uncomfortable to be the object of so much scrutiny and intrigue. At the lavish banquet that awaited us in the long dining room I managed but a few morsels of food and had it not been for the support of my aunt, doubt I could have lasted out that long day. I felt an actress playing a part, dreading the finale and the evening's final outcome.

Tonight would be every bit as bad as I could imagine. When the dreaded time came and could no longer be put off, I suffered in silence as drunken guests encouraged by the distasteful Ty Saffrey and sour faced Pierce Tredavik, made lewd remarks to his lordship. It was little wonder I needed prompting by Aunt Sarah that it was time I retire to the master bedchamber.

Once there with the help of Decima and Florence I undressed and put on the delicate nightgown with its fragile lace trimmings, laid out for me on the bed, pulling tight the drawstring at the neck. Aunt Sarah came and brushed out my hair, taking my cold hands in hers and leading me to the ancient heavily carved marriage bed. Once I had climbed between the crisp sheets, she smoothed flat the heavy covers.

'Nothing your brother could do would make amends for the devilish sacrifice you've had to make as a result of his folly,' she sighed.

'Tis a sad night for you, my sweet Layunie.' She made sure the maids were out of sight and cautiously withdrew something from her bodice, placing the tiny object in my hand. I went to look but she put her hand over mine.

'Pray place this where twill cause his lordship to think he's taken your virginity.' Her eyes held mine and an understanding passed between us, she put a comforting arm round my shoulder before kissing my cheek and reluctantly leaving me alone.

The unpleasant task done, I lay back against the pillows my head turned away from the door, waiting as if for death itself to arrive. I heard the door creak open and a rush of bawdy laughter came from outside. I heard Trevoran's footsteps as he came across to the bed, the mattress dipped, and a bony hand cruelly gripped my face turning it round. I was face to face with my tormentor, with his other hand he ripped my nightdress from neck to hem.

Savage lust filled his eyes as he scanned my naked body, he thrust his hand between my legs and I bit my lip with humiliation as he violated my body, trying to pull away in horror as he bit at my breasts like a wild animal lifting his head, eyes gleaming with delight. His probing hands pinched and hurt and when I could endure no more and cried out, he increased the torment. I screamed in anguish and prayed silently his bestial onslaught end, as I endured the ghastly needs of his vile body pounding and thrusting on top of me.

'Remember I bought you, body and soul, and I'll use you how I wish,' he hissed, squeezing my breast.

I felt physically nauseated; aware too as I suffered this final degradation that it was an impotent old man who so misused me. His pathetic attempt at lovemaking went on it seemed forever, in the end I lay like stone, hands tightly clenched, eyes fixed upon the blue fabric gatherings of the canopy above the bed. I had no option but to endure his demands until finally he rolled off me, gasping hoarsely. The sick ritual of imagined union over. I wondered if Aunt Sarah's bead like pouch had performed its task, if so, there would be blood on the sheets but not through any penetration befitting a groom on his wedding night.

I turned away pulling at the covers to shield my nakedness, turning away from him, listening to his laboured breath as he moved closer, smelt its sour stench as he mocked in my ear. 'Now you know what to expect every night, my sweet wife.' He lay back on the pillows and the sound of his measured breath settled into a rasping rhythm, whilst I lay curled up, my body smarting from the punishment it had endured and wondered if truly he believed our marriage consummated.

The candle spluttered and died, and the embers of the meagre fire no longer glowed, there were no sounds at all, the great house was absolutely still. I lay enclosed in a sanctuary of darkness; too frightened to make even now the slightest of movement lest I wake my bed companion. Fear gripped tight the pit of my stomach. My heart sank with despair. I remembered that last glimpse of Jarren as he was dragged away in chains from the Falmouth Customs House, what further horrors would he suffer and what of John? I could imagine George and

Nancy awaiting his return in the taproom of the Star worried beyond measure when he failed to come home. Accompanying these dark thoughts, the pitiful sight of Josh dying in Jarren's arms. Stealthily I moved closer the edge of the bed and bit hard my lip, my silent tears seeping into the lace edged pillow.

Wide-eyed I lay held in my waking nightmare, pondering Jarren's fate, hoping with all my heart that Giles and the crew of the *Rosemary* had sailed safe out from Falmouth. So much pain, all of it caused by the vile old man beside me, who in the eyes of the world I was bound to by the tethers of marriage. I felt my face grow red in anger, everything good Trevoran had destroyed, the weeks of passion at Rosecarren, the future we'd been setting sail for, all gone. Protectively I placed my hands on the slight swell of my abdomen, and knew without a doubt that the love child conceived at Nancledra I must protect at all cost.

As dawn broke the faintest strand of light crept across the wooden floor, filtering in through a tiny opening at the foot of the drawn drapes. I watched its path until exhausted I fell into a fretful sleep, only to awake in horror as I felt Trevoran's hands upon my body once again. I recoiled in disgust, easing myself off the bed, watching as his eyes took in my nakedness. I bent and clutched up the remnants of my nightdress, holding them to me in a vain attempt to gain some modesty. Trevoran gave an unpleasant laugh. 'Pah, you'll save for tonight, my precious wife,' he drawled with a look of contempt, and reached over to lift his heavy brocade robe from the chair beside the bed. As he stood his eyes caught sight of the crimson stain on the sheet, he looked directly at me, his piercing gaze held mine for an eternity, did he guess some trickery had taken place, I could not fathom his expression. I was held by his gaze, mesmerised, desperate to give no hint of any emotion and after a prolonged silence, he looked away and made his way to the door leaving me alone, trembling with cold and humiliation on this first morning of our marriage.

CHAPTER NINE

Wretched, with no news of Jarren, each night I was forced to endure the same ritual, to lie suffering the indignities of Trevoran's futile attempts at lovemaking, sickened by his impotent thrusting. Used at night, I saw little of Trevoran through the day and rarely did he dine with us. Usually my mealtimes shared only with Aunt Sarah in a chill room with a high vaulted ceiling. The long windows faced northwards and were heavily draped thus the room always seemed in half-darkness whatever the time of day. Stark of much furniture, two places were set at each end of an exceedingly long dining table. We ate in silence, neither of us appreciating the food set before us, nor the fine wine of which there was plenty.

In limbo, Aunt Sarah and myself waited out the long hours always conscious of being watched, both of us incarcerated in the house, at present unable to even walk in the grounds for it had rained incessantly each day from morning to dusk, and always a maid or one of Ty Saffrey's coarse lackeys with an excuse to be in earshot where ever we went. I tried to draw Florence, the little maid who helped me dress, into conversation but neither she nor Bessie who lit the fire each morning would say more than was civil. In total frustration one morning as Florrie brushed out my hair, I asked her, 'Who in this house besides his lordship would know where those who were with me at the time I was captured were taken?' Flustered for a moment, she couldn't bring herself to look at my reflection in the mirror, setting down the brush and hastily picking up the striped lavender morning dress she'd laid out on the bed earlier. She paused clearly uncertain whether to answer my question or flee. Thankfully she stayed.

'Tis not for me to say, ma'am.' Briefly our eyes met, and she saw how desperately I sought an answer to my question, I caught a glimpse of pity in her eyes and willed her to tell me something, anything.

'Well, I reckons only Mr Saffrey and Laurence Landy, his lordship's manservant, would know such things; confides in old Landy he does, makes the old man feel superior.' Her voice gained in confidence. 'We've heard nothing below stairs, only likes how you'm were captured. Mr Landy don't mix with the likes of us, thinks himself above a servant, got too big headed, cook says. He's been with the master for years, master treats him badly, poor devil, but you'll not get anything you want to know from him, nor that good for nothing Mr Saffrey, so don't bother asking.'

Before I could ask more, Decima knocked and came into the room, for it was her duty to help me dress. Luckily Florrie stopped talking as she entered and bobbing a curtsey quickly took her leave.

Mid-morning, the rain finally stopped. I unfastened my window and threw it wide open, breathing in the rustic smell of autumn and the familiar scent of the river. I watched the rippling waters of the Fal running high on an incoming tide, a poignant reminder of my days at Rosecarren. As I was about to turn away, a sound came from somewhere beneath my window and I looked down. A heavily cloaked figure was making his way across the leaf strewn lawns. At the same time a small sailing craft emerged from downriver, its sails clearly seen through the thicket of trees on the near bank, I watched as it was tied up alongside the wooden jetty. The man spoke to someone aboard, turned and quickly made his way back to the house. The man was Lawrence Landy, Trevoran's manservant.

My door opened and Aunt Sarah came in, I beckoned her come and stand beside me. Together we watched as Trevoran and Ty Saffrey came into view striding purposefully down towards the jetty. Lawrence Landy followed a short distance behind and helped them on board. He unfastened the ropes and threw them to a heavily bearded sailor standing on deck, briefly pausing to watch as the wind caught the craft's sails. Slowly it began makings its way to the centre of the Fal, setting a course up the golden-banked river. Trevoran stood at the bow and I shrank back into my room for he seemed to be looking directly up at my window, as though he knew I was watching his departure.

The morning sickness that by some miracle I had managed to hide from the servants, seemed to rise up and threatened to overwhelm me. I ignored it, an idea formed in my mind. I moved forward, my gaze following Landy as he made his way back towards the house. I grasped hold Aunt Sarah's hands.

'I must know where Jarren is being held, with Trevoran and Ty Saffrey out of the house, I intend to find out.' She opened her mouth to speak but I gave her no chance to voice her misgivings.

'I believe I know a way to find out.' I intently watched to see by which door Landy entered the house.

Taking Aunt Sarah's hand in mine, I led her towards my door and looked out, no one was about, stealthily we crept out.

'I won't ask where you're taking me,' she queried, struggling to keep up as I hurried to the far end of the landing and the door leading to the back stairs. I hoped this would lead us down and close to the door I'd seen Landy enter by. With their master out, it seemed the lackeys whose task it was to watch us were less vigilant, for as far as I could tell no one was watching us right now. Holding up the front of my skirts and petticoats I led the way down.

Cautiously I paused to peer from the narrow, arched entrance at the foot of the stairs and realised I didn't have the least idea where we were! No door led into the gardens. The flagstone passage was bereft of any furnishings; it was stark and chill with no rugs or tapestries. Sparse single candleholders broke the bleakness of the walls and along its length three small windows let in only tiny shafts of light. The smell of freshly baked bread hung in the air, bringing with it instant memories of Alice and the kitchen at Wellowmead. There was a murmur of voices and someone singing with a happy lilt in their voice before they stopped abruptly.

A door was opened and slammed shut, my heart thumped in fear and Aunt Sarah caught hold my arm and pulled me back up the stairs to a half landing. Footsteps passed close by and I crept down to see who it was. I saw the back of a man casually strolling down the passage, it was Laurence Landy. In his left hand he was swinging a bottle, at the end of the passage he turned right and disappeared from sight. I stepped forth with Aunt Sarah, intent on following him. Our soft slippers were silent upon the flagged floor as tentatively we peeped around the corner and caught sight of him once more. He was quite unaware of our presence, or our hasty retreat behind a pillar as his pace slowed and he stopped before a door. With his free hand he fumbled in his pocket for a key, then disappeared inside, time no doubt to indulge in a little of his master's excellent wine. I hoped he partook of the whole bottle and decided to change my plan, with Landy out of the way for what I hoped was a considerable time; instead of questioning the manservant I would search Trevoran's study.

I whispered to Aunt Sarah, 'I planned to confront Lawrence Landy and demand he tell me if he knows where Jarren is being held, but instead it's to Trevoran's study we're going now.' She looked horrified.

'Layunie, is it wise, what if we're caught in there? Mrs Treave or any of the servants could find us.' She pulled her hand from mine and stood defiantly, hands on hips. ''Tis sheer foolishness, I won't let you take the risk.' I looked away my resolve as strong as ever.

'It matters to me, Aunt, I need to know where Jarren is, I know its futile to think I can help him, but please I must find out, hopefully Landy will stay where he is awhile, and remember as mistress of this house I am free to go where I please. Mrs Treave may well tell his lordship if she finds us, but I doubt the servants would, it's a chance I must take.'

We retraced our steps, passing my room as we made our way to the great staircase, none would find it curious to see us here as often at this time of day we made our way down to the morning room or library. Two maids busy about their tasks took little notice of us, only standing aside to bob a curtsey as we passed, of the two lackeys usually hanging about there was no sign.

'Have you thought of the consequences if we're caught?' Aunt Sarah whispered, as we reached the study, looking decidedly uneasy as I placed my hands on the golden handles of the twin doors.

'We won't,' I replied, and determinedly entered the dark panelled, oppressive room. I ushered Aunt Sarah in and closed the doors, my eyes now fixed on Trevoran's huge carved desk strewn with papers. I urged Aunt Sarah to help as hurriedly I began leafing through the reams of documents, quickly reading through those I thought might hold some mention of Jarren. Several were heavily crested, one from the Sheriff of Cornwall stated an act had been passed in 1715 for holding the Assize Courts for the county of Cornwall at a convenient place namely Bodmin, another from the Lord High Chancellor, confirmed from 1716 the assize would be held alternatively at Bodmin and Launceston, I passed these to Aunt Sarah.

'So, the maid at Falmouth had been right!' I sighed.

Exposed now was a rolled document, its seal looked freshly broken. I unfolded it, in an elegant hand was written confirmation from Harrison Carter the keeper of Bodmin Gaol as to his receiving and holding the prisoners Polverne and Penrose until his lordship decreed what charges would be brought against them. Until such time he would house them at his lordship's pleasure and give them correction as deemed necessary, he would await instructions as to how to proceed at the next quarter sessions. I have housed the prisoners in that part of the gaol known as the dark house and hope this pleases you. This was written as a postscript underneath his signature, and although I had no idea what the dark house was, I knew it boded ill.

'Tis Bodmin, Aunt, and the wretched man who is its keeper is in Trevoran's pocket.' I sank down onto Trevoran's leather button backed seat, disheartened beyond belief.

A dog barked making me jump, the only dogs I knew of here belonged to Ty Saffrey. I pulled back the drapes and glanced out, three huge black beasts were chasing each other around on the lawns. I let the drape fall and cast my eyes once more over the letter and passed it to Aunt Sarah, she quickly read it before replacing it beneath the others.

'Let's be gone, Layunie,' she pleaded agitated, skirts rustling as she made her way to the door. I followed and we were about to leave when came the sound of approaching footsteps and voices. Horrified we stood, staring wide-eyed at one another. Swiftly I turned the ornate key that protruded from the lock. The voices came closer, finally were outside, the handles moved downwards, impatiently tried several times. When they did not yield and open, Trevoran swore loudly, shouting for the lackeys to gain entry. The splintering of wood followed heavy pounding on the doors. We ran over to the window and struggled to open it but found it impossible. Even though we knew it was futile to hide behind the drapes we did, clinging together awaiting the inevitable.

The dogs quickly found us once the doors were opened, I heard footsteps striding across the room, Ty Saffrey commanded their silence in a manner which caused the black beasts to whimper and cower on the floor as the drapes were thrown back. Trevoran stepped forward; his steel cold gaze met mine. 'So, madam, what brings you secretly to my study.' He cast a look at his desk. 'To find out where Polverne's being held, is that it?'

Ty Saffrey standing behind him gave me a mocking sneer, and I raised my head higher meeting Trevoran's gaze, darting a look of contempt at his companion. Trevoran turned his attention to Aunt Sarah. 'You, madam, shall leave my house just as soon as I can arrange it, I'll not have my wife's conspirator in my midst a moment longer than necessary.'

I gasped, and reached out for my aunt, saw the shocked look on her face and begged, 'Pray, let her stay.' But it was of no use; the loathsome man ignored my plea.

He spun round on the lackeys waiting at the door. 'Just how did these two manage to be in here without your knowledge?' There was silence as the two men shifted uneasy and hung their heads in remorse. 'Escort each to their own room and make sure they stay there, by rights I should turn you both out.' The yellowed whites of Trevoran's eyes were startlingly prominent, his bead-like pupils darted around the room fixing upon each of us in turn. The two lackeys hurried forward and ungraciously I was manhandled along with Aunt Sarah out of the study, the sleeve of my dress torn as I struggled against such indignity. Aunt Sarah retaliated by forcefully biting the hand upon her arm, causing her tormentor is yell out an oath in pain. I heard Trevoran order Ty Saffrey ride to Polmabe and fetch Pierce Tredavik.

'Tell him he is needed to escort my wife's aunt to Bath immediately.' The door slammed shut and I could hear no more.

In a fever of high temper, I paced the room infuriated at my treatment, beyond desolate at the thought of being parted from Aunt Sarah, my only source of comfort through these dark days. Florrie brought to my room a light lunch on a tray and whilst the door was open I heard a commotion further along the passage. There was no mistaking Ty Saffrey's raised voice.

'No, it's not possible, I'm instructed you're forbidden any contact with Lady Trevoran.' Aunt Sarah gave a shrill cry of anguish and I ran to the door screaming for her, my path blocked by one of hard-faced lackeys. I saw her distraught face as she pleaded to be allowed speak with me, but to no avail. All I could do was call her name as they took her down to where Pierce Tredavik surely waited with the coach.

Bereft of Aunt Sarah's company, I fell into a melancholy, sitting day after day on the window seat in the morning room gazing trance-like down across the lawns to the river. Food I partook of solely for the benefit of Jarren's child growing within me. Tonight I would tell Trevoran I suspected I was with child. How would he receive this news! Impotent old man as he was, who'd take no maid's virginity or plant his seed again, was he the victim of his own delusions, tonight I would find out.

Already it was getting dark, the orange flames which licked around the logs burning in the elaborate marble fireplace could not penetrate the wintry chill of the room and I rang for Florrie to fetch me a shawl. Alone I clasped tight my hands then spread them gently over where the child lay within, a child whose father was young, strong and virile, whose heart was mine. I closed my eyes and could see the face I so adored, the wicked smile that played across his lips and sent a secret message to my heart, those so dark eyes which would beg me to love him.

A tear ran down my cheek as I sat in the near darkness feeling so alone in this vast house. I stared out into the bleakness and silently prayed Jarren would escape and rescue me. If only I could get help to him, if only we were both free, for if tonight my story was believed and we were still parted at our baby's birth, the unthinkable could happen, our love child born of an all-consuming passion in the hidden cottage at Nancledra would be acknowledged as Trevoran's heir.

Confined to my room I saw no one but Meryl my new lady's maid and Florrie. Florrie came later to prepare me for bed and was as subdued and quiet as I, she said but a few words and brushed my hair for a shorter while than usual, thankful to lay down the silver hairbrush and take her leave of me.

I heard the door open and his lordship's slippered feet upon the floor, felt the bed dip as he climbed in, felt his cold hand lifting the hem of my nightgown and I wrenched myself away. 'No, sir, I beseech you, for I suspect I am with child, take care not to distress me.' He let go at once as if his fingers were suddenly burnt, I could not see his expression for the single candle on the table beside the bed caused his face to be in shadow, but I felt his scrutiny. I lay still, staring upwards awaiting his response; he said nothing, and his silence terrified me. His wizened body remained motionless, then to my relief he was gone from my bed and from the room. Leaving me to ponder what lay ahead on the morrow.

In fact no sooner was I dressed but a knock came on my door and Mrs Treave ushered into my room an elderly gentlemen with a slightly arched back. She introduced him as Sir Kyle Pellow, his lordship's physician, he was accompanied by an elderly black-clad crone whom she informed me was the local midwife Lily Merren. I shrunk back against the pillows for I thought she had more the looks of a witch than a midwife, her odd black rimmed eyes never leaving my face as with a wild gesture she drew the thick drapes around the bed with her skeleton like fingers.

'His lordship wishes me to confirm if you are indeed with child,' she wheezed, coughing as she removed her gloves and handing them to Mrs Treave. I noticed she seemed a little unsteady on her feet and as she came closer could plainly tell she was somewhat inebriated. My stomach tensed; this was a dangerous time. I'd talked much of this moment with Aunt Sarah before she left; for we both knew an astute midwife would discover my deception. Perchance I should be grateful fate dictated I be examined by Lily Merren this very morning. I had no doubt she was a fine midwife no matter her appearance, for Trevoran would only have the best, and she must have come recommended by Sir Kyle Pellow, but I hoped this morning Mrs Merren was not as perceptive as when her mind was not befuddled with brandy or the like.

Mrs Treave remained in the room talking to Sir Pellow as I lay on the bed hidden by the drapes and submitted to a very brief examination. I closely observed the midwife's face and could detect no sign of suspicion as to my child having been conceived prior to the time my marriage decreed. When she'd finished, she stood up and took hold a bedpost to steady herself, grateful it seemed that her task was complete. Mrs Treave asked if she was finished and pulled back the drapes from around my bed. Lilly

Merran left my side, bobbing a quick curtsey, nodding to Mrs Treave and confirming my condition to Sir Pellow who gallantly congratulated me before taking his leave with her, anxious to convey the good tidings to his lordship, leaving me momentarily alone with the usually austere housekeeper. She surprised me, for she seemed a little less cold, her manner towards me a little softer.

'Congratulations, ma'am,' she exclaimed and just for a second, I caught a flicker of a smile on her thin lips, it seemed she was happy to learn her master was to have an heir.

The nightly visits ended. I knew not whether he believed it was his child I carried or not, I saw not even fleeting glimpses of him during the following days and questioned Florrie as to his absence.

'He's away to Bodmin, expected back tomorrow so Mrs Treave says.' Her matter of fact tone quite unaware of the significance of her words, for my heart contracted in fear at the mention of Bodmin.

'There's something else miss, cook says I'd best not tell you, but you'm been fair to me you have, tis only fair you know. Jeb he's the coachman's son, well his dad works over at Polmabe. I met him in Feock yester morning and he says your aunt gave Pierce Tredavik the slip at Wellington when they stopped to change horses.' She paused, and I sat down to savour this piece of news, grateful she had told me.

'Thank you, Florrie, is there any more you know?'

'Only that Jeb's father was sent quick about to search the streets of Wellington looking for your aunt, but she'd simply vanished.'

Long after she'd left me, I pondered where my aunt had gone and who she could seek help from in this corner of Somerset.

The days that followed were solitary, the reality of not knowing what was happening outside this godforsaken place unbearable. Trevoran returned but I learnt nothing of his visit to Bodmin. I existed entombed here dreading those evenings when I could not eat alone in my room, those late afternoons when Mrs Treave would appear with strict orders from his lordship that my presence was expected at dinner. A cheerless affair at the best of times an ordeal at others for on some occasions we would be joined in the cold dining room by Ty Saffrey, the men making good my discomfiture. I was ignored for the most part, the blatant subject of private witticisms by my table companions at others, always thankful when the time came to take my leave of them.

Without Aunt Sarah's company the long winter days dragged by. The boredom and uncertainty of the future making me withdraw further into myself. There was a change in Mrs Treave's manner towards me, her icy attitude had melted, she became anxious that, as mistress of the house, I take an interest in the housekeeping and brought to the morning room one day six heavily bound ledgers, enquiring if I would like to inspect them and instruct her as to future menu's and so forth, but they held no interest for me and I sensed her disappointment at my indifference.

I continued to walk out every day whatever the weather and however much Mrs Treave advised against it. Heavily wrapped against the cold in my warmest of cloaks, I'd escape the house I felt entombed in. Time for me was standing still; frost replaced the morning dew, the leaves long gone from the trees these cold days of winter. I had just returned from one of these walks when Mrs Treave herself hurried forth and helped me from my cloak. 'The master wishes to speak with you,' she stated. 'He's been waiting quite a while now, in the study, mistress.' Her tone implied I should waste no time in joining him and briskly she hurried me on my way. Such a summons gave me a feeling of unease, was he to delight in telling me some horrific fact as to Jarren's fate. I longed for news of Jarren but dreaded it coming from Trevoran and before I knocked on the door braced myself against what I may hear.

When I entered, he was pouring himself a brandy from an overly large decanter. As usual he was impeccably dressed; but the brown knee length coat with copious side pleats and wide cuffed sleeves seemed to overwhelm the shrivelled body upon which they were worn. 'Ah! So, you've returned,' he exclaimed and walked over to his desk picking up a letter and handing it to me. 'This is for you.' I saw the seal was broken and shot him a look of disgust.

'Surely you recognised my father's handwriting?' I retorted, clutching the letter tightly in my hand, wishing to read it alone in the privacy of my room.

'I had to be sure,' he answered, and raised his voice as I turned to leave. 'One other matter, it seems you are too much on your own, I am engaging a companion for you.' I stopped and turned to stare at him in disbelief, a companion was the last thing I required, the dull monotony of my life I wished to endure on my own, not have some prattling female accompanying me wherever I went. His eyes bore into mine as if to challenge my refusal.

'It will be someone I deem a proper influence on you, the position has been posted in Truro and you will be

introduced to the successful applicant later this week.'
My face flushed scarlet.

'No, sir, I will endure no female spy of your choosing.'

A coal fell from the fire and ended the ensuing silence; Trevoran replaced it with brass tongs and looked across to where I stood eyes blazing with fury.

'I have no desire for a companion, pray put yourself to no further trouble on my behalf.' I stood defiantly feeling slightly lightheaded in this one room in the house that was over hot. Trevoran sat down and took a sip of brandy.

'I will compromise with you, you may interview the applicants yourself, should you find any of them to your liking, I will abide by your choice, turn them all away at your will, the idea came from Mrs Treave not from me, the necessary arrangements have been made, now, madam, you may go.'

I didn't hesitate to do so, almost colliding with Lawrence Landy as I opened the door; no doubt he'd been listening to every word we'd spoken.

Once inside my room, I sat down and unfolded the letter, as I did so I noticed a scent which filled the room, causing me to catch my breath. The memory it provoked so potent that for a moment I closed my eyes and could almost bring myself to believe I was back in the wild garden a Rosecarren.

Someone had placed in the middle of the mantle a vase of wild white roses. Impatiently I tugged at the bell pull, desperate to know where they came from. With heart pounding I paced the room waiting for Florrie to give me an explanation, the letter from my father cast aside to read later.

At last she came red faced and out of breath. 'Oh! Miss Layunie, I've so much to tell, been waiting for you, then Decia got me busy and I never saw you return.' I went over and took hold her hand, almost dragging her away from the door so none could hear us.

'Where did these roses come from?' I begged, with undisguised eagerness.

'They're come from yer aunt, miss, to remind you of somewheres, so she told me.'

'You've seen my aunt, where pray?' I gasped in amazement.

She took a deep breath. 'Well, ma'am, as you know Thursdays is my morning off. This morning I was walking down past the bell tower into Feock when I heard a coach rumbling along the lane and stood aside to let it pass. To my surprise it stopped beside me, proper worried me it did, then I heard your aunt calling my name from the lowered window. Said she'd remembered me Thursday mornings off, she opened the door and ordered me get in, asked could she trust me to get the roses to you and to be sure you got this.' She withdrew a little package from her pocket, tied with a red ribbon and handed it to me.

'She asked after you, mistress, and I told her how you fared, of the baby and that, twasn't long I was with her, just a few moments really. I told them in the kitchen the flowers came from one of old Mrs Whittle's neighbours, she's the old lady I was gone down to visit, said I thought you might like them. Tis a strange time for roses, cook remarked, but no one else took any notice, twas near midday so they were all busy.'

She glanced at the roses and I smiled. 'Thank you, Florrie, I'm most grateful to you.' For a moment we were silent.

'Your aunt sent her love and I was to tell you all will come right.' As she made her way to the door, I thanked her again, watching as she left, wondering if my aunt's words could possibly come true.

As the door closed, in haste I untied the red ribbon. Inside the outer parchment was a long missive written in Aunt Sarah's distinctive hand.

Dear Niece,

Have faith, no doubt you have heard I managed to escape the enforced journey to Bath, Pierce Tredavik is I'm sure most annoyed with my managing to accomplish this. From Wellington I caught a coach back down to Hayle and thence to St Ives. Knowing I must get word to your good friends there who must be out of their minds with worry. Poor Nancy was most upset when I told her the full story of what happened and the circumstances of your capture, she'd had no news of John other than what she'd heard from Simon when he returned from Falmouth. Her father had sought to find out where they were being held but to no avail, she knows now though and is most fearful for John. She is here where I am staying at present.

My dear, I do not want to distress you but myself and another have managed to gain entry to Bodmin Jail and have visited Jarren and John Penrose. I cannot describe to you just how deplorable the conditions there are, you will hear more of this shortly, through another source, but for the moment I will say no more. I have written to your father telling him how things are between you and Trevoran and have had no reply. I also wrote to Charles who did have the grace to answer, if only to say how sorry he is in the part he had to play in your misfortune.

I stopped reading and hastily thrust the letter inside a shawl lying across a nearby stool, for I could hear people talking. I went over and opened the door. Two maids were giggling as they placed new candles in the candelabra on the polished oak table outside. I closed the door and retrieved Aunt Sarah's letter. *I hope I am doing the right thing in trusting Florrie, she always seemed most honest and trustworthy, which is why you will have to wait to hear further news of Jarren, but only for a short while. I will mention no names only to tell you a certain ship sailed out through Falmouth harbour unhindered that fateful day. My thoughts are with you, be brave. Jarren said the scent of the roses would remind you of times past. I hope these come near to those he described. His love he sends you, he wills you to keep strong, all is not lost and you are always in his thoughts, he will find a way so you can be together again, of that you can be certain.*

Layunie my dear, destroy this letter now the moment you finish reading it.

Your loving aunt Sarah.

So this was how things fared and although it was a comfort to know Aunt Sarah was nearby, I was saddened by what seemed, in part, a bleak hopelessness in her letter. I sank downhearted onto the rug before the fire and read the letter twice more before tearing it into tiny fragments, watching as the orange and yellow flames devoured them. It was then I opened the box around which the letter had been wrapped, inside was a purse of gold coins. For this I was most grateful. I had no money, and money was always useful. Aunt Sarah, ever thoughtful, shrewdly knew one day it may help buy my freedom, or bribe others to help Jarren. I hid the purse between the folds of two dresses packed away in the press; placed there as my belly swelled so I could no longer wear them. Intrigued, I pondered from whom I would hear more of Jarren. Aunt Sarah's letter had left so many unanswered questions, a feeling of frustration welled up inside me. I wanted to go myself to Bodmin, knew too who I'd seek out to help Jarren and John to escape, the infamous Jack Swannell. Our seizure by Ruskin Tripper meant he'd kept his freedom, it had been he the excise were seeking that night, but Jarren's free spirit that was forfeited, to be held prisoner chained in some filthy cell.

By the time Florrie returned to help me dress for dinner, I'd read the letter Trevoran had given me from my father. I think he knew others would read it before me and was guarded in its content, only making the most general of references to the way things were with himself, a little news of Charles, and of some of our neighbours in Bath and Wellow who'd asked to be remembered to me. I welcomed this contact with home and noted the date on which it was sent and found Trevoran had kept it from me for two months at least. How I hated the man.

Mrs Treave knocked and informed me my presence was expected at dinner that night and that his lordship had two guests. To my dismay I had to suffer the company of both Ruskin Tripper and Pierce Tredavik. It was a frosty affair, outnumbered by my enemies I sat and ate in the cold dining room, grateful as always when at last I could take my leave of them and be gone from their unwelcome company.

CHAPTER TEN

A dreary week followed when the wind blew through the bare branches of the trees, and the weather was so inclement I was forced to stay indoors. The monotony was broken when the morning came for those poor souls who had applied for the position of companion were to be interviewed.

They were much alike, all timid uninteresting individuals, drab in dress and manner looking like obedient rabbits ready to say or do whatever was demanded of them. I would have had no use of any of them even if I had indeed desired a companion. Although this change in my daily routine had expelled some of the boredom it had been a tedious morning, and thankfully only three young women remained to be interviewed when I returned to the drawing room after a light luncheon. Mrs Treave was already seated behind a rather ugly table looking very formidable and I felt a little sorry for those who entered through the door opposite to be confronted by her stiff and formal composure. Due to my lack of interest, Mrs Treave had taken on the responsibility for the initial questions asked of the interviewees, and surveyed the references from their previous employers. When summoned to question them myself, I had little to ask and soon tired of the pretence.

I had seated myself in a large comfortable chair by the casement window, thus they were unable to see my weariness in this task.

How lucky it was I was seated so, for the housekeeper was unable to observe the look of utter astonishment on my face as the last but one of the interviewees came demurely into the room. It was none other than Nancy from the Star in St Ives. She introduced herself as Nancy Crago and seated herself with composure before the table. Impeccably dressed, her red hair swept back, neatly hidden beneath her bonnet, her round face and familiar freckles held in a suitably sombre expression, as with modesty she began to answer Mrs Treave's questions, even her strong accent was less pronounced. Aunt Sarah had worked wonders, I tried to suppress a smile, but it was impossible.

Well prepared for the kind of questions she would be asked, Nancy replied with confidence and conviction. I admit had I not known that none of what she said was true, I myself would have been totally convinced. Once or twice Mrs Treave turned to me and I smiled seemingly a little more interested in this candidate than I was in the others. Nancy handed over her reference from her previous employer and having read it and nodding with approval, Mrs Treave brought the letter over and handed it to me.

The notepaper bore the very impressive insignia of the Earl of Sedgebrooke who resided at Friars Moreton in Sussex. Mrs Treave watched as I read the glowing reference as to Nancy's capabilities. I wondered who on earth the Earl of Sedgebrooke was as I handed the reference back. The interview finished, I myself asked Miss Crago to wait outside, and with a polite gesture of thanks, Nancy left the room. Mrs Treave reached to ring the silver bell for the next person to enter, but as she did, I told her, 'I have a mind that Miss Crago seemed a most pleasant and capable person who may indeed be an agreeable companion.' She seemed relieved but insisted the last candidate be called.

Silently I prayed Miss Bryne would not be suitable, but in fact her references were impeccable, she had been companion to one of the counties most distinguished families which greatly impressed Mrs Treave, so much so my heart sank as she asked her to wait outside. The decision thankfully rested with me and I had the greatest pleasure in instructing Mrs Treave that Miss Crago was to be engaged for the position starting as soon as possible.

Two days later Jeb was sent down to collect Nancy from the Harrow Inn where the coach from Truro would set her down. From the drawing room I waited and watched. Time dragged by until I finally saw Jeb returning up the drive with the old shabby open carriage used for such purposes, he reigned the horses to the left and the coach disappeared along the drive leading to the side of house. Nancy would be entering by the servant's quarters and I waited restless and impatient, wondering how long it would be before she and I would be alone.

Feigning interest in a book, I sat beside the fire until at last Mrs Treave knocked and in a very formal manner escorted my new companion into the room. Nancy stood modestly head a little bowed as I greeted her. I told Mrs Treave to leave us as I would like to discuss with Miss Crago the general routine her days would follow here and learn a little about her previous employer.

As the door clicked shut, I was on my feet and we were hugging, holding each other tight, tears hurriedly wiped away by both of us, and for the first time in weeks I found myself smiling. 'I cannot believe you're here, it's a miracle, you're a natural actress, Nancy, how on earth did this come about? Pray tell me everything.'

We seated ourselves on the window seat and she grasped my hands. 'I am here because of your aunt, I came back with her to Truro, she happened to overhear two dowager duchesses gossiping discussing the position here and sought to fetch me from St Ives and coach me in a manner which would impress whoever was interviewing me, and of course Lord Sedgebrooke was most willing to help in this enterprise. I will tell you more of her circumstances and his lordship later, but first and most importantly your aunt charmed and bribed one of the turnkeys and just this week he smuggled us into Bodmin Gaol.'

She paused wiping away fresh tears. 'Layunie, I saw John, Jarren too.'

My heart lurched, and she squeezed my hands tighter. 'Pray tell me all and spare me no details however awful,' I insisted, watching as Nancy bit her lip and took a deep breath.

'Be brave, it's not good tidings I have for you. Jarren's not kept within the main gaol with John, he's in a small building set apart from the other prisoners. Twas safest we saw Jarren first and were smuggled in early one morning and taken down an unlit staircase into intense darkness. We stopped and I had to beg the turnkey hold his lantern closer to the grill in the cell door, and even then, all I could see was just a bundle of rags lying on filthy straw. Slowly I realised that the rags clothed a person and that beneath a heavy growth of beard it was

Jarren who lay there, filthy and unkempt.' She paused. 'Do you truly want to know all that I saw?'

I nodded and she continued.

'The turnkey who'd taken us into this loathsome part of the gaol tried to pull me away the moment Jarren lifted his head. I hung on to the iron grill for dear life determined not to move, knowing Jarren had recognised me. His fetters dragged on the floor as he fought to stand, so short the chains he could but take a couple of steps forward, but the steely look in his eyes conveyed all I needed to know, for it told me Jarren's spirit was unbroken, his voice strong as he spoke my name.'

A noise outside meant she had to stop talking and I waited breathless for all to go quiet once more so she could continue.

'As he spoke so I was wrenched away and prodded back to where Aunt Sarah waited, a handkerchief covering her mouth in an attempt to lessen the stench of the place. She placed a further coin in the turnkey's palm which gained us a little more time with John, a further coin offered meant we could speak with him alone away from the prying eyes and ears of others.'

Thus, through a succession of interruptions by Mrs Treave and her menus for the morrow, Polly the under maid with her candles and even Lawrence Landy looking for his master, I learnt more of how things fared at Bodmin Gaol. Of how my beloved Jarren was held, shackled at all times, in a dank windowless cell away from the other prisoners and dragged out into the yard and beaten regularly on the orders of Trevoran.

When they'd been taken to see John, Aunt Sarah and Nancy had been made to wait in a small room beside the arched entrance to the gaol and John had been brought to them there. He was weak, his bare feet shuffling along the floor as he was pushed forward, his face sunken by lack of food. So hungry, poor soul, he'd devoured what they'd brought in minutes, hiding some in his ragged shirt, vowing to get it to Jarren.

They'd had precious little time with him, and Nancy wiped away tears as she recounted how she'd wept in John's arms as he'd held her to his wasted body. It seemed Jarren had attempted two escapes when first they were brought there, both times he'd been caught, savagely flogged and starved by a merciless gaoler brought down from Launceston at the bequest of Trevoran. Just two days before it had grieved John sorely to see Jarren hauled out into the exercise yard and tugged round by the shackles, paraded up and down in front of Trevoran, who'd then ordered the keeper have the prisoner be cleaned up before the visit of the high sheriff the next day. John had managed to get close enough to speak with Jarren in the yard and learnt he'd already conceived another plan to escape.

When screams of pain echoed from some far region of the gaol the turnkey had hastily returned. Roughly he'd pushed Aunt Sarah aside and forcibly parted John and Nancy. Protesting loudly, John had been led away. The brute had returned, hurriedly hastening Nancy and Aunt Sarah's departure, ushering them out through a small side gate into the lane leading to Fore St. Their visit over.

Mrs Treave knocked on the door and came in clearly pleased to see me conversing with my new companion. Sadly, although I longed to know more, there was no time to talk further for we must dress for dinner. Trevoran had insisted on our joining him.

It was impossible to talk with Nancy alone during the rest of the evening. That night I tossed and turned in bed, my mind beset with dreadful images of Jarren caged like some wild animal.

The next morning was cold, yet the wintry sun made it possible for Nancy and I, mid-morning, to escape the confines of the house and company of others. Heavily cloaked against the cold we resisted the temptation to link arms as we walked down towards the river. Out of the corner of my eye I saw Ty Saffrey on his horse watching us from afar and pulled a face at him.

Nancy's giggle was infectious, and we struggled to keep our composure, knowing we were being scrutinised as we walked on down towards the river. Once there we seated ourselves on an ornamental stone seat and I begged Nancy tell me if Simon had indeed conveyed my message to her.

'Indeed he did, told us how he'd stood with a crowd of other folk gathered outside the Customs House trying to see what all the commotion was about. He was told two men been had been dragged out and taken away before he'd arrived, and that now the crowd was waiting to know what was going to happen to the women prisoner taken inside earlier. He'd no idea the men were Jarren and John and was truly shocked to see you emerge with Ruskin Tripper. Rode straight home he did, sleeping in a hayloft overnight. My father could tell something was amiss the moment Simon entered the courtyard exhausted. He tried to keep those in the taproom inside so he could talk with Simon in private, but they'd already gathered in the doorway, and Jenny had to push her way them so she could be there at his side. Still seated on his horse, Simon told us the sorry tale. Where Jarren and John were bound he knew not, only that you had left Falmouth escorted by Ruskin Tripper and the blue coats.

'There was nothing could be done at first, then some days later Father went with Adam and Simon up to Bodmin after they learnt it was there they'd been taken, only to be turned away, neither prisoners were allowed contact with anyone. Discreetly your aunt came down to St Ives, staying not at the Star but at the Feathers in Lelant. You had told her so much about us she thought it only right to come and tell us where John and his friend were being held, and where you'd been taken. Whilst she was still staying in Lelant, and although Father was against it, I sold the brandy hidden in the cellar of John's cottage, knowing the money may come in useful, and pleaded with your aunt to take me back with her to Truro, which she did. It was then by an amazing stroke of luck your aunt overheard the dowagers' conversation. She lost no time in applying for the position on my behalf, using the name Nancy Crago. Every day she groomed me in the duties involved in being a companion to someone in your position. I could but hope I would be invited for an interview and that it was you who would choose to whom the position was given.'

'I nearly didn't attend the interviews but thank goodness I did. I know Mrs Treave would have given it to the last applicant, but all is well, I was there, and it's such a great joy to have you here.'

Indeed, it was good to have Nancy at Trevoran Court and immediately she seemed to fit into the household as though she'd always been here. No one, not even Mrs Treave, in the weeks that followed suspected Nancy had never held the position of companion.

Together we spent hours alone talking of Jarren and John, of the past and the future when the day came they'd somehow be free, but still we had no word of how they fared.

After a dreary Christmas, the weeks dragged on, now heavily with child they were made bearable only by Nancy's presence and her optimism for the future that never wavered. In mid-January there were heavy falls of snow, with blizzards that isolated Trevoran Court, cutting it off from the world outside. Icy winds blew upriver and severe frosts endeavoured to keep a thick blanket of snow lying on the ground for many weeks making it impossible for Trevoran's physician or midwife able to attend me.

In late February as the snows cleared Aunt Sarah wrote to Trevoran begging to be allowed to return, she was concerned for my wellbeing and that of his child. A child she knew would be born much sooner than Trevoran anticipated. She enclosed also a letter my father had written, insisting she be allowed to visit, demanding I have her support and company during these last months as my time drew near. The day he received these letters, Trevoran had insisted I join him for dinner, angrily pacing the room as I entered, the elegant cut of his clothes distorted by his bent and withered figure. He threw both letters at me from across the room and as I bent to retrieve them, spoke to me with a disdainful sneer.

'Do not think for one moment, madam, that I'd have that woman in my house again, you have no need of your scheming relative here.'

Hot tears pricked my eyelids.

'Enough,' Trevoran growled, and so we sat and endured another silent meal in the icy dining room.

The following day I learned from Florrie that Jeb who had left the employ of Pierce Tredavik and now worked in the stables here, had been sent to the village to collect Lily Merren. Immediately I was worried should she raise some suspicion as to how far advanced my pregnancy was and inform Trevoran. Unable now to concentrate on the day's menus given to me by Mrs Treave for approval, I left Nancy with her in the drawing room and went to look from the window of the library where there was a clear view of the drive, and thus prepare myself for Lily Merren's arrival.

I heard a movement in the room and looked round to see that in my distracted state of mind I had failed to notice Pierce Tredavik sprawled awkwardly in one of the two high backed chairs before the fire, a brandy glass in hand. I barely acknowledged him; over the months our mutual dislike for one another had become more apparent. Aunt Sarah had been right when she said his bitterness towards me stemmed from the fact the child I carried would deny him his inheritance. His presence made me feel uncomfortable and I decided to return to Nancy and took one last fleeting glance out of the window.

Moments later I cried out in shock for Pierce had silently crept up behind me and grasped my arm. Roughly he spun me round, pushing me backwards against the wall between the windows with such force I was breathless. He placed his right hand across my mouth stifling my screams and with the other held my wrist tightly against the wall; he thrust his face contorted with malice close to mine, the smell of brandy on his breath overwhelming as I struggled to free myself. He removed his hand from my mouth his fingers now tightening around my throat. Unable to utter a sound such was my terror I stared into his green eyes ablaze with fury, his face so close to mine as he spat out the words.

'I vow, trollop, to prove you're nothing more than a smuggler's whore and the child in your belly Polverne's bastard, think hard, mistress, on how my uncle will feel at being made such a fool of and what punishment he will inflict on Polverne and you.' His tirade abruptly stopped, footsteps could be heard, and the library door opened. Pierce momentarily tightened his grip round my throat and viciously pushed me backwards as Trevoran and Ty Saffrey entered the room. He drew quickly away but not before his manner towards me had been noted, the surprise on their faces clearly evident. Trevoran walked over to his nephew his eyes darting between us.

'Do you see fit, sir, to tell me what goes on here?'

And white-faced, Peirce spluttered unconvincingly, 'A mere disagreement, nothing important, Uncle.'

With an air of distain, he walked over to the table and picked up his hat and cane before sauntering from the room. Trevoran made to go after him, then turned his current like eyes on me. I felt sure he was going to insist on an explanation and all at once the room seemed both hot and cold, the mantelpiece with its ornate mirror above swam before my eyes as I tried to quell my beating heart. I took a step forward reaching for the table to steady myself only to feel myself slipping to the ground and being caught in the strong arms of Ty Saffrey.

I was carried upstairs, and Mrs Treave fussed over me as I lay abed, clearly anxious both for the child I carried and my own wellbeing. Lilly Merren arrived soon after and stayed for three days. I could tell those around me were worried I'd miscarry. As a result of their concern, Trevoran relented. He wanted his heir safely born, and two days after I left my bed he summoned me to his study, announcing stiffly that he had written to Aunt Sarah stating she be allowed return until the child was born, and only until then.

It seemed an age until she arrived, early one frosty morning, just after the fire had been lit in my room and Florrie had drawn back the drapes. As she came through the door, she exclaimed with a mischievous smile, 'I can't believe the old tyrant's let me come back.' She hurried across the room, at the same time unclasping her heavy velvet cloak and handing it to the departing Florrie. With the wide skirts of her blue travelling dress clutched in her hands to still them, she ran into my outstretched arms.

I half laughed, half wept with joy as we hugged each other. Then she led me over to the window seat as far away as possible from prying ears. We sat down and she took my hand in hers. 'I'm sorry, Layunie, but I bring you no news of Jarren if that's what you've been hoping for. Since my visit with Nancy I have tried but can gain no admittance to the place, even bribery has not gained me entry, which is most strange.'

Disappointed I took the handkerchief she offered and wiped away a tear. 'I love him so much, Aunt, and fear he's being mistreated cruelly in Bodmin, Nancy told me how things are there, it's been such an age since we were together, sometimes I fear I'll never see him again.'

'Hush now, it'll all come right, first there's the baby to be born and then afterwards we can plan and contrive ways to correct your dreadful situation. Have faith in

Jarren too, he'll not linger in that dark hole a day longer than necessary.'

A short while later Nancy joined us, delighted to see Aunt Sarah, but disappointed too she brought no new word from Bodmin. We giggled like schoolgirls as Aunt Sarah mimicked the two dowagers discussing the post of companion that had brought her here. After a while I summoned Florrie and asked breakfast be brought to my room, listening in silence, trying hard to quell the flame of resentment which stirred within me, as Aunt Sarah told me Charles was engaged to a shipping heiress from Bristol.

The bitterness in my heart only softened when I reflected that without my brother and his gambling debts, I should never have set out upon the nightmare journey which led to my meeting Jarren that cold dark night as the horses thundered across Bodmin Moor.

Knowing that the birth would be two months earlier than expected, Aunt Sarah set upon the task of encouraging Mrs Treave to begin preparing the nursery for nothing had been done in this direction. She exuded such enthusiasm that Mrs Treave complied with all her suggestions and the empty nursery suite with its adjoining rooms was duly set in good order. On the day it was finished I sat in the old rocking chair beside the window, feeling strangely alone as if all around me was unreal, I didn't want my child to be here in this nursery, however pleasant, I wanted him or her to be free.

To my delight during one of our sombre evenings, Trevoran announced he was travelling to London on business and that together with other matters he had to attend to, would be gone for a little over a month. One shareholders' meeting he'd purposely brought forward so he would be back in Cornwall for the birth of his heir. Ty Saffrey would be in charge of the estates here whilst he was gone. He left two days later. With my husband away life was much more pleasant, the servants more relaxed and the formidable Mrs Treave seemed to become less remote and aloof with every day that passed.

One afternoon as I walked in the grounds with Aunt Sarah and Nancy, we began to make the most outrageous plan. It would be almost impossible to implement, an outrageous idea, but the seed was sown. I was so desperate to know how Jarren fared and Nancy just as anxious as I about her John, so as we walked together beside the river, it became exciting just to believe that maybe Nancy could contrive to visit Bodmin and see our menfolk.

To begin with our plan rested on Ty Saffrey allowing her to visit her pretend grandmother in Truro. We would need Florrie's help, for she would need to have received a note brought to the servants quarters by a pedlar or such, asking for Nancy to come home at once on the pretext that her grandmother was ill. If our plan worked, it would need much preparation and was highly dangerous. Florrie was eager to help, glad of the small amount of money I placed in her hand.

We talked about it for days before, in front of other maids in the dining room, Florrie gave Nancy the slip of paper saying someone had just left the message at the kitchen door. Nancy who'd written the note herself earlier, pretended to study it and with the slip of paper in hand approached Ty Saffrey, who to our surprise agreed to the visit, the only stipulation being that she must return the same day.

The following morning, we tightly packed a basket with clothes and food. Stealthily I procured from Trevoran's study a bottle of his finest brandy, this we hoped would be enough to bribe the turnkey. I dare not take more in case Lawrence Landy became suspicious when he returned with his master.

Nancy left before dawn, Ty Saffrey allowed Jeb to take her in the gig to the Kings Head, in time for her to catch the early morning post chaise to Truro. Little did Ty Saffrey know but in fact she'd change coach at the Black Horse Inn to go further up country. Nancy had been relieved to hear from Florrie that Jeb had orders to collect her from the Kings Head in the evening when the last post chaise returned from Truro. There was no way she could be late back, aware the predicament she would be in and the suspicion this would cause.

It was the longest day I had ever known, the light rain that began to fall after lunch had grown heavier and drove against the windows. Neither Aunt Sarah nor I could eat supper, watching from the drawing room window hoping and praying Nancy would make it back to the Kings Head in time for Jeb to collect her.

Relief surged through us when at last we heard the gig approaching, pacing back and forth we waited, knowing Nancy had been deposited at the servants' entrance. After hurrying through the maze of corridors, she arrived in the drawing room, wet through to the skin but so pleased to be safely back. Although we insisted she put on dry clothes, she didn't bother to change but sat before the fire in the drawing room looking tired and bedraggled. he removed her cloak and bonnet and set them aside, Aunt Sarah added more coal to fire.

'Well, pray tell me, how fare our menfolk?' I asked with trepidation.

'Not good, not good at all.' I could tell she was tired and whatever she'd seen had dispirited her.

'You managed to see them?' Aunt Sarah coaxed.'

'Only John.'

Nancy shivered and I begged her move closer to the fire. 'The bottles of Trevoran's brandy managed to bribe the turnkey and gain me entry.' She looked over to my Aunt.

'I went up to the same brute as on our previous visit, having waited and approached him as he left the Three Cups in Fore Street. He insisted on taking the silver ring from my finger as payment also, and insinuated there'd be a higher price to pay next time. Once inside, I was taken through a different door than last time, one leading off the main courtyard, told not to wander off and left in near darkness. The stench was stifling. The turnkey returned and ushered me down a passage past caged prisoners. Grey emancipated faces peered out; skeletal hands were thrust through the bars begging for food. Some called out as I passed whilst the sunken eyes of others looked at me vacant and empty, all hope of life gone.'

Clearly distressed, Nancy brushed a tendril of wet hair back from her face. 'The turnkey handed me a candle and lit it from a sconce further down the passage. I followed him until he stopped and opened a cell door lined with iron. Inside was John, he looked far dirtier and thinner than before, scrambling to his feet from the vile straw-covered floor, hair and beard grown wild, clearly pleased but also anxious at my being there. For a moment the turnkey lingered, loath to leave us alone, watching through the grill as I handed John the parcel of food and clothes, certain both would be taken away immediately I'd gone, and begged John eat whilst I was there.'

Nancy smiled and a faint blush of pink coloured her cheeks. The short time she'd had alone with John had clearly been very precious.

'John told me,' she hurried on, 'that Harrison Carter, Keeper of the Keys, had been away from Bodmin, and that in his absence the daily routine, however bad had been abandoned, no one had seen Jarren for weeks and John feared for his friend daily as the conditions had grown steadily worse.' She stood up agitated and paced up and down before the fire, she took a deep breath. 'Something happened as I made to leave the gaol.' Her voice faltered, and for a moment I thought she was going to cry, but she hurried on. 'The turnkey returned in great temper. He dragged me brutally from John's arms. John protested, striking the man who retaliated by hitting him hard on the jaw, twas awful, blood poured from John's mouth and nose as he fell backwards against the wall. I was pushed roughly out of the cell and dragged back to the courtyard. The turnkey drew back the bolts on the gate through which he had smuggled me in, and was about to open it, then cursed as impatient rapping came from the other side, and the door opened. Tis then I near fainted, outside was a group of soldiers on horseback. A pock-marked captain stood in the gateway and handed the reins of his horse to another, he glared red faced at the brute beside me, ordering the main gates be opened. I could but stand watching as many hands rushed to the other side of the courtyard and heaved aside the huge gates. The captain stood where he was as his men made their way round to the main entrance and clattered nosily into the courtyard. Tis then I hoped he would remove himself from the gateway making it possible for me to take my leave of the place, but no he stayed standing where he was, leaving me no option other than to stand beside the turnkey and watch the group of soldiers.'

She paused; breathless wiping away tears, then hurried on. 'A man emerged from the group, not a soldier, and unlike the others still on horseback astride a black stallion. Purposefully he rode towards us, halfway across the courtyard he dismounted, to my horror it was Ruskin Tripper.'

I gasped in disbelief and Aunt Sarah visibly paled.

Nancy hesitated and I all but held my breath waiting for her to continue; when she did it was almost in a whisper.

'I bowed my head, aware of his scrutiny, sick with terror, hoping the wide brim of my hat would hide my face and relieved my flame red hair was well hidden beneath my old bonnet. Twas by the grace of God my presence there was not challenged, it most probably would have been if the turnkey hadn't callously kicked me bellowing out as he did so, "Be off, wench, and make sure to do a better job with yer sewing, you lazy bitch." There was much laughter and having spat on the ground in front of me, viciously he shoved me out through the gate. Banging it shut and sliding the bolts across it.'

Nancy started trembling as she continued, 'I fled then, running with all my might down Fore St, hiding until the coach was due and I could come home, terrified I would be sought out by Tripper.' She stood up and paced the floor.

'I have thought of nothing since, what if he comes here and recognises me? I sat opposite him at supper just weeks ago, what if he tells Trevoran he saw me at Bodmin?'

She buried her face in her hands and I reached out to comfort her, the troubled look on Aunt Sarah's face mirroring my own thoughts. We tried as best we could to offer words of comfort, inwardly feeling less than confident and more than a little uneasy. How long would it be before we knew?

I dreaded Trevoran's return, and now even more so, each day seemingly to pass even slower than before. I felt no pity only relief upon receiving a letter stating his lordship had a severe chill and was advised by his London physician to remain at his town house. Three weeks passed, I woke each morning dreading word would come heralding his return. My child would be born any day now, I didn't want him here, there was no place in my heart to feel compassion for my husband's ills. My greatest wish being he would remain away long enough so my child would be born in his absence, and as the days passed it seemed this wish would be granted.

My pains began early one afternoon in the yellow drawing room when thankfully the house was quiet, and Aunt Sarah and I were alone with no servants fussing about their tasks. That my time had come filled me with both dread and joy for I longed to hold in my arms Jarren's child. We had a well devised plan to ensure no suspicion be aroused when my child entered the world almost two months earlier than my marriage decreed. Calmed by Aunt Sarah's unflustered manner, together we made our way the short distance to the library for it was from here, as we'd previously discussed, I would utter a loud cry for help, pretending to have misplaced my footing on the library steps and tumbled to the floor. She helped me lay down on the floor, took a book from the nearest shelf and placed it open on the rug beside me. The exquisitely carved library steps, she pushed along to where I lay. The house was silent, I was gripped by pain once more and Aunt Sarah knelt down putting a comforting hand on my brow.

'Twill be a good while yet,' she soothed. 'Remember what we rehearsed, and all will be well.' Then getting up quickly she left. I waited in the gloomy book-lined room, with its damask drapes and furniture from a previous century, the heavy smell of polish pervading the air; the only sound the spitting of the fire.

When I judged the time was right, I let out a heart-rending cry, a cry which echoed my innermost feelings. I wanted Jarren here, now, to be cradled in his arms, my fears quenched by his loving care. As if in response to my cry, Aunt Sarah's footsteps could soon be heard as she ran along the passage and into the library, crying out in what none would suspect but pure alarm. She tugged furiously at the bell pull and a startled waif-like housemaid answered, quickly sent scurrying off to fetch Mrs Treave who came hurrying into the library bereft of her usual composure. 'What in heaven's names happened?' she demanded, genuinely overwhelmed by the sight before her eyes.

'I've had a fall,' I sobbed and clutched my stomach in real pain, 'I think the child...' My voice tailed off and Mrs Treave shouted to Florrie standing open-mouthed in the doorway to tell Jeb go at once with the trap and fetch Lilly Merren from the village.

Florrie returned breathless saying Jeb had left, whilst a flustered Mrs Treave instructed her regarding the preparations needed and Florrie hastened away to fulfil them. Helped to my feet by Aunt Sarah and Mrs Treave, I was led slowly upstairs and put to bed, sinking into the soft down mattress relieved our story had gone unqueried, panicked by the waves of pain which seemed to ebb and flow like the tide steadily growing stronger. A cold compress was held across my forehead by Aunt Sarah, as anxiously we awaited the arrival of the crow-like Lily Merren.

Dressed in black, hunched over, she hobbled in, throwing off her tattered shawl and ordering Aunt Sarah from my bedside. I closed my eyes shrinking back against the pillows as I felt her hands examine me, heard the click of her tongue as she quipped, 'Tis a great fuss you're making, maid, infant will come when it's ready.' She ordered Florrie draw the drapes and bank up the fire, an army of maids scuttled to and fro busying themselves about my room with pewter jugs and piles of linen. Three maids struggled in carrying a heavy cradle with a carved hood, grateful to place their heavy burden down at the foot of my bed.

I knew not what time of day it was by now or cared as I twisted and turned in almost constant pain. Lily Merren's haggard face with sunken bird like eyes a ghastly vision as she peered at me without uttering a single word of comfort. I tried to imagine myself away from this house, this room, to imagine I was miles from here walking hand and hand with Jarren through the long grass to the cottage in the hollow at Nancledra, but the pain was too great and there was no escape.

The heat was suffocating, vaguely I remember Mrs Treave pacing up and down wringing her hands, worried no doubt that Trevoran's heir was coming early. I heard her endlessly telling Aunt Sarah she wished his lordship here, and I so grateful he wasn't! Swept along now by a timeless void of pain.

Aunt Sarah mopped my brow and Nancy held tight my hand. I glimpsed their faces full of sympathy as I struggled on through what seemed hours of torment, until at last lost in the throes of torture I heard, as if it were another person, myself crying out as I gave birth, heard my son's first lusty cry.

Exhausted but overjoyed I lay, beads of perspiration trickling down my face, reaching out as the tiny bundle was wrapped and placed in my arms. I kissed the tiny brow of Jarren's son, the fruits of our passion held lovingly in my arms, as Lily Merren's coarse hands kneaded my belly once more to bring the final indignities of childbirth to an end.

Brandy was brought and a toast made to my son. 'An heir for his lordship,' Mrs Treave proudly announced raising her glass.

'Thomas Pierce Trevoran.' She raised her glass and spoke the name decreed by his lordship immediately he knew I was with child.

For only a brief moment, Aunt Sarah left my bedside. But time enough for Lily Merren to lean over my bed, bringing her face close to mine, so close I could smell the brandy fresh on her breath. Even in the oppressive heat of my room I shivered and sensed the malice in her manner, none could hear as she chortled.

'A big strong boy you have, yer ladyship, unless I'm much mistaken, you'll not need the parson here for an early christening.' A tremor of unease ran through me, and I lay still ignoring her, wishing her gone from my room and my life.

To my relief, Mrs Treave ordered the little waiflike maid Daisy, to tell Jeb bring the trap and take Lily Merren back to the village. Cradling my newborn son, exhausted I lay back against the pillows listening as Lily informed Mrs Treave she knew a young Feock woman who'd be a suitable wet nurse. It was agreed Jeb fetch Theresa Drym back with him, I had no say in the matter and neither it seemed did Theresa Drym. Word came the trap was waiting. I watched Lily Merren boldly help herself to another glass of brandy, casting a sly look in my direction as she threw her shawl round her shoulders. At last she hobbled out followed by Mrs Treave leaving me alone with Aunt Sarah.

'Lily Merren suspects something,' I half whispered, half cried and recounted the old woman's words, handing my infant son to Aunt Sarah before struggling to sit up.

'She'll be well paid to suspect nothing nor blab her suspicions to anyone,' she stated firmly, placing the sleeping infant in his cradle, and patting my hand.

Exhausted once again, I sank back upon my pillows, my mind a mixture of relief that it was all over and anxiety for the days to come. Somehow, I managed to drift off to sleep. When I woke it was to see by the glowing embers of the fire, someone seated in the low chair beside the hearth my infant to her breast. I sat up, hot burning jealousy coursing through me. I wished myself other than the grand lady of this hateful establishment so I could feed my own child. I saw the turn of her head as she glanced towards me and as though sensing my feelings, quickly she rose and brought Thomas to me. Although it was dark and I could not see her properly, I felt an affinity with her, a liking for the yet unknown Theresa Drym who gently handed my precious son to me as the rain rattled against the windows on this his first day of life.

Thomas was fretful throughout the night, but I could tell even knowing her but this short time, there could be no person more capable or more to my liking than this kindly girl only a little younger than myself. Her bruised and battered appearance, when at first light the drapes were drawn apart, came as a total surprise. For the neat and tidy little soul with round face and pleasing smile, whose dark hair was tucked securely under a white lacy cap, had recently suffered greatly, one side of her face was painfully swollen, neck and wrists a multitude of ugly purple bruises. Shocked I watched as she busied herself with Thomas, when she lay him in his cradle, I ordered her come stand beside my bed and gently tried to coax out of her who'd done her such harm.

Theresa meekly stood before me; she bowed her head and said almost so softly I couldn't hear, 'It was my pa, he beat me when he found out my condition, kept it hidden for nearly nine months I had, wrapped up for winter and like, but finally he found out, called me dreadful names, and when I wouldn't tell him whose it was, he lost his temper and kept hitting me so I'd tell him but I never, and after he stopped, I begged him let me stay but he wouldn't and threw me out.'

Distraught she paused sobbing, and I patted the bed for her to sit down encouraging her to continue. 'Pray, if you want to, tell me all what's happened, I'll not judge you, maybe I could send someone to see your pa and tell him how distressed you are.' She gave me a weak smile.

'It would do no good, ma'am, he meant every word he said and every punch I received was well aimed. It mattered not to him that it was well past midnight when I fled the cottage; he knew I had nowhere I could go in Feock. I ran across the fields to Devoran and my young man's home.' She took a handkerchief from her pocket and wiped her eyes.

'Davy signed ships papers for the *Parmir* and set sail from Falmouth months ago, he knew naught of the baby. He'd of married me if he had, that I do know.' Her voice trembled, and I hoped what she said was true.

'When I reached his mother's cottage, grudgingly she took me in, gripped I was with the most dreadful pain, but she offered little sympathy until blood seeped through my petticoats and Davy's younger brother was sent to fetch old Lil. That night our daughter was stillborn, perfect little thing she was. Davy's dad never said a word to me, grudgingly I was let stay on in the Martin's cottage, twas made to feel I'd brought shame on them.'

She stopped and wiped away more tears.

'After all, said his mother more than once, she only had my word it was Davy's child I'd lost, so having spent just that two nights under their roof, when I was sent for to come here twas as if to a blessed sanctuary.'

Here was a kindred soul, like me she was parted from the man she loved. I shared something with this girl, understood her, held no harsh judgement against her, for I was no better than her. We would suit well together and indeed for a blessed three weeks our lives progressed into a peacefully routine.

Trevoran had sent his congratulations upon the safe arrival of his heir, but was thankfully still too ill to travel. He issued no instructions as to Aunt Sarah's leaving, for which we were most pleased. Then late one morning, the first morning I had ventured up and was happily helping Theresa bathe Thomas, Nancy entered the nursery bringing with her the dreaded letter heralding the return of my husband and unnamed houseguests at the end of next week.

Mrs Treave arranged everything; I merely approved her preparations for the guests and endorsed the splendid menus she set before me during the week leading up to Trevoran's return. Too soon that day dawned, there was nothing I could do but wait for his arrival with a feeling of foreboding. Aunt Sarah and Nancy joined me in the yellow drawing room, where we sat grouped together before one of the long casement windows. From here we had a clear view of the winding drive, a dejected trio we were indeed, for we made little conversation each of us lost within our own thoughts, each with our own reasons to feel no joy in his return.

The day wore on broken only by the light luncheon Mrs Treave laid out for us in the dining room. A little before dusk the blue and yellow plumes adorning the heads of Trevoran's finest horseflesh, and the coach with its striking emblems upon the doors came into sight bowling along the drive. As it swung round underneath the great canopied entrance, I fleetingly glimpsed three occupants in the coach, but it was the outrider almost hidden from view on the other side of the coach who caught our attention. I saw Nancy's face grow pale and I prayed we could somehow be mistaken, and hoped with all my heart we were.

Ill at ease, I joined Mrs Treave in the huge marbled hall where the servants were lined up to welcome the return of their master. Two footmen held open the doors and reluctantly I went out into the mellow sunshine to greet my husband and his guests. Trevoran's wizened appearance had increased, his skin yellower, he looked older and thinner, his step a little uncertain as he came towards me. I saw his eyes take in every detail of my dress before he spoke. 'Layunie, may I introduce my cousin Simon Trevoran and his wife Isabella.'

Simon Trevoran was tall, thin with a small head and prominent nose, he took my hand and kissed it in a very gentlemanly fashion, but as he did so for a moment his smile waned and I saw a menacing look in his ice blue eyes. Isabella gave me a weak smile and stepped a little closer to her husband. For a moment there was silence, then the outrider strode up the steps removing his tricorn hat and unclasping his cloak. I had not been mistaken, it was my tormentor, he who had taken my love from me, robbed me of my precious hopes and dreams, destroyer of my life, whose presence here would so trouble Nancy too. Suddenly my legs felt weak, the last thing I remember before fainting is the sly smile on the lips of Simon Trevoran as I looked upon the fox-like face of Ruskin Tripper. Still a little weak from childbirth, I fainted.

The next thing I remember is waking in my own room with Nancy gently patting my arm and saying softly, 'Layunie, wake up, I'm sorry but its time you got up to dress for dinner, his lordship insists you go down, he was quite adamant of it, he came in just a while ago and looked at you himself he did.'

I struggled to sit up still feeling lightheaded and unwell. 'Was it Simon Trevoran carried me up here?' I queried, and she nodded.

'I've a feeling he's another bad 'un, like Pierce Tredavik, twas his manner and the way he most ungraciously tipped you onto the bed, when he thought no one was looking.' I could tell her loyalty to me had been sorely hurt by his actions. She hurried on, 'His lordship went up to the nursery earlier to see Thomas, twas a brief visit and afterwards he was most insistent you attend his guests tonight, I've let you sleep longer than I should, I'd better ring for Florrie to come and attend you.'

This done she sat despondently on my bed, and my newly regained energy built up over the last few weeks totally deserted me.

'I'll stay out of sight,' Nancy sighed. 'I fear being recognised by Ruskin Tripper from that day in Bodmin.' She bit her lip and searched my face for words of comfort, but as I lay looking up at the gathered canopy above my bed, no thoughts came to calm her fears or mine. I too worried should he catch sight of her, and as Florrie helped me dress, I could think only that nothing could be more odious than being seated at the same table as Trevoran and his house guests.

My aunt arrived distressed just as Florrie was fastening the last button of my rose taffeta dress, she had had the misfortune to step from her room as Trevoran was passing, and seen the surprised look on his face, curtly he had bidden her come to his study the next morning at noon.

'Alas, I fear he hasn't forgotten what he stated, that I could stay only until his heir was born. I saw by his expression he didn't expect to find me still here.' And like her I feared tomorrow's summons meant she would be asked to leave.

Thus there was no joy on that first night of my husband's homecoming. Theresa brought Thomas in and I kissed him goodnight, I could see in him a likeness to Jarren and took him from her arms, holding him close as if gaining support from this tiny bundle and handed him back. From Aunt Sarah I received firm words of advice and agreed to try and cast my woes aside, to concentrate on playing my role of mistress of this house so well as to convince our guests that it would be useless trying to pursue any ideas for my imminent removal from this position. Florrie finished pinning my hair and fastened the Trevoran diamonds around my throat, I stole a last look in the mirror and gazed momentarily at the sad eyed sophisticated young woman who stared back. The gong sounded in the great hall below and I gathered my energy to begin the charade.

Trevoran was waiting at the bottom of the main staircase as I made my way down; he was dressed in an elaborate coat and knee breeches of green velvet. I remembered what had been considered by the dowagers in Bristol and Bath the characteristics of good breeding, a straight back and confident carriage of the head, and confidently stepped from the stair onto the marble floor. Trevoran's fleshy lips gave me a wan smile as he held out his left arm to escort me to the dining room.

We sat each end of the dining table with Simon Trevoran to my right and Isabella to my left, next to Isabella sat Ruskin Tripper and next to Simon was Pierce Tredavik, indeed my enemies were all here tonight, even Ty Saffrey made an appearance making his apologies as he spoke on some urgent matter with Trevoran.

The atmosphere was utterly oppressive, the room cold as always, the flames of the candles dancing wildly in the many drafts coming from the long casement windows, the smouldering fire inadequate. I so longed for each course to be over, listening as they made conversation amongst themselves. I was totally ignored, a matter I found most pleasing for I had nothing to say to those responsible for Jarren and John being in that hellhole at Bodmin. It was an effort even to eat in their presence and Isabella's forced laughter at the silliest of remarks severely grated on my nerves.

For much of the meal I stared down at my plate, when I looked up briefly, I caught a look in Trevoran's eye that told me he found my predicament here at table most amusing. A cruel curl was also on the lips of Simon Trevoran as a silence now descended around the table.

Trevoran spoke shattering this silence when he asked Ruskin Tripper abruptly, 'Tell me pray, what are the conditions like in Bodmin at present? I hear they're worse than ever.' With bowed head I listened as with obvious pleasure Tripper delighted in explaining with great detail just how appalling the conditions were. The inmates he described as little more than animals and were treated as such. Isabella, to my disgust, found this statement hilariously funny and I cast her a cutting glance that brought her tirade of laughter to a close. Tripper then followed through with a further vivid description of the filth and degradation suffered by the inmates. Simon sniggered and Pierce Tredavik mumbled something under his breath as Tripper boasted further.

'But of course, much worse than all this is the treatment they receive in the dark house.' I glanced up and saw the beady eyes of Trevoran steadily watching for my reaction. At the mention of the dark house, my resolve to be strong deserted me. I could take no more and pushing back my chair I stood up and looked at those around the table with utter contempt. Fighting back tears, face burning crimson and quite overcome, I hurried towards the door, hating myself for having succumbed to their intended humiliation. A manservant hurried forward to open the door and even then, as I made my way out of the room, I heard the grating voice of Isabella begging Ruskin Tripper for further revelations.

A roar of laughter came from behind the now closed doors, and feeling utterly defeated, I abandoned any sense of protocol, gathering up my skirts and running wildly through the house to the sanctuary of my room. Only upon reaching it did I change my mind as to where I was to seek the solitude I craved, and crept quietly into the nursery. I stood beside Thomas's cradle and look down on my sleeping son, gently I picked him up and held his little body close to mine drawing comfort from him, stroking his tiny forehead threading my finger through one of his tiny hands. I placed him still sleeping back in his cradle blowing him a kiss before I turned to leave, suddenly feeling sickened as a thought entered my mind and struck terror in my heart. Would Trevoran visit my bedroom tonight?

I rang for Florrie who prepared me for bed, she could tell something was wrong but knowing her place behaved as she should busying herself with the usual routine. To my relief she bushed my hair a lesser time than usual, both of us silent for I had no heart for conversation. When she left, I lay determined to stay awake terrified least I heard the soft padding of Trevoran's feet upon the wooden floor or the light of his candle beneath my door.

It wakened me, the touch of his cold hand upon my breast and I shrunk away revolted, instinctively bringing both hands up in horror to push him away. I tried to turn and climb from the bed but was imprisoned in his claw-like grip. 'You are my wife,' he hissed, as the candle gutted and plunged the room into darkness.

My head was flung backwards as he pulled away the pillows and threw them to the floor, his face above me now, the smell of his sour breath made me reach as his fleshy lips came crushing down on mine hard and dispassionate. With one hand he roughly tore at my nightdress and I felt a hand hot and clammy moving across my thigh, felt his teeth upon my body, his fingers pinched at my nipples. I fought to be free of him, twisting my head from side to side, kicking out wildly mortified as his skinny legs straddled my body, whilst as before I endured his impotent thrustings.

Finally done with me, Trevoran raised his bony body, rolled off, and slept soundly whilst I lay awake bruised and bitten, with no child of Jarren's in my belly to bring these nightly visits to an end.

Trevoran left my bed before break of day, the bed dipped as he sat on its edge. I feigned sleep, terrified lest he suspect I was awake and sought to abuse me further. Only after he'd closed the door and been gone awhile did I sleep, and only for a short time. I woke with my body sore and aching and summoned Florrie. I needed her to tend me and wished to be dressed and gone from my room before the housemaids came and witnessed my plight.

'Tis a crying shame, yur ladyship,' Florrie scolded, dipping a square of clean linen into a bowl of tepid water and wiping my bitten flesh.

'Pray God he'll not be doing this to you every night, ma'am.' She saw the bed sheets were bloodied where my skin had been cruelly clawed and dragged them from the bed, replacing them with fresh linen. ''Tis'nt the place for housemaids to knows all what goes on,' she stated, and her kindness brought a lump to my throat.

'Thank you, Florrie,' I sighed, as she brought out my lavender day dress and began to see me suitably attired, loosening what fastenings she could. She gave me an embarrassed half smile wishing to say more to console me but knowing it wasn't her place to do so.

Hardly able to walk so painful my limbs, I made my way along to Aunt Sarah's room and broke down in tears, confiding in her Trevoran's treatment of me, showing her some of my bruises and hideous bite marks, what she saw appalled her.

Long before the other guests had risen, we ate breakfast with Nancy, though in all truth I wasn't hungry. Afterwards Nancy discreetly left me alone with my aunt for the rest of the morning, sensing this could well be one of the last mornings my Aunt Sarah would spend here.

Well before noon she was summoned to Trevoran's study, and ready for battle swept from her room a vision in russet silk, outraged at his treatment of me. An irate Aunt Sarah was a good match for Trevoran and even as I made my way to the top of the grand staircase, I could hear their raised voices. I slowly made my way down listening to Trevoran shout abuse at my aunt and her retaliate and rebuke him for his treatment of me. Ty Saffrey had also heard the raised voices and walked briskly past me across the marbled pillared hall and made his way to the study.

'Take this squawking witch away and get her out of my house.' I heard Trevoran order, and Ty Saffrey emerged from the study propelling my aunt back to her room in the most undignified manner.

I followed behind them beseeching Saffrey treat my Aunt with more respect. He shouted to two lackeys who emerged from below stairs to accompany him, issuing orders that they stay with my aunt until she leave the Court, which would be as soon as the arrangements could be made. Ty Saffrey opened the door to her room and thrust her inside. The lackeys positioned themselves either side of the door and Saffrey left making a mock bow to me. Walking off with a jaunty step, ordering Florrie pack my aunt's belongings immediately as she was leaving.

Aunt Sarah paced the room her face red with temper. 'I shall have more words with your father, while Charles dallies with his heiress your life here with that despicable man is nothing short of scandalous.'

I walked over to the door mindful of the eaves dropping lackeys outside. Upon opening the door, I found Ty Saffrey himself leaning against the doorframe. Our eyes locked, his mouth twitched with amusement and I angrily slammed the door shut.

Dejected we sat on the window seat and watched as two maids came in and hurriedly folded and packed away Aunt Sarah's clothes.

'I shall stop in Truro; I have friends there who I can prevail upon to let me stay awhile.' She lowered her voice. 'I have one or two ideas which I hope will contrive to help you and Jarren, and if they don't, well, be sure other ideas will come, child.'

A knock came on the door and Mrs Treave entered. 'Jeb's waiting, I've been sent to say as soon as your aunt is ready his lordship wants her gone.' Having delivered this curt message, she nodded to Aunt Sarah and quickly withdrew.

Another tearful parting, we were joined by Nancy and Theresa who brought Thomas in to say goodbye. I decided we would all go down and see her off and, like the others, gasped in disbelief as we emerged into the hazy sunshine and saw the ramshackle conveyance waiting in the drive. Jeb touched his forelock and looked embarrassed. ''Tis what the master ordered,' he grumbled as he helped my aunt climb up into the old wooden dogcart laden with her trucks, a final humiliation she would not take lightly.

As we stood to wave her goodbye, a horse and rider cantered from the direction of the stables, it was Ruskin Tripper. He raised his tricorn hat to us as he passed and spurred on his jet-black stallion, galloping down the drive his cloak billowing out behind him as he disappeared from sight. I hated that man just as much as I hated Trevoran. I looked at Nancy and saw the frightened look on her freckled face.

Jeb eased the horses forward and with a jolt the cart began to move. Holding Thomas in my arms, I ran forward and held Aunt Sarah's hand, holding on to it for as long as I could. When I had to let go, Nancy put a comforting arm around my shoulder. In utter despair, Aunt Sarah and I shouted our last goodbyes. Then sadly I watched as she left Trevoran Court once more.

CHAPTER ELEVEN

Following Aunt Sarah's departure, I could but hold on to my dream of freedom, closing my eyes against the present purgatory in which I lived.

Simon and the insipid Isabella stayed on week after week and all this time I continued to endure Trevoran's nightly visits and recoiled at his very opening of the door.

From several snide innuendos made, I knew Simon doubted Thomas's parentage. Then one evening, Florrie came to dress me for dinner and was far from her usual sunny self. She was red face and subdued, I could sense she was far from happy. I watched her reflection in the mirror as she came over and began unpinning my hair, she picked up the silver backed hairbrush and before she'd even begun, I asked, 'Something's bothering you, Florrie, I know you far too well for you to disguise it.' She paused and her eyes reflected in the mirror met mine. I turned around. She took two steps back and stood forlorn, hands clasped tight together.

'Oh! mistress, tis ashamed of meself I am, but believe me, on and on at me all day she been, tried I did to ignore her until I could take no more, that Isabella Trevoran she be nothing more than a nosey parker, keep asking me what I know of you and his lordship's sleeping habits, tis none of her business.' With the corner of her apron she wiped away a tear that was trickling down her cheek. I watched her waif-like shoulders heave as she tried in vain to stifle her sobs.

'Well I says to er, for I'm proper fed up her following me around, best you ask 'is lordship yerself, ma'am, if it so important you be knowing such things, I says, turned me back on her and left her standing in the middle of the blue drawing room, mouth open, aghast at me speaking out in such a fashion. Should have kept me big mouth shut, she'll summon Mrs Treave and demand I'm dismissed, I knows that's what she'll do.'

She began to cry and as I stood to comfort her, rapid knocking came on the door. I was scarce given time to say enter before the door opened. With a face like thunder Mrs Treave came in, she hesitated and looked somewhat aggrieved by the sight of my comforting the distraught Florrie, but quickly regained her composure, but it was I spoke who spoke first.

'If you wish to speak to me about what took place a short while ago between Isabella Trevoran and Florrie, my instructions are that Florrie is to receive no punishment. Isabella Trevoran is entirely at fault over this.' I walked over to the door holding it wide open in a gesture of dismissal.

'I do not know what Isabella has told you but pray, Mrs Treave, forget the matter, return to your duties, and I insist his lordship is not bothered with this nonsense, I hope I have made myself clear.' With a disdainful tilt of the head that clearly showed she was put out at these instructions, and having shot a look of sheer contempt at Florrie, she withdrew, the sound of her keys jangling on her belt finally fading away. I reassured Florrie that all would be well, I was mistress of this house, there would be no repercussions, for Isabella could hardly admit to his lordship what information she was trying to get Florrie to disclose. However, I sincerely hoped this matter would go no further and would chastise Mrs Treave if it were otherwise.

For me, later that evening the atmosphere around the table was even chillier than usual, though his lordship was I felt sure unaware of any more awkwardness than was normal, for polite conversation I had never indulged in.

The next day Simon approached Nancy, probing for details of a similar nature and demanding to know the circumstances surrounding Thomas's premature birth. Hence my days were spent constantly uneasy in mind for I dreaded the prospect that Simon would hunt out and question the witch-like Lilly Merren.

With this fear uppermost in mind, I begged Theresa Drym seek out the old crone and find out in conversation if anyone from the big house had come calling. I managed to persuade Theresa to plead with Mrs Treave be allowed a few hours off the following day, twas after all quite a long time she'd been here now, and she'd asked for no leave since her arrival the night of Thomas's birth.

Mrs Treave, run off her feet with his lordship declaring more guests were arriving on the morrow, grudgingly granted her two hours off. A wet nurse was no help where housework was concerned and there was plenty for the housemaids to be busy with. An unquestioningly kind soul, Theresa had readily agreed to find about what she could, setting out for Feock the next day mid-morning. I sat before the casement window in the nursery, Thomas asleep warm upon my lap, waiting impatiently for her return.

At last she came into sight walking up the drive, and a short while afterwards hurriedly came into the nursery bobbing a brief curtsey, catching her breath as she spoke. 'Old Lil's not been seen these last three weeks or more, her cottage all shuttered up. Jonas the blacksmith found her old dog tied up outside his yard one morning, reckoned she scarpered pretty quick over something, that's what them in the village says.'

Relief swept over me, and I hugged Thomas closer stroking his dark curly hair so much like his father's, which was proving to be yet another worry! Thankfully for now at least, thoughts of Simon Trevoran or Pierce Tredavik questioning Lily Merren could be forgotten.

Our guests the next day were of little interest to me. I expected the usual assortment of elderly county gentry; old men who repulsed me with their lewd comments that Trevoran let go unchallenged. When the gentlemen left us after dinner I knew what to expect, the dowagers dripping with jewellery would gather like vultures and endlessly gossip regarding the social intrigues of Truro, having in the past forsaken any attempts to draw me into their conversations. I was happy to remain an outsider and could well imagine myself the subject their tittle-tattle.

The following evening, I descended the grand staircase into the hall ablaze with candlelight, dutifully placing my hand lightly on the crooked arm Trevoran so gallantly stood forward and offered me. It was whilst walking amongst our guests making the pleasantries expected of me, that I noticed there were two persons unknown to me. A handsome rugged man who wore no wig but his own greying hair tied back, his clothes well cut but not elegant as were the other guests, no satin breeches or exquisitely embroidered coat, but the charcoal grey he wore suited him well. He was younger too, around the mid-forties and clearly uncomfortable in his present surroundings, the only person I saw speak with him was the odiously ever-present Ruskin Tripper. By the man's side, her hand visibly trembling as she took his arm, a dark haired young woman much the same age as myself, her plain blue dress with simple lace at the elbows, lack of jewellery other than silver cross, betrayed the fact she was not of the same social standing as the other guests.

Uncertain as to how to greet me, she bobbed a deep curtsey and I saw two of the plump dowagers look at each other, lower their eyes abruptly and turn their backs to her with distain. As the gong sounded, I saw Isabella hide a smile behind her fan and whisper something in Simon's ear, thus instantly I warmed to the unknown young woman giving her a welcoming smile. In the far corner of the room I saw a sly look pass between Ruskin Tripper and Ty Saffrey. I felt uneasy, there was something different about tonight, who were these two strangers so sadly out of place here, and what had made Trevoran invite them here?

As the meal progressed so I sensed the conversation around the table a little forced, there seemed an air of expectancy which made me wary, furtive glances were cast my way. Trevoran spoke my name and I looked down the table at my wizened husband seated at the other end, seemingly even more jaundiced in his gold satin attire, his eyes glinting maliciously in the candle-light. He paused, fork half raised to his mouth, conversation ceased as if in anticipation. 'My dear, I've been most neglectful in not introducing you to our new guests.' He gestured with his fork in the direction of the strangers at table. 'This is Harrison Carter, Keeper of the Keys at Bodmin Gaol, and his daughter Suzannah.'

In the silence that followed, I looked upon the face of Harrison Carter with disbelief and horror, it was he who held my love incarcerated in the dark house, filthy and starved of food, deprived of all decency. I remembered seeing the letter that bore his name in Trevoran's study. Trevoran's expression was pure evil, he set his fork down and the clink it made upon his plate emphasised the silence of those present. Simon patted his mouth with his napkin and enquired, 'Tis a most dreadful place and full of the most uncouth of villains, what say you, Mr Carter sir, is that not so?' Trevoran resumed eating with gusto, satisfied at my humiliation. The silence that followed was only broken by Isabella's nervous laughter. I sat numbed by this new knowledge and knew Suzannah sensed my pain. Further down the table someone made a toast and I heard the clink of glasses, how distant I felt from those present. I watched them as if from afar, saw Ty Saffrey set his glass on the table, his gaze never leaving Suzannah, but it was Harrison Carter who surprised me with a lingering look of compassion.

Suzannah stole a glance at me and a lump came to my throat. Pierce sat back in his chair clearly enjoying every minute of my discomfort. 'I say, Mr Carter, pray tell us of the punishments these villains suffer, from what I've heard they'd break even the most stubborn of creature.'

Harrison Carter leaned a little forward over the table and stared directly at Pierce. 'Be minded, sir, I speak not of my work when away from the gaol.' It pleased me it was Pierce Tredavik who looked away first stabbing at a piece of meat on his plate.

An awkward pause in conversation followed, before the bulbous nosed exceedingly stout Robert Westerleigh spoke of the growing troubles at the Whealdonna mine. He was a coarse, extremely wealthy landowner, a somewhat infrequent visitor here as his business interests often conflicted with those of Trevoran.

The conversation around the table became dominated by the Whealdonna mine, roof timbers had collapsed, two young men killed, and the miners led by Owen Pengle were refusing to work even if this meant they starved. I listened but took no interest other than to sympathise with the unknown Owen Pengle and the miners. I wished Suzannah had been seated closer to me so I could have conversed with her; instead we exchanged a mutual smile as the meal continued.

Talk of the Whealdonna mine continued; from what was being discussed I gathered Trevoran and Richard Westerleigh were principle shareholders. 'No doubt Solomon Wendron will be rubbing his hands together with glee,' someone spluttered, and I looked up as a deathly hush descended around the table. Trevoran purposefully banged down his glass, his jaundiced eye seeking out the speaker.

'Tis no business of Solomon Wendron unless of course his men have been ordered to whip up trouble.' He took the stem of his glass between his fingers, twisting it round spilling some of the contents on Mrs Treave's pristine white tablecloth.

'The troublemakers must be sorted out and the mine worked, I intend to call a shareholder's meeting at Porthpean House to ensure this is done and swiftly.'

Trevoran's statement was greeted with approval by all, my only thought being that my father had often spoken of Porthpean House so I knew it to be in St Austell and dearly hoped this would keep my husband from his home and from my bed.

I scarce touched cook's caramel peaches, grateful when the meal was over, wondering perchance could I be so bold as to ask Harrison Carter how Jarren fared, but knew in my heart this would be nigh on impossible and unfair to the man himself, should I approach him.

As we rose from table, so I saw to my disappointment Harrison Carter take his daughter's arm and sensed he had no wish to stay. I watched Trevoran briefly exchange words with him acknowledging whatever excuse I felt sure had been made. Simon Trevoran and Ty Saffrey swaggered over to join them. I saw Trevoran's power and authority assert itself in his manner.

Harrison Carter bowed and Suzannah curtseyed as they prepared to leave. Just then Robert Westerleigh said something under his breath and everyone laughed, this provoked Trevoran to turn his back to me for a second, all attention on Robert Westerleigh, he turned back too late to see me pass my newly embroidered handkerchief to Suzannah or that I mouthed the words. 'Give this to Jarren Polverne.' Her father witnessed all this and looked away his expression unfathomable. I felt indifferent to his knowledge of my behaviour, he held my love wrongly imprisoned in his filthy gaol. Abruptly they were gone, Suzannah and myself exchanging a fleeting glance as hastily her father escorted her away.

It was four days later Trevoran left for St Austell accompanied by Ty Saffrey. It was with immense pleasure I watched them leave, peering out from behind the drapes as Harry the elder, one of his lordships powdered footmen, dressed in his best livery of gold and green lowered the steps of the coach, and Trevoran together with my ginger headed enemy Ty Saffrey climbed aboard. Harry folded the steps and closed the door bearing its owner's hateful crest and moments later dust rose from the parched drive as the coach set off for St Austell.

Thankful of their departure, together with Nancy I made my way up to the nursery for it had become a habit of ours to sit within the confines of this cosy room away from the rest of the household. Here I could sit rocking my precious lovechild and talk freely of Jarren, and Nancy of John Penrose. Theresa Drym had become a friend to us both, here we found sanctuary, somewhere where Isabella never ventured.

The nursery was one place I was safe from Isabella's persistent questions as to if I was yet with a second child. I found her presence every day more suffocating for she was forever spying on me, only leaving Trevoran Court when Simon took her visiting Pierce Tredavik at Polmabe, where for sure the three of them conspired to plot against me and my son.

The following Monday was one such a day, Simon and Isabella having left shortly before noon. The weather, hot and sultry, made the afternoon pass all too slowly, with Thomas grisly with the heat unable to settle until Theresa finally sang him asleep. Weary I left Nancy with Theresa and went to my room, I meant only to lie down for a brief while but when I awoke it was dusk. Someone was knocking frantically at my door but before I could answer, Florrie ran through to my dressing room fetching out my black woollen cloak. 'Oh, miss, hurry, tis something most wonderful happened.'

There was no time to question her as I slipped on my shoes, hastily a cloak was fastened about me and without the slightest hesitation my hand was taken firmly in hers as she led me along the corridor and down the back stairs, entering a maze of passages until we emerged into the night through a tiny doorway. Keeping close the ivy-clad wall we came to the stable block. As we approached, Jeb's uncle, who worked in the gardens, stood touching his forelock as the excited Florrie bade me hurry inside and up the rough open tread stairs with the poorly fitting door at the top. As I pushed it open, Florrie hurried back down the stairs and closed the outer door leaving me on my own.

It was very dark. I supposed these to be the living quarters of the stable hands. By the yellow glow of a tallow candle I could make out the shape of meagre furnishings and a makeshift bed made up on a pile of straw. Bewildered, my eyes adjusted to the dim light and I saw the bed boasted fine white linen edged in lace.

I had no chance to query this before footsteps sounded on the stairs and the latch lifted, shadows cast by the candle danced wildly hither and thither. My heart missed a beat as Jarren stepped into the room. As if in a dream I ran into his arms burying my face against his shirt, clinging to him, unable to believe he was really here. Held in his arms, I was near lifted off my feet as he stroked my hair and whispered my name over and over again burying his face in my hair. I looked up and he bent his head to kiss me. I put my arms round his wasted body, but whatever he'd endured his brown eyes still held their sparkle and his lips upon mine sent a tremble through me, a knowingness of the passion to come.

'We haven't much time, my love, but we'll use it well.'

Once again, his mouth was on mine hot and impatient, and I responding wantonly helpless against the desperate need that was in both of us. It took no time to shed our clothes, Jarren unlacing my dress and letting it fall to the ground and I tearing off his shirt and breeches until both naked we lay upon the bed in a frenzy of unbridled passion, my body pressed deep into the feather mattress by a real man.

Gasping for breath our passion spent we lay beside each other, my face buried in the hollow of his neck. Then with aching tenderness we made love again until our lust was truly satisfied, only afterwards as we lay at peace, still and silent, my head on his shoulder my arm draped across his chest, knowing time could not stand still, and that these precious moments would soon be over, did I ask, 'How came about tonight, who must I thank for your presence?'

He smiled, running his finger down my naked body. 'Tis Suzannah Carter the keeper's daughter and the rioters at Par, my love. The keepers gone there, a miner was killed last night, and the mob went wild. Alas the heat has brought sickness throughout the gaol, the turnkeys too ill themselves to bother with the prisoners. Suzannah took the key and crept over to the dark house to give me your handkerchief, told me she'd seen you and how sorry she'd felt knowing I was here. Early yesterday Trevoran travelled from St Austell up to Bodmin for talks with her father. Word had come the miners were gathering at Whealdonna again. When he arrived, they both left immediately in the keeper's coach with outriders, leaving Jeb behind at the gaol. Suzannah heard talk from the kitchens that Jeb had sympathy towards you and that his lady friend was your maid, she broached him with a plan and cautiously he agreed.'

Jarren sat up one arm resting on a pillow, I stroked his back ever mindful of the scar on his shoulder, hardly able to believe he was here. 'Suzannah has a forbidden romance she's concealing from her father, it's with one of the dragoons, and thought to do her bit for love, seeing as you, my dearest wife, looked so unhappy at the dinner she and her father attended and were deeply humiliated at.'

Entwined we lay in the darkness for the tallow was now long spent. 'I'll never be able to thank her enough.'

'Don't go back, stay free we can run away together and take Thomas with us.' Sadly, even as I spoke these words, I knew it was not to be.

'I gave Suzannah my word I would return, for she has taken upon herself a great risk in arranging this meeting, she sought to get her beloved allow me wash away the filth of the gaol and provided me with these clothes so I could see you. I must go back.'

I respected Jarren's honesty and knew he would never break his word, for a short while time itself seemed to stay still. We lay content, in sweet oblivion to the reality that soon my love would be taken from me, back to the place that would shut out both his light and freedom.

'Tell me of our son,' he begged as I stroked his face and threaded my fingers through the fringe of black curls, near covering his eyes.

'Thomas is strong and fine and like his father, a joy to have for he is a happy baby and is a part of you always with me.' Jarren gave me that special smile of his I so loved, and the flame of passion engulfed us once again.

A knock came on the door and Florrie called my name. 'Tis time Jeb be setting off back, mistress.' Reluctantly I answered and hurriedly we dressed, the knowledge that the memories of tonight would have to last until we were both free.

Footsteps came on the stair, and Jarren gathered me in his arms, his breath warm against my forehead. We shared one last lingering kiss, the knocking on the door became more persistent and then with Jeb he was gone into the night.

* * * * * * * * * * * * * * * * * * * *

How dull the days seemed now, and none could persuade me to break free from the melancholy that filled me. I knew with certainty that tonight would never be repeated for Jeb confessed to having helped Suzannah and her dragoon elope later that same evening he'd brought Jarren to Trevoran Court.

Trevoran returned home one week later. Owen Pengle and the miners after much argument and persuasion had been satisfied finally with new safety measures at the Whealdonna mine. Thankfully, Trevoran had not resumed his nightly visits to my bedchamber, but once more I was forced to dine with him, Simon and Isabella.

Simon grew ever more bitter towards me with each day that passed, bragging openly in front of the servants he was the true heir to the Trevoran Estate.

One night at dinner, Trevoran seemed weary, the pallor of his skin more jaundiced than usual. Simon persistently jested with him whether I was with child, and I sensed Trevoran getting more than a little tired of being questioned so. Irritated, he was quarrelsome with his manservant, and pushed his plate aside, picking up his glass and leaving the room. I saw Simon give Isabella a meaningful look, and not wishing to be left seated with this distasteful couple, hastened to withdraw myself from their company.

Twas scarce moments later I heard raised voices followed by the sound of breaking glass. I retraced my steps; from within the dining room a heated quarrel was taking place between my husband, who must have returned there, Simon and Isabella. I sent away the servants who lingered in the corridor outside, happy to loiter and listen to the argument within so they could report to the others below stairs. Daisy I ordered come with me and withdrew further down the corridor.

'Were you in the dining room, if so, what provoked his lordship?'

Daisy looked down at the floor embarrassed. 'He came back, the master, and caught Mr Simon calling little Thomas a bastard.' We could hear now Isabella's high-pitched screeching as she joined Simon quarrelling heatedly with his Lordship. I dismissed Daisy and slowly made my way up to my room thinking it best to be safely out of the way. By noon the next day, Simon and Isabella had left Trevoran Court.

After their departure we never had visitors not even Ruskin Tripper. Apart from his morning ride around the estate, Trevoran became a recluse. A small concession occurred a few times during that summer, for Nancy had been allowed to accompany Mrs Treave into Feock. Jeb would set them down at the Feathers and pick them up a little later. In a brief conversation with the inn-keeper, Nancy mentioned she came from the St Ives, and himself being a St Ives man he remembered her father and the Star Inn.

Months slipped by, the seasons came and went, four years of life and me a prisoner, with no word of Jarren or John Penrose. I was permitted no communication with the outside world, if letters came for me, Trevoran never sanctioned them to reach me.

Thomas was nearly four when Trevoran had a seizure which left him paralysed and in an invalid chair. His temper and pettiness increased with his confinement to the chair, wheeled around with reverence by Lawrence Landy. Whenever I upset him in the slightest, by eating too slowly at dinner or too fast, not having my hair arranged to his liking, or for the most ridiculous of reasons, I'd be forbidden to see Thomas and locked in my room. Sometimes, just as at present, I was locked in for days on end with only Nancy or Florrie permitted to bring me food, and one of the maids to light the fire and change my bed linen. There was no point in dressing or Florrie arranging my hair; instead I just combed it loose as Jarren always liked it best. If Theresa could, she would smuggle Thomas in to see me, my little boy running into my arms for illicit hugs and kisses.

Surprisingly, Trevoran still visited my bedchamber at least once a week and was placed in my bed by one of his new hateful personal servants. Why he came I do not know, only that his bony fingers still pawed at me. I was repulsed by his presence, his breath stank, and at times his breathing so shallow I thought him dead.

Matters came to a head one night when instead of lying like a stone until he'd finished his groping, the smell of his breath on my face made me retch and in disgust, I pushed his hands away from me, sickened by him. In fury he grasped my hair with his good hand, and I hauled myself from the bed tugging my hair from his grasp. Trevoran half pulled from the bed, fell back against the pillows and furiously rang the bedside bell.

Lawrence Landy himself came and helped his master from my room, Trevoran in such a temper I surely thought he would die of anger. But it was I who was to suffer, for Florrie shook me awake the next morning with news that left me desolate.

Having been taken from my room, Trevoran had roused the whole household, and ordered arrangements be made for Thomas and his new nanny whom he'd appointed but last week – a person I'd not even met! – leave today for his townhouse in London. The new nanny, whey faced and sour of disposition so Florrie said, wanted the kindly Theresa Drym dismissed but Thomas threw such a tantrum as to upset his lordship, so she'd been allowed retain her employment and accompany them as well. Trevoran together with Pierce Tredavik and a handful of servants had set out to accompany them to London before dawn.

I felt complete disbelief then anger. So, this is my punishment? He would take my son away from me.

Praying she was wrong, barefoot and clad only in my nightgown, I ran from my room, along the corridor and up the narrow stairs to the nursery suite. 'I must see for myself they have truly gone,' I shouted at Florrie. I reached the top stair and flung open the door, staring round me in horror for the nursery suite held only an echoing silence.

In cold fury I flew down the stairs and burst into Trevoran's study. Lawrence Landy was there seated at a side table writing in a ledger, the pathetic little man could tell me no more than I already knew. In temper I ran over and pulled Trevoran's precious books from their shelves and onto the floor, then set about destroying his priceless family heirlooms, dragging the ancient tapestry with the family crest from the wall, throwing his mother's ornate vases to the floor, destroying everything in his room I could, whilst Lawrence Landy half rose from his seat ashen faced. I looked at the weasel and seized his pot of ink throwing it at Trevoran's portrait that hung above the fireplace. Exhausted I turned my attention to the newly lit fire and picked out a log only alight at one end plunging it into the pile of books on the floor. In seconds they were ablaze and taking one last look around ran from the room leaving Lawrence Landy in the doorway shouting for help as the whole study burst into flames.

Nancy found me hysterical, half crying, half laughing, huddled in the furthest corner of the yellow drawing room, which was quickly filling up with smoke. I heard the muffled voice of Ty Saffrey call out. 'Have you found her, woman?' As coughing and spluttering he staggered through the smoke a handkerchief to his mouth. He pulled me up and seized both of us by the elbows pushing us towards the long casement windows, he opened one, guiding us through and out into the fresh air, then he was gone. I sat shivering, clad only in my nightgown, with Nancy beside me on the steps leading down to the lawns, sobbing uncontrollably as black smoke drifted out from the windows.

Quite still I sat feeling detached from the sounds around me, the mayhem within, with servants running to and fro with pails of water trying to save their master's house from burning down. Ty Saffrey shouting his orders at the minions. For my part I wouldn't have cared had the whole house burnt down, indeed it would have served Trevoran right if it did.

After the fire in the study had been quenched, a messenger was dispatched to inform Trevoran of my behaviour, by the evening of the next day the same person duly returned with a letter instructing Lawrence Landy to have me locked alone in my room until his lordship's return. The horrid little man enjoyed the power his master had bestowed on him and issued these orders to Mrs Treave who could do nothing but insist they be carried out immediately.

Trevoran did not return for three weeks. Restless and bored into almost a stupor, my spirit of rebellion deserted me. I had been incarcerated in this room before but never deprived of Nancy's company, or of the gossip I shared with Florrie and Theresa Drym, however unladylike this may be.

Not Florrie but Meryl did for me, bringing my food and other necessities, her pale oval face with high brow bore, as always, the superior servant look that Florrie and I so detested, and often exchanged humorous remarks about.

On the day Trevoran returned, I spent my time gazing out of the casement window in my room, down across the lawns and through the trees to the river, watching the assorted ships on the Fal pass by. I wondered if any on board gave a second glance at the huge house with many windows, peeping out from behind the trees. Today there was hardly a ripple on its peaceful waters as silently it flowed passed my prison.

It was thus gazing from the window I saw Trevoran's return for he came not by coach but sailed down river from Truro. I saw his boatman tie up at the wooden quay and Ty Saffrey and Lawrence Landy stride down across the lawns to greet him. He cast not a look at my window as Landy wheeled him with great difficulty from the boat along the gravel path. Trevoran looked in ill temper as several times the wheels caught and the chair became stuck fast, with Ty Saffrey having to help free them. They passed beneath the balcony and out of sight. There was no sign of Thomas or Theresa Drym. I sat in the window seat anxiously awaiting the summons that would surely come.

None came, but hardly any time passed before I heard much activity, voices and hammering from somewhere further down the corridor, it seemed endless and I couldn't possibly imagine what it could be. Then Ty Saffrey without knocking unlocked my door, and with a jewelled finger he beckoned me follow him. Reluctantly I did so, compelled by curiosity to meekly obey; it was as we approached the grand staircase that I saw it, a rough wooden screen, hastily built with a door and small hatch set into it. I stared in horror at this hideous structure. Ty Saffrey impeccably dressed in russet breeches and matching coat leaned against the wall and watched me, a sardonic smile playing on his lips.

'You and your companion will remain on this floor and in this wing until his lordship decides otherwise.'

I stared at him in disbelief, then my heart sank for the sound of more hammering could be heard. I spun round only to find my arm firmly grasped, Ty Saffrey held me tight to him, his breath hot on my face as he sneered. 'Yes, mistress, it's indeed what you fear, the entrance from this wing to the nursery is being closed off.' I tried to pull free, but he wasn't finished with me.

'Mrs Treave is to personally deal with the supervision of young Master Thomas's nurturing and wellbeing when he returns here, dismissing those no longer needed.' Was he insinuating Theresa who I so liked, and Thomas adored, would be sent from the house? Pray God no. I kicked out catching him unawares and ran along the corridor and up the nursery stairs. Ty Saffrey followed spluttering obscenities no lady should hear and quickly caught up with me, wrenching my hand away from the nursery door. I had to make sure Thomas truly wasn't here. He brutally hauled me downstairs as I kicked and screamed at him in anger. Once we got to my room, he dragged me inside and let go his grip on my arm. Beyond caring, I reached out and clawed at his face, drawing blood, he reeled back and in fury raised his hand to me, only just managing to hold in check his urge to hit me, as the fire of hatred blazed in his eyes.

'Your precious son is still in London and for the present is to remain there.' He put his hand to his face. 'Don't ever do that to me again, be his lordship's wife or no I'll make you sorry.' I raised my chin and stared back at him undaunted by his threatening words, watching as blood trickled down his face.

I was thankful to hear footsteps and Nancy appeared bearing a tray with my lunch. Saffrey gave me a malevolent smile as he backed towards the door. 'One more

thing, his lordship wishes you told, the unused rooms
on this floor are to be made ready as you require, for
neither you or your companion if she stays will be
permitted anywhere else.' He strutted from the room
slamming shut the door. Nancy set down the tray
knowing already my situation; she ran over and put her
arms around me sharing my grief.

'What more can he do to me?' I fumed, shocked by
this new turn of fortune.

'Tis only a matter of time,' she soothed. 'Twill all end
one day, our menfolk will see to that.' I took her hand
so grateful for her companionship.

I could eat nothing and fell into a melancholy from
which none could rouse me, my only comfort being my
trust in Theresa to care for my son, and in fetching the
two keepsake rings from their hiding place to clasp
tightly in my hand as I slept, remembering the man who
gave them to me what seemed an age ago.

Nancy saw to the refurbishment of the unused
rooms. Day after day we would sit in the newly furnished drawing room, Nancy trying to busy herself with
embroidery and I staring out towards the river in a
world of my own, growing thinner and weaker with
every week that passed.

Florrie managed to tell us when Thomas had been
brought back down to Cornwall. At first, I watched in
hope of seeing Thomas in the grounds with Theresa
taking one of their daily walks, but not once did I see
them, so large the estate no doubt she was forbidden
from bringing him within my sight.

Thus summer slipped into autumn, my only gladness
being that Trevoran's nightly visits to my bed ceased, for
which I was most grateful. My relationship with Mrs

Treave which for a short while had begun to mellow, her having such a great fondness for Thomas, had become restrained once more following the fire. Her concern for my health as I grew weaker was obvious, no doubt she feared what the consequences would be should I weaken further and die. She had sensed my closeness to Florrie and it seemed made sure other servants newly appointed and unknown to me brought our meals to the hatch and carried out the household tasks in this part of the wing. Told not to communicate to either myself or Nancy they carried out their daily routine in silence forbidden to answer any of the questions I repeatedly asked.

It was to Mrs Treave I turned, desperate for word of him, seeking the reassurance as to his wellbeing I so badly needed. This she gave but was sparse of words and was clearly uncomfortable answering my questions.

One day during the last week of September, I opened my eyes and saw it was Florrie not sulky Meryl who came to my room drawing back the drapes. I had no time to speak with her before Mrs Treave knocked and entered. Seeing I was still abed, without asking my permission she ushered in a tall thin bearded man dressed in sombre black, who viewed me through grave wrinkled eyes. Mrs Treave carried his cape over her arm, she offered to take the small black bag he carried but this he dismissed and placed it on the table beside my bed, he introduced himself as Benedict Carrick Trevoran's London physician.

'Whilst here your husband has informed me of his concern for you, he believes you've not been eating, is that correct?'

I eased myself up and lay back against the pillows, the frosty eyes of Mrs Treave silencing any truth I may impart. 'I have little appetite,' I replied, and saw the housekeeper loosen her clenched hands.

'It's important you keep up your strength, especially now with your son so afflicted with the measles.'

It was impossible to disguise my horror, or that this was the first I'd heard of it, in dismay I grasped his hand. He looked round at Mrs Treave clearly perplexed, then turned his back on her and looked at me with compassion, closing his other hand over mine. 'I'm so sorry, my dear, I thought you knew.' Behind him I saw Mrs Treave's back stiffen.

'I have left a potion with his nurse and will call twice daily on him, be assured I will do my absolute best for young Master Thomas.'

I looked directly into his eyes and pleaded, 'I beg you take me to see my son, I want to see Thomas, I beseech you, make them let me see him, make them.' I began to struggle from the bed. Bewildered and embarrassed, he eased his hand from my grasp and picked up his bag, I clutched hold his arm as he went to move away, kneeling before him hysterically begging him to take me to Thomas. He stood for a moment hesitant in what to do, unused to such a blatant cry for help, then shaking his head he hastened to the door uttering questions to Mrs Treave I knew she wouldn't answer.

Once they'd left, I remained staring at the closed door, my mind in turmoil. Nancy swept into the room and did her best to comfort me as now I tugged desperately at the bell pull in a hope of summoning Florrie, anyone, even Meryl so I could question them.

'I had a right to know my son was ill, he needs me I should be with him,' I yelled at Nancy. No one came and consumed with frustration, I ran down the corridor banging with my fists against the new more elegantly contrived screen, still no one came; the house was engulfed in a morbid silence.

Exhausted, I leant against the screen and slid to the floor sobbing, Trevoran had won, my spirit crushed, only Jarren could save me now for if anything happened to Thomas, I would rather be dead than live here. Nancy brought a shawl and placed it around my shoulders, she left me alone, knowing I was beyond her help, my sorrow too deep.

Twas an age before I heard approaching footsteps on the other side of the screen. I rose stealthily as the key was placed in the lock and holding tight my nightgown stood behind the opening door, thus taking a startled Florrie by surprise. The tray she carried fell to the floor, shattering the crockery and spilling the hot broth on the polished floor. Our eyes conveyed a mutual understanding, and I wasted no time in running through the door and on towards the stairs that led up to the nursery.

A startled Theresa rose from a low stool as I burst through the door, at once she gathered Thomas gently up and handed him to me. I cradled him close, his fever obvious, his body limp and clammy, face and arms covered with telltale red spots. Despite my beating heart, I sat quite calm now, dipping the square of linen Theresa handed me into a bowl of cold water and bathing Thomas's brow to sooth him, wishing he would open his eyes and give me some sign that he was getting better, that the fever was breaking, as it had with Jarren after the shot was removed from his shoulder. 'Tis good you're here, ma'am, tis a mother's love he needs.' She smiled down at us and discreetly went into an adjoining room leaving us alone.

When they came twas like an army as the many feet sounded on the stair, I was taken hold of by two liveried servants, crying out as others tried to wrench Thomas from me. I fought to hold on to him running to the farthest part of the nursery darting from side to side before they succeeded and handed him back to Theresa. I was led from the nursery suite, struggling like a wild woman and dragged back to my room where Trevoran was seated in his hideous chair waiting for me.

Too distraught was I to notice what he held in his good hand, too late to avoid the agony as the whip sliced through my nightgown and into the flesh of my back. I could only scream again and again at the biting pain inflicted by my brute of a husband. I sought to escape, falling as I tried to flee from him, petrified as Trevoran shouted orders to Lawrence Landy. By now I was too weak to stand, only drag myself along the floor trying to escape the menacing creak of the wheels as his chair followed my every move. Time after time he struck me, the whip coiling itself round my body. I raised my hands to protect my face and tasted my own blood, reached out in the vain effort of pulling myself under the heavy walnut table, but I was too exhausted and overcome lay still on the floor my nightgown scarlet red with my own blood.

The lashing stopped, I glimpsed Trevoran, his face a caricature of pure evil. I remember Lawrence Landy's look of horror, heard someone screaming as though in the far distance, smelt my own blood as I rested my face against the floor and fell gratefully into unconsciousness.

I can recall little of the days which followed, only briefly remembering the muffled voices that at times surrounded me, seemingly coming from somewhere in the far distance. I heard my own cries as hands held me whilst my wounds were cleansed; salve was rubbed into my broken flesh making me scream with pain. I felt the agony each time fresh linen was applied to the wounds and struggled to raise my hands and pushed away the spoon, as I was forced to swallow beef tea and lukewarm broth brought by well-meaning souls.

Finally one morning, I came out of my strange half world and awoke weak but with my senses restored, the delirium had passed. Slowly I managed to pull myself up and lie back against the pillows. I shuddered for my back throbbed and smarted causing me unbelievable agony. I hesitated to move further for my ribs hurt as I breathed, but I was thankful to be alive. In the semi darkness I saw Nancy asleep in the chair by the window, and for the moment decided against waking her, instead closing my eyes and in the quietness remembered the horrific manner in which Trevoran had inflicted his fury, leaving me so close to death.

I thought of Thomas and could wait no longer for news of him and raised my head a little to call across the room to Nancy. She woke startled and realising it was I who'd woken her, gathered up her skirts and ran over to the bed tugging furiously at the bell pull. 'Tis a miracle you've come back to us,' she soothed gently taking my hands in hers. 'We didn't think you'd make it so poorly you were.'

'How's Thomas?' I asked, in a voice barely audible and watched, as her expression grew serious.

'Trevoran's taken him to London to a top physician recommended by Bennedick Carrick, he was real poorly when they left, there's been no word since.'

I began to cry, and she put a comforting arm round my shoulders. 'Trevoran's money will see he gets the best treatment, Theresa's with him, he's a strong little boy I'm sure he'll be alright.' A knock came on the door and Nancy went to open it.

Florrie hurried in still fastening her apron, her delight at seeing I was better replaced with compassion as she saw my tears and knew at once I'd asked after Thomas. She understood my sorrow and came over fussing with the bedclothes. 'Oh! Tis so good to see you better, mistress, twas a time...' The sentence went unfinished and her face reddened, I reached out and took her hand, looking at both of them.

'I take it that brute of a husband of mine summoned no outside help to aid in my recovery, so it's to the both you I owe my life. Trevoran has Thomas, no doubt he cared not if I lived or died.' I knew this to be true by the look that passed between them.

Florrie went over and drew back the damson drapes just a little. 'Tis a good beginning to the day, you being so much better, I'll away to the kitchen and bring you both up something warming, little Daisy be up by now and she'll be pleased to hear you'm better.' She bobbed a curtsey and was gone. I was grateful to her for indeed, for the first time in days, I felt hungry.

'Tell me all that's happened,' I begged Nancy, and lay back against the pillows my eyes shut, whilst she brought a chair over and sat beside my bed.

'There was mayhem the night Trevoran attacked you, Lawrence Landy was terrified you were dead, he made to feel if you had a pulse but Trevoran wouldn't let him near you, struck his hand away with the whip. I came in to see you lying lifeless on the floor.'

Nancy's voice trembled with emotion and I reached out and touched her arm as she swallowed hard and carried on. 'Trevoran shouted at Landy to wheel him away and I summoned Florrie to help me carry you to your bed, no one else came to help us, twas so lifeless you were we stayed up with you through that first night terrified. Not until the next morning dare we peel the blood-soaked nightdress from you and bring ourselves to clean the weals Trevoran inflicted. He sent no one to ask after your wellbeing and by noon the next day had left for London taking Thomas with him, together with that pie-faced nanny and Theresa, the rest of the household followed the next day. Trevoran Court is practically shut up; Florrie says dust shrouds have been placed over the furniture in most of the principle rooms. Mrs Treave looked in on you but briefly before leaving with them, her thoughts on her master's treatment of you hidden behind her usual composure. Only a few servants are left here apart from Ty Saffrey and the rest of the estate workers, the rest have all been removed to London. We are still confined here in the West Wing, Ty Saffrey has a lackey posted by the partition at all times of the day and night, their coarse attentions to Florrie and little Daisy as they come and go most tiresome.'

She paused for breath just as Florrie returned, struggling through the door with a wide silver tray, which she set down beside the bed, I begged her stay and join us, but she wouldn't. ''Tis things I must get on with, mistress,' she'd declared her cheeks reddening, the bridge between mistress and servant sometimes difficult to cross. As she turned to leave I remembered the night Jarren came here, it would burn in my heart forever, I had Jeb and Florrie to thank for that and now she had helped Nancy with my care, I thought of her more as a friend than servant.

Slowly I grew stronger, the pain as I walked gradually receding as each day passed. Nancy moved the most comfortable chair over by the casement window and it was here I would sit hoping desperately for word of my son. Thus, I felt a mixture of anticipation and fear when one afternoon I heard an exchange of voices outside my room, one of them male I recognised immediately as belonging to the arrogant Ty Saffrey. Moments later he boldly strode into my room without knocking and made a mock bow.

'Lady Trevoran, tis good indeed to see you much recovered,' he drawled, his lips pursed as if to smirk as I strove to stand up.

It hurt to do so and inwardly I hated myself, but unashamedly I begged him for news of Thomas.

'Of your son I have no word, that's not why I'm here,' he said coldly. 'I forwarded a letter sent to you on to his lordship, he returned it and advised me you may receive it.' He withdrew a folded piece of paper from his pocket and stepped forward, I made to snatch it from his hand, and he drew back. 'Patience, Lady Trevoran, patience,' he purred, making great play of handing it to me once more, his insolence quite undisguised. I turned away and sat again in the chair finding it difficult to fight back the tears of humiliation.

'You may go, Mr Saffrey, you have completed your task,' I snapped, my voice brusque and dismissive, quietly waiting until he'd left before wiping the tears from my eyes and unfolding what I found to be a black edged letter.

My heart sank as I recognised Aunt Sarah's familiar hand, I had always feared such a letter and now it had come. It was dated at the beginning of the previous month. She had written to tell me my father had died at Wellowmead our family home of a heart seizure during his sleep, thankfully she thought it unlikely he had felt any pain and was glad to have been staying with him during the previous two months. There came now a passage in the letter that had been stuck through in different ink. I studied it hard managing to make out some of the words. Words, which repeatedly expressed my father's remorse at my unhappiness.

For a moment I put the letter down my eyes brimming with tears, never ever had I blamed him, it was Charles I blamed. I read on, Charles and his wife were in India so the only close relative at the funeral had been Aunt Sarah; she expressed her sorrow at having to impart this news in such a manner but knew it futile to ask his lordship's permission to visit with me, as ever her thoughts were with me. Folded within her letter was another, that being from Kirby and Browslow, my father's solicitors. My father's small estate and our house in Wellow was left to Charles, this was totally as I'd expected, Charles being his only son. There was a list of items; mainly my mother's which the bank was holding for me but nothing more. Indeed, although Trevoran had paid off Charles's gambling debts and father's creditors, it seemed little capital remained. With great sadness I read through both letters again, another bond with the past forever lost.

CHAPTER TWELVE

Only as summer approached once more did I feel fully recovered from Trevoran's brutal beating. None of his household had returned from London so I knew not how Thomas fared, that he would have received the best attention my husband's money could buy, my only comforting thought.

Then quite unexpectedly at long last word reached us from beyond the confines of Trevoran Court, coming one afternoon as I was sitting with Nancy in the summerhouse by the river under the watchful eye of Ty Saffrey. He sat perched behind his desk before the mullioned window of the land agent's office, his crop of red hair clearly visible. Nancy and I had been reminiscing about my first days at the Star after Jarren and I escaped Ruskin Tripper and the revenue, fleeing for our lives along the beach below Chy-an-Mor to the safety of her father's inn. She'd laughed as I confessed how jealous of Jenny I'd been, her flagrant flirting with Jarren and obvious resentment of me had caused me much distress. I could see Jenny in my mind's eye even now and although I knew there had never ever been anything between them, felt a certain relief that she had found her own beau in Simon.

Twas Jeb who passed the scrap of paper on to Florrie, she hurried straight to find us in the summerhouse and whispered she had something for me. Mindful we were being watched she made to gather up the tray from the wooden table, slipping the note in my hand as she did so. I tucked it up my sleeve glancing at Nancy; heart pounding I glanced up and saw Ty Saffrey striding across the lawns.

With difficulty I hid the turmoil of emotions that instantly welled up and threatened to unsettle my calm composure. Florrie bobbed a curtsey and before Ty Saffrey reached us hurried off. I took no notice of him as he approached, twas only when he spoke, I looked in his direction.

'Tis time I escorted you back to the house,' he stated in his usual brusque manner, casting a quizzical eye on the departing figure hastily making her way back to the house, and then at me whose face burnt red under his scrutiny. I stood up looking down as I smoothed out the folds of my olive-green skirts in what I hoped seemed a leisurely fashion.

I linked my arm through Nancy's and began walking back, not across the lawns but following the gravel path, ever-conscious Saffrey followed only a few paces behind, his brown polished boots crushing the stones beneath them.

Once in my room I sat with Nancy on the bed and removed the fragile piece of paper from my sleeve, twas creased and dirty, and clinging to it a vile smell. On it was scribbled faintly the words *be ready* followed by the letter *t* that was all, for the fragile scrap of paper had become ripped the remaining letters missing, below the word *be* was the initials *J.P.* and however hard I tried to piece the paper together twas impossible to read more. I handed it to Nancy who eagerly scrutinised the message. My heart sang, my beloved Jarren was alive.

'This means Jarren's got something planned, pray to God it includes John,' she whispered, jumping up with excitement, clutching the note close to her chest. When she handed the note back to me her face was flushed with anticipation. I kissed the tiny scrap of paper that could possibly herald our liberty, wishing only that Thomas was here with me but knowing Jarren would do everything he could to reunite us with our son once we were free. Unable to believe after so long that word had come from Jarren, I paced the room unable to rest. Finally, Nancy stood guard by the door whilst I hid the note with the two rings and bag of coins behind the woven tapestry on the wall. The prospect of finally leaving this place had come so unexpectedly upon us, it was hard to comprehend. But indeed, we would be ready, must be ready for the missing letters on the note made it imperative we be ready at any hour of the days to follow.

As usual if I particularly wanted to see Florrie, infuriatingly it was always Meryl who brought our meals and did for us. When questioned she said Florrie had been given some urgent task to perform by Libby Toms. Libby Toms held the position of housekeeper whilst Mrs Treave was in London and was almost as formidable.

Sleep that night was impossible for I tossed and turned waiting to find out how Jeb had come by the note. In the morning again it was Meryl who drew back the drapes and brought my breakfast tray. I requested she ask Florrie to come to my room, but it seemed Florrie was otherwise occupied. Libby Toms had order-ed the servants into a frenzy of activity. My heart sank on hearing this, and I prayed to God it wasn't my

husband's imminent return that had set her about preparing the house, silently I pleaded, not now, that would
be too unfair.

I felt so claustrophobic I sent word we be allowed to
spend time in the garden, surprised when this was granted
for it was a concession not often agreed to, and after all
we had only been there yesterday. Ty Saffrey came himself
to escort us downstairs, for some reason we were not
allowed on the stretch of land which fronted the river,
two of Ty Saffrey's lackeys accompanied us making sure
we didn't do so. We walked through the rose garden, and
then shivered as the path led us under a canopy of trees
shielding us from the sun, when we emerged from this we
were almost at the entrance of the courtyard. I looked
back; the lackeys were some way behind us now and on
impulse caught hold Nancy's hand as we turned a corner,
dragging her down an overgrown path that led to the
back to the stables.

Breathless we waited, when Saffrey's men realised
we'd vanished they caused a great commotion hollering
the place down as they looked for us, shouting for others
to join them. No doubt terrified of Ty Saffrey's wrath.

When the scurry of activity died down and all was
quiet, I told Nancy to stay hidden and crept out determined to find Jeb. The courtyard and stable blocks
seemed deserted and I prayed Jeb hadn't been called
away to help search for us, relieved to find him alone,
whistling away busy in the stable of a grey stallion his
back towards me.

I pushed aside the half door and stepped silently onto
the hay-strewn floor, rays of sunlight streaming into the
hot dust speckled interior. I watched as Jeb thrust his
pitchfork into a bale of hay, then almost drop it with

surprise at seeing me standing almost behind him. He lowered the fork and touched his cap, but I had no time to observe the necessities of propriety and begged him tell me who gave him the scrap of paper.

Unfortunately, Pierce Tredavik who to my knowledge had not visited Trevoran Court since his Uncles departure, chose just that moment to do so. He must have ridden under the archway and into the courtyard very quietly for so intent was I in listening as Jeb told me of the dishevelled man who'd been lying in wait to see him by the west gatehouse, that neither of us heard the hooves on the cobbles until it was too late. Dismounting just outside the open stable door, whip in hand, Pierce chided, 'Fraternising with the stable lads now are we? Be careful, Layunie, one bastard fobbed off as his lordship's heir is quite enough.' A disdainful sneer blighted his features. Oh! How I loathed him.

Jeb quickly stepped through the doorway and took hold the reins of Tredavik's lively chestnut stallion, leading it off to a stable on the opposite side of the yard. Tredavik's eyes held mine and in a deliberately slow manner he pulled off his black riding gloves then stood tapping his whip against his right boot.

'Can't wait to tell my uncle of your little escapade,' he mocked triumphantly. 'I'm about to leave for London, Layunie, and will tell him the moment I get there.'

His over familiarity with the use of my name, was infuriating in the extreme. My face reddened, I knew he'd take great pleasure in telling Trevoran and scolded myself inwardly at being found here. Frustrated also at not learning more from Jeb. I could utter no plausible reason why I was here for it was common knowledge

I loathed horse riding and, on any account, would not have been permitted to do so even if it were otherwise.

We stood two enemies staring at each other with undisguised hatred, and it was he who glanced away first. Boldly I stepped out into the courtyard and turned my back on him, purposefully walking back towards the rose gardens, leaving the unfortunate Jeb to bear Tredavik's wrath.

Nancy crept out from where she'd remained hidden and walked beside me. I spoke not a word and Nancy knew better than to question me, as somehow I struggled to hold back tears of anger and overwhelming helplessness. Jarren must come soon for I could not live like this much longer.

In silence we made our way back towards the house stopping momentarily to sit beneath the bower of a large oak tree, looking innocently surprised when almost immediately one of Ty Saffrey's men spied us, and pulling a dirty handkerchief from his pocket to dab his forehead ordered us return to the house.

Once safely ushered inside, we overheard talk amongst the servants that Storpe was due to return, together with other members of the household, this was the reason our walk earlier had been restricted. I had had little to do with Storpe, a hook-nosed disdainful fellow who dealt with Trevoran's legal matters.

Later I witnessed his arrival as I drew in the casement window of my room, closing it against the cool breeze that had found its way up from the coast. Looking down and across the lawns my gaze was held by the sight of white sails drifting beyond the trees, silently drawing in beside the Trevoran jetty with the responding scurry of activity below. I watched Storpe and a procession of tired green and gold liveried footmen as they made their way to the house, followed by a couple of giggling maids clutching up their skirts as they ran to catch up. I watched as Jeb took the cart along the narrow strip of track beside the river to the jetty, praying that Theresa and Thomas were returning also. On impulse as Storpe came closer and passed almost underneath my window, I unfastened the catch and threw it open.

'How fares my son, Mr Storpe?' I implored, not caring who heard. All eyes were upon me, as Storpe at first appeared to ignore my plea, then abruptly stopped and looked up, his bulbous watery eyes totally cold, his jowled face red from embarrassment or fury I could not tell.

'You have no son, madam, no son,' he spluttered, before continuing on, ignoring me as I screamed at him to tell me more, the pitying look on the faces of the servants giving me no cause for comfort, the giggling maids subdued now as meekly they followed the others.

On whose orders I know not, only that twas Meryl that continued to do for us and even then, this was under the watchful eye of one of Ty Saffrey's men. Our meals were left for us at the hatch, but it made no difference for I couldn't eat, my mind focused solely on my son and Storpe's words. *'You have no son.'* Did this mean that my lovely baby boy had died? Distraught, I hammered on the partition demanding Storpe be brought to me but there was no response. Libby Toms distressed by my frantic behaviour tried to pacify me and I begged Florrie be allowed bring my meals, but I never saw her and three days later Storpe and the others were gone along with more of Trevoran's possessions and Meryl, who I wasn't displeased to see leave.

It was when I saw Florrie struggling down to the jetty with her heavy carpetbag, one of the last to leave, that my heart wrenched with despair. She set it down and looked up at my window wiping away tears with the back of her hand. I cried too, overwhelmed with the shock and sorrow of her leaving. Florrie had been a good friend as well as a loyal servant, I knew how much she loved Jeb, knew they'd begun to make plans for the future, taking her away from here was so unjust my heart broke for her. There would be no goodbye kiss from Jeb, he was nowhere in sight. In the distance the figure of Storpe stood supervising the loading of the ship. I watched as Florrie disappeared from view and took the handkerchief Nancy held out for me, turning to look back across to the river, as the sails were unfurled. I clutched at the window, lightheaded and upset beyond words, dismayed when I saw a gloating Ty Saffrey watching me from the gravel path below.

* * * * * * * * * * * * * * * * * * *

Life settled back to its usual succession of boring days though we were ever ready should we receive further word from Jarren. We had a new maid, who'd come down from the London house and appeared mortified at being left behind here in Cornwall. I learnt this from Daisy who'd imparted this piece of gossip to me as she laid out my clothes the day after Storpe and the others departed.

'She doesn't mix with no one, or talk to no one below stairs, not a soul, right misery that Ruby is,' Daisy exclaimed. 'Speaks so little it's a wonder anyone knows her name, upset cause she got herself a young man in London is all I heard from cook.'

With me, Ruby was tight lipped and unresponsive to my plea for information as to my son, she flounced around carrying out her duties ill-tempered and rude in manner. When I happened to overhear a sharp exchange of words between her and Libby Toms on the stairs beyond the partition, heard the warning from Libby Toms she'd be dismissed if her sullen way continued, I had an idea, and placed upon the tray Ruby was about to collect two gold coins retrieved from the little leather pouch Aunt Sarah had given me; twas a gamble but knowing now how much the girl wanted to get back to her sweetheart in London, one worth taking.

I placed my hand over the money once she'd seen it, her eyes round as saucers eyes glinting with the prospect of receiving such a sum.

'How fared my son in London? Was Thomas alive when you set out on your journey here?' I asked.

'I only been there a couple of months and I ain't seen no little 'un at all, if one had been there, I'd have seen it,' Ruby responded dourly. I raised my hand and greedily she snatched up the coins. Tossing her head in the air she walked meaningfully from my room, no doubt to collect her things from the attic and be gone. Once more I grieved for Thomas, turning over in my mind Storpe's words a thousand times, Ruby's too, until it seemed they must mean my son had died of the measles in London.

We never saw Ruby again and Daisy took over her duties. These were sad days and to recount how many times I retrieved and unfolded that tattered piece of paper and re-read it is impossible to recall. What word the letter t was to form I never fathomed. A week passed and then another, a new girl took on Daisy's previous duties; she'd also come from the London house. A shy creature who fled quickly from my presence, and with whom I had no conversation.

Then came that night, the memory of what happened stills brings a glow of warmth to my cheeks and a quickening of my heartbeats, for I awoke in the dead of night as a rough calloused hand was lightly placed across my mouth. 'Tis me Jarren,' a voice whispered, so recognisable I nearly died, as his warm breath brushed my face. With urgency his lips sought mine and swiftly he pulled aside the bed covers to lie beside me, unlacing the ties on my cambric nightdress and letting it fall open. I gasped and cried out softly filled with wanton lust as Jarren explored my body and I his, like so long ago, dismayed when abruptly he drew away and climbed from the bed. He leant over me and kissed my forehead.

'There's time for pleasuring later, my sweet, we must be gone; John Penrose is waiting down by the river, go fetch Nancy, then get yourself dressed.'

I slipped from the bed and for a brief moment wound my arms around his waist. 'I thought you'd never come for me,' I murmured, my words lost as I nestled in the warmth of his body. With resolve he took hold my arms and gently pushed me away.

'Fetch our son and Nancy now,' he urged.

'Thomas isn't here,' I spluttered. 'Trevoran's taken him away, I've had no word, he was ill when he took him, I'm not sure if he's still alive even.' I saw the pained look on Jarren's face before I crept across the room to fetch Nancy, opening the door enough to hear the rhythmic snoring of one of Ty Saffrey's lackeys posted on guard the other side of the partition.

Terrified lest I made some sound, I crept into Nancy's room and shook her awake, putting a finger to her lips and taking her hand in mine. 'Tis happening now; Jarren's here with John. You're to come to my room, get dressed as quickly as you can.' Stunned into wakefulness, as I closed her door she was already out of bed.

When I returned, Jarren helped as hurriedly I shed my nightgown and struggled into my petticoats and the plainest of dresses. I fetched out the thickest of my cloaks and Jarren placed it gently about my shoulders. Twas then I retrieved the keepsake rings from their hiding place along with Aunt Sarah's little bag of money. I handed him the gold ring with its strange crest, the ring he'd given me as we fled through the woods the day Joshua was killed, he kissed it solemnly before sliding it slowly onto his finger.

'Tell me more of our son later,' he said in a voice heavy with emotion, for we mustn't tarry, it's time we were gone.' I saw his sigh of relief when Nancy silently entered the room. Hastily he pulled aside the heavy drapes covering the open window and ushered us towards it.

'I found the doors of the balcony sealed and nailed shut, this window is the only way I could gain entry and help you escape from. I watched earlier and saw you looking down from it towards the river.' He held out his hand and helped me climb from a chair, out through the casement to sit petrified on the ivy-covered ledge.

'I'll hold the rope steady,' he whispered calmly. 'Be brave and let go the window then hold tight the rope with both hands, my arms will be around you, you can't fall, twill be alright, I promise, I'll come back for you, Nancy, and you do the same.'

The prospect of doing such a thing frightened me beyond belief. 'What if—' I began to say but Jarren wasn't listening, already his hands were reaching for the rope. His dark eyes bade I do as he bid and taking a deep breath, I did as he'd ordered, I dare not look down. Petrified I clutched the rope and slowly descended, grateful when I felt the ground beneath my feet. Jarren climbed back up and moments later Nancy was standing safely beside me.

Jarren shook free the rope, curling it loosely round his right hand, urging us to follow as he ran towards a nearby coppice. The pungent smell of the river and the cool damp air caught in my throat making me breathless as I fought to keep up. We made our way further on, to a place where the trees dipped into the river; under these a small boat was moored on the muddy bank; beside it, John stood anxiously waiting ready to cast off.

Nancy ran to him and they stood arms entwined, quite still, reunited at last. I heard her sobbing with joy and Jarren and I slowed our pace giving them a moment alone.

Then some way off a dog barked startling us all, wasting no time, Jarren lifted me into the boat stealing a quick kiss as John tenderly picked up Nancy and placed her on the wooden seat beside me.

'Tis good to see you, John,' I sighed, as nimbly he jumped on board.

'And you, Miss Layunie,' he replied, steadying the boat as Jarren pushed off from the bank, both men losing no time in taking a set of oars. Neither showed any sign of the weakness they must feel from their sufferings in Bodmin. The waters of the Fal slipped quickly by as we followed the outline of its dark tree lined banks. I hugged Nancy with joy, then turned my gaze once more upon the man I loved, a lump came to my throat, praise God we were free.

The bound oars were almost soundless as they cut through the choppy waters, the breeze quickening as we travelled further down river, each of us watchful, listening, praying none had been alerted to our leaving or that a revenue cutter would appear on the river. I sensed where we were heading, as swiftly we slid past tree-shrouded creeks. Jarren and John were beginning to tire now, the years of deprivation suffered in Bodmin sapping their strength. At last Jarren drew in his oars and John likewise. It pained me to see Jarren so weak and John slumped forward now against his oars. Jarren turned, saw his friend so and told him to rest, stating with confidence and giving me a broad smile, 'I know these waters; we're almost there.' It wasn't long before he began to steer the boat closer the bank on our right, catching hold the cascade of branches above us and gliding the boat beneath them. My hands gripped the side of the boat as it struck against the protruding roots of trees reaching out into the river. It was dark, this enclosed world that led into our hidden creek, but I was overwhelmed to be here once again. The boat bumped against the bank as the water became too shallow and Jarren jumped ashore. At this early hour the creek had that familiar eerie feel to it, a low mist hung over the water, damp and clinging, the faint lapping of the tide against the muddy bank suddenly bringing Joshua to mind and with it the memory of his terrible death. I shivered as Jarren reached for my hand, carefully helping me out of the boat, he saw tears form in my eyes and held me close.

'Tis of Joshua you're thinking, mourn him we must, but tis the future we must look to.' I gripped his jacket then slipped my arms beneath it and round his waist feeling the warmth of his body, his shirt damp with sweat clinging to his back, loath to let him go.

'I know, but he was such a good true friend,' I murmured.

'Indeed he was, maid,' he whispered back softly.

I sought the comfort only Jarren could give me, our return here brought with it a sadness, not only the memory of Joshua, but of that fine morning when we left this haven, setting out for our wedding from this very shore, the Fortunes Fair at Penryn and our midnight wedding at St Gluvius, the promise of the future which lay ahead and the horror which followed.

After John pulled the boat ashore, we set out for the cottage. 'It's but a few minutes more,' Jarren said to comfort Nancy as together we struggled to keep up with our menfolk, our velvet slippered feet sinking into the muddy path. Faint fingers of dawn crept over the sky as we passed the stark ruins of Rosecarren. Then suddenly twas impossible to go further, the patch of ground from the cottage leading down to the creek always overgrown and was no more, the dense forest had closed in and reclaimed it, the cottage almost completely lost from sight. John slumped against a tree and Jarren handed him a hip flask. He shook his head, but Nancy persuaded him to drink from it, the dark rum trickling down his beard as she held it to his mouth. It began to rain the squally misty rain so beloved of Cornwall and Jarren looked at his friend with concern.

'We must press on,' he urged. 'A couple of hours rest will do you good and it will be yours to have shortly.' I watched as John pulled himself together and nodded in agreement. Jarren drew a knife from his belt, its blade glinting in the dawn light as he began physically fighting a path through the overgrown tangle of brier and forest.

The cottage door hung half open, time and the elements had taken their toll, Jarren wrenched the door from its hinges and threw it aside. Sadly, the cottage afforded little shelter, the floor upstairs and the roof all but collapsed, now a pile of rubble on the floor. Only the walls and stout chimney remained. Above us in the far corner part of the floor hung precariously from the wall at a slant, twas to reach here we picked our way through the debris grateful to find somewhere to shelter from the rain.

John stumbled wearily over a heap of rotten timbers and slid to the floor resting his head against the cob wall.

'Here, friend, have a drink,' Jarren insisted, handing him the hip flask and John gratefully took a swig of rum, then passed it on to Nancy managing a weak smile, by the time she had taken it from his hand he was asleep.

I wanted to ask so much, and Jarren sensing this put his arm round me, deftly un-braiding my hair and letting it fall free. 'Be patient, I'll tell you all there is to know, my sweet, but not now, suffice that Giles should have the *Rosemary* anchored down at Mylor waiting for us. At last I get to take my bride to Porth Tallus.' He looked across at Nancy.

'Giles will take you and John further up the coast to Looe, there's a cottage for you there, one of my uncle's by the boatyard.' He looked anxiously at John clearly troubled.

'Alas we can't linger here however much John needs to rest, you'll be missed shortly, if not already and it won't be long before there'll be a thorough search both up and down the Fal for none will want to face Trevoran's wrath, they'll hope to find you before he gets to find out.' He took hold a twig lying on the floor and began to make a pattern in the dirt.

'Tis John I'm worried about,' Nancy sighed, as she stroked her sweetheart's face. 'Will he be alright, Jarren?' Her tear-filled eyes seeking the reassurance I hoped he give.

'Twill be fine, food is what he needs and the love of a good woman, I know tis brutal but in a minute or so we must be on our way, to stay here longer would be foolish.' Loath to wake John, we tarried a few minutes longer, then Jarren gently shook his friend awake.

'Not much further, we'll cut across the headland and soon be there, and you can rest, my friend.'

He put his arm round John's waist supporting him as we began to trudge on through the dense woodland, the cottage left behind once more. We set out making our way through the trees away from the river, and here suddenly we came across a pedlar his quizzical face quite deformed and horrible. He was slumped against a tree as if in a stupor but as we passed I saw his eyes alert with mischief. A knot of fear tightened in my stomach, I'd seen him once before at Trevoran Court, Ty Saffrey holding him by the scruff of the neck and hauling him off the estate. It was difficult to know if he'd seen me then or not. Jarren ignored him half-carrying John as we hurried past but try as I might the image of the pedlar stayed with me. I needed to tell Jarren I'd seen him before but now wasn't the right time.

Twas a relief when at last through the trees I caught sight an expanse of water and upon its mirrored surface the *Rosemary* waiting, sails unfurled. Jarren paused, setting John down upon a fallen tree to rest.

'Praise God she's here, soon we'll be truly free.' He raised his hands to his mouth about to signal those on board, and then stopped; someone was coming. We drew back a little into the shadows watching as a pony came into sight trotting along the track beside the creek drawing behind it a wagon, an old woman heavily shawled cursed the animal as she passed, we watched relieved when a little further on, still cursing she disappeared down a narrow lane and out of sight.

Jarren gave the signal which was answered by the same low whistle. We watched as a small boat was lowered, it caused ripples on the still water as it came towards us. Two hefty sailors lifted John on board, the rest of us wasting no time in clambering aboard, my gaze fixed on the shore as we left it behind, my heart fearful should our escape somehow be prevented. Not until we were safely on board the *Rosemary* hugged by Giles and warmly greeted by those of his men who knew Jarren from days past, did I feel safe. Giles hurried us below deck his men anxious to get under way, could this really be happening were we really to be free?

Hastily Giles sought a cabin for John and Nancy. Totally exhausted, John staggered unable to stand, he leaned against Giles for support, his face ashen unable to move his limbs, feet dragging on the floor. It pained me to see him so and Nancy's face portrayed her fears as she waited, eyes glazed with tears, watching as Giles gently lay John on the wooden bunk trying to make him as comfortable as he could, asking a sailor bring another blanket and water to the cabin.

We took our leave now, as Nancy sat beside the already sleeping John her hand in his. Giles hurried back on deck but telling Jarren first we were to have his cabin as before.

Once Jarren closed the door behind us I asked the question I'd been longing to, 'How come you escaped?'

But Jarren was tired. 'Later, Layunie, I'll tell you in good time.' I rested my head against his chest, feeling the motion of the ship as she slipped out from Mylor and rounded the headland into the Carrick Roads, knowing I wouldn't feel we were out of danger till we'd made safe passage out between the two castles and were far from Falmouth.

'Rest, little one, all will be well,' Jarren soothed lifting me onto the wide bunk and climbing in beside me. I nestled into his harsh woollen coat oblivious to the clinging smell of Bodmin Gaol, waking with a start when Giles returned later, bringing with him a bundle of clean clothes.

'Take these, cuz, there's a barrel of water up on deck waiting for you, and that's an order, you smell dreadful.' Jarren eased himself up and dutifully followed his cousin, looking back to blow me a kiss as he did so.

Alone I lay on the bunk too frightened something would go wrong to be entirely happy. Jarren returned smelling much better than he had, and without the heavy growth of beard, he looked more like the Jarren I knew. We were joined by Giles who brought with him a small cask of rum and three tumblers, setting them down upon the locker with its gold gilt rail.

'Have we passed out of Falmouth waters?' I questioned, and Giles gave me a broad grin.

'Indeed we have, indeed we have.'

I hugged them both in turn; tears of joy streaming down my face, hoping upon hope that this time our luck would hold.

'I'll never be able to repay you; you know that, don't you,' Jarren told him, 'tis funny but I believe we've succeeded this time, I feel it in my bones, we're free.' He hugged me to him, and I so prayed he was right.

Giles let out a good measure of rum into the tankards. 'I know you'd do the same for me, it's the bond of blood coursing through our veins that binds together.'

'On my honour I would,' Jarren replied. 'A toast to all of us aboard the *Rosemary*, may she sail into safe waters.' We raised our glasses clinking them together as the ship ploughed on through the sea into deeper waters far offshore, the rum warming my aching body and bringing a glow to my cheeks.

Later we joined Giles and food was brought to us, cold meat and thick chunks of bread, served in the same low ceiled room where an age ago, Giles had unrolled the map of Cornwall. I remembered how I'd studied the coastline with excited anticipation, listened as he told us of our destination, watched as he pointed out where we would land and the place where we were to begin our new lives, before fate had altered everything.

'A toast to your freedom,' Giles declared, pouring Jarren another measure, which he downed in one swallow, Giles refilling his glass not once but twice.

'And a toast to Jacky Swannell,' Jarren said, putting his arm round me. 'We all cursed him when old Tripper found us, but tis trumps he came up in the end, God save his soul if he's got one,' he joked, and I looked on puzzled waiting for some kind of explanation.

'I'll tell you later,' was all he teased, stifling a yawn.

'Away with you now, tis bed you need cuz,' Giles said, 'we'll talk more tomorrow.'

In all truth I was finding it hard to keep awake, relieved to follow Jarren to Giles' cabin, welcoming its familiar smell of beeswax and tobacco, remembering the time we'd spent here, the night we were wed. Jarren took my hand and gently squeezed my fingers, a silent shared moment of memory forever ours.

'Tis but one thing I need from my cabin, then it's all yours,' Giles said, pulling the drawer beneath the bunk open and taking out a clean shirt.

Footsteps sounded overhead, I shuddered clutching hold of Jarren, instantly jolted back to that morning at Trehallan's Quay.

'Have no fear, Layunie, tis a small trusted crew on board, men from St Ives.' Giles's meaning was perfectly clear, but my heart still beat a little faster.

Jarren clambered onto the bunk and lay sprawled in the middle his eyes closed. Giles turned towards me and winked mischievously. 'Layunie, you look as lovely as ever, alas I must say no more, for he can be a jealous brute.' Jarren opened his eyes and looked over pulling me possessively towards the bunk, with his brown eyes twinkling with laughter he moved over and made room for me.

'Come here, wife,' he ordered, patting the bed grinning broadly at Giles as he left us alone closing the door tightly shut behind him.

I climbed in and curled up beside him our arms entwined his lips on mine, soft and comforting. There'd be no lovemaking tonight for we were both more than tired, I lay not even removing my dress, happy to stay thus, lulled to sleep by the rhythmic roll of the *Rosemary*.

We were awakened at dawn by a loud knocking on the door. Without waiting, two ragtag sailors pushed it open and struggled in, carrying between them a heavy wooden tub with rope handles three quarters full of steaming water. Jarren raised his head to look at them sleepily nodding his thanks, whilst I felt my face redden as they touched their forelocks in an embarrassed greeting on leaving. I snuggled closer to Jarren stroking his face, sharing a moment of closeness with him, a short while ago a time like this I'd despaired of ever enjoying again.

Softly I traced the rugged scar on his shoulder, remembered our first lovemaking at Nancledra, and tingled with desire. He kissed the palm of my hand and I saw in his dark eyes the same memory; with urgency he tilted my chin upwards bringing my face closer to his. My heart quickened as his mouth sought mine hard and demanding, as with one hand he began unlacing my dress, growing ever more impatient as he fought to free me of it, cursing the tiny hooks and eyes until finally the bodice slipped from my shoulders. We could wait no longer and in a flurry of discarded clothes we sought to satisfy each other's needs, his touch upon my body setting it on fire, unleashing pent up passion and wanton lust, the aching want in my belly rose, a want so strong twas one only Jarren could satisfy, his need for me bringing us both to the height of abandoned fulfilment until truly satisfied we lay exhausted and naked upon the rumpled bunk.

Twas Jarren broke the contented silence. 'Tis another child I'll give you, tis saddened I am at having been deprived of knowing our first born.' The words spoken softly made me open my eyes, from under his fringe of black curls Jarren's dark eyes were serious, and I felt full of compassion.

'I fear he died of the measles, our little Thomas, he was taken away and I never saw him again.' Jarren listened, as choked with emotion I quietly repeated Storpe's words to me that fateful day and added, a lump in my throat, 'He was a lovely little boy, with such a look of you about him with his dark curls, if Trevoran doubted his parentage, he said nothing. I think his need for an heir was so great he didn't want to know the truth, even when those around him sought to plant suspicion in his mind.'

Softly Jarren kissed my forehead sharing my grief. 'They'll be more sons, my sweet, strong lusty sons that none shall take from us.' His words of comfort did little to soothe me, the memory of Thomas's loss too raw. We lay awhile in silence until Jarren pulled himself up and lay resting on one elbow, his fingers tracing the contours of my body.

'The water in the tub will soon go cold, and them who brought it will be sure displeased if it goes unused, best bathe now, wife, and I can take pleasure in watching.' I slipped from the bunk with its tangle of clothes and blankets and sank down into the lukewarm water, the mischievous smile on Jarren's face rewarded with a quick splash.

When I rose from the tub, Jarren wrapped me in a thick coarse towel, he caressed my shoulders, his thumbs making circles at the base of my neck, softly he kissed me and I turned, his body covered with droplets of cold water glistened invitingly. I let the towel slip and with unashamed urgency he took me there where we stood as daylight shone in through the tiny porthole.

Afterwards it was a rush to get ready. Giles knocked and called out for us to join him and just as we were about to do so, I took from the pocket of my cloak Aunt Sarah's little pouch of money, and gave it to Jarren.

'Tis your money, maid, I'll not be taking it from you,' he insisted, but I placed it inside his hand closing his fingers over it and would not take it back.

Twas all I could do but not cry when once more we were reunited with John and Nancy, pleased to see how much better John looked now he was rested and in fresh clothes. Giles bade us sit at the oblong table and food was carried in on a huge wooden tray. Without protocol we helped ourselves of mutton and potato pie, mortally hungry, it tasted delicious. There was little conversation as we ate and when at last our hunger was satisfied, we sat back and Jarren laid his hand on my shoulder and looked across the table.

'Have you told Nancy the manner our escape?' he asked John.

'No, I've done nothing but sleep, there's been no time.'

I wondered then just how long he'd taken to recuperate and stole a glance at Nancy noticing the unmistakeable tinge of a blush upon her freckled cheeks. Giles refilled our tankards.

'We shall die of curiosity if you don't tell us soon,' Nancy exclaimed, and we both looked at Jarren to enlighten us.

'Tis luck that finally freed us, luck and the help of a brave man.' He looked down at the table and then across to John.

'But we must not forget the help we received from others when times were really hard, when plans painstakingly made, we were forced to abandon more than once.' I felt his sadness, a bitterness that lingered, was eager to learn more but half afraid to listen, almost holding my breath as I waited for my love to continue.

'I'll tell of our actual escape all in good time, what led up to it began with many small changes. I overheard the turnkeys talking as to how Trevoran had set up residence in London, thus his visits to Bodmin ceased, but he left strict orders that I was still to remain in the dark house. Whenever Ruskin Tripper came to Bodmin, as commanded by Trevoran, Harrison Carter had me taken from my cell still fettered in ball and chain and dragged out into the middle of the courtyard, often I'd be left there without food or water chained to the grills of the underground cells, forbidden to be moved until nightfall.' His voice rose and it was obvious how embittered he felt at such treatment. 'Twas insufferable the power that man had over us because of Trevoran.' He banged the table with his fist making the pewter plates jump and ale leap from the tankards.

John spoke now taking up their story. 'It was shortly after one of these visits that Harrison Carter's daughter returned to Bodmin, pregnant with her blue coat's child. After eloping they'd married in Exeter; when her man was posted to far-off Dorchester, she'd sought reconciliation with her father. With her husband's blessing she returned to Bodmin before her time came. It's because of her we had extra rations and our filthy rags exchanged for better, the extra food mightily appreciated, and the turnkeys, liking Suzannah, didn't tell.'

Jarren reached for my hand and drew me over to sit on his knee. 'Your aunt, after Trevorans's mistreatment, returned to Truro and met a beau who gained her access to visit us, I'll tell you more of this later.'

My mouth dropped opened in amazement but knowing Aunt Sarah I shouldn't really be surprised.

Just then one of the Giles's crew knocked and entered, he asked should he alter course and briefly Giles left us to go up on deck. Whilst he was gone, the same two ragtag sailors who'd brought us the tub of water came and cleared away our empty plates. When Giles returned, he leant forward across the table and smiled at Nancy. 'I have kept in touch with your father and all in St Ives, Kate out at Gwithian too. Have no fear all are well.'

'Thank you, Giles.' Nancy beamed with joy and I felt so glad for her.

Jarren resumed telling us their story. ''Tis so much to tell all at once, ladies, suffice to say we made many, many plans to escape but tis like a fortress Bodmin, escape seemed impossible our plans always foiled. Then about two weeks or so ago I was hauled out into the yard, held under the pump to be doused with water when the smell of me got too offensive for the turnkeys. As they led me back, I heard horses ridden hard approaching the main gates, these were hurriedly opened. Ruskin Tripper rode into the courtyard; in one of his black-gloved hands he held the reins of two other horses, two men were draped across their backs. A platoon of dragoons followed through clattering across the cobbles. Tripper ordered the prisoners untied, the ropes were cut through and they fell to the ground, twas then I saw one was Jack Swannell.' Jarren paused and took a sup of ale. I looked at Nancy the name Jack Swannell was one we remembered so well; it had been he they were looking for back then when the revenue searched Trehallan's Quay.

Jarren could see what I was thinking. 'Twasn't his fault we were captured, Layunie, we free traders are always being pursued by the revenue. We're no different from Jack.' He looked at John who nodded in agreement. I felt chastised.

'The poor devils lay where they'd fallen in the dirt, for a moment I thought they were dead, so much blood was seeping through their clothes. Tripper issued an order and Jack was roughly pulled to his feet, too weak to stand he fell to his knees. A dragoon stepped forward and struck him across the face with the back of his hand, another dismounted and forced him to stand up. On Tripper's orders they let Jack fall to the ground there to be kicked unmercifully whilst Tripper watched. Twas brutal. Us prisoners began to jeer and cause a commotion; we made such a din that Tripper's horse reared up almost unseating him. In fury he lashed out at Jack with his whip. Harrison Carter appeared and tried to take control. Jack was picked up and carried off to the dark house, his companion likewise. We were silenced, the turnkeys hastened my return there too, a trail of fresh blood was wet upon the earth floor, still warm underfoot. I had been the lone prisoner here, now my silent tomb was engulfed with muffled cries torn from Jack in the agony of torture. When the turnkeys left, I tried calling Jack's name but got no response I was to learn later they'd left him for dead.'

I shuddered; however bad I'd imagined Bodmin to be it was far, far worse. I listened shocked as Jarren continued, Giles seated now at the top of the table.

'Once they realised Jack might live, I was given the task of feeding him, I and the man captured with him, Ralph Trevenna. Jack was a sick man and the turnkeys wanted nothing to do with him, something foreign he had so they said, and not caring if I lived or died, still shackled wrist to ankles ordered me take over their duties in his cell. I did my best for him but only a miracle would save him.'

Jarren's voice became bitter, knuckles white as he gripped his fists together. 'Unlike me, kept in Bodmin at Trevoran's insistence, Jack and Ralph were to be escorted to Launceston for the next quarter sessions, both would hang. Jack had killed a revenue officer in a fierce battle off Porthleven, Ralph seriously wounding another. Twas as they completed the run they'd been caught. I was there trying to spoon foul-smelling gruel into Jack's mouth when Harrison Carter told them their fate. "I'll never last till then," Jack had half laughed. "Old Judge Potter will have to do without me, or him." He'd nodded in Ralph's direction, for Ralph had given one of the turnkeys a black eye and been flogged for it, the wounds had festered, with a high fever Ralph trembled uncontrollably. "We'll both be long dead before—" He'd had to break off coughing, blood dribbling from his mouth. Harrison Carter withdrew putting a handkerchief to his mouth as Jack struggled to sit up on the damp straw.

'After he'd gone Jack beckoned me closer. "Think, man, t'would be a good way for you to escape, you and John Penrose." He'd paused fighting for breath. "You ever bin before Judge Potter?" he asked. And indeed, both John and I had many years earlier, so I nodded, and he continued.

"So if you and John took our places but didn't manage to escape on the journey and went up before him, he'd know twas you not me, and send you back here, he'd have to. The dragoons knows we'm too ill to escape, be off their guard a bit, tis worth a try, all it needs is them two skull brains to be drunk as usual when they comes for us, like as not twill be well before dawn only the escort party up and about. Harrison Carter'll not get from his bed to see us off, rest of um tucked up in bed, bribe um with this." From a hidden pocket he eased out a bag of gold sovereigns. "We'll change places, tis little difference in rags we'm in, and we're not unalike."

'He looked over at Ralph, his skin sallow and covered in sweat, a large battered hat half obscuring his face. "Twill be a miracle if he makes it through the next few days, better hope tis soon them take us, what say you to my idea?" Jack slumped against the wall, green pus oozed through his shirt where Ruskin Tripper's whip had caught him, he rested his head against the slime covered the wall. "Tis because of me you're here, they was looking for me not you, get out this place, make a plan, go, take a chance at freedom."

As we listened, above us the crew went about their business oblivious to the sad tale Jarren was recounting, the screeching of gulls breaking the silence as we waited to hear more.

'Sometimes lady luck shines down on those who need it, for Giles chose this most appropriate of times to visit Bodmin, that's how he knew to have the *Rosemary* anchored at Mylor waiting should we succeed. As it was, I had but four days to keep Jack and Ralph alive, how much longer they tarried after we'd gone I'll never know.'

He stopped speaking, silent for a moment staring at the table deep in thought. I knew he cared deeply for those poor souls they'd left behind.

'I bribed the turnkeys Scammel and Toms with Jack's gold; John was smuggled across to the dark house on the night required. Twas then we bade Jack and Ralph goodbye.

'Long before dawn the escort came, we were dragged out into the courtyard, the rags we wore so covered in grime they differed not from those of our doomed companions. Ralph's hat shielded John's face from scrutiny. I just had to hope my incarceration in the dark house and beard made me unrecognisable and that the dragoons would have no doubt that Scammel was handing over the correct prisoners. Unshackled, roughly we were heaved up onto the backs of the waiting horses, we didn't need to feign weakness and with heads bowed sat, as though barely conscious, waiting as the dragoon commander ordered the main gates be opened. Our horses restless to begin their journey were led across the courtyard and out into the deserted streets of Bodmin, soon the town lay behind us and the darkened landscape opened out into a sweeping expanse of barren moorland.'

He looked across to John who continued. 'Knowing every nook and cranny of this desolate place, it was just a matter of biding our time. Bodmin Moor held no fears for us, unlike the dragoons wary of the treacherous bogs that claimed lives. Dawn broke as we trekked on through isolated hamlets, past slabs of weathered granite that told us, not them, just where we were. It was bitter cold, the sky darkened and the weather on Bodmin always quick to change did so, swallowing us up in a swiftly descending cloud, surrounding us in a thick swirling mist.

'We journeyed on, knowing not if the escort knew we had strayed from the given route, then as often happens for a moment or two the mist lifted. We came upon a stream, the escort commander put up his hand ordering the straggly line of dragoons to halt. Ignoring their half dead prisoners, glad for a chance to dismount they did so, venturing cautiously down the steep grassy bank to fill their flasks with spring water. Their commander did likewise, twas now we made our escape, untying their horses first. Too late they realised what was happening, we heard their shouts and frantic scrambling, fleeing the musket shot when it came. Frightened their horses galloped away and like us soon were quickly lost from sight in the descending mist. Our journey to Trevoran Court and the rescuing of the women we love proved easy after that!'

John grinned broadly and Jarren laughed hugging me to him. Looking up I saw the familiar twinkle in his so dark eyes as he scrutinised my face, a look so tantalizingly seductive that I read his mood. Without taking his eyes from my face, he gently pulled me to my feet then lifted me into his arms. I glimpsed the roguish look he gave our companions and kissed him, giggling uncontrollably as he carried me off to our cabin. I was so, so happy.

The next day Jarren tried to reassure me we were safe, but still I fretted especially when we went up on deck. Giles had told us he had taken the *Rosemary* out into deep water. It was here I'd feel a knot of fear as the wind tugged at my hair leaving the taste of salt on my lips. Unbidden, my eyes would search the iron grey sea, ever fearful I should sight a revenue sloop cutting through the sea, with the odious Ruskin Tripper at its bow, in tricorn hat and billowing black cloak. I could see him in my mind's eye, even imagine his fox-like features braced for the kill.

I tried as best I could not to let such thoughts spoil the pleasure of these moments, a time of peace when Jarren and I would stand together wrapped warm against the chill winds which filled the *Rosemary*'s sails, him softly brushing back tendrils of hair which danced about my face as we ploughed through the heaving sea. Precious moments when time stood still, a time that held with it the dawn of a new beginning. For we were sailing up the coast to Porth Tallus and Boswedden the safe sanctuary we'd been destined for all that time ago.

Each day our men grew stronger for Giles had made sure the *Rosemary* was well stocked with provisions. Both Nancy and I grateful to be free and with the men we loved, and little by little each day we were to learn how those we cared about fared.

Giles told me of Aunt Sarah's beau in Truro, a wealthy gentleman who was much enamoured of her and would likely as not ask for her hand any day. It was to Truro she'd gone after fleeing from Pierce Tredavik at the coaching inn. Giles had visited her modest abode, for by chance when out walking along the iron quay with her Hector, she'd spotted the *Rosemary* tied up alongside and caught sight of Giles recognising his likeness to Jarren.

I'd spoken to her many times of the *Rosemary* and of Giles. She knew immediately who he was and longed to find out if he had news of us. At the time, the lovelorn Hector had been most perplexed for being Aunt Sarah she'd run in and demanded paper and pen from a near-by bookshop, scribbling a note there and then, and sending the bewildered Hector to walk the gangplank and deliver it.

My eyes filled with tears of laughter, how typical of my impulsive aunt, I longed to see her and wondered when this would be possible and how.

Giles told Nancy further news of her folks in St Ives, of her father and the others at the Star. Jenny and Simon had two boys and another child on the way; they lived in now, running the inn for George. The regulars in the taproom forever asked if there was further word of us and Giles promised George would be told we were safe and where we were bound, but none of the others must know.

It was just before sunset on the third evening as I took a turn on deck with Jarren, we heard Giles shout orders to the crew. I watched, my cloak held tight about me, as they scurried back and forth, two of the crew climbed up the mast. The rigging ropes creaked and quivered, overhead canvas sail flapped wildly about in the quickening breeze. One of them hollered down to Giles who stepped forward to take the wheel, turning it gently but firmly, finally holding her steady. He'd altered course, instinctively I knew we were heading inland towards the coast.

As the *Rosemary* approached the coastline, the sea grew calm, the velvety dark waters barely stirring as we drew nearer the rugged shadow of the headland. A boat was lowered, and provisions taken on board, together with a small cabin trunk that held some quite delightful clothes. Jarren had joked when I took a peek inside, saying he had a good idea where they came from.

I remembered this now as I glanced over towards Giles and could but smile, remembering what Jarren had told me after supper last evening. 'Cousin Giles has found a lady love,' he whispered with a wide grin, for this clearly this amused him. 'Tis apparently the fair maid who keeps Boswedden aired and such, her name's Mercy Martin and he seems much taken with her, me thinks we'll see the *Rosemary* aplenty in the bay and anchored at Portlooe.'

I nestled closer to him eager now to begin the next part of our journey and to see our new home, and although I felt sad knowing we'd soon be parted from Nancy and her John, Jarren assured me they were to live not far away.

For some reason it was then I remembered the pedlar I'd seen on our way to Mylor, and the way he'd looked at me, and told Jarren.

'We're far away from any harm he could do us, twill soon be time to leave the *Rosemary*. Forget about him, my sweet, there's a lot of sea between us and Mylor now.' Indeed that was true and reassured, encircled in Jarren's arms, I gazed out across the sea, the night air holding a still and magical memory I would always remember.

Twas a sad parting for Nancy and myself; when we'd meet again, we must act as if strangers to those around us. We'd shared so much since first we'd met at the Star, supporting each other when our future and the lives of the men we loved seemed so unsure. For a moment our men folk left the two of us alone, their footsteps echoing on the wooden deck as we hugged each other too choked to speak. Nancy's freckled face was wet with tears as I wished her well promising to meet again with her soon.

Giles was anxious we shouldn't tally here with the *Rosemary* silhouetted against the horizon, all may appear quiet but there was always the danger that revenue cutters may be patrolling these waters, or bluecoats watching from the cliffs. He hugged both Jarren and myself, making me blush for, as always, I felt a little shy of him. Four of the crew waited in a boat below, one holding tight the rope ladder the others with oars at the ready, impatient to begin their task. Gathering my skirts around me, Jarren helped me warily over the side of the ship, and I clung tight the moving ladder as the *Rosemary* rose and fell with the gentle swell of the sea, terrified lest I miss my footing, grateful when I was safely on board with Jarren at my side.

Two of Giles's men pushed off from the side of the *Rosemary* and holding the side of the boat I looked up, raising my hand to wave goodbye. A sudden drenching with sea spray drew my eyes away, the boat rocked uncertainly before rhythmically the oars clipped the sea, as swiftly we made our way towards the shore. Once there I held my breath as we threaded our way through the jumble of rocks that jutted out precariously from beneath the cliff.

Skilfully the boat was brought alongside a small island of slate grey rock, and it was here Jarren decided we would go ashore. The boat was secured and steadied as Jarren lifted me out. Shivering and wet through I stood as the provisions on board were unloaded. Giles had instructed Jarren on the direction we must take to reach Boswedden and we set off across the rocks using them like stepping-stones to make our way to the foot of the cliff. Here we found the tiny stream Giles had mentioned with the two steep paths on either side barely visible through the foliage.

We were to take the path that led away to our right; well-worn steps had been carved out of the rock and earth. Jarren led the way taking hold my hand and pulling me up the steep and often almost non-existent steps that slowly began to even out and form a slippery path that wound its way upwards and round the face of the cliff. Breathless we reached the top; I waited chilled to the bone as Jarren returned to help the others who were carrying our provisions, helping to ease their burden as they struggled up quite some way behind.

Looking out to sea, the silhouette of the *Rosemary* indeed stood out against the horizon and I fretted, anxious to be on our way so the crew could return, and Giles set sail. I took hold of some of the smaller bundles they carried, and we started making our way as quickly as we could along the barren cliff top. Then I saw it, a lone building nesting in a small copse the spindly trees bowed by the wind surrounded and sheltered it, this must be Boswedden. As we came closer, I was sure, for it was as Giles had described. A long low building of thick cob walls, larger than a cottage, its roof with arched windows set into it making it quite distinctive. I loved it at first sight.

Once outside, Giles's men set down the trunk and other items they carried. Thanked by Jarren and myself they quickly turned to go, anxious to get back onboard the *Rosemary*. We stood for a moment looking out across Porth Tallus bay enjoying this very precious moment in time, for we were free.

Jarren took from his pocket the ornate key Giles had given him, he unlocked the door and raised the latch. Romantic as ever, he lifted me in his arms, pushing open the door, carrying me over the threshold and into our first home.

CHAPTER THIRTEEN

Thus, for the last twenty-one years, Boswedden has been our home. Thomas, I must tell you, your father Jarren, his black locks now peppered with grey, remains as ever the handsome Cornishman who stole that first kiss in the cellar at Tremaron. The laughter in his eyes and mischievous smile still much beloved by me and inherited by our sons; perchance, Thomas, you have it too.

But of course, none of this you would have known had it not been for two happenings in this past year of 1743. It is these that have set my mind to write down my story and try and right the wrongs you surely have been told about my character. I loved you very much and beg you believe this to be true. During these last months that I remain in Cornwall, tis been agreed between your father and myself I write it all down for you to judge me as you will. It is but only recently I heard you were living; this came as a great shock for I truly believed you had perished of the measles.

As I have written it down, pray believe it is the truth. You were taken from Trevoran Court by the man you thought to be your father so his physician could treat you in London. And I heartlessly told 'I had no son' by Storpe, Trevoran's manservant. His words have never left me for I took them to mean you had died of the measles at the place where you'd been taken.

As you, my first born, read these journals, I beg you believe that throughout the passing years you were never far from my thoughts, even after your three brothers were born. Jack, nine months after we came here, followed in quick succession by Matthew, Josh and your sister Crinnis, who is to be fourteen in but a little while. Trevoran's cruelty and my forced separation from you still brings tears to my eyes. Storpe's words 'You have no son' stark darts upon my heart.

Before I continue to tell you more of my present circumstance, firstly I must tell the remainder of my story.

I loved Boswedden from the very moment your father Jarren carried me over the threshold. Once Giles's men had gone, he lit a taper and by the little light it gave we could see our home was sparse of furniture. Unlived in for so long it smelt damp and fusty, the atmosphere sadly forlorn, but as I stood shivering with cold, my cloak and dress hanging heavy about me soaked with spray from the sea, I fell in love with my new home.

We set about making Boswedden our home. At first the villagers viewed us newcomers with undisguised suspicion, but Jarren worked his charm on those whose trust of outsiders mattered most. The fact that his uncle was Gabriel Galley down in Portlooe, a man well known and much respected, made it easier for us to become accepted into the tiny community of Porth Tallus.

Many times during those early days I'd find some small token of Boswedden's former resident, a quill beneath the settle, a scrap of paper with unreadable writing discarded at the back of a drawer and wondered what happened to the man who'd lost everything he possessed gambling at the card table.

We spent only a little of what remained of Aunt Sarah's money, hiding the rest well out of reach inside one of the numerous vaulted rafters. Soon Jarren was earning his living fishing, with John alongside him. Giles's father Gabriel providing their boat, another legacy from Boswedden's unlucky former owner.

Our first visitor to Boswedden had been Mercy Martin, Giles's apparent ladylove. Warily, I'd peeped from the window at the sound of someone approaching, wishing Jarren were there, relieved to see a young woman of about my age in a dark blue dress and black shawl, her cream bonnet askew. She struggled to control the bad-tempered mule harnessed to an over laden cart. I went out to help her almost getting bitten by the brutish mule as I helped restrain it. A bond was formed as we set about unloading the strange selection of furniture Jarren's Uncle Gabriel had sent up from Portlooe. Ill matched chairs and tables, two hideous armchairs, heavy cases surprisingly well packed with delicate china and the finest of cutlery. By the time our task was complete, I knew that I'd made my first friend here in Porth Tallus.

Only a short while later, Giles and Mercy wed in the tiny church on the quay in Portlooe near Harbour house. It was there Jarren's Uncle Gabriel lived, not forty paces from the quay, in a splendid house overlooking the busy harbour. He returned to his other house in Porthleven only when business matters decreed. And Harbour House was where Giles and Mercy made their home too and brought up their twin sons.

When I first met him, Jarren's Uncle Gabriel was much as I'd imagined, his eyes held the same depth of warmth, and although his hair was snowy white, he still remained a very handsome man, who at our first meeting waved aside my thanking him for providing us with a home, as though twas nothing. Over the coming years his home would become a meeting place where all would frequently gather, a house where there was much happiness and laughter, tears too when nigh on fifteen years ago the *Rosemary* was lost, driven by fierce gales onto the rocks at Pencarrow. Giles and the crew were lucky to escape with their lives, leaping into the perilous waters, clambering over the rocks to safety, watching helpless as she was smashed to pieces. Her silhouette upon a moonlit sea that first night we set foot upon Porth Tallus soil, a sight I shall never forget.

Angry and dismayed by her tragic loss, and with a badly injured arm, Giles was forced to stay ashore. Restless and ill-tempered, he gradually began taking over control of the boat yard Gabriel had acquired upriver, and as his father got older, gradually began to oversee all his many business interests.

One regret I have is that sadly I was never to see my dearest Aunt Sarah again. Six months after our arrival, Giles made it his business to seek her out when in Truro. He'd stood uncertain before the open door of the house he'd visited previously. There was mayhem within for that very day she was preparing to leave for her husband's estate in Scotland. Warmly she'd welcomed Giles into her near empty parlour, recounting how word had reached her of Jarren's escape, mine too from Trevoran Court, overjoyed that at last I was with the man I loved. Quickly she scribbled a short note wishing us well and giving her new abode as Manor Rising. But its exact location in Scotland she failed to write down. I kept that note in a wooden box beside my bed, but in all these years never saw her again.

With the passing of time, I knew your father and John were drawn back into the world of the free traders. Nancy and I spending many a night afeard they would be caught, but they never were, and I kept silent knowing it would do no good to try and change the man I loved.

It is time now to turn to the present and of the happenings that led me to write these journals. The first of these was the sudden death of Uncle Gabriel who'd been caught in a sudden squall whilst out fishing and subsequently caught a chill. At first it seemed no worse than the many other chills he'd suffered, but one night a week later Mercy sent word, summoning us to Harbour House. His condition had rapidly worsened. Eyes closed he lay in the four-poster bed, his breathing shallow and rasping, his cheeks and forehead afire with fever. Dr Tregonning came and having examined his patient stood looking gravely down on his old friend, watching silently whilst Mercy wiped his brow with a cool cloth. As he turned to speak with Giles, I saw sympathy in his eyes and my heart contracted in dismay, I knew then twas nothing he could do. By dawn, Jarren's most wonderful uncle and Giles's father had lost his struggle to live.

The sorrow we felt at his passing is too hard to put down in words. We mourned him, his funeral bringing no ending to our grief, nor the passing of time, an emptiness in our lives remains still.

The task of settling his business affairs and the sale of the property in Porthleven fell to Giles as his son. Accompanied by Jarren he left for Porthleven a week after the funeral. Mercy and I standing on the bridge of seven arches in Portlooe, watching as they began their sad journey.

On their return it was clear what they found hidden away in a carved wooden sea chest in Gabriel's house in Porthleven both troubled and excited them. Great bundles of age-old documents some which appeared to be land titlements, many bearing the name of Alimorante. The Spanish inscriptions and writings too complex and intricate for Giles with his little knowledge of the language to interpret, but he vowed to have them read, the correspondence too addressed to his father dated some fifty years previous.

Jarren seemed unsettled and disturbed by what they'd found, seeing his mother's name faded upon the parchment a potent reminder of the young woman who when dragged from the sea, had survived barely long enough to give him life before losing her own. To me her name brought an instant memory, the sight and smell of the wild white roses around the ruins of Rosecarren and her lonely solitary grave.

Once back in Portlooe, they'd brought the chest by pony and cart up to Boswedden for we had no servants to pry. And after telling us of its contents, Jarren had sat brooding and silent, Giles too.

Long after Giles and Mercy had gone home and the rest of your brothers and sister had gone to bed, Jarren sat quite still, watching as candlelight flickered on the chest's elaborate broken clasp. Finally, he went over and lifted the heavy lid.

'Look on this, Layunie,' he called to me, and thrust a yellowed document into my hand. Twas a simple message written in the hand of his uncle and addressed to Giles. It read:

"Upon hearing of my dear sister's death, I locked this chest forever, though I have not the heart to destroy its contents, but pray take no notion to act upon your findings within, t'would be too dangerous to do so."

The need to know more about the documents contained in the chest became an obsession with both Giles and Jarren and it was this desire to know more that set us on the road to Liskeard barely three weeks later. A scholar was to be found there who Giles hoped would be able to translate the documents. It was also the week of the May fair and Mercy and I begged go with them climbing into the back of the wagon with the thickest of cloaks wrapped around us as long before dawn, we began our journey.

As the sun rose so it brought warmth to our bones, dispelling the clinging fingers of mist that followed us along gutted lanes leading inland. When we reached the edge of the market place in Liskeard, Jarren helped Mercy and myself down from the wagon. I stood smoothing out my rumpled skirts my legs stiff and aching, as he gave me a parting kiss and pressed some coins in my hand.

'In a while wait for us here, tis impossible to say how long we'll be gone, a little patience I beg, sweet wife, for we go in seek of a possible fortune.'

I placed my hand on the front of his jacket and reached up to kiss him knowing he and Giles were eager to be gone. I sensed the excitement in them, dreaded that today would somehow change our lives forever. Jarren saw my frown.

'Don't go fretting now,' were his parting words, on his face that special smile, and I raised my hand to wave as he and Giles disappeared through the mingling crowds. Mercy linked her arm in mine, the sight of the market stalls and smell of the baker's fare leading us happily into its midst. I sensed she too was worried but as we watched the brightly clothed juggler delighting his raggedly clad audience, like me she could but smile.

After a while, I left Mercy choosing ribbons for a new bonnet and thought it best to return to where we were to meet our menfolk, resting a while on a low cob wall until they returned. It was here my senses were jolted and heartbeat quickened, as I thought I recognised across the square a once familiar face. For a moment I lost sight of her and felt pure panic, my eyes searching though the crowds to seek her out, and then I did; many years had passed but I was certain who she was. A group of rowdy drunkards scattered as a fine coach with resplendent coat of arms upon its doors stopped before the entrance of the inn where she stood. A liveried servant jumped down and opened the door of the coach and she handed her small charge into the outstretched arms of a lady within. The door was shut, and she stood back as the coachman whipped up the horses and was gone.

I watched as another coach jolted forward and took its place, an array of luggage was being brought forth and realised it too was about to depart. I darted through the crowds, touching the waiting woman on her shoulder as she stood with her back to me talking to a young servant girl.

Theresa May turned around, as recognition dawned, the shock at seeing her old mistress made her gasp, I quelled the word she would have spoken with a finger to my lips. To my dismay, I saw the coachman make ready to be off, the young girl she'd been talking to giving us a strange look as she climbed aboard.

'Theresa, pray, a minute of your time.' Still clearly shocked she let me draw her away where none could hear us.

'What happened to my son after he was taken away, did he suffer much before he died?'

She looked at me bewildered. 'Your son never died; who told you such a wicked lie?' I swayed and held on to her arm lightheaded with the shock of what she'd said.

'I hear he be down at Trevoran Court now, that place all been shut up since the old master died years back, Thomas be Lord Trevoran now, not liking Cornwall he's stayed up in London if gossip has it right. I'll tell you mistress, old master wouldn't have yer name mentioned, told Thomas bad things of you. Demented with anger he was when you went, paid a fortune to have you found is what I heard from Mrs Treave, but I told young Thomas you was a fine lady I did, told him how much you loved him, hated the way them about the old master blackened yer name.'

'If we could be having you now, miss,' the coachman barked, the horses shifting impatient on the cobbles.

'Pray swear you'll tell no one you've seen me,' I begged, fearful now, so many years and no one, not a single person from the past I'd seen. We walked the short distance back to the coach.

'Don't worry, I'll not tell a soul, you were a good mistress. I'm off back to London, Lady Sibland's been ter a funeral, tis her daughter I'm nanny to. Mistress is a flighty piece, tis the last relative they got lives down here, I doubt I'll be in these parts again for I'm to be wed myself. Tis luck you saw me, milady, it must be a shock, you thinking your little boy dead for all these years and now hearing he's not.'

The others were already seated as Theresa Drym took her place among them, I received curious stares from her companions before abruptly the coachman closed the door and sprung up onto his seat, she held out her hand and I grasped it before she sat back.

'Step aside, miss,' a voice growled and the be-whiskered coachman eased the horses forward through the milling crowd. I stood long after they'd departed, oblivious to all around me, unable to believe the words she'd spoken, the shock of what I'd been told. You, Thomas, had survived, and I unaware of it all these years.

I went back to the place where we'd agreed to meet, desperate to tell Jarren what I'd learned and share with him the truth she'd told me but knew this impossible until we were alone. This was a very private matter, so when Mercy struggled towards me clutching her many purchases, I feigned a sense of normality quite worthy of an accomplished actress.

Thankfully, it was only a little while later I glimpsed Jarren and Giles impatiently pushing their way through the crowds, and waited expectantly, longing to know what they'd learnt. Stepping eagerly into Jarren's outstretched arms as though we were young sweethearts.

'Twould seem there's a fortune to be ours if we seek it out, and we must, Layunie, we must.' He kissed me passionately lifting me off my feet.

'But your uncle wrote—' I looked up and saw the glint of challenge in his eyes, knew then no words I spoke would persuade him from pursuing this new found venture, heard Giles saying much the same to Mercy. Giles gathered up Mercy's goods and Jarren took hold my hand hastily guiding me through the crowds back to the wagon. The young ragamuffin who'd run forward as we'd arrived offering to take care of the horse, accepting gratefully the coin Jarren tossed him.

My thoughts as we jolted along the rutted track leading out of Liskeard dwelt on my meeting with Theresa. If I was quieter than usual no one noticed both Jarren and Giles vying to impart to us what they'd learnt from the rolled parchments, which Giles now held tightly in his hand. They had so much to tell and I must confess twas hard not to get caught up with their excitement and passion, for in essence the documents left no doubt that disinherited though Jarren's mother Rosario had been when she married Matthew Galley, provision had been made for any issue from that marriage. The scholar had found a passage in her father Georges Jose's own hand, and faint and barely readable though it was, the instructions laid down in it broached no question, gave notice also of other bequest and the name of who to seek out should such a claim be brought. The scholar had read with difficulty through the faded script, translating the scrawled place names written in spidery writing that ran down the edge of the faded map. The map showed large parcels of land, a separate document badly discoloured bore tithe like deeds, it was Jarren's belief that these parcels of land, as his mother's only son were his. The name nominated by Rosario's father to be called upon half obliterated by a watermark, and surely, he must be long dead, for the date barely decipherable upon the parchment was the year 1687.

Twas it seemed much the same provision made for Giles, clearly his father was blamed for Rosario having met with Jarren's father, bitter cruel words had been read today for the first time since a vindictive hand had written them, they had upset Giles and it was easy now to understand why his father had wanted the past forgotten.

By the time we reached Portlooe, already they were deciding what to do about the vast amount of land, to which it seemed they had legal claim. I thought of my sons waiting impatiently at home wondering what we had learnt today, knew they too would be enthralled in the mystery. Inside I felt a knot of fear, it went hand in hand with the knowledge that I would be happy go with Jarren to these far-off foreign parts, if asked, and knew it to be inevitable that he would.

And he did, Thomas, over a year has passed since our journey to Liskeard, one moment I am fearful for the future, the other as excited as your father at this new adventure. We are all to go, Giles, Mercy, their sons and your three brothers, all of us except Crinnis, for she is to stay in Cornwall with Nancy and John. I miss her sorely already, for they have left Portlooe to join Nancy's father and his new wife who moved some ten years since to run a coaching inn. Just where I cannot say. It is there we shall join them on our return. Sadly, Boswedden has been sold to raise money for our voyage, Harbour House likewise and the boatyard too. Pray God all this is not in vain.

After we'd returned from Liskeard that day and were alone, I told your father of my meeting with Theresa, he was filled with compassion as I told him what she'd said, and later as I lay beside him softly crying, he cradled me in his arms, twas there I stayed until the dawn crept across the bay.

The next morning when I came downstairs, he was standing in the open doorway gazing out to sea, he turned as I reached the final stair and came towards me. 'Don't go fretting to see him will you, maid, best leave Thomas there in his fine house thinking it's rightfully his, no doubt his mind's been poisoned against you and me, let matters rest as they are, the past could still bring us trouble.'

I knew in my heart he was right. So I threw myself into the planning and organising of our great adventure. Indeed this took up much of my time, shedding a tear as the hideous chairs Mercy and I had struggled with all those years ago were bought and collected by a little old man from Polperro in a purple coat, a tiny monkey on his shoulder. But still I longed somehow reach out to you.

It was our son Jack who persuaded Jarren let me write these journals, and Jack who promised he'd make sure they'd be given into your hands only. Tis brave of him to take the risk and I love him for it. He will bring them to you just before we set sail.

I write this today the ninth day of May in the year 1743. It will be my last entry for we are quite ready now. There has been so much to tell but at last my task is over. I have written these journals sitting here at the window of Boswedden in my favourite tapestry chair or seated upon the grassy slopes overlooking Porth Tallus bay. You know the truth of me now, and above all else I hope to have gained your respect. Twill be a tearful parting I take from my beloved Boswedden, we have heard that all in Porth Tallus will be turning out to wish us well, tis almost too much, the parting from all that is familiar. A kindly soul is to sail us down to Falmouth for it alas must be from there we set sail, and in truth I feel more fearful of that place than whatever lies before us, tis a place I dread to revisit, the last time I was there forever in my memory. Your father Jarren bloodied and shackled in leg irons dragged from the Customs House, Trevoran gloating, his current eyes fixed upon me, standing triumphant waiting to escort me to Trevoran Court to begin the nightmare that was my existence.

There is one person whom I need not fear, for he I know will not be on the quay seated on his black stallion, fox-like features sharp beneath his tricorn hat, cloak splayed out around him. Last year we learnt that Ruskin Tripper was dead, killed by the shot of a desperate free trader. Nancy and I joined our men folk round the table in the 'Jolly Sailor' and drank a toast to his good riddance.

It is strange to think of you our son as the new Lord Trevoran, and I can but pray you have inherited from Jarren and myself some traces of humanity and love, your predecessor to the title of Lord Trevoran so sorely lacked. I sincerely hope those dependent on the Trevoran estates have found their lives changed for the better, the man you thought to be your father was not a good master to them. Memories fade with time and my life at Trevoran Court seems such a long time ago, happiness is what I've got now, and by God's grace so let it continue. I wish you well, Thomas, you are forever in my thoughts.

I trust having read the brief letter I enclosed with these journals that you read them and are persuaded not to judge me harshly.

Your loving mother Layunie Polverne.

CHAPTER FOURTEEN

Thomas read the journals in rapt fascination, drawn into them, the neat writing reaching out to him across the years, each one bringing vividly to life his mother's changing fortunes. Whatever arrangements he'd made for the day completely forgotten.

He was interrupted only briefly by the arrival of the irate captain of the *Martingale*. Fog had delayed her sailing and his unruly crew now refused to sail on her when it lifted. 'In fear of their lives, they says,' the old seadog spluttered. ''Tis being said the ship's unfit for such a long voyage, should be another from the Trevoran Line setting sail.'

Privately, Captain Hicks agreed with his men, she wasn't the sturdiest of ships, that's why he'd come here in person to beg its owner the *Charlotte May* be made ready instead. The four-master, the pride of his lordship's line, would take the voyage in her stride.

The impudence of the man outraged Thomas, although he knew only too well, having visited her but a week ago, the poor state of the *Martingale*. However the captain was sent quickly on his way, told to deal with his crew as he saw fit, the door of the study slammed shut behind him.

Ill-tempered at being disturbed, Thomas strode across the study and took a glance out the window, hoping the mist had lifted. He tugged the bell pull for

Molly to make up the fire, cussed the still present mist, for the *Martingale* would be a day late in sailing.

As Molly left, he ordered his meals be served to him in the study, something quite unheard of, and caused quite a stir below stairs. Twas much later at dusk before she was summoned again to close the drapes and light the candles in the candelabra, whilst MaryJane made up the fire.

'Tis a lot of old books he's been given keeping him in there,' she gossiped downstairs as the bell rang again and his lordship told Jacobs he was dismissed for the evening.

In perfect peace, Thomas had read on into the night until finally he'd finished every journal. Slowly, he closed the last book and sat overwhelmed, clutching its rough cover tightly in his hand, shocked by the implications of what he'd leant. Feeling a surge of love for the person in whose hand they were written.

Restless, he drew aside the drapes, staring out at the dark landscape, that cold remote disciplinarian he'd regarded as his father was not his sire! Of this he was glad, quite believing the man he'd thought to be his father capable of the torturous life forced upon his mother. He sat down again lost in thought, reaching forward to prod the dying embers of the fire, throwing on more logs until the reflection of the flames danced upon his highly polished boots. Now he knew why his uncle Pierce Tredavik and cousin Simon hated him so.

One by one he took the journals and threw them onto the fire, waiting till the flames abated before adding another, his mother was right, they must be destroyed now.

With this task completed, he took from his pocket a key and went over and opened the top right-hand draw of his desk, pressing the secret latch that opened a hidden compartment. He reached in and took out a small miniature of his mother he'd been given as a child by Mrs Treave. How she'd come by it he'd never asked, but had always treasured it, always keeping it safely hidden. He gazed down at the face of the beautiful young woman it portrayed, remembering the sweet smell of her perfume, the only thing he remembered.

A log spluttered, shattering the silence, and he glanced up about to replace the miniature before stopping, jolted by the realisation upon which ship his father, mother and the others were to set sail, the only ship in port sailing to the place they were most likely destined. The *Martingale*.

'They couldn't have known she belonged to the Trevoran Line,' he said aloud, and cursed the cruel trick that fate had played on him.

In one swift movement, Thomas replaced the miniature and closed the drawer locking it firmly, slipping the key in his pocket. Deep in thought, he slumped down into the leather seat behind his desk and poured a large measure of brandy.

His eyes rested on the last dying embers of the fire, the clasp on one of the journals still managing to glitter amongst the ashes, his soul sank with misery and despair, knowing that possibly the sailors on board were right and that his ship was unfit for the long journey, and that the mist could lift at any time and the *Martingale* sail. He got up and vigorously tugged at the tapestry bell pull, waiting, glass in hand, twice refilling it, growing ever impatient as the minutes passed, his mind a turmoil of decisions until finally his housekeeper entered, candle in hand, by then it was too late. 'I've had a change of mind, go back to your bed,' he snapped.

'If you're sure, sir.' Mrs Berwick quickly withdrew, wondering at the hour and the master's ill temper.

Knowing now just what he was going to do, Thomas took pen to paper and wrote a short note to Captain Hicks. He then went to the library and opened the safe, withdrawing from it a silver casket, wrapping it in cloth before setting off to the stables. His eyes grew accustomed to the dark and having scraped open one of the ill-fitting doors, he prodded awake the lad sleeping on a pallet beside the stall of a newly born foal. He instructed him on what he wanted done and then mounted the steep wooden steps to the living quarters two at a time to find Jeb and shook him awake.

Jeb had been at Trevoran Court ever since Thomas could remember, there was no protocol between them, and he spoke to him as if to a friend. 'I need your help and desperately quick,' he stated as Jeb roused himself to wakefulness, and rubbing his eyes stood up.

'I want you to take this note and package and find Captain Hicks, if he's not on the *Martingale* he'll be in lodgings nearby, someone will know where he is, this package is intended for a woman. With her is her husband and three sons, they are passengers on the *Martingale*. The name is Pearce. Take Orion, young Sam's making him ready now, it's very important, the matter I'm sending you on, be as quick as you can.'

Jeb struggled into his clothes whilst Thomas waited below in the stable, Orion saddled and ready to mount the moment his head groom appeared.

'Come straight to me on your return,' Thomas stated firmly, hastily handing the package and folded sealed note to Jeb who placed them in the canvas saddlebag.

'None ud make it quicker than me, sir,' Jeb bragged, easing the giant chestnut thoroughbred forward and out into the lane rapidly quickening his pace until horse and rider disappeared into the mist shrouded darkness. For a long while after he'd gone, Thomas stood where he was, breathing in the heavy scent of the nearby woods, threads of mist chilling him to the bone.

Pray God the mist lingers, he thought. The *Charlotte May* he knew was made ready to sail, but for a much shorter voyage, he knew the amount of disruption the orders he'd dispatched would bring, twas unheard of before. He was sure it would be welcomed no doubt by Captain Hicks, but the wrath of Captain Sinclair he'd surely have to face.

He strode back and through the great hall, although twas still early the under maids were already about their duties and he was curiously relieved they'd not touched the fire in his study. He took up the poker and raked through the ashes, retrieving the clasp which still managed to shine, separating out others blackened by the fire, sifting through the embers with the poker making sure every page of the journals was burnt, thankful he'd just finished this when little Mary came in to re-lay the fire. He felt like a child as he lifted the lid of a small iron box on his desk and with his handkerchief wrapped around his hand placed his still warm keepsakes inside, all that was left of a lifetime so carefully written down for him.

Already impatient for Jeb's return, he made for his bedchamber, rang for his valet who helped him change as though twas normal for his master not to sleep in his bed but wish to change his clothes. And with only the slightest look of curiosity, Mrs Berwick herself served him breakfast. His manner to all was sullen and quiet, for in truth he was in turmoil. Should he have gone himself, no, t'would have complicated matters more, he'd have been tempted to find his mother, Jarren and his brothers. It still shocked him the knowledge he was the son of a free trader, an escapee from Bodmin, the rebel and hero so lovingly written about by his mother, from the journals he knew them all so well, but he himself a stranger to them still.

Restless he went to the Land Office and took from the hook the key to the West Wing, the doors leading to it had always been closed and locked, the contents removed long ago. Mrs Treave had told him many years before that the rooms here were left to fall into disrepair, the man he'd thought his father decreed they be left thus, his fathers will so strong Thomas had not thought to go there even after his death. His footsteps echoed in the hollow emptiness, dust lay thick upon the floors, the stark rooms fusty with the smell of a place long abandoned. Remembering the description of it in the journals, he found the room which must have been his mother's and stood by the casement window lost in thought; twas a strange feeling, the knowledge that so much unhappiness had been suffered here.

Thankfully, the great house was still shrouded in mist, but slowly as he stood there the grassy lawns began to become clearer and through the gaps in the trees, he saw glimpses of the river.

As he left the West Wing, faint rays of sunlight crept across the lawns and danced upon the river, the desire to saddle up one of his fine horses and ride to Falmouth foremost in his mind, he couldn't stand to wait for Jeb's return. With determination he walked towards the stables, about to call out to Sam when he heard the unmistakeable sound of hoofbeats on the drive.

Thomas quickened his pace and arrived at the stables just as Sam ran forward to take hold Orion's reins and Jeb slid from the saddle. 'Tis all being done, master, just as you instructed, right rumpus it caused, the two cap'ns hollering at each other something awful. As I left though things ad calmed down an' Capt'n Hicks crew were unloading her cargo and t'other way round, both ships being made ready to sail on the afternoon's tide, mist allowing. Can't be done no quicker, I was to tell you, sir, and the little package, sir, safe with Capt'n Hicks.'

Thomas patted Jeb's shoulder in a gesture of gratitude. 'Well done, you made good time and my thanks to you for it, go to yer bed, man, I'll not be needing you again today. I'll get Ben to see to any needs regarding the horses.' If Jeb was curious as to the master's strange behaviour, he said nothing, gladly seeking his well-earned rest.

Resolute that he'd done his duty, Thomas returned to the house, desperately trying to dislodge the need he felt to ride to Falmouth. Their journey delayed by the fog, somewhere in Falmouth his mother, father and family were spending these last hours preparing for their voyage. A hazardous one to be sure, and even after the *Charlotte May* reached the port of San Peruano, they still faced a further voyage around the coast until they reached the tiny speck on the globe which was their destination. Apprehension lay heavy in his stomach.

He sat in his study pondering on what he'd learned, disturbed finally by his valet reminding him of the meeting in Truro of the Mine Owners Committee he was to preside over.

'Damn the mine owners,' he cussed, his loyal valet looking upon his master with surprise, indeed it was strange times they were experiencing above stairs, and this further proof that something was amiss.

Thomas knew he should go to the meeting in Truro, it was important, but he was unable to focus his mind on the day's business. His rivals would be there bidding against each other for a stake in the new mine at Lanner. He had no choice other than to go, if he wanted a stake in it of any worth.

With this in mind, Thomas tried to set aside all thoughts of his mother and the newly read journals. Barely a quarter of an hour later, his valet was brushing a strand of hair from the sleeve of his fashionable blue coat, and Lord Thomas, without so much as a word to Parker, picked up his gloves and strode from the room, leaving the man bewildered at his master's bad humour. The valet glanced out of the casement window watching as old Ben brought the coach and horses to a halt before the canopied entrance of the hall. Moments later it was bowling down the drive leaving a cloud of dust in its wake.

Thomas sat back in the coach feeling wretched, wondering how things fared in Falmouth. The familiar lush green countryside still covered in a slight mist as he passed by, of no account, his thoughts elsewhere. As they neared the end of the long lane leading from the Trevoran Estate, old Ben slowed the horses. Thomas knew that it was here his decision would have to be made, the lane forked left for Falmouth and right for Truro. As Ben manoeuvred the horses to take the right fork, he lowered the window of the carriage and shouted up to him, 'Make for Falmouth instead, and quicken the pace where you can.' Ben acknowledged reacting immediately, skilfully changing the direction the team of chestnuts was to take.

Although impatient to reach his destination, Thomas still had no idea what he sought to do when he got there, only that he must be there when the *Charlotte May* sailed, perchance to gain a glimpse of his mother, all of them, just this once.

It seemed an age but in truth Ben made Falmouth in excellent time. At the top of the hill leading down to the harbour the sight he longed to see came into view. Tied up alongside Custom House quay the *Charlotte May*. Beside her on the quay between the throng of horses and wagons, a noisy crowd was gathering as the crew made final preparations to set sail. Ben stopped a little way off and sought his master's instructions.

'Take us up to the farthest end of Westpoint Quay,' Thomas ordered, having made up his mind this would be a quiet vantage point from where to watch.

Once Ben had brought the carriage to a halt, Thomas lowered the window and breathed in deeply almost able to taste the potent smell of the seaweed and salt water. He felt the damp breeze ruffle his hair as he watched the newly hazy sun dancing on the water, cast his eye along the harbour with its maze of masts and rigging, the ships clinging some four deep to the quay. He had a good view of the *Charlotte May* even catching a glimpse of Capt'n Hicks busy on deck and sensed before long the ship would be underway for the tide was high already. He stepped down onto the quay and waited as gulls screeched overhead and two red-sailed schooners sailed silently by.

His thoughts returned to the journals, what he'd read had shocked and saddened him, above all angered him. If only he'd asked more questions, defied his lordship by asking of her, if only Theresa May hadn't been dismissed whilst he was still so young. They'd poisoned his mind against her, all of them! His father, Pierce, Simon even old Landy. He admired his mother; it took spirit to follow your heart, to give up everything for the love of a man so far beneath her birthright.

As he thought this, a vision of Autumn Povey from Devoran came to mind, dancing barefoot beside the Fal, her fair hair flying out around her shoulders. A solitary companion when younger, he missed her friendship, for time and status had made it impossible.

CHAPTER FIFTEEN

Standing on the deck of the *Charlotte May* as the ropes holding her were cast off, Layunie and Jarren looked down on the crowds gathered on the quay below. Layunie not quite believing this day had finally come. Slowly the fine four-master slipped her moorings. She wiped away a tear, this a moment both of sadness and excitement. Sadness, for she wished Crinnis and the others could have been here, excitement in what lay ahead.

She smiled, happily watching as Jack and his bothers walked along the deck to join Giles and Mercy, leaving her and Jarren alone. Jack had kept his promise and delivered her journals into Thomas's hands, of that she was glad. She felt the breeze tug at her hair, felt the glow it brought to her cheeks, she rested her arms on the ship's rail, happy their voyage was finally begun, warmed by Jarren's closeness, safely encircled in his arms.

Both were silent as the ship made her way past the Customs House with its terrible memories. For a moment, the others forgotten, the searing pain of the last time they were there too strong to be denied.

Deep in thought, she was startled when someone tapped her shoulder. Jarren, ever protective, turned and stepped forward ready to challenge the intruder, wondering what the sailor wanted. 'Tis no harm I mean to you, mistress, Capt'n Hicks asked me to give you this, ma'am.' The toothless sailor grinned, handing her what seemed a box wrapped in linen, he took a wary look at Jarren, touched his forelock and quickly took his leave of them.

Puzzled, Layunie unwrapped the linen and looked at the silver casket inside with amazement. 'I recognise this, it was mine!' She looked at Jarren mystified. Carefully she opened the lid, inside it still held what had been her collection of jewels, left behind when she'd fled Trevoran Court. A narrow blue velvet box rested at the bottom, inside it the priceless sapphire and diamond heirloom Trevoran's bony fingers had placed around her throat. Beneath this was a folded note, carefully she opened it out.

Do with these what you will, have no qualms should you need them for barter. Signed, your loving son, Thomas Trevoran.

Layunie quickly shut the lid from prying eyes, and Jarren hid it once more within the linen, with one hand she reached out to steady herself as the deck moved beneath her feet with the swell of the sea.

'I don't understand how—'

It was then she looked towards the quay and saw the Trevoran coach, even after all this time the distinctive coat of arms made her clutch Jarren's arm with alarm.

'Tis him,' she said, almost in a whisper. And Jarren's eyes followed her gaze.

There he saw standing quite still watching the ship depart, a young man, finely dressed to be sure, but in looks so much like himself. He felt Layunie tremble and took hold her hand, aware the depth of emotion she was feeling at their son's presence on the quay. He leant forward and whispered in her ear, 'Take comfort, my sweet, he came because he understood, he read the truth by your own hand, that's why he's here.' He put a comforting arm around her shoulders and raised his other arm, in a final gesture of farewell to his first-born son.

In a voice choking with emotion, Layunie cried out to Thomas across the ever-widening stretch of water.

'I never forgot you and never stopped loving you.'

Words that were carried faintly to shore on a gust of wind, precious words that Thomas would always treasure. He raised his hand in acknowledgement and so did she, waving to him until he was indistinguishable upon the quay.

The wind filled the huge canvas sails of the *Charlotte May*, and held lovingly once more in Jarren's arms, Layunie clutched hold the silver casket, content the journals so painstakingly written had served to right the past and forge a new bond between her and her son. She wiped the tears from her eyes and rested her head against Jarren's chest as gently he stroked her face, his rough hand soft against her cheek.

'Maybe one day when we return, you'll get to meet him,' he soothed, and on impulse pulled the clasps from her hair, setting loose the tumbling curls. To him she barely looked older than she had all those years ago on Bodmin Moor. Layunie looked up at the man she so loved, his dark eyes still twinkled mischievously, still held that hint of wickedness that made him Jarren. He gave her that special smile she loved so well, bending to kiss her lips but briefly before they were joined once again by their excited sons. Later she would tell them of Thomas's presence on the quay and of the gift he'd sent and of how much it meant to her that he was there.

From the shore, Thomas watched as gracefully the finest of his ships slipped out of Falmouth harbour between the twin castles of Pendennis and St Mawes, out to face the Atlantic. An ache filled his heart, but strangely he felt at peace, overcome with the satisfaction that his decision to be here had been right. Alone, he stood watching until the ship was but a speck on the horizon, taking those on board far away from the shores of Cornwall, praying one day they'd return safe home.

The End.

CPSIA information can be obtained
at www.ICGtesting.com
Printed in the USA
LVHW042006040820
662390LV00006B/905

9 781839 751233